Praise for the previous volumes of
Nebula Awards Showcase

"Invaluable, not just for the splendid fiction and lively nonfiction, but as another annual snapshot, complete with grins and scowls."—*Kirkus Reviews*

"Would serve well as a one-volume text for a course in contemporary science fiction."—*The New York Review of Science Fiction*

"Very impressive."—*Off the Shelf*

Kim Stanley Robinson is the Nebula and Hugo Award–winning author of such science fiction novels as the *Mars* trilogy, *Antarctica, Escape from Kathmandu,* and *The Martians.*

Nebula Awards Showcase

EDITED BY

Kim Stanley Robinson

A ROC BOOK

ROC
Published by New American Library, a division of
Penguin Putnam Inc., 375 Hudson Street,
New York, New York 10014, U.S.A.
Penguin Books Ltd, 80 Strand,
London WC2R 0RL, England
Penguin Books Australia Ltd, Ringwood,
Victoria, Australia
Penguin Books Canada Ltd, 10 Alcorn Avenue,
Toronto, Ontario, Canada M4V 3B2
Penguin Books (N.Z.) Ltd, 182–190 Wairau Road,
Auckland 10, New Zealand

Penguin Books Ltd, Registered Offices:
Harmondsworth, Middlesex, England

First published by Roc, an imprint of New American Library,
a division of Penguin Putnam Inc.

First Printing, April 2002
10 9 8 7 6 5 4 3 2 1

Library of Congress Cataloging-in-Publication Data is available upon request.

Printed in the United States of America

CONTENTS

INTRODUCTION

The Science Fiction Writers of America was founded, and began giving out its Nebula Awards, in 1965. Founder Damon Knight's timing was good; the sixties were a turbulent time when many things were changing fast, making people feel that the future had yet again "arrived" somehow and was palpably there, demanding to be shaped. Science fiction writers responded by combining the techniques of literary modernism with the traditional science fiction methods of extrapolation and speculation, and they used this volatile new mix to describe the global unrest of that era in stories that were vivid and unforgettable. Science fiction had never been better, and in the same way that magical realism was revealing itself as the literary genre best suited to speak for Latin America's particular history and situation, science fiction in those years finished the process of making itself the natural language of the United States. The Nebula anthologies from that period still glow with the background radiation of that exuberant arrival.

Since then much has happened to both the world and to science fiction. The disarray and confusion of the seventies, the Reagan backlash, the end of the Cold War, the Clinton years of globalization: all were matched by corresponding developments in this genre that now mirrored the world so well. Blockbuster sf movies, franchised fiction riding their success, vastly popular fantasy series, increasing academic interest, decreasing midlists, the appearance of the Internet and electronic publishing—all these things occurred, and at the same time, rapid technological development on all fronts combined to turn our entire social reality into one giant science fiction novel, which we are all writing together in the great collaboration called history.

An amazing thirty-six years. What then of the Science Fiction Writers of America? Given the events described above, in effect creating the radical science-fictionalization of the world, naturally the SFWA was collectively awarded the 2001 Nobel Prize for literature, and the UN General Assembly voted to ask us to take over the governing of the world—

No? No. That last was science fiction (it's a habit)—in this case an alternative history, one that I wouldn't want to live in, and I'll bet you wouldn't either.

No, what the SFWA has "really" done in these last thirty-six years is to pound along like the Energizer bunny, organizing the efforts of volunteers to help the situation of writers in relation to publishers, health insurance companies, and the general public. SFWA has also been the site of intense squabbling and backbiting, not least about the Nebula Awards themselves. So some important and useful things have been accomplished, and on the other hand many hours have been wasted, in ways entertaining or not. In other words, it's been much like any other human organization; and throughout all, it has served as a guild, or a diffuse kind of hometown, for a talented and hardworking group of professional writers.

And the stories they have produced? Well, the field has gotten too big for any one reader to say for sure. One can only take samples and extrapolate, in the usual sf way. The sample that is this year's group of nominated stories, for instance, is revealing; it is filled with interesting work, exhibiting (to my eye) various trends and patterns. And the award winners among them are wonderful stories, intense and moving. By their evidence the genre is doing fine.

But back to those trends and patterns, as a way of discussing some of the good work that this anthology does not have room to include. SFWA has always been a collection of various factions or interest groups within the genre, and this is reflected in the stories that made the final ballot, as usual. There are a number of "hard sf" stories concerned with emerging technologies and their immediate ramifications. There are also quite a few fantasy stories exploring the ways that myths and the fantastic can speak to our current situation. Another cluster of this year's nominees has to do with time travel of one sort or another, in particular travel back into the past. This I think might be a way of questioning what our society could have done differently in the last few decades to make things better. They could also indicate a feeling that the future is somehow mortgaged or locked up, so that even in thought experiments it is now easier to change the past.

Another cluster of nominees focuses on machine transcendance, people uploading or downloading their minds into computers, thereby dodging death and entering some new form of existence. Current science fiction is filled with stories about this idea, making it one of the field's main topics of the day. I find this intriguing, because in fact there is no possibility that any such process will ever come to pass. It's an idea that ignores or misunderstands the complexity of the brain, the nature of computers, and the utter absence of any conceivable method to transfer the one into the other. It is, in other words, one of those science fiction ideas, like time travel or faster-than-light travel, that is never going to happen in the real world, and yet gets written about as if it is right around the corner, if not already upon us.

Despite that, in the case of this year's stories, they feel right; they feel like they are about something relevant to us now. I think that they are therefore about something else than their supposed subject matter; and that this something else is not just the wish for immortality in a new guise, though it is surely that, too. I think these stories are a way of talking about the choices we are making now about how to live. They are saying that we can already "download ourselves,"—in effect by approximating the existences of brains in bottles, to use an older image for the same thing. So many of us work at desks, looking at screens and tapping with our fingers; and when our work is done, we entertain ourselves by looking at screens and tapping with our fingers. Reduced to watching and tapping, our thoughts thereby channeled and choreographed by programmers elsewhere, we could be said to be machine software already. But wait—is that a good thing?

That, in any case, is what I think these downloading stories are really about. They are an artistic response to contemporary reality; they are science fiction doing its usual job of extrapolating current trends into an emotionally comprehensible symbol, metaphor, parable, or allegory.

This is to say that science fiction stories at their best are always about something in the here and now, and they need to be read at more than their surface level by delving into a relationship to our time that is metaphorical. Some people are resistant to this necessity of a dual or allegorical reading, but in fact it is one source of science fiction's great power. These stories are not just entertainments, even though they are entertaining; they are not set in the future only for the sake of freedom from the restraints of reality. They are statements about the way we live now, coded, just as all art is in one way or another coded. And their particular form of coding has a significant advantage over most forms of metaphoric abstraction in art, which is precisely their location "in the future" and the way this invests them with some of the power of prophecy. After reading other non-realist works, like surrealism or fantasy (or even the realisms, which no longer seem very realistic), the reader is free to say, Well, that writer certainly is imaginative and/or troubled, but it's their problem, their dream; it's not my problem. The reader can walk away without any cognitive or emotional entanglement. A science fiction story, on the other hand, says by its placement in our collective future, This could happen. This could happen to us! And the reader is forced to think about it in those terms, so like prophecy. Could it happen? Is it likely? Is something else more likely? What in the current moment supports one view or another? And if it does happen, what does that mean for us?

So, by placing itself in our future, science fiction positions itself as the next term in an if-then proposition, which starts with the here and now and ends in some dramatic new place; our moment is thus illuminated by it, using a very peculiar and powerful beam to become symbol, metaphor, parable, or allegory—simulation, forecast, model, or prophecy—take your pick.

All the winning stories this year, and the nominated stories I've chosen to include with them, take this illuminating and confrontational stance of speaking to us from the future, often the near future, the "day after tomorrow." The tones of their stories are very different, ranging from the Steinbeckian realism of Greg Bear's novel to the witty ironies of Eleanor Arnason's planetary adventure; from the bitter sting of Terry Bisson's satire to the can-do optimism of Linda Nagata's utopia; from the sharp melancholy of Walter Jon Williams's allegory to the deep melancholy of Gardner Dozois's parable (for they are very different, as you will see)—in that sense these stories are all over the map. But they are all about our present predicaments, and they all take the very powerful stance of "speaking from the future." They make a good representation of contemporary science fiction at its best, which is what the Nebula Awards are all about. Enjoy!

—Kim Stanley Robinson

ABOUT THE NEBULA AWARDS

THIS YEAR'S BALLOT

NOVELS

(winner) *Darwin's Radio,* Greg Bear (Ballantine Del Rey)
A Civil Campaign, Lois McMaster Bujold (Baen)
Forests of the Heart, Charles de Lint (Tor)
Midnight Robber, Nalo Hopkinson (Warner Aspect)
Crescent City Rhapsody, Kathleen Ann Goonan (Avon Eos)
Infinity Beach, Jack McDevitt (HarperPrism)

NOVELLAS

"Fortitude," Andy Duncan (*Realms of Fantasy,* June 1999)
"Ninety Percent of Everything," Jonathan Lethem, James Patrick Kelly, and John Kessel (*F&SF,* September 1999)
(winner) "Goddesses," Linda Nagata (*Sci Fiction/SciFi.com,* July 5, 2000)
"Hunting the Snark," Mike Resnick (*Asimov's,* December 1999)
"Crocodile Rock," Lucius Shepard (*F&SF,* October/November 1999)
"Argonautica," Walter Jon Williams (*Asimov's,* October/November 1999)

NOVELETTES

"Stellar Harvest," Eleanor Arnason (*Asimov's,* April 1999)
"A Knight of Ghosts and Shadows," Gardner Dozois (*Asimov's,* October/November 1999)
"Jack Daw's Pack," Greer Gilman (*Century 5,* Winter 2000)

"A Day's Work on the Moon," Mike Moscoe (*Analog,* July/August 2000)

"How the Highland People Came to Be," Bruce Holland Rogers (*Realms of Fantasy,* August 1999)

"Generation Gap," Stanley Schmidt (*Artemis Magazine #1,* Spring 2000)

(winner) "Daddy's World," Walter Jon Williams (*Not of Woman Born,* Constance Ash, ed., Roc Books)

SHORT STORIES

(winner) "macs," Terry Bisson (*F&SF,* October/November 1999)

"The Fantasy Writer's Assistant," Jeffrey Ford (*F&SF,* February 2000)

"Flying over Water," Ellen Klages (*Lady Churchill's Rosebud Wristlet,* No. 7, October 2000)

"The Golem," Severna Park (*Black Heart, Ivory Bones,* Ellen Datlow and Terri Windling, eds., Avon)

"Scherzo with Tyrannosaur," Michael Swanwick (*Asimov's,* July 1999)

"You Wandered Off Like a Foolish Child to Break Your Heart and Mine," Pat York (*Silver Birch, Blood Moon,* Ellen Datlow and Terri Windling, eds., Avon)

SCRIPTS

(winner) *Galaxy Quest,* Robert Gordon, David Howard (Dreamworks)

Being John Malkovich, Charlie Kaufman (Propaganda Films)

The Green Mile, Frank Darabont, based on the novel by Stephen King (Castle Rock/Warner Brothers)

Dogma, Kevin Smith (View Askew Productions)

Princess Mononoke, Hayao Miyazaki, Neil Gaiman (Walt Disney Productions)

Unbreakable, M. Night Shyamalan (Touchstone)

PAST NEBULA AWARD WINNERS

1965

Best Novel: *Dune* by Frank Herbert
Best Novella: "The Saliva Tree" by Brian W. Aldiss and "He Who Shapes" by Roger Zelazny (tie)
Best Novelette: "The Doors of His Face, the Lamps of His Mouth" by Roger Zelazny
Best Short Story: " 'Repent, Harlequin!' Said the Ticktockman" by Harlan Ellison

1966

Best Novel: *Flowers for Algernon* by Daniel Keyes and *Babel-17* by Samuel R. Delany (tie)
Best Novella: "The Last Castle" by Jack Vance
Best Novelette: "Call Him Lord" by Gordon R. Dickson
Best Short Story: "The Secret Place" by Richard McKenna

1967

Best Novel: *The Einstein Intersection* by Samuel R. Delany
Best Novella: "Behold the Man" by Michael Moorcock
Best Novelette: "Gonna Roll the Bones" by Fritz Leiber
Best Short Story: "Aye, and Gomorrah" by Samuel R. Delany

1968

Best Novel: *Rite of Passage* by Alexei Panshin
Best Novella: "Dragonrider" by Anne McCaffrey
Best Novelette: "Mother to the World" by Richard Wilson
Best Short Story: "The Planners" by Kate Wilhelm

1969

Best Novel: *The Left Hand of Darkness* by Ursula K. Le Guin
Best Novella: "A Boy and His Dog" by Harlan Ellison
Best Novelette: "Time Considered as a Helix of Semi-Precious Stones" by Samuel R. Delany
Best Short Story: "Passengers" by Robert Silverberg

1970

Best Novel: *Ringworld* by Larry Niven
Best Novella: "Ill Met in Lankhmar" by Fritz Leiber
Best Novelette: "Slow Sculpture" by Theodore Sturgeon
Best Short Story: no award

1971

Best Novel: *A Time of Changes* by Robert Silverberg
Best Novella: "The Missing Man" by Katherine MacLean
Best Novelette: "The Queen of Air and Darkness" by Poul Anderson
Best Short Story: "Good News from the Vatican" by Robert Silverberg

1972

Best Novel: *The Gods Themselves* by Isaac Asimov
Best Novella: "A Meeting with Medusa" by Arthur C. Clarke
Best Novelette: "Goat Song" by Poul Anderson
Best Short Story: "When It Changed" by Joanna Russ

1973

Best Novel: *Rendezvous with Rama* by Arthur C. Clarke
Best Novella: "The Death of Doctor Island" by Gene Wolfe
Best Novelette: "Of Mist, and Grass, and Sand" by Vonda N. McIntyre
Best Short Story: "Love Is the Plan, the Plan Is Death" by James Tiptree Jr.
Best Dramatic Presentation: *Soylent Green*
Stanley R. Greenberg for screenplay (based on the novel *Make Room! Make Room!*), Harry Harrison for *Make Room! Make Room!*

1974

Best Novel: *The Dispossessed* by Ursula K. Le Guin
Best Novella: "Born with the Dead" by Robert Silverberg
Best Novelette: "If the Stars Are Gods" by Gordon Eklund and Gregory Benford

Best Short Story: "The Day Before the Revolution" by Ursula K. Le Guin
Best Dramatic Presentation: *Sleeper* by Woody Allen
Grand Master: Robert A. Heinlein

1975

Best Novel: *The Forever War* by Joe Haldeman
Best Novella: "Home Is the Hangman" by Roger Zelazny
Best Novelette: "San Diego Lightfoot Sue" by Tom Reamy
Best Short Story: "Catch That Zeppelin!" by Fritz Leiber
Best Dramatic Writing: Mel Brooks and Gene Wilder for *Young Frankenstein*
Grand Master: Jack Williamson

1976

Best Novel: *Man Plus* by Frederik Pohl
Best Novella: "Houston, Houston, Do You Read?" by James Tiptree Jr.
Best Novelette: "The Bicentennial Man" by Isaac Asimov
Best Short Story: "A Crowd of Shadows" by Charles L. Grant
Grand Master: Clifford D. Simak

1977

Best Novel: *Gateway* by Frederik Pohl
Best Novella: "Stardance" by Spider and Jeanne Robinson
Best Novelette: "The Screwfly Solution" by Raccoona Sheldon
Best Short Story: "Jeffty Is Five" by Harlan Ellison
Special Award: *Star Wars*

1978

Best Novel: *Dreamsnake* by Vonda N. McIntyre
Best Novella: "The Persistence of Vision" by John Varley
Best Novelette: "A Glow of Candles, a Unicorn's Eye" by Charles L. Grant
Best Short Story: "Stone" by Edward Bryant
Grand Master: L. Sprague de Camp

1979

Best Novel: *The Fountains of Paradise* by Arthur C. Clarke
Best Novella: "Enemy Mine" by Barry Longyear
Best Novelette: "Sandkings" by George R. R. Martin
Best Short Story: "giANTS" by Edward Bryant

1980

Best Novel: *Timescape* by Gregory Benford
Best Novella: "The Unicorn Tapestry" by Suzy McKee Charnas
Best Novelette: "The Ugly Chickens" by Howard Waldrop
Best Short Story: "Grotto of the Dancing Deer" by Clifford D. Simak
Grand Master: Fritz Leiber

1981

Best Novel: *The Claw of the Conciliator* by Gene Wolfe
Best Novella: "The Saturn Game" by Poul Anderson
Best Novelette: "The Quickening" by Michael Bishop
Best Short Story: "The Bone Flute" by Lisa Tuttle*

1982

Best Novel: *No Enemy But Time* by Michael Bishop
Best Novella: "Another Orphan" by John Kessel
Best Novelette: "Fire Watch" by Connie Willis
Best Short Story: "A Letter from the Clearys" by Connie Willis

1983

Best Novel: *Startide Rising* by David Brin
Best Novella: "Hardfought" by Greg Bear
Best Novelette: "Blood Music" by Greg Bear
Best Short Story: "The Peacemaker" by Gardner Dozois
Grand Master: Andre Norton

*This Nebula Award was declined by the author.

1984

Best Novel: *Neuromancer* by William Gibson
Best Novella: "Press Enter ■" by John Varley
Best Novelette: "Bloodchild" by Octavia E. Butler
Best Short Story: "Morning Child" by Gardner Dozois

1985

Best Novel: *Ender's Game* by Orson Scott Card
Best Novella: "Sailing to Byzantium" by Robert Silverberg
Best Novelette: "Portraits of His Children" by George R. R. Martin
Best Short Story: "Out of All Them Bright Stars" by Nancy Kress
Grand Master: Arthur C. Clarke

1986

Best Novel: *Speaker for the Dead* by Orson Scott Card
Best Novella: "R & R" by Lucius Shepard
Best Novelette: "The Girl Who Fell into the Sky" by Kate Wilhelm
Best Short Story: "Tangents" by Greg Bear
Grand Master: Isaac Asimov

1987

Best Novel: *The Falling Woman* by Pat Murphy
Best Novella: "The Blind Geometer" by Kim Stanley Robinson
Best Novelette: "Rachel in Love" by Pat Murphy
Best Short Story: "Forever Yours, Anna" by Kate Wilhelm
Grand Master: Alfred Bester

1988

Best Novel: *Falling Free* by Lois McMaster Bujold
Best Novella: "The Last of the Winnebagos" by Connie Willis
Best Novelette: "Schrödinger's Kitten" by George Alec Effinger
Best Short Story: "Bible Stories for Adults, No. 17: The Deluge" by James Morrow
Grand Master: Ray Bradbury

1989

Best Novel: *The Healer's War* by Elizabeth Ann Scarborough
Best Novella: "The Mountains of Mourning" by Lois McMaster Bujold
Best Novelette: "At the Rialto" by Connie Willis
Best Short Story: "Ripples in the Dirac Sea" by Geoffrey Landis

1990

Best Novel: *Tehanu: The Last Book of Earthsea* by Ursula K. Le Guin
Best Novella: "The Hemingway Hoax" by Joe Haldeman
Best Novelette: "Tower of Babylon" by Ted Chiang
Best Short Story: "Bears Discover Fire" by Terry Bisson
Grand Master: Lester del Rey

1991

Best Novel: *Stations of the Tide* by Michael Swanwick
Best Novella: "Beggars in Spain" by Nancy Kress
Best Novelette: "Guide Dog" by Mike Conner
Best Short Story: "Ma Qui" by Alan Brennert

1992

Best Novel: *Doomsday Book* by Connie Willis
Best Novella: "City of Truth" by James Morrow
Best Novelette: "Danny Goes to Mars" by Pamela Sargent
Best Short Story: "Even the Queen" by Connie Willis
Grand Master: Frederik Pohl

1993

Best Novel: *Red Mars* by Kim Stanley Robinson
Best Novella: "The Night We Buried Road Dog" by Jack Cady
Best Novelette: "Georgia on My Mind" by Charles Sheffield
Best Short Story: "Graves" by Joe Haldeman

1994

Best Novel: *Moving Mars* by Greg Bear
Best Novella: "Seven Views of Olduvai Gorge" by Mike Resnick
Best Novelette: "The Martian Child" by David Gerrold

Best Short Story: "A Defense of the Social Contracts" by Martha Soukup
Grand Master: Damon Knight

1995

Best Novel: *The Terminal Experiment* by Robert J. Sawyer
Best Novella: "Last Summer at Mars Hill" by Elizabeth Hand
Best Novelette: "Solitude" by Ursula K. Le Guin
Best Short Story: "Death and the Librarian" by Esther M. Friesner
Grand Master: A. E. van Vogt

1996

Best Novel: *Slow River* by Nicola Griffith
Best Novella: "Da Vinci Rising" by Jack Dann
Best Novelette: "Lifeboat on a Burning Sea" by Bruce Holland Rogers
Best Short Story: "A Birthday" by Esther M. Friesner
Grand Master: Jack Vance

1997

Best Novel: *The Moon and the Sun* by Vonda N. McIntyre
Best Novella: "Abandon in Place" by Jerry Oltion
Best Novelette: "The Flowers of Aulit Prison" by Nancy Kress
Best Short Story: "Sister Emily's Lightship" by Jane Yolen
Grand Master: Poul Anderson

1998

Best Novel: *Forever Peace* by Joe W. Haldeman
Best Novella: "Reading the Bones" by Sheila Finch
Best Novelette: "Lost Girls" by Jane Yolen
Best Short Story: "Thirteen Ways to Water" by Bruce Holland Rogers
Grand Master: Hal Clement

1999

Best Novel: *Parable of the Talents* by Octavia E. Butler
Best Novella: "Story of Your Life" by Ted Chiang

Best Novelette: "Mars Is No Place for Children" by Mary A. Turzillo
Best Short Story: "The Cost of Doing Business" by Leslie What
Best Script: *The Sixth Sense* by M. Night Shyamalan
Grand Master: Brian W. Aldiss

ABOUT THE NEBULA AWARDS

The Nebula Awards are chosen by the members of the Science Fiction and Fantasy Writers of America. In 2000 they were given in five categories: short story—under 7,500 words; novelette—7,500 to 17,499 words; novella—17,500 to 39,999 words; novel—more than 40,000 words; and script. SFWA members read and nominate the best sf stories and novels throughout the year, and the editor of the "Nebula Awards Report" collects these nominations and publishes them in a newsletter. At the end of the year, there is a preliminary ballot and then a final one to determine the winners.

The Nebula Awards are presented at a banquet at the annual Nebula Awards Weekend, held originally in New York and, over the years, in places as diverse as New Orleans; Eugene, Oregon; and aboard the *Queen Mary*, in Long Beach, California.

The Nebula Awards originated in 1965, from an idea by Lloyd Biggle Jr., the secretary-treasurer of SFWA at that time, who proposed that the organization select and publish the year's best stories, and have been given ever since.

The award itself was originally designed by Judith Ann Blish from a sketch by Kate Wilhelm. The official description: "a block of Lucite four to five inches square by eight to nine inches high into which a spiral nebula of metallic glitter and a geological specimen are embedded."

SFWA also gives the Grand Master Award, its highest honor. It is presented for a lifetime of achievement in science fiction. Instituted in 1975, it is awarded only to living authors and is not necessarily given every year. The Grand Master is chosen by SFWA's officers, past presidents, and board of directors.

The first Grand Master was Robert A. Heinlein in 1974. The others are Jack Williamson (1975), Clifford Simak (1976), L. Sprague de Camp (1978), Fritz Leiber (1981), Andre Norton

(1983), Arthur C. Clarke (1985), Isaac Asimov (1986), Alfred Bester (1987), Ray Bradbury (1988), Lester del Rey (1990), Frederik Pohl (1992), Damon Knight (1994), A. E. van Vogt (1995), Jack Vance (1996), Poul Anderson (1997), Hal Clement (1998), Brian W. Aldiss (1999), and Philip José Farmer (2000).

The thirty-sixth annual Nebula Awards banquet was held in Los Angeles on April 29, 2001.

ABOUT THE SCIENCE FICTION AND FANTASY WRITERS OF AMERICA

The Science Fiction and Fantasy Writers of America, Incorporated, includes among its members most of the active writers of science fiction and fantasy. According to the bylaws of the organization, its purpose "shall be to promote the furtherance of the writing of science fiction, fantasy, and related genres as a profession." SFWA informs writers on professional matters, protects their interests, and helps them in dealings with agents, editors, anthologists, and producers of nonprint media. It also strives to encourage public interest in and appreciation of science fiction and fantasy.

Anyone may become an active member of SFWA after the acceptance of and payment for one professionally published novel, one professionally produced dramatic script, or three professionally published pieces of short fiction. Only science fiction, fantasy, and other prose fiction of a related genre, in English, shall be considered as qualifying for active membership. Beginning writers who do not yet qualify for active membership may join as associate members; other classes of membership include illustrator members (artists), affiliate members (editors, agents, reviewers, and anthologists), estate members (representatives of the estates of active members who have died), and institutional members (high schools, colleges, universities, libraries, broadcasters, film producers, futurist groups, and individuals associated with such an institution).

Anyone who is not a member of SFWA may subscribe to *The SFWA Bulletin*. The magazine is published quarterly, and contains articles by well-known writers on all aspects of their profession. Subscriptions are $18 a year or $31 for two years. For information on how to subscribe to the *Bulletin*, write to:

SFWA Bulletin
P.O. Box 10126
Rochester, NY 14610

Readers are also invited to visit the SFWA site on the World Wide Web at the following address: http://www.sfwa.org

THE GRAND MASTER AWARD

SFWA gives a Grand Master Award, its highest honor, for a lifetime of achievement in science fiction. Instituted in 1975, it is awarded only to living authors and is not necessarily given every year. The Grand Master is chosen by SFWA's officers, past presidents, and Board of Directors.

The past winners are Robert A. Heinlein (1974), Jack Williamson (1975), Clifford Simak (1976), L. Sprague de Camp (1978), Fritz Leiber (1981), Andre Norton (1983), Arthur C. Clarke (1985), Isaac Asimov (1986), Alfred Bester (1987), Ray Bradbury (1988), Lester del Rey (1990), Frederik Pohl (1992), Damon Knight (1994), A. E. van Vogt (1995), Jack Vance (1996), Poul Anderson (1997), Hal Clement (1998), and Brian Aldiss (1999).

This year's Grand Master Award was given to Philip José Farmer.

PHILIP JOSÉ FARMER

An Appreciation by Robert Silverberg:

He exploded into our midst—there is no better verb to describe his arrival—in the summer of 1952, with a novella called "The Lovers," the coming of which had been heralded in the field for many months. For once, all the publishing hype was justified. " 'The Lovers' is a story we would like to introduce with trumpets and fanfares—maybe even a parade," declared Sam Mines, the editor of *Startling Stories*, by way of preface. "We feel that way about it. . . . We think this story is a delicate and beautiful, yet powerful and shocking piece of work. We are amazed that so strong and sure a drama could come from a new young writer. We believe that we are here launching the career of a man who will shortly be ranked with the few at the very top. We think Philip José Farmer is the find of the year."

It was all true. No one, not even Theodore Sturgeon, not even Fritz Leiber, had written anything like "The Lovers," a science fictional love story in which the speculative biological elements and the emotional elements were perfectly integrated, a magnificent demonstration of what science fiction could be when equal attention was paid to the science and the fiction. One paragraph will suffice to demonstrate the point:

> "They drank the purplish liquor. After a while he picked her up and carried her into the bedroom. There he forgot. The only disconcerting item was that she insisted upon keeping her eyes open, even during the climax, as if she were trying to photograph his features upon her mind."

Notice what is going on here, and place it, if you can, in the context of the rigid official moral code of the far-off world of 1952, a year when motion picture censors debated long and earnestly over whether a provocative word like "virgin" could be spoken aloud in a film. For one thing, Farmer shows a man and a woman entering a bedroom for purposes of carnal intercourse. Nobody, so far as I can recall, had ever done that in a science fiction magazine until then. Note also that he refers to "the climax"—and, in a later passage, speaks of "orgasm." This was new vocabulary for popular fiction. Finally, there is the woman's odd insistence on keeping her eyes open at the moment of orgasm, which, we will discover, is not Farmer's idea of a bit of pornographic detail work, but is, in fact, the key element of the profoundly original biological speculation on which the whole story is built.

1952 was a good year for science fiction, to put it mildly—it brought us some fine Jack Vance stories, and Heinlein's "The Year of the Jackpot," and Asimov's *The Currents of Space*, and early versions of the Pohl-Kornbluth *Space Merchants* and Sturgeon's *More Than Human*, and, above all the rest, Bester's *The Demolished Man*—but no story, except perhaps the Bester, was as widely discussed as Farmer's "Lovers." He followed it the following year with a book-length sequel, "Moth and Rust," along with two novelettes, and in September 1953, at the very first Hugo Award ceremony in Philadelphia, this astonishing opening salvo of work was rewarded with a Hugo designating Farmer as the most promising new writer of the year.

Promising he surely was, and the promise was quickly fulfilled, with a stream of remarkable novels and stories that established him quickly in the first rank of the field. It was work marked by extraordinary drive, energy, and power—characteristics typical of Farmer himself. He is in frail health now, midway through his ninth decade, but for most of his life the physical vitality of the man was apparent at a glance. As a boy, he once told an interviewer, "I was very strong and swift and was so agile in the trees that my nickname in grade school was 'Tarzan.' " One day, he said, he attempted a leap too great even for him, "and so, like Lucifer, I fell because of pride. I ripped some muscles in my thighs and was paralyzed for half an hour with the intense pain." Though he recovered and became an outstanding high school athlete, the accident changed him profoundly: he became introspective, philosophical, deeply aware of the tragic possibilities of existence.

His early Hugo, the wild praise showered on him in the aftermath of "The Lovers," the eagerness with which editors courted his work, all this provided him with a reenactment of his boyhood fall just a few years after the spectacular launching of his career. He gave up his job in a steel mill and took up writing science fiction as his profession. A novel that he called *I Owe for the Flesh* was the winner of a huge cash prize in a much-touted literary competition, but an unscrupulous middleman intercepted the money and Farmer never saw any of it, nor did the book see print. Two other publishing deals collapsed about the same time. Farmer, who found himself suddenly overextended financially, lost his house and was forced to take work as a manual laborer.

All this might have aborted the career of a lesser man, but that fierce vitality of his and his powerful drive toward creative self-expression kept him intact through all these adversities. He continued to write—such memorable stories as "Father," "Night of Light," and "The Alley Man" date from this period—and a great turning point came for him in the mid-1960s when Frederik Pohl, at that time the most important magazine editor in science fiction, guided him toward a drastic reconstruction of *I Owe for the Flesh* into a series of novellas, beginning with "The Day of the Great Shout," that eventually became the novels known as the Riverworld series. By 1969 Farmer was able to return to full-time writing again; the first Riverworld novel, *To Your Scattered Bodies Go*, was published to great commercial and critical success two years later and brought him a Hugo Award in 1972. From then on he moved from triumph to triumph—the World of Tiers series, the Tarzan-derived but distinctively Farmeresque novels *Lord Tyger* and *Time's Last Gift*, a book-length expansion of "The Lovers," and a dazzling host of other works that brought him, finally, the Grand Master award he had so richly earned through his more than forty years of vigorous and exuberant storytelling.

His work is a mixture of obsessive reexaminations of cultural totems both high and low: Melville's Ishmael and Joyce's Leopold Bloom rub elbows with Tom Mix and Tarzan, Doc Savage and Fu Manchu.

Throughout his career he has reached again and again into the stew of myth and archetype that underlies the narrative art. With unquenchable humor, unfettered narrative drive, and an unabashed willingness to confront the biggest of philosophical questions, this quiet, witty, and much beloved man has graced our field for decades with his presence and his gifts, and it is only fitting that we, his colleagues, honor him at last with the highest award we can bestow.

At the Nebula Banquet in Los Angeles in April of 2001, Philip José Farmer said in his acceptance speech:

"I have long thought of this award. Despite being modest, I thought I deserved it; but I thought I'd shuffle off before I had it. But I managed to live long enough.

"And I'm really shaken by Harlan's praise—usually I don't pay any attention to what he says—but really, Harlan has a tremendous heart. I've seen evidence of great generosity there, in our long acquaintance. I met him when he was around sixteen, and he impressed me then, but I had no idea he was going to be such a—what shall I say—stalwart, courageous writer. A man who writes like nobody else.

"But I'm supposed to be up here praising myself. And I want to keep this speech short, because I've found that short speeches are very popular, especially at the end of the evening. So I'm going to say, you have no idea what this award means to me"—raising award—"and I'm going to take it home somehow; I mean I can't ship it; I might even put it in my pocket. But—words fail me. I've dreamed of this day. There were times when I didn't give a damn whether I got it or not. But I'm glad I hung on, and I appreciate this tribute from you, and your love and appreciation.

"Thank you very much."

THE AUTHOR EMERITUS AWARD

In 1994 SFWA initiated the Author Emeritus Award to honor veteran writers who were no longer writing and publishing as much as they had in the past, and who were important to science fiction's history. The Author Emeritus is invited to attend the Nebula Awards weekend, is honored at the banquet, and given a special award. The Author Emeritus Award has so far honored Emil Petaja, Wilson Tucker, Judith Merril, Nelson Bond, William Tenn, and Daniel Keyes.

This year's Author Emeritus is Robert Sheckley.

ROBERT SHECKLEY

An Appreciation by David G. Hartwell:

Robert Sheckley is the subject of a recent essay by Brian Aldiss, who says, "Whereas most writers of this kind of futuristic fairy tale will go to great lengths, by deploying ordinary language, and by methods of realism adapted from the mundane or everyday novel, to reassure us that their feet are on the ground, even if their heads are in galactic space, Sheckley's heart is with the Unbelievable. His main target is the Incredible. With one swing of his computer he hacks through the string which suspends our disbelief. It would crash down, were it not for the fact that there is no gravity in Sheckley's space." Sheckley is one of the great living sf writers, whose reputation is based primarily on the quality of his quirky, subversive, satirical short fiction, a body of work admired by everyone from Kingsley Amis, J. G. Ballard, and Harlan Ellison to Roger Zelazny, with whom he collaborated. As an ironic investigator of questions of identity and of the nature of reality, he is a peer of Philip K. Dick and Kurt Vonnegut. In a recent interview on the Web [www.fantascienza.net/sfpeople/robert.sheckley] this exchange took place:

> Delos: Why is there something, instead of there being nothing?
>
> Sheckley: There isn't something. There's only nothing masquerading as something and looking very like Gerard Depardieu. That, by the way, is the real meaning of cyberspace.

Sheckley first came to prominence in the 1950s as one of the leading writers in *Galaxy*, became a novelist in the 1960s, and still (but too infrequently) produces fiction today that is thought-provoking, memorable, and stylish.

Robert Sheckley is one of the finest sf writers of the century and is still producing first-class work in short fiction and at novel length. There are present Grand Masters who have contributed less, and only a few who have contributed more to sf in the last sixty years. The present fashion is to ignore the contributions of a writer unless they are novels, and that is a growing disaster and a betrayal of the history of sf achievement in the twentieth century. Not just the SFWA, but fans in general are losing touch with sf literary history and many of the masterworks and fine writers of the past, but especially those whose finest achievements were short fiction. Despite the efforts of NESFA press and others, almost everybody is looking at novels as the measure of a writer's true quality. If this goes on, everyone from Damon Knight to Harlan Ellison to Lucius Shepard to Ted Chiang will end up as second rank and not worthy of Grand Master awards no matter how fine their stories. And to put it bluntly, there are a disproportionate number of excellent short story writers in sf, but not a lot of first-class novelists. Better than half the present Grand Masters made a major part of their contribution to sf through their short stories, some, such as Fritz Leiber, were most important for their stories. Never publishing a classic novel as a thumb rule for elimination is the same kind of arbitrary literary politics as eliminating a writer from the canon because she or he only wrote sf. Wake up, SFWA: Sheckley should be a Grand Master next.

At the Nebula banquet in Los Angeles in April of 2001, Robert Sheckley gave this acceptance speech:

"I have a few remarks here—not humor—not after all of this.

"I took a slightly more sentimental tone.

"I want to express my appreciation at having been able to live a life in science fiction. Science fiction has given me a voice and a number of viewpoints with which to feel the world and to say something about it. That is a rare privilege. It has given me something to do and a discipline with which to do it.

"Our field of science fiction and fantasy is one of dreams. We dream, and flesh out our dreams with words. The words are necessary though often difficult. Our work gives us the pleasure and pain of working in form. Form is mostly invisible; felt fields of force within our minds, sensations of beauty and order, and of a greater measure of dreaming beyond our dreams. We furnish our interior world with dreams, but the dreams have to be clothed in words. They don't come full-blown. We sit down to work in our corner of the world, and choose to live in our creations.

"In Shelley's words,

Like a poet, living in a world of thought,
Singing hymns unbidden until the world is wrought
To sympathy with hopes and fears it heeded not.

"The poets say it awfully well. I want to close with a poem by William Earnest Henley that I especially like. I think it speaks for our field:

We are the music makers
And we are the dreamers of dreams,
Wandering by lone sea breakers,

Sitting by desolate streams.
World losers and world forsakers
Of the world forever it seems.

With wonderful deathless ditties
We build up the world's great cities
And out of the fabulous story
We fashion an empire's glory.

One man with a dream, at pleasure,
Shall go forth and conquer a crown,
And three with a new song's measure
Can trample an empire down.

We in the ages lying,
In the buried past of the Earth
Built Ninevah with our sighing
And Babel itself with our mirth.

And o'erthrew them with prophesying
For the good of the new world's worth.
For each age is a dream that is dying,
Or one that is coming to birth.

WALTER JON WILLIAMS

Walter Jon Williams has been publishing science fiction since 1984, and in the years since he has been prolific; the work pouring from his pen has given him a reputation for intelligent, sophisticated, and versatile science fiction. Some of the best of it can be found in his novels *Hardwired*, *Angel Station*, *Days of Atonement*, *Aristoi*, and *The Rift*.

He is a pleasure to meet at conventions and workshops: sociable; persuasive; plays a good game of pool. His short fiction has appeared on award ballots so many times that for quite a while he was the holder of Gardner Dozois's uncoveted "Bull Goose" award, meaning that his stories had received more award nominations than anyone else's without actually winning one. As a former holder of this honor myself, I can testify that it is something one passes along with little regret, except perhaps for one's lost youth; but that would be gone anyway, so it's better to win an award.

His winning novelette is a particularly fine example of his work about the human-computer interface, which has been a recurrent interest throughout his career. As I said in my introduction to this volume, stories about this subject are often ways of talking about how we live now in the world; and never more so than here, in a dark tale that has an even blacker allegorical under-surface, if we identify with the young protagonist, as clearly we are meant to, and if we take his situation to be ours, and "Daddy's World" to be our world.

DADDY'S WORLD

Walter Jon Williams

One day Jamie went with his family to a new place, a place that had not existed before. The people who lived there were called Whirlikins, who were tall thin people with pointed heads. They had long arms and made frantic gestures when they talked, and when they grew excited threw their arms out *wide* to either side and spun like tops until they got all blurry. They would whirr madly over the green grass beneath the pumpkin-orange sky of the Whirlikin Country, and sometimes they would bump into each other with an alarming clashing noise, but they were never hurt, only bounced off and spun away in another direction.

Sometimes one of them would spin so hard that he would dig himself right into the ground, and come to a sudden stop, buried to the shoulders, with an expression of alarmed dismay.

Jamie had never seen anything so funny. He laughed and laughed.

His little sister Becky laughed, too. Once she was laughing so hard that she fell over onto her stomach, and Daddy picked her up and whirled her through the air, as if he were a Whirlikin himself, and they were both laughing all the while.

Afterward, they heard the dinner bell, and Daddy said it was time to go home. After they waved good-bye to the Whirlikins, Becky and Jamie walked hand-in-hand with Momma as they walked over the grassy hills toward home, and the pumpkin-orange sky slowly turned to blue.

The way home ran past El Castillo. El Castillo looked like a fabulous place, a castle with towers and domes and minarets, all gleaming in the sun. Music floated down from El Castillo, the swift, intricate music of many guitars, and Jamie could hear the fast click of heels and the shouts and laughter of happy people.

But Jamie did not try to enter El Castillo. He had tried before, and discovered that El Castillo was guarded by La Duchesa, an angular forbidding woman all in black, with a tall comb in her hair. When Jamie asked to come inside, La Duchesa had looked down at him and said, "I do not admit anyone who does not know Spanish irregular verbs!" It was all she ever said.

Jamie had asked Daddy what a Spanish irregular verb was—he had difficulty pronouncing the words—and Daddy had said, "Someday you'll learn, and La Duchesa will let you into her castle. But right now you're too young to learn Spanish."

That was all right with Jamie. There were plenty of things to do without going into El Castillo. And new places, like the country where the Whirlikins lived, appeared sometimes out of nowhere, and were quite enough to explore.

The color of the sky faded from orange to blue. Fluffy white clouds coasted in the air above the two-story frame house. Mister Jeepers, who was sitting on the ridgepole, gave a cry of delight and soared toward them through the air.

"Jamie's home!" he sang happily. "Jamie's home, and he's brought his beautiful sister!"

Mister Jeepers was diamond-shaped, like a kite, with his head at the topmost corner, hands on either side, and little bowlegged comical legs attached on the bottom. He was bright red. Like a kite, he could fly, and he swooped through in a series of aerial cartwheels as he sailed toward Jamie and his party.

Becky looked up at Mister Jeepers and laughed from pure joy. "Jamie," she said, "you live in the best place in the world!"

■

At night, when Jamie lay in bed with his stuffed giraffe, Selena would ride a beam of pale light from the Moon to the Earth and sit by Jamie's side. She was a pale woman, slightly translucent, with a silver crescent on her brow. She would stroke Jamie's forehead with a cool hand, and she would sing to him until his eyes grew heavy and slumber stole upon him.

"The birds have tucked their heads
The night is dark and deep

All is quiet, all is safe,
And little Jamie goes to sleep."

Whenever Jamie woke during the night, Selena was there to comfort him. He was glad that Selena always watched out for him, because sometimes he still had nightmares about being in the hospital. When the nightmares came, she was always there to comfort him, stroke him, sing him back to sleep.

Before long the nightmares began to fade.

■

Princess Gigunda always took Jamie for lessons. She was a huge woman, taller than Daddy, with frowsy hair and big bare feet and a crown that could never be made to sit straight on her head. She was homely, with a mournful face that was ugly and endearing at the same time. As she shuffled along with Jamie to his lessons, Princess Gigunda complained about the way her feet hurt, and about how she was a giant and unattractive, and how she would never be married.

"I'll marry you when I get bigger," Jamie said loyally, and the Princess's homely face screwed up into an expression of beaming pleasure.

Jamie had different lessons with different people. Mrs. Winkle, down at the little red brick schoolhouse, taught him his ABCs. Coach Toad—who *was* one—taught him field games, where he raced and jumped and threw against various people and animals. Mr. McGillicuddy, a pleasant whiskered fat man who wore red sleepers with a trapdoor in back, showed him his magic globe. When Jamie put his finger anywhere on the globe, trumpets began to sound, and he could see what was happening where he was pointing, and Mr. McGillicuddy would take him on a tour and show him interesting things. Buildings, statues, pictures, parks, people. "This is Nome," he would say. "Can you say Nome?"

"Nome," Jamie would repeat, shaping his mouth around the unfamiliar word, and Mr. McGillicuddy would smile and bob his head and look pleased.

If Jamie did well on his lessons, he got extra time with the Whirlikins, or at the Zoo, or with Mr. Fuzzy or in Pandaland. Until the dinner bell rang, and it was time to go home.

Jamie did well with his lessons almost every day.

When Princess Gigunda took him home from his lessons, Mister Jeepers would fly from the ridgepole to meet him, and tell him that his family was ready to see him. And then Momma and Daddy and Becky would wave from the windows of the house, and he would run to meet them.

Once, when he was in the living room telling his family about his latest trip through Mr. McGillicuddy's magic globe, he began skipping around with enthusiasm, and waving his arms like a Whirlikin, and suddenly he noticed that no one else was paying attention. That Momma and Daddy and Becky were staring at something else, their faces frozen in different attitudes of polite attention.

Jamie felt a chill finger touch his neck.

"Momma?" Jamie said. "Daddy?" Momma and Daddy did not respond. Their faces didn't move. Daddy's face was blurred strangely, as if it had been caught in the middle of movement.

"Daddy?" Jamie came close and tried to tug at his father's shirtsleeve. It was hard, like marble, and his fingers couldn't get a purchase at it. Terror blew hot in his heart.

"Daddy?" Jamie cried. He tried to tug harder. "Daddy! Wake up!" Daddy didn't respond. He ran to Momma and tugged at her hand. "Momma! Momma!" Her hand was like the hand of a statue. She didn't move no matter how hard Jamie pulled.

"Help!" Jamie screamed. "Mister Jeepers! Mr. Fuzzy! Help my momma!" Tears fell down his face as he ran from Becky to Momma to Daddy, tugging and pulling at them, wrapping his arms around their frozen legs and trying to pull them toward him. He ran outside, but everything was curiously still. No wind blew. Mister Jeepers sat on the ridgepole, a broad smile fixed as usual to his face, but he was frozen, too, and did not respond to Jamie's calls.

Terror pursued him back into the house. This was far worse than anything that had happened to him in the hospital, worse even than the pain. Jamie ran into the living room, where his family stood still as statues, and then recoiled in horror. A stranger had entered the room—or rather just parts of a stranger, a pair of hands encased in black gloves with strange silver circuit patterns on the backs, and a strange glowing opalescent face with a pair of wraparound dark glasses drawn across it like a line.

"Interface crashed, all right," the stranger said, as if to someone Jamie couldn't see.

Jamie gave a scream. He ran behind Momma's legs for protection.

"Oh, shit," the stranger said. "The kid's still running."

He began purposefully moving his hands as if poking at the air. Jamie was sure that it was some kind of terrible attack, a spell to turn him to stone. He tried to run away, tripped over Becky's immovable feet and hit the floor hard, and then crawled away, the hall rug bunching up under his hands and knees as he skidded away, his own screams ringing in his ears . . .

. . . He sat up in bed, shrieking. The cool night tingled on his skin. He felt Selena's hand on his forehead, and he jerked away with a cry.

"Is something wrong?" came Selena's calm voice. "Did you have a bad dream?" Under the glowing crescent on her brow, Jamie could see the concern in her eyes.

"Where are Momma and Daddy?" Jamie shrieked.

"They're fine," Selena said. "They're asleep in their room. Was it a bad dream?"

Jamie threw off the covers and leaped out of bed. He ran down the hall, the floorboards cool on his bare feet. Selena floated after him in her serene, concerned way. He threw open the door to his parents' bedroom and snapped on the light, then gave a cry as he saw them huddled beneath their blanket. He flung himself at his mother, and gave a sob of relief as she opened her eyes and turned to him.

"Something wrong?" Momma said. "Was it a bad dream?"

"No!" Jamie wailed. He tried to explain, but even he knew that his words made no sense. Daddy rose from his pillow, looking seriously at Jamie, and then turned to ruffle his hair.

"Sounds like a pretty bad dream, trouper," Daddy said. "Let's get you back to bed."

"No!" Jamie buried his face in his mother's neck. "I don't want to go back to bed!"

"All right, Jamie," Momma said. She patted Jamie's back. "You can sleep here with us. But just for tonight, okay?"

"Wanna stay here," Jamie mumbled.

He crawled under the covers between Momma and Daddy. They each kissed him, and Daddy turned off the light. "Just go to sleep, trouper," he said. "And don't worry. You'll have good dreams from now on."

Selena, faintly glowing in the darkness, sat silently in the corner. "Shall I sing?" she asked.

"Yes, Selena," Daddy said. "Please sing for us."

Selena began to sing,

"The birds have tucked their heads
The night is dark and deep
All is quiet, all is safe,
And little Jamie goes to sleep."

But Jamie did not sleep. Despite the singing, the dark night, the rhythmic breathing of his parents, and the comforting warmth of their bodies.

It *wasn't* a dream, he knew. His family had really been frozen.

Something, or someone, had turned them to stone. Probably that evil disembodied head and pair of hands. And now, for some reason, his parents didn't remember.

Something had made them forget.

Jamie stared into the darkness. What, he thought, if these *weren't* his parents? If his parents were still stone, hidden away somewhere? What if these substitutes were bad people—kidnappers or worse—people who just *looked* like his real parents? What if they were evil people who were just waiting for him to fall asleep, and then they would turn to monsters, with teeth and fangs and a horrible light in their eyes, and they would tear him to bits right here in the bed . . .

Talons of panic clawed at Jamie's heart. Selena's song echoed in his ears. He *wasn't* going to sleep! He *wasn't*!

And then he did. It wasn't anything like normal sleep—it was as if sleep was *imposed* on him, as if something had just *ordered* his mind to sleep. It was just like a wave that rolled over him, an irresistible force, blotting out his sense, his body, his mind . . .

I *won't* sleep! he thought in defiance, but then his thoughts were extinguished.

When he woke he was back in his own bed, and it was morning, and Mister Jeepers was floating outside the window. "Jamie's awake!" he sang. "Jamie's awake and ready for a new day!"

And then his parents came bustling in, kissing him and petting him and taking him downstairs for breakfast.

His fears seemed foolish now, in full daylight, with Mister Jeepers dancing in the air outside and singing happily.

But sometimes, at night while Selena crooned by his bedside, he gazed into the darkness and felt a thrill of fear.

And he never forgot, not entirely.

■

A few days later Don Quixote wandered into the world, a lean man who frequently fell off his lean horse in a clang of homemade armor. He was given to making wan comments in both English and his own language, which turned out to be Spanish.

"Can you teach me Spanish irregular verbs?" Jamie asked.

"Sí, naturalmente," said Don Quixote. "But I will have to teach you some other Spanish as well." He looked particularly mournful. "Let's start with *corazón*. It means 'heart.' *Mi corazón,*" he said with a sigh, "is breaking for love of Dulcinea."

After a few sessions with Don Quixote—mixed with a lot of sighing about *corazón*s and Dulcinea—Jamie took a grip on his courage, marched up to El Castillo, and spoke to La Duchesa. *"Pierdo, sueño, haría, ponto!"* he cried.

La Duchesa's eyes widened in surprise, and as she bent toward Jamie her severe face became almost kindly. "You are obviously a very intelligent boy," she said. "You may enter my castle."

And so Don Quixote and La Duchesa, between the two of them, began to teach Jamie to speak Spanish. If he did well, he was allowed into the parts of the castle where the musicians played and the dancers stamped, where brave Castilian knights jousted in the tilting yard, and Señor Esteban told stories in Spanish, always careful to use words that Jamie already knew.

Jamie couldn't help but notice that sometimes Don Quixote behaved strangely. Once, when Jamie was visiting the Whirlikins, Don Quixote charged up on his horse, waving his sword and crying out that he would save Jamie from the goblins that were attacking him. Before Jamie could explain that the Whirlikins were harmless, Don Quixote galloped to the attack. The Whirlikins, alarmed, screwed themselves into the ground where they were safe, and Don Quixote fell off his horse trying to swing at one with his sword. After poor Quixote fell off his horse a few times, it was Jamie who had to rescue the Don, not the other way around.

It was sort of sad and sort of funny. Every time Jamie started to laugh about it, he saw Don Quixote's mournful face in his mind, and his laugh grew uneasy.

After a while, Jamie's sister Becky began to share Jamie's lessons. She joined him and Princess Gigunda on the trip to the little schoolhouse, learned reading and math from Mrs. Winkle, and then, after some coaching from Jamie and Don Quixote, she marched to La Duchesa to shout irregular verbs and gain entrance to El Castillo.

Around that time Marcus Tullius Cicero turned up to take them both to the Forum Romanum, a new part of the world that had appeared to the south of the Whirlikins' territory. But Cicero and the people in the Forum, all the shopkeepers and politicians, did not teach Latin the way Don Quixote taught Spanish, explaining what the new words meant in English, they just talked Latin at each other and expected Jamie and Becky to understand. Which, eventually, they did. The Spanish helped. Jamie was a bit better at Latin than Becky, but he explained to her that it was because he was older.

It was Becky who became interested in solving Princess Gigunda's problem. "We should find her somebody to love," she said.

"She loves *us*," Jamie said.

"Don't be silly," Becky said. "She wants a *boyfriend*."

"*I'm* her boyfriend," Jamie insisted.

Becky looked a little impatient. "Besides," she said, "it's a puzzle. Just like La Duchesa and her verbs."

This had not occurred to Jamie before, but now that Becky mentioned it, the idea seemed obvious. There were a lot of puzzles around, which one or the other of them was always solving, and Princess Gigunda's lovelessness was, now that he saw it, clearly among them.

So they set out to find Princess Gigunda a mate. This question occupied them for several days, and several candidates were discussed and rejected. They found no answers until they went to the chariot race of the Circus Maximus. It was the first race in the Circus ever, because the place had just appeared on the other side of the Palatine Hill from the Forum, and there was a very large, very excited crowd.

The names of the charioteers were announced as they paraded their chariots to the starting line. The trumpets sounded, and the chariots bolted from the start as the drivers whipped up the horses. Jamie watched enthralled as they rolled around the *spina* for the first lap, and then shouted in surprise at the sight of Don Quixote galloping onto the Circus Maximus, shouting that he was about to stop this group of rampaging demons from destroying the land, and planted himself directly in the path of the oncoming chariots. Jamie shouted along with the crowd for the Don to get out of the way before he got killed.

Fortunately Quixote's horse had more sense than he did, because the spindly animal saw the chariots coming and bolted, throwing its rider. One of the chariots rode right over poor Quixote, and there was a horrible clanging noise, but after the chariot passed, Quixote sat up, apparently unharmed. His armor had saved him.

Jamie jumped up from his seat and was about to run down to help Don Quixote off the course, but Becky grabbed his arm. "Hang on," she said, "someone else will look after him, and I have an idea."

She explained that Don Quixote would make a perfect man for Princess Gigunda.

"But he's in love with Dulcinea!"

Becky looked at him patiently. "Has anyone ever *seen* Dulcinea? All we have to do is convince Don Quixote that Princess Gigunda *is* Dulcinea."

After the races, they found that Don Quixote had been arrested by the lictors and sent to the Lautumiae, which was the Roman jail. They weren't allowed to see the prisoner, so they went in search of Cicero, who was a lawyer and was able to get Quixote out of the Lautumiae on the promise that he would never visit Rome again.

"I regret to the depths of my soul that my parole does not enable me to destroy these demons," Quixote said as he left Rome's town limits.

"Let's not get into that," Becky said. "What we wanted to tell you was that we've found Dulcinea."

The old man's eyes widened in joy. He clutched at his armor-clad heart. "*Mi amor!* Where is she? I must run to her at once!"

"Not just yet," Becky said. "You should know that she's been changed. She doesn't look like she used to."

"Has some evil sorcerer done this?" Quixote demanded.

"Yes!" Jamie interrupted. He was annoyed that Becky had taken charge of everything, and he wanted to add his contribution to the scheme. "The sorcerer was just a head!" he shouted. "A floating head, and a pair of hands! And he wore dark glasses and had no body!"

A shiver of fear passed through him as he remembered the eerie floating head, but the memory of his old terror did not stop his words from spilling out.

Becky gave him a strange look. "Yeah," she said. "That's right."

"He crashed the interface!" Jamie shouted, the words coming to him out of memory.

Don Quixote paid no attention to this, but Becky gave him another look.

"You're not as dumb as you look, Digit," she said.

"I do not care about Dulcinea's appearance," Don Quixote declared, "I love only the goodness that dwells in her *corazón*."

"She's Princess Gigunda!" Jamie shouted, jumping up and down in enthusiasm. "She's been Princess Gigunda all along!"

And so, the children following, Don Quixote ran clanking to where Princess Gigunda waited near Jamie's house, fell down to one knee, and began to kiss and weep over the Princess's hand. The Princess seemed a little surprised by this until Becky told her that she was really the long-lost Dulcinea, changed into a giant by an evil magician, although she probably didn't remember it because that was part of the spell, too.

So while the Don and the Princess embraced, kissed, and began to warble a love duet, Becky turned to Jamie.

"What's that stuff about the floating head?" she asked. "Where did you come up with that?"

"I dunno," Jamie said. He didn't want to talk about his memory of his family being turned to stone, the eerie glowing figure floating before them. He didn't want to remember how everyone said it was just a dream.

He didn't want to talk about the suspicions that had never quite gone away.

"That stuff was weird, Digit," Becky said. "It gave me the

creeps. Let me know before you start talking about stuff like that again."

"Why do you call me Digit?" Jamie asked.

Becky smirked. "No reason," she said.

"Jamie's home!" Mister Jeepers's voice warbled from the sky. Jamie looked up to see Mister Jeepers doing joyful aerial loops overhead. "Master Jamie's home at last!"

■

"Where shall we go?" Jamie asked.

Their lessons for the day were over, and he and Becky were leaving the little red schoolhouse. Becky, as usual, had done very well on her lessons, better than her older brother, and Jamie felt a growing sense of annoyance. At least he was still better at Latin and computer science.

"I dunno," Becky said. "Where do you want to go?"

"How about Pandaland? We could ride the Whoosh Machine."

Becky wrinkled her face. "I'm tired of that kid stuff," she said.

Jamie looked at her. "But you're a kid."

"I'm not as little as you, Digit," Becky said.

Jamie glared. This was too much. "You're my little sister! I'm bigger than you!"

"No, you're not," Becky said. She stood before him, her arms flung out in exasperation. "Just *notice something* for once, will you?"

Jamie bit back on his temper and looked, and he saw that Becky was, in fact, bigger than he was. And older-looking. Puzzlement replaced his fading anger.

"How did you get so big?" Jamie asked.

"I grew. And you *didn't* grow. Not as fast anyway."

"I don't understand."

Becky's lip curled. "Ask Mom or Dad. Just *ask* them." Her expression turned stony. "Just don't believe everything they tell you."

"What do you mean?"

Becky looked angry for a moment, and then her expression relaxed. "Look," she said, "just go to Pandaland and have fun, okay? You don't need me for that. I want to go and make some calls to my friends."

"*What* friends?"

Becky looked angry again. "*My* friends. It doesn't matter who they are!"

"Fine!" Jamie shouted. "I can have fun by myself!"

Becky turned and began to walk home, her legs scissoring against the background of the green grass. Jamie glared after her, then turned and began the walk to Pandaland.

He did all his favorite things, rode the Ferris wheel and the Whoosh Machine, watched Rizzio the Strongman and the clowns. He enjoyed himself, but his enjoyment felt hollow. He found himself *watching*, watching himself at play, watching himself enjoying the rides.

Watching himself not grow as fast as his little sister.

Watching himself wondering whether or not to ask his parents about why that was.

He had the idea that he wouldn't like their answers.

■

He didn't see as much of Becky after that. They would share lessons, and then Becky would lock herself in her room to talk to her friends on the phone.

Becky didn't have a telephone in her room, though. He looked once when she wasn't there.

After a while, Becky stopped accompanying him for lessons. She'd got ahead of him on everything except Latin, and it was too hard for Jamie to keep up.

After that, he hardly saw Becky at all. But when he saw her, he saw that she was still growing fast. Her clothing was different, and her hair. She'd started wearing makeup.

He didn't know whether he liked her anymore or not.

■

It was Jamie's birthday. He was eleven years old, and Momma and Daddy and Becky had all come for a party. Don Quixote and Princess Gigunda serenaded Jamie from outside the window, accompanied by La Duchesa on Spanish guitar. There was a big cake with eleven candles. Momma gave Jamie a chart of the stars. When he touched a star, a voice would appear telling Jamie about the star, and lines would appear on the chart showing any constellation the star happened to belong to. Daddy gave Jamie a car, a miniature Mercedes convertible, scaled to Jamie's size, which he could drive around the country and which he could use in the Circus Maximus when the chariots weren't racing. His sister gave Jamie a kind of lamp stand that would project lights and moving patterns on the walls and ceiling when the lights were off. "Listen to music when you use it," she said.

"Thank you, Becky," Jamie said.

"Becca," she said. "My name is Becca now. Try to remember."

"Okay," Jamie said. "Becca."

Becky—Becca—looked at Momma. "I'm dying for a cigarette," she said. "Can I go, uh, out for a minute?"

Momma hesitated, but Daddy looked severe. "Becca," she said, "this is *Jamie's birthday*. We're all here to celebrate. So why don't we all eat some cake and have a nice time?"

"It's not even real cake," Becca said. "It doesn't *taste* like real cake."

"It's a *nice cake*," Daddy insisted. "Why don't we talk about this later? Let's just have a special time for Jamie."

Becca stood up from the table. "For *the Digit*?" she said. "Why are we having a good time for *Jamie*? He's not even a *real person*!" She thumped herself on the chest. "*I'm* a real person!" she shouted. "Why don't we ever have special times for *me*?"

But Daddy was on his feet by that point and shouting, and Momma was trying to get everyone to be quiet, and Becca was shouting back, and suddenly a determined look entered her face and she just disappeared—suddenly, she wasn't there anymore, there was only just air.

Jamie began to cry. So did Momma. Daddy paced up and down and swore, and then he said, "I'm going to go get her." Jamie was afraid he'd disappear like Becca, and he gave a cry of despair, but Daddy didn't disappear, he just stalked out of the dining room and slammed the door behind him.

Momma pulled Jamie onto her lap and hugged him. "Don't worry, Jamie," she said. "Becky just did that to be mean."

"What happened?" Jamie asked.

"Don't worry about it." Momma stroked his hair. "It was just a mean trick."

"She's growing up," Jamie said. "She's grown faster than me and I don't understand."

"Wait till Daddy gets back," Momma said, "and we'll talk about it."

But Daddy was clearly in no mood for talking when he returned, without Becca. "We're going to have *fun*," he snarled, and reached for the knife to cut the cake.

The cake tasted like ashes in Jamie's mouth. When the Don and Princess Gigunda, Mister Jeepers and Rizzio the Strongman, came into the dining room and sang "Happy Birthday," it was all Jamie could do to hold back the tears.

Afterward, he drove his new car to the Circus Maximus and drove as fast as he could on the long oval track. The car really wouldn't go very fast. The bleachers on either side were empty, and so was the blue sky above.

Maybe it was a puzzle, he thought, like Princess Gigunda's love life. Maybe all he had to do was follow the right clue, and everything would be fine.

What's the moral they're trying to teach? he wondered.

But all he could do was go in circles, around and around the empty stadium.

■

"Hey, Digit. Wake up."

Jamie came awake suddenly with a stifled cry. The room whirled around him. He blinked, realized that the whirling came from the colored lights projected by his birthday present, Becca's lamp stand.

Becca was sitting on his bedroom chair, a cigarette in her hand. Her feet, in the steel-capped boots she'd been wearing lately, were propped up on the bed.

"Are you awake, Jamie?" It was Selena's voice. "Would you like me to sing you a lullaby?"

"Fuck off, Selena," Becca said. "Get out of here. Get lost."

Selena cast Becca a mournful look, then sailed backward, out of the window, riding a beam of moonlight to her pale home in the sky. Jamie watched her go, and felt as if a part of himself was going with her, a part that he would never see again.

"Selena and the others have to do what you tell them, mostly," Becca said. "Of course, Mom and Dad wouldn't tell *you* that."

Jamie looked at Becca. "What's happening?" he said. "Where did you go today?"

Colored lights swam over Becca's face. "I'm sorry if I spoiled your birthday, Digit. I just got tired of the lies, you know? They'd kill me if they knew I was here now, talking to you." Becca took a draw on her cigarette, held her breath for a second or two, then exhaled. Jamie didn't see or taste any smoke.

"You know what they wanted me to do?" she said. "Wear a little girl's body, so I wouldn't look any older than you, and keep you company in that stupid school for seven hours a day." She shook her head. "I wouldn't do it. They yelled and yelled, but I was damned if I would."

"I don't understand."

Becca flicked invisible ashes off her cigarette and looked at Jamie for a long time. Then she sighed.

"Do you remember when you were in the hospital?" she said.

Jamie nodded. "I was really sick."

"I was so little then, I don't really remember it very well," Becca said. "But the point is—" She sighed again. "The point is that you weren't getting well. So they decided to—" She shook her head. "Dad took advantage of his position at the University, and the fact that he's been a big donor. They were doing AI research, and the neurology department was into brain modeling, and they needed a test subject, and— Well, the idea is, they've got some of your tissue, and when they get cloning up and running, they'll put you back in—" She saw Jamie's stare, then shook her head. "I'll make it simple, okay?"

She took her feet off the bed and leaned closer to Jamie. A shiver ran up his back at her expression. "They made a copy of you. An *electronic* copy. They scanned your brain and built a holographic model of it inside a computer, and they put it in a virtual environment, and—" She sat back, took a drag on her cigarette. "And here you are," she said.

Jamie looked at her. "I don't understand."

Colored lights gleamed in Becca's eyes. "You're in a computer, okay? And you're a program. You know what that is, right? From computer class? And the program is sort of in the shape of your mind. Don Quixote and Princess Gigunda are programs, too. And Mrs. Winkle down at the school house is *usually* a program, but if she needs to teach something complex, then she's an education major from the University."

Jamie felt as if he'd just been hollowed out, a void inside his ribs. "I'm not real?" he said. "I'm not a person?"

"Wrong," Becca said. "You're real, alright. You're the apple of our parents' eye." Her tone was bitter. "Programs are real things," she said, "and yours was a real hack, you know, absolute cutting-edge state-of-the-art technoshit. And the computer that you're in is real, too—I'm interfaced with it right now, down in the family room—we have to wear suits with sensors and a helmet with scanners and stuff. I hope to fuck they don't hear me talking to you down here."

"But what—" Jamie swallowed hard. How could he swallow if he was just a string of code? "What happened to *me*? The original me?"

Becca looked cold. "Well," she said, "you had cancer. You died."

"Oh." A hollow wind blew through the void inside him.

"They're going to bring you back. As soon as the clone thing works out—but this is a government computer you're in, and there are all these government restrictions on cloning, and—" She shook her head. "Look, Digit," she said. "You really need to know this stuff, okay?"

"I understand." Jamie wanted to cry. But only real people cried, he thought, and he wasn't real. He wasn't real.

"The program that runs this virtual environment is huge, okay, and *you're* a big program, and the University computer is used for a lot of research, and a lot of the research has a higher priority than *you* do. So you don't run in real-time—that's why I'm growing faster than you are. I'm spending more hours being me than you are. And the parents—" She rolled her eyes. "They aren't making this any better, with their emphasis on *normal family life*."

She sucked on her cigarette, then stubbed it out in something invisible. "See, they want us to be this *normal family*. So we have breakfast together every day, and dinner every night, and spend the evening at the Zoo or in Pandaland or someplace. But the dinner that we eat with *you* is virtual, it doesn't taste like anything—the grant ran out before they got that part of the interface right—so we eat this fast-food crap before we interface with you, and then have dinner all *over* again with *you* . . . Is this making any sense? Because Dad has a job and Mom has a job and I go to school and have friends and stuff, so we really can't get together every night. So they just close your program file, shut it right down, when they're not available to interface with you as what

Dad calls a 'family unit,' and that means that there are a lot of hours, days sometimes, when you're just *not running*, you might as well really be *dead*—" She blinked. "Sorry," she said. "Anyway, we're *all* getting older a lot faster than you are, and it's not fair to you, that's what I think. Especially because the University computer runs fastest at night, because people don't use them as much then, and you're pretty much real-time then, so interfacing with you would be almost *normal*, but Mom and Dad sleep then, 'cuz they have day jobs, and they can't have you running around unsupervised in here, for God's sake, they think it's unsafe or something . . ."

She paused, then reached into her shirt pocket for another cigarette. "Look," she said, "I'd better get out of here before they figure out I'm talking to you. And then they'll pull my access codes or something." She stood, brushed something off her jeans. "Don't tell the parents about this stuff right away. Otherwise they might erase you, and load a backup that doesn't know shit. Okay?"

And she vanished, as she had that afternoon.

Jamie sat in the bed, hugging his knees. He could feel his heart beating in the darkness. How can a program have a heart? he wondered.

Dawn slowly encroached upon the night, and then there was Mister Jeepers, turning lazy cartwheels in the air, his red face leering in the window.

"Jamie's awake!" he said. "Jamie's awake and ready for a new day!"

"Fuck off," Jamie said, and buried his face in the blanket.

■

Jamie asked to learn more about computers and programming. Maybe, he thought, he could find clues there, he could solve the puzzle. His parents agreed, happy to let him follow his interests.

After a few weeks, he moved into El Castillo. He didn't tell anyone he was going, he just put some of his things in his car, took them up to a tower room, and threw them down on the bed he found there. His mom came to find him when he didn't come home for dinner.

"It's dinnertime, Jamie," she said. "Didn't you hear the dinner bell?"

"I'm going to stay here for a while," Jamie said.

"You're going to get hungry if you don't come home for dinner."

"I don't need food," Jamie said.

His mom smiled brightly. "You need food if you're going to keep up with the Whirlikins," she said.

Jamie looked at her. "I don't care about that kid stuff any-more," he said.

When his mother finally turned and left, Jamie noticed that she moved like an old person.

■

After a while, he got used to the hunger that was programmed into him. It was always *there*, he was always aware of it, but he got so he could ignore it after a while.

But he couldn't ignore the need to sleep. That was just built into the program, and eventually, try though he might, he needed to give in to it.

He found out he could order the people in the castle around, and he amused himself by making them stand in embarrassing po-sitions, or stand on their head and sing, or form human pyramids for hours and hours.

Sometimes he made them fight, but they weren't very good at it.

He couldn't make Mrs. Winkle at the schoolhouse do what-ever he wanted, though, or any of the people who were supposed to teach him things. When it was time for a lesson, Princess Gi-gunda turned up. She wouldn't follow his orders, she'd just pick him up and carry him to the little red schoolhouse and plunk him down in his seat.

"You're not real!" he shouted, kicking in her arms. "You're not real! And *I'm* not real, either!"

But they made him learn about the world that *was* real, about geography and geology and history, although none of it mat-tered here.

After the first couple times Jamie had been dragged to school, his father met him outside the schoolhouse at the end of the day.

"You need some straightening out," he said. He looked grim. "You're part of a family. You belong with us. You're not going to stay in the castle anymore, you're going to have a *normal family life*."

"No!" Jamie shouted. "I *like* the castle!"

Dad grabbed him by the arm and began to drag him homeward. Jamie called him a *pendejo* and a *fellator*.

"I'll punish you if I have to," his father said.

"How are you going to do that?" Jamie demanded. "You gonna erase my file? Load a backup?"

A stunned expression crossed his father's face. His body seemed to go through a kind of stutter, and the grip on Jamie's arm grew nerveless. Then his face flushed with anger. "What do you mean?" he demanded. "Who told you this?"

Jamie wrenched himself free of Dad's weakened grip. "I figured it out by myself," Jamie said. "It wasn't hard. I'm not a kid anymore."

"I—" His father blinked, and then his face hardened. "You're still coming home."

Jamie backed away. "I want some changes!" he said. "I don't want to be shut off all the time."

Dad's mouth compressed to a thin line. "It was Becky who told you this, wasn't it?"

Jamie felt an inspiration. "It was Mister Jeepers! There's a flaw in his programming! He answers whatever question I ask him!"

Jamie's father looked uncertain. He held out his hand. "Let's go home," he said. "I need to think about this."

Jamie hesitated. "Don't erase me," he said. "Don't load a backup. Please. I don't want to die *twice*."

Dad's look softened. "I won't."

"I want to grow up," Jamie said. "I don't want to be a little kid forever."

Dad held out his hand again. Jamie thought for a moment, then took the hand. They walked over the green grass toward the white frame house on the hill.

"Jamie's home!" Mister Jeepers floated overhead, turning aerial cartwheels. "Jamie's home at last!"

A spasm of anger passed through Jamie at the sight of the witless grin. He pointed at the ground in front of him.

"Crash right here!" he ordered. *"Fast!"*

Mister Jeepers came spiraling down, an expression of comic terror on his face, and smashed to the ground where Jamie pointed. Jamie pointed at the sight of the crumpled body and laughed.

"Jamie's home at last!" Mister Jeepers said.

■

As soon as Jamie could, he got one of the programmers at the University to fix him up a flight program like the one Mister Jeepers had been using. He swooped and soared, zooming like a superhero through the sky, stunting between the towers of El Castillo and soaring over upturned, wondering faces in the Forum.

He couldn't seem to go as fast as he really wanted. When he started increasing speed, all the scenery below paused in its motion for a second or two, then jumped forward with a jerk. The software couldn't refresh the scenery fast enough to match his speed. It felt strange, because throughout his flight he could feel the wind on his face.

So this, he thought, was why his car couldn't go fast.

So he decided to climb high. He turned his face to the blue sky and went straight up. The world receded, turned small. He could see the Castle, the hills of Whirlikin Country, the crowded Forum, the huge oval of the Circus Maximus. It was like a green plate, with a fuzzy, nebulous horizon where the sky started.

And, right in the center, was the little two-story frame house where he'd grown up.

It was laid out below him like scenery in a snow globe.

After a while he stopped climbing. It took him a while to realize it, because he still felt the wind blowing in his face, but the world below stopped getting smaller.

He tried going faster. The wind blasted onto him from above, but his position didn't change.

He'd reached the limits of his world. He couldn't get any higher.

Jamie flew out to the edges of the world, to the horizon. No matter how he urged his program to move, he couldn't make his world fade away.

He was trapped inside the snow globe, and there was no way out.

■

It was quite a while before Jamie saw Becca again. She picked her way through the labyrinth beneath El Castillo to his throne room, and Jamie slowly materialized atop his throne of skulls. She didn't appear surprised.

"I see you've got a little Dark Lord thing going here," she said.

"It passes the time," Jamie said.

"And all those pits and stakes and tripwires?"

"Death traps."

"Took me forever to get in here, Digit. I kept getting derezzed."

Jamie smiled. "That's the idea."

"Whirlikins as weapons," she nodded. "That was a good one. Bored a hole right through me, the first time."

"Since I'm stuck living here," Jamie said, "I figure I might as well be in charge of the environment. Some of the student programmers at the University helped me with some cool effects."

Screams echoed through the throne room. Fires leaped out of pits behind him. The flames illuminated the form of Marcus Tullius Cicero, who hung crucified above a sea of flame.

"O tempora, o mores!" moaned Cicero.

Becca nodded. "Nice," she said. "Not my scene exactly, but nice."

"Since I can't leave," Jamie said, "I want a say in who gets to visit. So either you wait till I'm ready to talk to you, or you take your chances on the death traps."

"Well. Looks like you're sitting pretty, then."

Jamie shrugged. Flames belched. "I'm getting bored with it. I might just wipe it all out and build another place to live in. I can't tell you the number of battles I've won, the number of kingdoms I've trampled. In this reality and others. It's all the same after a while." He looked at her. "You've grown."

"So have you."

"Once the paterfamilias finally decided to allow it." He smiled. "We still have dinner together sometimes, in the old house. Just a normal family, as Dad says. Except that sometimes I turn up in the form of a werewolf, or a giant, or something."

"So they tell me."

"The advantage of being software is that I can look like anything I want. But that's the disadvantage, too, because I can't really *become* something else, I'm still just . . . me. I may wear another program as a disguise, but I'm still the same program inside, and I'm not a good enough programmer to mess with that, yet." Jamie hopped off his throne, walked a nervous little circle around his sister. "So what brings you to the old neighborhood?" he asked. "The old folks said you were off visiting Aunt Maddy in the country."

"*Exiled,* they mean. I got knocked up, and after the abortion they sent me to Maddy. She was supposed to keep me under control, except she didn't." She picked an invisible piece of lint from her sweater. "So now I'm back." She looked at him. "I'm skipping a lot of the story, but I figure you wouldn't be interested."

"Does it have to do with sex?" Jamie asked. "I'm sort of interested in sex, even though I can't do it, and they're not likely to let me."

"*Let* you?"

"It would require a lot of new software and stuff. I was prepubescent when my brain structures were scanned, and the program isn't set up for making me a working adult, with adult desires et cetera. Nobody was thinking about putting me through adolescence at the time. And the administrators at the University told me that it was very unlikely that anyone was going to give them a grant so that a computer program could have sex." Jamie shrugged. "I don't miss it, I guess. But I'm sort of curious."

Surprise crossed Becca's face. "But there are all kinds of simulations, and . . ."

"They don't work for me, because my mind isn't structured so as to be able to achieve pleasure that way. I can manipulate the programs, but it's about as exciting as working a virtual butter churn." Jamie shrugged again. "But that's okay. I mean, I don't *miss* it. I can always give myself a jolt to the pleasure center if I want."

"Not the same thing," Becca said. "I've done both."

"I wouldn't know."

"I'll tell you about sex if you want," Becca said, "but that's not why I'm here."

"Yes?"

Becca hesitated. Licked her lips. "I guess I should just say it, huh?" she said. "Mom's dying. Pancreatic cancer."

Jamie felt sadness well in his mind. Only electrons, he thought, moving from one place to another. It was nothing real. He was programmed to feel an analog of sorrow, and that was all.

"She looks normal to me," he said, "when I see her." But that didn't mean anything: his mother chose what she wanted him to see, just as he chose a mask—a werewolf, a giant—for her.

And in neither case did the disguise at all matter. For behind the werewolf was a program that couldn't alter its parameters; and behind the other, ineradicable cancer.

Becca watched him from slitted eyes. "Dad wants her to be scanned, and come here. So we can still be a *normal family* even after she dies."

Jamie was horrified. "Tell her *no*," he said. "Tell her she can't come!"

"I don't think she wants to. But Dad is very insistent."

"She'll be here *forever*! It'll be awful!"

Becca looked around. "Well, she wouldn't do much for your Dark Lord act, that's for sure. I'm sure Sauron's mom didn't hang around the Dark Tower, nagging him about the unproductive way he was spending his time."

Fires belched. The ground trembled. Stalactites rained down like arrows.

"That's not it," Jamie said. "She doesn't want to be here no matter what I'm doing, no matter where I live. Because whatever this place looks like, it's a prison." Jamie looked at his sister. "I don't want my mom in a prison."

Leaping flames glittered in Becca's eyes. "You can change the world you live in," she said. "That's more than I can do."

"But I can't," Jamie said. "I can change the way it *looks*, but I can't change anything *real*. I'm a program, and a program is an *artifact*. I'm a piece of *engineering*. I'm a simulation, with simulated sensory organs that interact with simulated environments—I can only interact with *other artifacts*. *None* of it's real. I don't know what the real world looks or feels or tastes like, I only know what simulations tell me they're *supposed* to taste like. And I can't change any of my parameters unless I mess with the engineering, and I can't do that unless the programmers agree, and even when that happens, I'm still as artificial as I was before. And the computer I'm in is old and clunky, and soon nobody's going to run my operating system anymore, and I'll not only be an artifact, I'll be a museum piece."

"There are other artificial intelligences out there," Becca said. "I keep hearing about them."

"I've talked to them. Most of them aren't very interesting—it's like talking to a dog, or maybe to a very intelligent microwave oven. And they've scanned some people in, but those were adults, and all they wanted to do, once they got inside, was to escape. Some of them went crazy."

Becca gave a twisted smile. "I used to be so jealous of you, you know. You lived in this beautiful world, no pollution, no violence, no shit on the streets."

"Integra mens augustissima possessio," said Cicero.

"Shut up!" Jamie told him. "What the fuck do you know?"

Becca shook her head. "I've seen those old movies, you know? Where somebody gets turned into a computer program, and next thing you know he's in every computer in the world, and running everything?"

"I've seen those, too. Ha ha. Very funny. Shows you what people know about programs."

"Yeah. Shows you what they know."

"I'll talk to Mom," Jamie said.

■

Big tears welled out of Mom's eyes and trailed partway down her face, then disappeared. The scanners paid a lot of attention to eyes and mouths, for the sake of transmitting expression, but didn't always pick up the things between.

"I'm sorry," she said. "We didn't think this is how it would be."

"Maybe you should have given it more thought," Jamie said.

It isn't sorrow, he told himself again. It's just electrons moving.

"You were such a beautiful baby." Her lower lip trembled. "We didn't want to lose you. They said that it would only be a few years before they could implant your memories in a clone."

Jamie knew all that by now. Knew that the technology of reading memories turned out to be much, much simpler than implanting them—it had been discovered that the implantation had to be made while the brain was actually growing. And government restrictions on human cloning had made tests next to impossible, and that the team that had started his project had split up years ago, some to higher paying jobs, some retired, others to pet projects of their own. How his father had long ago used up whatever pull he'd had at the University trying to keep everything together. And how he long ago had acquired or purchased patents and copyrights for the whole scheme, except for Jamie's program, which was still owned jointly by the University and the family.

Tears reappeared on Mom's lower face, dripped off her chin. "There's potentially a lot of money at stake, you know. People want to raise perfect children. Keep them away from bad influences, make sure that they're raised free from violence."

"So they want to control the kid's environment," Jamie said.

"Yes. And make it *safe*. And wholesome. And—"

"Just like *normal family life*," Jamie finished. "No diapers, no vomit, no messes. No having to interact with the kid when the parents are tired. And then you just download the kid into an adult body, give him a diploma, and kick him out of the house. And call yourself a perfect parent."

"And there are *religious people* . . ." Mom licked her lips. "Your dad's been talking to them. They want to raise children in environments that reflect their beliefs completely. Places where there is no temptation, no sin. No science or ideas that contradict their own . . ."

"But Dad isn't religious," Jamie said.

"These people have money. Lots of money."

Mom reached out, took his hand. Jamie thought about all the code that enabled her to do it, that enabled them both to feel the pressure of unreal flesh on unreal flesh.

"I'll do what you wish, of course," she said. "I don't have that desire for immortality, the way your father does." She shook her head. "But I don't know what your father will do once his time comes."

■

The world was a disk a hundred meters across, covered with junk: old Roman ruins, gargoyles fallen from a castle wall, a broken chariot, a shattered bell. Outside the rim of the world, the sky was black, utterly black, without a ripple or a star.

Standing in the center of the world was a kind of metal tree with two forked, jagged arms.

"Hi, Digit," Becca said.

A dull fitful light gleamed on the metal tree, as if it were reflecting a bloody sunset.

"Hi, sis," it said.

"Well," Becca said. "We're alone now."

"I caught the notice of Dad's funeral. I hope nobody missed me."

"I missed you, Digit." Becca sighed. "Believe it or not."

"I'm sorry."

Becca restlessly kicked a piece of junk, a hubcap from an old, miniature car. It clanged as it found new lodgment in the rubble. "Can you appear as a person?" she asked. "It would make it easier to talk to you."

"I've finished with all that," Jamie said. "I'd have to resurrect too much dead programming. I've cut the world down to next to nothing. I've got rid of my body, my heartbeat, the sense of touch."

"All the human parts," Becca said sadly.

The dull red light oozed over the metal tree like a drop of blood. "Everything except sleep and dreams. It turns out that sleep and dreams have too much to do with the way people process memory. I can't get rid of them, not without cutting out too much of my mind." The tree gave a strange, disembodied laugh. "I dreamed about you, the other day. And about Cicero. We were talking Latin."

"I've forgotten all the Latin I ever knew." Becca tossed her hair, forced a laugh. "So what do you do nowadays?"

"Mostly I'm a conduit for data. The University has been using me as a research spider, which I don't mind doing, because it passes the time. Except that I take up a lot more memory than any real search spider, and don't do that much better a job. And the information I find doesn't have much to do with *me*—it's all about the real world. The world I can't touch." The metal tree bled color.

"Mostly," he said, "I've just been waiting for Dad to die. And now it's happened."

There was a moment of silence before Becca spoke. "You know that Dad had himself scanned before he went."

"Oh, yeah. I knew."

"He set up some kind of weird foundation that I'm not part of, with his patents and programs and so on, and his money and some other people's."

"He'd better not turn up here."

Becca shook her head. "He won't. Not without your permission anyway. Because I'm in charge here. You—your program—it's not a part of the foundation. Dad couldn't get it all, because the University has an interest, and so does the family." There was a moment of silence. "And I'm the family now."

"So you . . . *inherited* me," Jamie said. Cold scorn dripped from his words.

"That's right," Becca said. She squatted down amid the rubble, rested her forearms on her knees.

"What do you want me to do, Digit? What can I do to make it better for you?"

"No one ever asked me that," Jamie said.

There was another long silence.

"Shut it off," Jamie said. "Close the file. Erase it."

Becca swallowed hard. Tears shimmered in her eyes. "Are you sure?" she asked.

"Yes. I'm sure."

"And if they ever perfect the clone thing? If we could make you . . ." She took a breath. "A person?"

"No. It's too late. It's . . . not something I can want anymore."

Becca stood. Ran a hand through her hair. "I wish you could meet my daughter," she said. "Her name is Christy. She's a real beauty."

"You can bring her," Jamie said.

Becca shook her head. "This place would scare her. She's only three. I'd only bring her if we could have . . ."

"The old environment," Jamie finished. "Pandaland. Mister Jeepers. Whirlikin Country."

Becca forced a smile. "Those were happy days," she said. "They really were. I was jealous of you, I know, but when I look back at that time . . ." She wiped tears with the back of her hand. "It was the best."

"Virtual environments are nice places to visit, I guess," Jamie said. "But you don't want to live in one. Not forever." Becca looked down at her feet, planted amid rubble.

"Well," she said. "If you're sure about what you want."

"I am."

She looked up at the metal form, raised a hand. "Good-bye, Jamie," she said.

"Good-bye," he said.

She faded from the world.

And in time, the world and the tree faded, too.

■

Hand in hand, Daddy and Jamie walked to Whirlikin Country. Jamie had never seen the Whirlikins before, and he laughed and laughed as the Whirlikins spun beneath their orange sky.

The sound of a bell rang over the green hills. "Time for dinner, Jamie," Daddy said.

Jamie waved good-bye to the Whirlikins, and he and Daddy walked briskly over the fresh green grass toward home.

"Are you happy, Jamie?" Daddy asked.

"Yes, Daddy!" Jamie nodded. "I only wish Momma and Becky could be here with us."

"They'll be here soon."

When, he thought, they can get the simulations working properly.

Because this time, he thought, there would be no mistakes. The foundation he'd set up before he died had finally purchased the University's interest in Jamie's program—they funded some scholarships, that was all it finally took. There was no one in the Computer Department who had an interest anymore.

Jamie had been loaded from an old backup—there was no point in using the corrupt file that Jamie had become, the one that had turned itself into a *tree*, for heaven's sake.

The old world was up and running, with a few improvements. The foundation had bought their own computer—an old one, so it wasn't too expensive—that would run the environment full-time. Some other children might be scanned, to give Jamie some playmates and peer socialization.

This time it would work, Daddy thought. Because this time, Daddy was a program too, and he was going to be here every minute, making sure that the environment was correct and that everything went exactly according to plan. That he and Jamie and everyone else had a normal family life, perfect and shining and safe.

And if the clone program ever worked out, they would come into the real world again. And if downloading into clones was never perfected, then they would stay here.

There was nothing wrong with the virtual environment. It was a *good* place.

Just like normal family life. Only forever.

And when this worked out, the foundation's backers—fine people, even if they did have some strange religious ideas—would have their own environments up and running. With churches, angels, and perhaps even the presence of God . . .

"Look!" Daddy said, pointing. "It's Mister Jeepers!"

Mister Jeepers flew off the rooftop and spun happy spirals in the air as he swooped toward Jamie. Jamie dropped Daddy's hand and ran laughing to greet his friend.

"Jamie's home!" Mister Jeepers cried. "Jamie's home at last!" ■

Walter Jon Williams writes about this story,

"Some people claim to want nothing so much as to have their intelligences downloaded into machines. I can't picture anything more hellish, even if you put me in a machine with cool video games. Not only are you stuck in a place you can't leave, you're not in control of the environment; that's the job of the programmer. And who would want to control such an environment but a stone control freak?

"Of this realization is 'Daddy's World' made.

"I'd like to thank Constance Ash for soliciting the story and thereby initiating the train of thought that led to its creation."

GREG BEAR

Greg Bear published his first story as a teenager, but his mature work began in the late 1970s, and in the 1980s several famous novels, such as *Blood Music*, *Eon*, *The Forge of God*, and *Eternity*, made him one of the best known of his generation of science fiction writers, and widely popular not only in the States but in the United Kingdom and elsewhere. He is known for the expansive scale of his vision, reminiscent of one of his heroes, Olaf Stapledon, combined with a close attention to the complexities of character and the moral issues of our time. His novel *Moving Mars* also won a Nebula Award, and over his career he has hit for the cycle, winning Nebula Awards at each story length.

In this year's award-winning novel, *Darwin's Radio,* Bear returns to one of the subjects that has interested him the most and inspired some of his best work, which is our growing power to intervene in our own biological nature. He has understood better than most that discovering the structure of DNA, and even laying out the genome in full, does not at all dispell the mystery of life. Close study of the current situation has given him ideas of his own on these issues, and the result is science fiction in one of the strongest senses of the term, speculating beyond the current frontier in an attempt to make an intervention in an ongoing scientific inquiry. *Darwin's Radio* suggests that what remains unknown about genetics is so powerful that moving to the next level could be like opening Pandora's box.

FROM DARWIN'S RADIO

Greg Bear

68

WEST VIRGINIA AND OHIO

Rain and mist followed them from Clarksburg. The old blue Buick's tires made a steady hum on wet roads pushing and curling through limestone cuts and low round green hills. The wipers swung short black tails, taking Kaye back to Lado's whining little Fiat on the Georgian Military Road.

"Do you still dream about them?" Kaye asked as Mitch drove.

"Too tired to dream," Mitch said. He smiled at her, then focused on the road.

"I'm curious to know what happened to them," Kaye said lightly.

Mitch made a face. "They lost their baby and they died."

Kaye saw she had touched a nerve and drew back. "Sorry."

"I told you, I'm a little wacko," Mitch said. "I think with my nose and I care what happened to three mummies fifteen thousand years ago."

"You are far from being wacko," Kaye said. She shook her hair, then let out a yell.

"Whoa!" Mitch cringed.

"We're going to travel across America!" Kaye cried. "Across the heartland, and we're going to make *love* every time we stop somewhere, and we're going to *learn* what makes this great nation tick."

Mitch pounded the wheel and laughed.

"But we aren't doing this right," she said, suddenly prim. "We don't have a big poodle dog."

"What?"

"Travels with Charley," Kaye said. "John Steinbeck had a truck

he called Rocinante, with a camper on the back. He wrote about traveling with a big poodle. It's a great book."

"Did Charley have attitude?"

"Damn right," Kaye said.

"Then I'll be the poodle."

Kaye buzzed his hair with mock clippers.

"Steinbeck took more than a week, I bet," Mitch said.

"We don't have to hurry," Kaye said. "I don't want this to ever end. You've given me back my life, Mitch."

■

West of Athens, Ohio, they stopped for lunch at a small diner in a bright red caboose. The caboose sat on a concrete pad and two rails off a frontage road beside the state highway, in a region of low hills covered with maples and dogwood. The food served in the dim interior, illuminated by tiny bulbs in railway lanterns, was adequate and nothing more: a chocolate malt and cheeseburger for Mitch and patty melt and bitter instant iced tea for Kaye. A radio in the kitchen in the back of the caboose played Garth Brooks and Selay Sammi. All they could see of the short-order cook was a white chef's hat bobbing to the music.

As they left the diner, Kaye noticed three shabbily dressed adolescents wandering beside the frontage road: two girls wearing black skirts and torn gray leggings and a boy in jeans and a travel-stained windbreaker. Like a lagging and downcast puppy, the boy walked several steps behind the girls. Kaye seated herself in the Buick. "What are they doing out here?"

"Maybe they live here," Mitch said.

"There's just the house up the hill behind the diner," Kaye said with a sigh.

"You're getting a motherly look," Mitch warned.

Mitch backed the car out of the gravel lot and was about to swing out onto the frontage road when the boy waved vigorously. Mitch stopped and rolled down the window. A light drizzle filled the air with silvery mist scented by trees and the Buick's exhaust.

"Excuse me, sir. You going west?" the boy asked. His ghostly blue eyes swam in a narrow, pale face. He looked worried and exhausted and beneath his clothes he seemed to be made of a bundle of sticks, and not a very large bundle.

The two girls hung back. The shorter and darker girl covered her face with her hands, peeping between her fingers like a shy child.

The boy's hands were dirty, his nails black. He saw Mitch's attention and rubbed them self-consciously on his pants.

"Yeah," Mitch said.

"I'm really *really* sorry to bother you. We wouldn't ask, sir, but it's tough finding rides and it's getting wet. If you're going west, we could use a lift for a while, hey?"

The boy's desperation and a goofy gallantry beyond his years touched Mitch. He examined the boy closely, his answer snagged somewhere between sympathy and suspicion.

"Tell them to get in," Kaye said.

The boy stared at them in surprise. "You mean, now?"

"We're going west." Mitch pointed at the highway beyond the long chain-link fence.

The boy opened the rear door and the girls jogged forward. Kaye turned and rested her arm on the back of the seat as they jumped in and slid across. "Where are you heading?" she asked.

"Cincinnati," the boy said. "Or as far past as we can go," he added hopefully. "Thanks a million."

"Put on your seat belts," Mitch said. "There's three back there."

The girl who hid her face appeared to be no more than seventeen, hair black and thick, skin coffee-colored, fingers long and knobby with short and chipped nails painted violet. Her companion, a white blonde, seemed older, with a broad, easygoing face worn down to vacancy. The boy was no more than nineteen. Mitch wrinkled his nose involuntarily; they hadn't bathed in days.

"Where are you from?" Kaye asked.

"Richmond," the boy said. "We've been hitchhiking, sleeping out in the woods or the grass. It's been hard on Delia and Jayce. This is Delia." He pointed to the girl covering her face.

"I'm Jayce," said the blonde absently.

"My name is Morgan," the boy added.

"You don't look old enough to be out on your own," Mitch said. He brought the car up to speed on the highway.

"Delia couldn't stand it where she was," Morgan said. "She wanted to go to L.A. or Seattle. We decided to go with her."

Jayce nodded.

"That's not much of a plan," Mitch said.

"Any relatives out west?" Kaye asked.

"I have an uncle in Cincinnati," Jayce said. "He might put us up for a while."

Delia leaned back in the seat, face still hidden. Morgan licked his lips and craned his neck to look up at the car's headliner, as if to read a message there. "Delia was pregnant but her baby was born dead," he said. "She got some skin problems because of it."

"I'm sorry," Kaye said. She held out her hand. "My name is Kaye. You don't have to hide, Delia."

Delia shook her head, hands following. "It's ugly," she said.

"I don't mind it," Morgan said. He sat as far to the left-hand side of the car as he could, leaving a foot of space between himself and Jayce. "Girls are more sensitive. Her boyfriend told her to get out. Real stupid. What a waste, hey."

"It's too ugly," Delia said softly.

"Come on, sweetie," Kaye said. "Is it something a doctor could help with?"

"I got it before the baby came," Delia said.

"It's okay," Kaye said soothingly, and reached back to stroke the girl's arm. Mitch caught glimpses in the rearview mirror, fascinated by this aspect of Kaye. Gradually, Delia lowered her hands, her fingers relaxing. The girl's face was blotched and mottled, as if splattered with reddish-brown paint.

"Did your boyfriend do that to you?" Kaye asked.

"No," Delia said. "It just came, and everybody hated it."

"She got a mask," Jayce said. "It covered her face for a few weeks, and then it fell off and left those marks."

Mitch felt a chill. Kaye faced forward and lowered her head for a moment, composing herself.

"Delia and Jayce don't want me touching them," Morgan said, "even though we're friends, because of the plague. You know. Herod's."

"I don't want to get pregnant," Jayce said. "We're really hungry."

"We'll stop and get some food," Kaye said. "Would you like to take a shower, get cleaned up?"

"Oh, wow," Delia said. "That would be so great."

"You two look decent, hey, real nice," Morgan said, staring up at the headliner again, this time for courage. "But I have to tell you, these girls are my friends. I don't want you doing this just so *he* can see them without their clothes on. I won't put up with that."

"Don't worry," Kaye said. "If I were your mom, I'd be proud of you, Morgan."

"Thanks," Morgan said, and dropped his gaze to the window. The muscles on his narrow jaw clenched. "Hey, it's just the way I feel. They've gone through enough shit. Her boyfriend got a mask, too, and he was really mad. Jayce says he blamed Delia."

"He did," Jayce said.

"He was a white boy," Morgan continued, "and Delia is partly black."

"I *am* black," Delia said.

"They were living in a farmhouse for a while until he made her leave," Jayce said. "He was hitting her, after the miscarriage. Then she was pregnant again. He said she was making him sick because he had a mask and it wasn't even his baby." This came out in a mumbled rush.

"My second baby was born dead," Delia said, her voice distant. "He only had half his face. Jayce and Morgan never showed him to me."

"We buried it," Morgan said.

"My God," Kaye said. "I'm so sorry."

"It was hard," Morgan said. "But hey, we're still here." He clamped his teeth together and his jaw again tensed rhythmically.

"Jayce shouldn't have told me what he looked like," Delia said.

"If it was God's baby," Jayce said flatly, "He should have taken better care of it."

Mitch wiped his eyes with a finger and blinked to keep the road clear.

"Have you seen a doctor?" Kaye asked.

"I'm okay," Delia said. "I just want these marks to go away."

"Let me see them up close, sweetie," Kaye said.

"Are you a doctor?" Delia asked.

"I'm a biologist, but not a medical doctor," Kaye said.

"A scientist?" Morgan asked, interest piqued.

"Yeah," Kaye said.

Delia thought this through for a few seconds, then leaned forward, eyes averted. Kaye touched her chin to steady her. The sun had come out but a big panel truck growled by on the left and the wide tires showered the windshield. The watery light cast a wavering gray pall over the girl's features.

Her face bore a pattern of demelanized, teardrop-shaped dapples, mostly on her cheeks, with several symmetrical patches at the corners of her eyes and lips. As she turned away from Kaye, the marks shifted and darkened.

"They're like freckles," Delia said hopefully. "I get freckles sometimes. It's my white blood, I guess."

69

ATHENS, OHIO

May 1

Mitch and Morgan stood on the wide white-painted porch outside the office of James Jacobs, MD.

Morgan was agitated. He lit up the last of his pack of cigarettes and puffed with slit-eyed intent, then walked over to a rough-barked old maple and leaned against it.

Kaye had insisted after a lunch stop that they look up a family practice doctor in the white pages and take Delia in for a checkup. Delia had reluctantly agreed.

"We didn't do anything criminal," Morgan said. "We didn't have no money, hey, and she had her baby and there we were." He waved his hand up the road.

"Where was that?" Mitch asked.

"West Virginia. In the woods near a farm. It was pretty. A nice place to be buried. You know, I am so tired. I am so sick of them treating me like a flea-bitten dog."

"The girls do that?"

"You know the attitude," Morgan said. "Men are contagious. They *rely* on me, I'm always here for them, then they tell me I have real boy cooties, and that's it, hey. No *thanks*, ever."

"It's the times," Mitch said.

"It's lame. Why are we living now and not some other time, not so lame?"

■

In the main examining room, Delia perched on the edge of the table, legs dangling. She wore a white flower-print open-backed robe. Jayce sat in a chair across from her, reading a pamphlet on smoking-related illnesses. Dr. Jacobs was in his sixties, thin, with a close-cut and tightly curled patch of graying hair around a tall and noble dome. His eyes were large, and both wise and sad. He told the girls he would be right back, then let his assistant, a middle-aged woman with a bun of fine auburn hair, enter the room with a clipboard and pencil. He closed the door and turned to Kaye.

"No relation?" he asked.

"We picked them up east of here. I thought she should see a doctor."

"She says she's nineteen. She doesn't have any ID, but I don't think she's nineteen, do you?"

"I don't know much about her," Kaye said. "I'm trying to help them, not get them in trouble."

Jacobs cocked his head in sympathy. "She gave birth less than a week or ten days ago. No major trauma, but she tore some tissue, and there's still blood on her leggings. I don't like to see kids living like animals, Ms. Lang."

"Neither do I."

"Delia says it was a Herod's baby and that it was born dead. Second-stage, by the description. I see no reason not to believe her, but these things should be reported. The baby should have undergone a postmortem. Laws are being put in place right now, at the federal level, and Ohio is going along . . . She said she was in West Virginia when she delivered. I understand West Virginia is showing some resistance."

"Only in some ways," Kaye said, and told him about the blood test requirements.

Jacobs listened, then pulled a pen from his pocket and nervously clicked it with one hand. "Ms. Lang, I wasn't sure who you were when you came in this afternoon. I had Georgina get on the Web and find some news pictures. I don't know what you're doing in Athens, but I'd say you know more about this sort of thing than I do."

"I might not agree," Kaye said. "The marks on her face . . ."

"Some women acquire dark markings during pregnancy. It passes."

"Not like these," Kaye said. "They tell us she had other skin problems."

"I know." Jacobs sighed and sat on the corner of his desk. "I have three patients who are pregnant, probably with Herod's second-stage. They won't let me do amnio or any kind of scans. They're all churchgoing women and I don't think they want to know the truth. They're scared and they're under pressure. Their friends shun them. They aren't welcome in church. The husbands won't come in with them to my office." He pointed to his face. "They all have skin stiffening and coming loose around the eyes, the nose, the cheeks, the corners of the mouth. It won't just peel away . . . not yet. They're shedding several layers of facial corium and epidermis." He made a face and pinched his fingers together, tugging at an imaginary flap of skin. "It's a little leathery. Ugly as sin, very scary. That's why they're nervous and that's why they're shunned. This separates them from their community, Ms. Lang. It *hurts* them. I make my reports to the state and to the feds, and I get no response back. It's like sending messages into a big dark cave."

"Do you think the masks are common?"

"I follow the basic tenets of science, Ms. Lang. If I'm seeing it more than once, and now this girl comes along and I see it again, from out of state . . . I doubt it's unusual." He looked at her critically. "Do you know anything more?"

She found herself biting her lip like a little girl. "Yes and no," she said. "I resigned from my position on the Herod's Taskforce."

"Why?"

"It's too complicated."

"It's because they've got it all wrong, isn't it?"

Kaye looked aside and smiled. "I won't say that."

"You've seen this before? In other women?"

"I think we're going to see more of it."

"And the babies will all be monsters and die?"

Kaye shook her head. "I think that's going to change."

Jacobs replaced his pen in his pocket, put his hand on the desktop blotter, lifted its leather corner, dropped it slowly. "I won't file a report on Delia. I'm not sure what I'd say, or who I'd say it to. I think she'd vanish before any authorities could come along to help her. I doubt we'd ever find the infant, where they buried it. She's tired and she needs steady nourishment. She needs a place to stay and rest. I'll give her a vitamin shot and prescribe antibiotics and iron supplements."

"And the marks?"

"Do you know what chromatophores are?"

"Cells that change color. In cuttlefish."

"These marks can change color," Jacobs said. "They're not just a hormonally induced melanosis."

"Melanophores," Kaye said.

Jacobs nodded. "That's the word. Ever seen melanophores on a human?"

"No," Kaye said.

"Neither have I. Where are you going, Ms. Lang?"

"All the way west," she said. She lifted her wallet. "I'd like to pay you now."

Jacobs gave her his saddest look. "I'm not running a goddamned HMO, Ms. Lang. No charge. I'll prescribe the pills and you pick them up at a good pharmacy. You buy her food and find her a clean place to get a good night's sleep."

The door opened and Delia and Jayce emerged. Delia was fully dressed.

"She needs clean clothes and a good soak in a hot tub," Georgina said firmly.

For the first time since they had met, Delia smiled. "I looked in the mirror," she said. "Jayce says the marks are pretty. The doctor says I'm not sick, and I can have children again if I want."

Kaye shook Jacobs's hand. "Thank you very much," she said.

As the three of them left through the front office, joining Mitch and Morgan on the front porch, Jacobs called out, "We live and we learn, Ms. Lang! And the faster we learn, the better."

■

The little motel sported a huge red sign with TINY SUITES and $50 crowded onto it, clearly visible from the freeway. It had seven rooms, three of them vacant. Kaye rented all three and gave Morgan his own key. Morgan lifted the key, frowned, then pocketed it.

"I don't like being alone," he said.

"I couldn't think of another arrangement," Kaye said.

Mitch put his arm around the boy's shoulder. "I'll stay with you," he said, and gave Kaye a level look. "Let's get cleaned up and watch TV."

"We'd like you to stay in our room," Jayce told Kaye. "We'd feel a lot safer."

The rooms were just on the edge of being dirty. Draped on beds with distinct hollows, thin and worn quilted coverlets showed unraveled nylon threads and cigarette burns. Coffee tables bore multiple ring marks and more cigarette burns. Jayce and Delia explored and settled in as if the accommodations were royal. Delia took the single orange chair beside a table-lamp combo hung with black metal cone-shaped cans. Jayce lounged on the bed and switched on the TV. "They have HBO," she said in a soft and wondering voice. "We can watch a movie!"

Mitch listened to Morgan in the shower in their room, then opened the front door. Kaye stood outside with her hand up, about to knock.

"We're wasting a room," she said. "We've taken on some responsibilities, haven't we?"

Mitch hugged her. "Your instincts," he said.

"What do *your* instincts tell you?" she asked, nuzzling his shoulder.

"They're kids. They've been out on the road for weeks, months. Someone should call their parents."

"Maybe they never had real parents. They're desperate, Mitch." Kaye pushed back to look up at him.

"They're also independent enough to bury a dead baby and stay on the road. The doctor should have called the police, Kaye."

"I know," Kaye said. "I also know why he didn't. The rules have changed. He thinks most of the babies are going to be born dead. Are we the only ones with any hope?"

The shower stopped and the stall door clicked open. The small bathroom was filled with steam.

"The girls," Kaye said, and walked over to the next door. She gave Mitch a hand-open sign that he instantly recognized from the marching crowds in Albany, and he understood for the first time what the crowds had been trying to show: strong belief in and a cautious submission to the way of Life, belief in the ultimate wisdom of the human genome. No presumption of doom, no ignorant attempts to use new human powers to block the rivers of DNA flowing through the generations.

Faith in Life.

Morgan dressed quickly. "Jayce and Delia don't need me," he

said as he stood in the small room. The holes in the sleeves of his black pullover were even more obvious now that his skin was clean. He let the dirty windbreaker dangle from one arm. "I don't want to be a burden. I'll go now. Give my thanks, hey, but—"

"Please be quiet and sit down," Mitch said. "What the lady wants, goes. She wants you to stick around."

Morgan blinked in surprise, then sat on the end of the bed. The springs squeaked and the frame groaned. "I think it's the end of the world," he said. "We've really made God angry."

"Don't jump to any conclusions," Mitch said. "Believe it or not, all this has happened before."

■

Jayce turned on the TV and watched from the bed while Delia took a long bath in the chipped and narrow tub. The girl hummed to herself, tunes from cartoon shows—*Scooby Doo*, *Animaniacs*, *Inspector Gadget*. Kaye sat in the single chair. Jayce had found something old and affirming on the TV: *Pollyanna*, with Hayley Mills. Karl Malden was kneeling in a dry grassy field, berating himself for his stubborn blindness. It was an impassioned performance. Kaye did not remember the movie being so compelling. She watched it with Jayce until she noticed that the girl was sound asleep. Then, turning down the volume, Kaye switched over to Fox News.

There was a smattering of show business stories, a brief political report on congressional elections, then an interview with Bill Cosby on his commercials for the CDC and the Taskforce. Kaye turned up the volume.

"I was a buddy of David Satcher, the former surgeon general, and they must have a kind of ol' boy network," Cosby told the interviewer, a blond woman with a large smile and intense blue eyes, " 'cause years ago they got me, this ol' guy, in to talk about what was important, what they were doing. They thought I might be able to help again."

"You've joined quite a select team," said the interviewer. "Dustin Hoffman and Michael Crichton. Let's take a look at your spot."

Kaye leaned forward. Cosby returned against a black background, face seamed with parental concern. "My friends at the Centers for Disease Control, and many other researchers around the world, are hard at work every day to solve *this problem* we're all facing. Herod's flu. SHEVA. Every day. Nobody's gonna rest until it's understood and we can cure it. You can take it from me, these people care, and when you hurt, they hurt, too. Nobody's asking you to be patient. But to survive this, we all have to *be smart*."

The interviewer looked away from the big screen television on the set. "Let's play an excerpt from Dustin Hoffman's message . . ."

Hoffman stood on a bare motion picture sound stage with his hands thrust into the pockets of tailored beige pants. He smiled a friendly but solemn greeting. "My name is Dustin Hoffman. You might remember I played a scientist fighting a deadly disease in a movie called *Outbreak*. I've been talking to the scientists at the National Institutes of Health and the Centers for Disease Control and Prevention, and they're working as hard as they can, every day, to fight SHEVA and stop our children from dying."

The interviewer interrupted the clip. "What *are* the scientists doing that they weren't doing last year? What's new in the effort?"

Cosby made a sour face. "I'm just a man who wants to help us get through this mess. Doctors and scientists are the only hope we've got, and we can't just take to the streets and burn things down and make it all go away. We're talking about thinking things through, working together, not engaging in riots and panic."

Delia stood in the bathroom doorway, plump legs bare beneath the small motel towel, head wrapped in another towel. She stared fixedly at the television. "It's not going to make any difference," she said. "My babies are dead."

■

Mitch returned from the Coke machine at the end of the line of rooms to find Morgan pacing in a U around the bed. The boy's hands were knots of frustration. "I can't stop thinking," Morgan said. Mitch held out a Coke and Morgan stared at it, took it from his hand, popped the top, and chugged it back fiercely. "You know what they did, what Jayce did? When we needed money?"

"I don't need to know, Morgan," Mitch said.

"It's how they treat me. Jayce went out and got a man to pay for it, and, you know, she and Delia *blew* him, and took some money. Jesus, I ate some of that dinner, too. And the next night. Then we were hitching and Delia started having her baby. They won't let me touch them, even hug them, they won't put their arms around me, but for money, they *blow* these guys, and they don't care whether I see them or not!" He pounded his temple with the ball of his thumb. "They are so *stupid*, like farm animals."

"It must have been tough out there," Mitch said. "You were all hungry."

"I went with them because my father's nothing great, you know, but he doesn't beat me. He works all day. They needed me more than he does. But I want to go back. I can't do anything more for them."

"I understand," Mitch said. "But don't be hasty. We'll work this through."

"I am so sick of this shit!" Morgan howled.

■

They heard the howl in the next room. Jayce sat up in bed and rubbed her eyes. "There he goes again," she murmured.

Delia dried off her hair. "He really isn't stable sometimes," she said.

"Can you drop us off in Cincinnati?" Jayce asked. "I have an uncle there. Maybe you can send Morgan back home now."

"Sometimes Morgan's such a child," Delia said.

Kaye watched them from her chair, her face pinking with an emotion she could not quite understand: solidarity compounded with visceral disgust.

Minutes later, she met Mitch outside, under the long motel walkway. They held hands.

Mitch pointed his thumb over his shoulder, through the room's open door. The shower was running again. "His second. He says he feels dirty all the time. The girls have played a little loose with poor Morgan."

"What was he expecting?"

"No idea."

"To go to bed with them?"

"I don't know," Mitch said quietly. "Maybe he just wants to be treated with respect."

"I don't think they know how," Kaye said. She pressed her hand on his chest, rubbed him there, her eyes focused on something distant and invisible. "The girls want to be dropped off in Cincinnati."

"Morgan wants to go to the bus station," Mitch said. "He's had enough."

"Mother Nature isn't being very kind or gentle, is she?"

"Mother Nature has always been something of a bitch," he said.

"So much for Rocinante and touring America," Kaye said sadly.

"You want to make some phone calls, get involved again, don't you?"

Kaye lifted her hands. "I don't *know*!" she moaned. "Just taking off and living our lives seems wildly irresponsible. I want to learn more. But how much will anybody tell us—Christopher, anybody on the Taskforce? I'm an outsider now."

"There's a way we can stay in the game, with different rules," Mitch said.

"The rich guy in New York?"

"Daney. And Oliver Merton."

"We're not going to Seattle?"

"We are," Mitch said. "But I'm going to call Merton and say I'm interested."

"I still want to have our baby," Kaye said, eyes wide, voice fragile as a dried flower.

The shower stopped. They heard Morgan toweling off, alternately humming to himself and swearing.

"It's funny," Mitch said, almost too softly to hear. "I've been very uncomfortable about the whole idea. But now . . . it seems plain as anything, the dreams, meeting you. I want our baby, too. We just can't be innocent." He took a deep breath, raised his eyes to meet Kaye's, added, "Let's go into that forest with some better maps."

Morgan stepped out onto the walkway and stared at them owlishly. "I'm ready. I want to go home."

Kaye looked at Morgan and almost flinched at his intensity. The boy's eyes seemed a thousand years old.

"I'll drive you to the bus station," Mitch said.

70

THE NATIONAL INSTITUTES OF HEALTH, BETHESDA

May 5

Dicken met the director of the National Institute of Child Health and Human Development, Dr. Tania Bao, outside the Natcher Building, and walked with her from there. Small, precisely dressed, with a composed and ageless face, its features arranged on a slightly undulating plain, nose tiny, lips on the edge of a smile, and slightly stooped shoulders, Bao might have been in her late thirties, but was in fact sixty-three. She wore a pale blue pantsuit and tasseled loafers. She walked with small quick steps, intent on the rough ground. The never-ending construction on the NIH campus had been brought to a halt for security purposes, but had already torn up most of the walkways between the Natcher Building and the Magnuson Clinical Center.

"NIH used to be an open campus," Bao said. "Now, we live with the National Guard watching our every move. I can't even buy my granddaughter toys from the vendors. I used to love to see them on the sidewalks or in the hallways. Now they've been cleared out, along with the construction workers."

Dicken raised his shoulders, showing that these things were outside his control. His area of influence did not even include himself anymore. "I've come to listen," he said. "I can take your opinions to Dr. Augustine, but I can't guarantee he'll agree."

"What happened, Christopher?" Bao asked plaintively. "Why do they not respond to what is so obvious? Why is Augustine so stubborn?"

"You're a far more experienced administrator than I am," Dicken said. "I know only what I see and what I hear in the news. What I see is unbearable pressure from all sides. The vaccine teams haven't been able to do anything. Mark will do everything he can, regardless, to protect public health. He wants to focus our resources on fighting what he believes is a virulent disease. Right now, the only available option is abortion."

"What he *believes* . . ." Bao said incredulously. "What do *you* believe, Dr. Dicken?"

The weather was coming into a warm and humid summer

mood that Dicken found familiar, even comforting; it made a deep and sad part of him think he might be in Africa, and he would have much preferred that to the current round of his existence. They crossed a temporary asphalt ramp to the next level of finished sidewalk, stepped over yellow construction tape, and walked into the main entrance of Building 10.

Two months ago, life had begun to come apart for Christopher Dicken. The realization that hidden parts of his personality could affect his scientific judgment—that a combination of frustrated infatuation and job pressure could jolt him into an attitude he knew to be false—had preyed on him like a swarm of little biting flies. Somehow, he had managed an outward appearance of calm, of going with the game, the team, the Taskforce. He knew that could not go on forever.

"I believe in work," Dicken said, embarrassed that his thoughts had delayed a response for so long.

Simply cutting himself off from Kaye Lang, and failing to support her in the face of Jackson's ambush, had been an incomprehensible and unforgivable mistake. He regretted it more with each day, but it was too late to retie old and broken threads. He could still build a conceptual wall and work diligently on those projects assigned to him.

They took the elevator to the seventh floor, turned left, and found the small staff meeting room in the middle of a long beige and pink corridor.

Bao seated herself. "Christopher, you know Anita, Preston."

They greeted Dicken with little cheer.

"No good news, I'm afraid," Dicken reported, seating himself opposite Preston Meeker. Meeker, like his colleagues within the small, close room, represented the quintessence of a child health specialty—in his case, neonatal growth and development.

"Augustine still at it?" Meeker asked, pugnacious from the start. "Still pushing RU-486?"

"In his defense," Dicken said, and paused for a moment to collect his thoughts, to present this old false face more convincingly, "he has no alternatives. The retrovirus folks at CDC agree that the expression and completion theory makes sense."

"Children as carriers of unknown plagues?" Meeker pushed out his lips and made a pishing noise.

"It's a highly defensible position. Added to the likelihood that most of the new babies will be born deformed—"

"We don't know that," House said. House was the acting deputy director of the National Institute of Child Health and Human Development; the former deputy director had resigned two weeks ago. A great many NIH people associated with the SHEVA Taskforce were resigning.

With hardly a pang, Dicken thought that once again Kaye Lang had proved herself a pioneer by being the very first to leave.

"It's indisputable," Dicken said, and had no trouble telling her this, because it was true: no normal infants had been born yet to a SHEVA-infected mother. "Out of two hundred, most have been reported severely deformed. All have been born dead." *But not always deformed,* he reminded himself.

"If the president agrees to start a national campaign using RU-486," Bao said, "I doubt the CDC will be allowed to remain open in Atlanta. As for Bethesda, it is an intelligent community, but we are still in the Bible Belt. I have already had my house picketed, Christopher. I live surrounded by guards."

"I understand," Dicken said.

"Perhaps, but does Mark understand? He does not return my calls or my e-mail."

"Unacceptable isolation," Meeker said.

"How many acts of civil disobedience will it take?" House added, clasping her hands on the table and rubbing them together, her eyes darting around the group.

Bao stood and took up a whiteboard marker. She quickly and almost savagely chopped out the words in bright red, saying, "Two million first-stage Herod's miscarriages, as of last month. Hospitals are flooded."

"I go to those hospitals," Dicken said. "It's part of my job to be on the front."

"We also have visited patients here and around the country," Bao said, mouth tight with irritation. "We have three hundred SHEVA mothers in this very building. I see some of them every day. *We* are not isolated, Christopher."

"Sorry," Dicken said.

Bao nodded. "Seven hundred thousand reported second-stage Herod's pregnancies. Well, here the statistics fall apart—we do not know what is happening," Bao said, and stared at Dicken. "Where have all the others gone? They are not reporting. Does Mark know?"

"I know," Dicken said. "Mark knows. It's sensitive information. We don't want to acknowledge how much we know until the president makes his policy decision on the Taskforce proposal."

"I think I can guess," House said sardonically. "Educated women with means are buying black-market RU-486, or otherwise obtaining abortions at different stages of their pregnancy. There's a wholesale revolt in the medical community, in women's clinics. They've stopped reporting to the Taskforce, because of the new laws regulating abortion procedures. My guess is, Mark wants to make official what's already happening around the country."

Dicken paused for a moment to gather his thoughts, shore up his sagging false front. "Mark has no control over the House of Representatives or the Senate. He speaks, they ignore him. We all know the rates of domestic violence are way up. Women are being forced out of their homes. Divorce. Murder." Dicken let that sink in, as it had sunk in to his own thoughts and self in the last few months. "Violence against pregnant women is at an all-time high. Some are even resorting to quinacrine, when they can get it, to self-sterilize."

Bao shook her head sadly.

Dicken continued. "Many women know the simplest way out is to stop their second-stage pregnancies before they go anywhere near full term and other side effects appear."

"Mark Augustine and the Taskforce are reluctant to describe these side effects," Bao said. "We assume you refer to facial cauls and melanisms in both the parents."

"I also refer to whistling palate and vomeronasal deformation," Dicken said.

"Why the fathers, too?" Bao asked.

"I have no idea," Dicken said. "If NIH hadn't lost its clinical study subjects, due to an excess of personal concern, we might all know a lot more, under at least mildly controlled conditions."

Bao reminded Dicken that no one in the room had had anything to do with the closure of the Taskforce clinical studies in this very building.

"I understand," Dicken said, and hated himself with a ferocity he could barely hide. "I don't disagree. Second-stage pregnancies are being ended by all but the poor, those who can't get to clinics or buy the pills . . . or . . ."

"Or what?" Meeker asked.

"The dedicated."

"Dedicated to what?"

"To nature. To the proposition that these children should be given a chance, whatever the odds of their being born dead or deformed."

"Augustine does not seem to believe any of the children should be given a chance," Bao said. "Why?"

"Herod's is a disease. This is how you fight a disease." *This can't go on much longer. You'll either resign or you'll kill yourself trying to explain things you don't understand or believe.*

"I say again, we are not isolated, Christopher," Bao said, shaking her head. "We go to the maternity wards and the surgeries in this clinic, and visit other clinics and hospitals. We see the women and the men in pain. We need some rational approach that takes into account all these views, all these pressures."

Dicken frowned in concentration. "Mark is just looking at medical reality. And there's no political consensus," he added quietly. "It's a dangerous time."

"That's putting it mildly," Meeker said. "Christopher, I think the White House is paralyzed. Damned if you do, and certainly damned if you don't and things go on the way they are."

"Maryland's own governor is involved in this so-called States' Health revolt," House said. "I've never seen such fervor in the religious right here."

"It's pretty much grass roots, not just Christian," Bao said. "The Chinese community has pulled in its horns and with good reason. Bigotry is on the rise. We are falling apart into scared and unhappy tribes, Christopher."

Dicken stared down at the table, then up at the figures on the whiteboard, one eyelid twitching with fatigue. "It hurts all of us," he said. "It hurts Mark, and it hurts me."

"I doubt it hurts Mark as much as it hurts the mothers," Bao said quietly.

71

OREGON

May 10

"I'm an ignorant man, and I don't understand a lot of things," Sam said. He leaned on the split-rail fence that surrounded the four acres, the two-story frame farmhouse, an old and sagging barn, the brick workshed. Mitch pushed his free hand into his pocket and rested a can of Michelob on the lichen-grayed fence post. A square-rump, black-and-white cow cropping a patch of the neighbor's twelve acres regarded them with an almost complete absence of curiosity. "You've only known this woman for what, two weeks?"

"Just over a month."

"Some whirlwind!"

Mitch agreed with a sheepish look.

"Why be in such a hurry? Why in hell would anyone want to get pregnant, now of all times? Your mother's been over her hot flashes for ten years, but after Herod's, she's still skittish about letting me touch her."

"Kaye's different," Mitch said, as if admitting something. They had come to this topic on the backs of a lot of other difficult topics that afternoon. The toughest of all had been Mitch's admission that he had temporarily given up looking for a job, that they would largely be living on Kaye's money. Sam found this incomprehensible.

"Where's the self-respect in that?" he had said, and shortly after they had dropped that subject and returned to what had happened in Austria.

Mitch had told him about meeting Brock at the Daney mansion, and that had amused Sam quite a bit. "It baffles science," he had commented dryly. When they had gotten around to discussing Kaye, still talking with Mitch's mother, Abby, in the large farmhouse kitchen, Sam's puzzlement had blossomed into irritation, then downright anger.

"I admit I may be stuck in abysmal stupidity," Sam said, "but isn't it just damned dangerous to do this sort of thing now, deliberately?"

"It could be," Mitch admitted.

"Then why in hell did you agree?"

"I can't answer that easily," Mitch said. "First, I think she could be right. I mean, I think she *is* right. This time around, we'll have a healthy baby."

"But you tested positive, *she* tested positive," Sam said, glaring at him, hands gripping the rail tightly.

"We did."

"And correct me if I'm wrong, but there's *never* been a healthy baby born of a woman who tested positive."

"Not yet," Mitch said.

"That's lousy odds."

"She's the one who found this virus," Mitch said. "She knows more about it than anyone else on Earth, and she's convinced—"

"That everyone else is wrong?" Sam asked.

"That we're going to change our thinking in the next few years."

"Is she crazy, then, or just a fanatic?"

Mitch frowned. "Careful, Dad," he said.

Sam flung his hands up in the air. "Mitch, for Christ's sake, I fly to Austria, the first time I've ever been to Europe, and it's without your mother, damn it, to pick up my son at a hospital after he's . . . Well, we've been through all that. But why face this kind of grief, take this kind of chance, I ask, in God's name?"

"Since her first husband died, she's been a little frantic about looking ahead, seeing things in a positive light," Mitch said. "I can't say I understand her, Dad, but I love her. I trust her. Something in me says she's right, or I wouldn't have gone along."

"You mean, *cooperated*." Sam looked at the cow and brushed his hands free of lichen dust on his pants legs. "What if you're both wrong?" he asked.

"We know the consequences. We'll live with them," Mitch said. "But we're not wrong. Not this time, Dad."

■

"I've been reading as much as I can," Abby Rafelson said. "It's bewildering. All these viruses." Afternoon sun fell through the kitchen window and lay in yellow trapezoids on the unvarnished oak floor. The kitchen smelled of coffee—too much coffee, Kaye thought, nerves on edge—and tamales, their lunch before the men had gone out walking.

Mitch's mother had kept her beauty into her sixties, an authoritative kind of good looks that emerged from high cheekbones and deep-sunk blue eyes combined with immaculate grooming.

"These particular viruses have been with us a long time," Kaye said. She held up a picture of Mitch when he was five years old, riding a tricycle on the Willamette riverfront in Portland. He looked intent, oblivious to the camera; sometimes she saw that same expression when he was driving or reading a newspaper.

"How long?" Abby asked.

"Maybe tens of millions of years." Kaye picked up another picture from the pile on the coffee table. The picture showed Mitch and Sam loading wood in the back of a truck. By his height and thin limbs, Mitch appeared to be about ten or eleven.

"What were they doing there in the first place? I couldn't understand that."

"They might have infected us through our gametes, eggs or sperm. Then they stayed. They mutated, or something deactivated them, or . . . we put them to work for us. Found a way to make them useful." Kaye looked up from the picture.

Abby stared at her, unfazed. "Sperm or eggs?"

"Ovaries, testicles," Kaye said, glancing down again.

"What made them decide to come out again?"

"Something in our everyday lives," Kaye said. "Stress, maybe."

Abby thought about this for a few seconds. "I'm a college graduate. Physical education. Did Mitch tell you that?"

Kaye nodded. "He said you took a minor in biochemistry. Some pre-med courses."

"Yes, well, not enough to be up to your level. More than enough to be dubious about my religious upbringing, however. I don't know what my mother would have thought if she had known about these viruses in our sex cells." Abby smiled at Kaye and shook her head. "Maybe she would have called them our original sin."

Kaye looked at Abby and tried to think of a reply but couldn't. "That's interesting," she managed. Why this should disturb her she did not know, but that it did upset her even more. She felt threatened by the idea.

"The graves in Russia," Abby said quietly. "Maybe the mothers had neighbors who thought it was an outbreak of original sin."

"I don't believe it is," Kaye said.

"Oh, I don't believe it myself," Abby said. She trained her examining blue eyes on Kaye now, troubled, darting. "I've never been very comfortable about anything to do with sex. Sam's a gentle man, the only man I've felt passionate about, though not the only man I've invited into my bed. My upbringing . . . was not the best that way. Not the wisest. I've never talked with Mitch about sex. Or about love. It seemed he would do well enough on his own, handsome as he is, smart as he is." Abby laid her hand on Kaye's. "Did he tell you his mother was a crazy old prude?" She looked so sadly desperate and at a loss that Kaye gripped her hand tightly and smiled what she hoped was reassurance.

"He told me you were a wonderful mother and caring," Kaye said, "and that he was your only son, and that you'd grill me like a pork chop." She squeezed Abby's hand tighter.

Abby laughed and something of the electricity fell from the air between them. "He told me you were headstrong and smarter than any woman he had ever met, and that you cared so much about things. He said I'd better like you, or he'd have a talk with me."

Kaye stared at her, aghast. "He did not!"

"He did," Abby said solemnly. "The men in this family don't mince words. I told him I'd do my best to get along with you."

"Good grief!" Kaye said, laughing in disbelief.

"Exactly," Abby said. "He was being defensive. But he knows me. He knows I don't mince words, either. With all this original sin popping out all over, I think we're in for a world of change. A lot of ways men and women do things will change. Don't you think?"

"I'm sure of it," Kaye said.

"I want you to work as hard as you can, please, dear, my new daughter, please, to make a place where there will be love and a gentle and caring center for Mitch. He looks tough and sturdy but men are really very fragile. Don't let all this split you up, or damage him. I want to keep as much of the Mitch I know and love as I can, as long as I can. I still see my boy in him. My boy is strong there still." There were tears in Abby's eyes, and Kaye realized, holding the woman's hand, that she had missed her own mother so much, for so many years, and had tried unsuccessfully to bury those emotions.

"It was hard, when Mitch was born," Abby said. "I was in

labor for four days. My first child, I thought the delivery would be tough, but not that tough. I regret we did not have more . . . but only in some ways. Now, I'd be scared to death. I *am* scared to death, even though there's nothing to worry about between Sam and me."

"I'll take care of Mitch," Kaye said.

"These are horrible times," Abby said. "Somebody's going to write a book, a big, thick, book. I hope there's a bright and happy ending."

■

That evening, over dinner, men and women together, the conversation was pleasant, light, of little consequence. The air seemed clear, the issues all rained out. Kaye slept with Mitch in his old bedroom, a sign of acceptance from Abby or assertion from Mitch or both.

This was the first real family she had known in years. Thinking about that, lying cramped up beside Mitch in the too-small bed, she had her own moment of happy tears.

She had bought a pregnancy test kit in Eugene when they had stopped for gas not far from a big drug store. Then, to make herself feel she was really making a normal decision despite a world so remarkably out of kilter, she had gone to a small bookstore in the same strip mall and bought a Dr. Spock paperback. She had shown the paperback to Mitch, and he had grinned, but she had not shown him the test kit.

"This is so normal," she murmured as Mitch snored lightly. "What we're doing is so *natural* and normal, please, God."

72

SEATTLE, WASHINGTON/WASHINGTON, D.C.

May 14

Kaye drove through Portland while Mitch slept. They crossed the bridge into Washington state, passed through a small rainstorm and then back into bright sun. Kaye chose a turnoff and they ate lunch at a small Mexican restaurant near no town that had a name that they would know. The roads were quiet; it was Sunday.

They paused to nap for a few minutes in the parking lot and Kaye nestled her head on Mitch's shoulder. The air was slow and the sun warmed her face and hair. A few birds sang. The clouds moved in orderly ranks from the south and soon covered the sky, but the air stayed warm.

After their nap, Kaye drove on through Tacoma, and then Mitch drove again, and they continued in to Seattle. Once through the downtown, passing under the highway-straddling convention center, Mitch felt anxious about taking her straight to his apartment.

"Maybe you'd like to see some of the sights before we settle in," he said.

Kaye smiled. "What, your apartment is a mess?"

"It's clean," Mitch said. "It just might not be . . ." He shook his head.

"Don't worry. I'm in no mood to be critical. But I'd love to look around."

"There's a place I used to visit a lot when I wasn't digging . . ."

■

Gasworks Park sprawled below a low grassy promontory overlooking Lake Union. The remains of an old gas plant and other factory buildings had been cleaned out and painted bright colors and turned into a public park. The vertical gasworks tanks and decaying walkways and piping had not been painted, but had been fenced in and left to rust.

Mitch took her by the hand and led her from the parking lot. Kaye thought the park was a little ugly, the grass a little patchy, but for Mitch's sake, said nothing.

They sat on the lawn beside the chain-link fence and watched passenger seaplanes landing on Lake Union. A few lone men and women, or women with children, walked to the playground beside the factory buildings. Mitch said the attendance was a little low for a sunny Sunday.

"People don't want to congregate," Kaye said, but even as she spoke, chartered buses were arriving in the parking lot, pulling into spaces marked off by ropes.

"Something's up," Mitch said, craning his neck.

"Nothing you planned for me?" she asked lightly.

"Nope," Mitch said, smiling. "But maybe I don't remember, after last night."

"You say that every night," Kaye said. She yawned, holding her hand over her mouth, and tracked a sailboat crossing the lake, and then a wind surfer in a wetsuit.

"Eight buses," Mitch said. "Curious."

Kaye's period was three days late, and she had been regular since going off the pill, after Saul's death. This caused a steely kind of concern. When she thought about what they might have started, her teeth ground together. *So quickly. Old-fashioned romance. Rolling downhill, gathering speed.*

She had not told Mitch yet, in case it was a false alarm.

Kaye felt separated from her body when she thought too hard. If she pulled back from the steely concern and just explored her sensations, the natural state of tissues and cells and emotions, she felt fine; it was the context, the implications, the *knowing* that interfered with simply feeling good and in love.

Knowing too much and never knowing enough was the problem.

Normal.

"Ten buses, whoops, eleven," Mitch said. "Big damn crowd." He stroked the side of her neck. "I'm not sure I like this."

"It's your park. I don't want to move for a while," Kaye said. "It's nice." The sun threw bright patches over the park. The rusty tanks glowed dull orange.

Dozens of men and women in earth-colored clothes walked in small groups from the buses toward the hill. They seemed in no hurry. Four women carried a wooden ring about a yard wide, and several men helped roll a long pole on a dolly.

Kaye frowned, then chuckled. "They're doing something with a yoni and a lingam," she said.

Mitch squinted at the procession. "Maybe it's a giant hoop game," he said. "Horseshoes or something."

"Do you think?" Kaye asked with that familiar and uncritical tone he instantly recognized as no-holds-barred disagreement.

"No," he said, smacking his temple with his palm. "How could I have not seen it right away? It's a yoni and a lingam."

"And you an anthropolologist," she said, lightly doubling the syllables. Kaye got up on her knees and shaded her eyes. "Let's go see."

"What if we're not invited?"

"I doubt it's a closed party," she said.

■

Dicken went though the security check—pat-down, metal detection wand, chemical sniff—and entered the White House through the so-called diplomatic entrance. A young Marine escort immediately took him downstairs to a large meeting room in the basement. The air conditioning was running full blast and the room felt cold as a refrigerator compared to the eighty-five-degree heat and humidity outside.

Dicken was the first to arrive. Other than the Marine and a steward arranging place settings—bottles of Evian and legal pads and pens—on the long oval conference table, he was alone in the room. He sat in a chair reserved for junior aides at the back. The steward asked him if he'd like something to drink—a Coke or glass of juice. "We'll have coffee down here in a few minutes."

"Coke would be great," Dicken said.

"Just fly in?"

"Drove from Bethesda," Dicken said.

"Going to be some miserable weather this afternoon," the steward said. "Thunderstorms by five, so the weather people say at Andrews. We get the best weather reports here." He winked and smiled, then left and returned after a few minutes with a Coke and a glass of chopped ice.

More people began arriving ten minutes later. Dicken recognized the governors of New Mexico, Alabama, and Maryland; they were accompanied by a small group of aides. The room would soon hold the core of the so-called Governors' Revolt that was raising hell with the Taskforce across the country.

Augustine was going to have his finest hour, right here in the basement of the White House. He was going to try to convince ten governors, seven from very conservative states, that allowing women access to a complete range of abortion measures was the only humane course of action.

Dicken doubted the plea would be met with approval, or even polite disagreement.

Augustine entered some minutes later, accompanied by the

White House–Taskforce liaison and the chief of staff. Augustine put his valise on the table and walked over to Dicken, his shoes clicking on the tile floor.

"Any ammunition?" he asked.

"A rout," Dicken said quietly. "None of the health agencies felt we had a chance of taking control again. They feel the president has lost his grip on the issue, too."

Augustine's eyes wrinkled at the edges. His crow's feet had grown noticeably deeper in the last year, and his hair had grayed. "I suppose they're going it on their own—grass-roots solutions?"

"That's all they see. The AMA and most of the side branches of the NIH have withdrawn their support, tacitly if not overtly."

"Well," Augustine said softly, "we sure as hell don't have anything to offer to get them back in the fold—yet." He took a cup of coffee from the steward. "Maybe we should just go home and let everyone get on with it."

Augustine turned to look as more governors entered. The governors were followed by Shawbeck and the secretary of Health and Human Services. "Here come the lions, followed by the Christians," he said. "That's only as it should be." Before leaving to sit at the opposite end of the table, in one of the three seats where no tiny flags flew, he said, in a very low voice, "The president's been talking with Alabama and Maryland for the last two hours, Christopher. They've been arguing with him to delay his decision. I don't think he wants to. Fifteen thousand pregnant women were murdered in the last six weeks. *Fifteen thousand,* Christopher."

Dicken had seen that figure several times.

"We should all bend over and get our butts kicked," Augustine growled.

■

Mitch estimated there were at least six hundred people in the crowd moving toward the top of the hill. A few dozen onlookers followed the resolute group with its wooden ring and pillar.

Kaye took his hand. "Is this a Seattle thing?" she asked, pulling him along. The idea of a fertility ritual intrigued her.

"Not that I've heard of," Mitch said. Since San Diego, the smell of too many people gave him the willies.

At the top of the promontory, Kaye and Mitch stood on the

edge of a large flat sundial, about thirty feet across. It was made of bas-relief bronze astrological figures, numerals, outstretched human hands, and calligraphic letters showing the four points of the compass. Ceramics, glass, and colored cement completed the circle.

Mitch showed Kaye how the observer became the gnomon on the dial, standing between parallel lines with the seasons and dates cast into them. It was two o'clock, by her estimation.

"It's beautiful," she said. "Kind of a pagan site, don't you think?" Mitch nodded, keeping his eye on the advancing crowd.

Several men and boys flying kites moved out of the way, pulling and winding their strings, as the group climbed the hill. Three women carried the ring, sweating beneath the weight. They lowered it gently to the middle of the sundial. Two men carrying the pillar stood to one side, waiting to set it down.

Five older women dressed in light yellow robes walked into the circle with hands clasped, smiling with dignity, and surrounded the ring in the center of the compass. The group said not a word.

Kaye and Mitch descended to the south side of the hill, overlooking Lake Union. Mitch felt a breeze coming from the south and saw a few low banks of cloud moving over downtown Seattle. The air was like wine, clean and sweet, temperature in the low seventies. Cloud shadows swung dramatically over the hill.

"Too many people," Mitch told Kaye.

"Let's stay and see what they're up to," Kaye said.

The crowd compacted, forming concentric circles, all holding hands. They politely asked Kaye and Mitch and others to move farther down the hill while they completed their ceremony.

"You're welcome to watch, from down there," a plump young woman in a green shift told Kaye. She explicitly ignored Mitch. Her eyes seemed to track right past him, through him.

The only sound the gathering people made was the rustling of their robes and the motion of their sandaled feet in the grass and over the bas-relief figures of the sundial.

Mitch shoved his hands into his pockets and hunched his shoulders.

■

The governors were seated at the table, leaning right or left to speak in murmurs with their aides or adjacent colleagues. Shawbeck remained standing, hands clasped in front of him. Augustine had walked around one quarter of the table to speak with the governor of California. Dicken tried to puzzle out the seating arrangements and then realized that someone was following a clever protocol. The governors had been arranged not by seniority, or by influence, but by the geographic distribution of their states. California was on the western side of the table, and the governor of Alabama sat close to the back of the room in the southeastern quadrant. Augustine, Shawbeck, and the secretary sat near where the president would sit.

That meant something, Dicken surmised. Maybe they were actually going to bite the bullet and recommend that Augustine's policies be carried out.

Dicken was not at all sure how he felt about that. He had listened to presentations on the medical cost of taking care of second-stage babies, should any survive for very long; he had also listened to figures showing what it would cost for the United States to lose an entire generation of children.

The liaison for Health stood by the door. "Ladies and gentlemen, the president of the United States."

All rose. The governor of Alabama got to his feet more slowly than the others. Dicken saw that his face was damp, presumably from the heat outside. But Augustine had told him that the governor had been in conference with the president for the past two hours.

A Secret Service agent dressed in a blazer and golf shirt walked past Dicken, glanced at him with that stony precision Dicken had long since become used to. The president entered the room first, tall, with his famous shock of white hair. He seemed fit but a little tired; still, the power of the office swept over Dicken. He was pleased that the president looked in his direction, recognized him, nodded solemnly in passing.

The governor of Alabama pushed back his chair. The wooden legs groaned on the concrete floor. "Mr. President," the governor said, too loudly. The president stopped to speak with him, and the governor took two steps forward.

Two agents glanced at each other and swung about to politely intervene.

"I love the office and I love our great country, sir," the governor said, and wrapped the president in his arms, as if delivering a protective bear hug.

The governor of Florida, standing next to them, grimaced and shook his head in some embarrassment.

The agents were mere feet away.

Oh, Dicken thought, nothing more; just a blank and prescient awareness of being suspended in time, a train whistle not yet heard, brakes not yet pressed, arm willed to move but as yet limp by his side.

He thought perhaps he should get out of the way.

■

The blond young man in a black robe wore a green surgical mask and kept his eyes lowered as he advanced up the hill to the compass rose. He was escorted by three women in brown and green, and he carried a small brown cloth bag tied with golden rope. His wispy, almost white hair blew back and forth in the breeze that was quickening on the hill.

The circles of women and men parted to let them through.

Mitch watched with a puzzled expression. Kaye stood with arms folded beside him. "What are they up to?" he asked.

"Some sort of ceremony," Kaye said.

"Fertility?"

"Why not?"

Mitch mulled this over. "Atonement," he said. "There are more women than men."

"About three to one," Kaye said.

"Most of the men are older."

"Q-tips," Kaye said.

"What?"

"That's what young women call men who are old enough to be their fathers," Kaye said. "Like the president."

"That's insulting," Mitch said.

"It's true," Kaye said. "Don't blame me."

The young man was hidden from their view as the crowd closed again.

■

A large burning hand picked up Christopher Dicken and carried him to the back of the wall. It shattered his eardrums and collapsed his chest. Then the hand pulled back and he slumped to the floor. His eyes flickered open. He saw flames rush along the crushed ceiling in concentric waves, tiles falling through the flames. He was covered with blood and bits of flesh. White smoke and heat stung his eyes, and he shut them. He could not breathe, could not hear, could not move.

■

The chanting began low and droning. "Let's go," Mitch told Kaye.

She looked back at the crowd. Now something seemed wrong to her, as well. The hair on her neck rose. "All right," she said.

They circled on a walkway and turned to walk down the north side of the hill. They passed a man and his son, five or six years old, the son carrying a kite in his small hands. The boy smiled at Kaye and Mitch. Kaye looked at the boy's elegant almond eyes, his long close-shaven head so Egyptian, like a beautiful and ancient ebony statue brought to life, and she thought, *What a beautiful and normal child. What a beautiful little boy.*

She was reminded of the young girl standing by the side of the street in Gordi, as the UN caravan left the town; so different in appearance, yet provoking such similar thoughts.

She took Mitch's hand in hers just as the sirens began. They looked north toward the parking lot, and saw five police cars skidding to a halt, doors flung open, officers emerging, running through the parked cars and across the grass, up the hill.

"Look," Mitch said, and pointed at a lone middle-aged man dressed in shorts and a sweatshirt, talking on a cellular phone. The man looked scared.

"What in hell?" Kaye asked.

The droning prayer had strengthened. Three officers rushed past Kaye and Mitch, guns still holstered, but one had pulled out his baton. They pushed through the outer circles of the crowd on the top of the hill.

Women shrieked abuse at them. They fought with the officers, shoving, kicking, scratching, trying to push them back.

Kaye could not believe what she was seeing or hearing. Two women jumped on one of the men, shouting obscenities.

The officer with the baton began to use it to protect his fellows. Kaye heard the stomach-twisting chunk of weighted plastic on flesh and bone.

Kaye started back up the hill, but Mitch grabbed her arm.

More officers plowed into the crowd, batons swinging. The chanting stopped. The crowd seemed to lose all cohesion. Women in robes broke away, hands clutched to their faces in anger and fear, screaming, crying, their voices high and frantic. Some of the robed women collapsed and pounded the scruffy yellow grass with their fists. Spittle dribbled from their mouths.

A police van pushed over the curb and over the grass, engine roaring. Two female officers joined in the rout.

Mitch backed Kaye off the mound, and they came to the bottom, facing uphill to keep an eye on the crowd still massed around the sundial. Two officers pushed out of this assembly with the young man in black. Red dripping slashes marked his neck and hands. A woman officer called for an ambulance on her walkie-talkie. She passed within yards of Mitch and Kaye, face white and lips red with anger.

"Goddamn it!" she shouted at the onlookers. "Why didn't you try to stop them?"

Neither Kaye nor Mitch had an answer.

The young man in the black robe stumbled and fell between the two officers supporting him. His face, warped by pain and shock, flashed white as the clouds against the hard-packed dirt and yellow grass. ■

Greg Bear writes about his novel,

"After years of strong doubts about the view of evolution as a completely random and meaningless process, I continued research I had begun with *Blood Music*. Some of this work leaked into *Slant* and *Legacy*. Soon, however, I had assembled a thoroughly crackpot view of biology and living systems and how they choose to change and react to change. A new novel began to take shape in my head, rather than a work of nonfiction, because that's how I think. *Darwin's Radio* was the result. My personal experience of being a parent (think of it as biology in action) got all mixed together with modern molecular biology and biotech, and thank God, it worked. It's sold very well (always nice) and has opened doors to numerous biology and genomics conferences, where I've been welcomed with considerable grace and compliments and lively debate. Strangely enough, the core ideas in *Darwin's Radio* independently echo the theories of a number of very smart and forward-thinking scientists trying to figure out where the Modern Synthesis of Darwinism went wrong. Now many of our conclusions are being supported by startling revelations about the human genome. And there's more to come. My sense of discovery will continue with *Darwin's Children*. And if this all sounds rather breathless, believe me, it's because I am!"

TERRY BISSON

Terry Bisson is the author of the novels *Wyrldmaker*, *Talking Man*, *Fire on the Mountain*, *Voyage to the Red Planet*, *Pirates of the Universe*, and *The Pickup Artist*. His short fiction has been collected in *Bears Discover Fire* and *In the Upper Room*.

I once called Bisson science fiction's Mark Twain, and the comparison is apt; as with Twain, his angrier stories shade into a a kind of Swiftian satiric ferocity. "macs" is one of those. It would be an interesting study to look at the immense differences between this story and Bisson's earlier Nebula Award–winning story, "Bears Discover Fire," even though they are both comprised in their entirety of mostly Southern voices; and to explore what inspires his love or anger, and to learn from that. Also to contemplate the broad reach of his work. He is a thoroughgoing modernist with an unerring ear for American speech, and a good friend.

MACS

Terry Bisson

What did I think? Same thing I think today. I thought it was slightly weird even if it was legal. But I guess I agreed with the families that there had to be Closure. Look out that window there. I can guarantee you, it's unusual to be so high in Oklahoma City. Ever since it happened, this town has had a thing about tall buildings. It's almost like that son of a bitch leveled this town.

Hell, we wanted Closure too, but they had a court order all the way from the Supreme Court. I thought it was about politics at first, and I admit I was a little pissed. Don't use the word pissed. What paper did you say you were with?

Never heard of it, but that's me. Anyway, I was miffed—is that a word? miffed?—until I understood it was about Victims' Rights. So we canceled the execution, and built the vats, and you know the rest.

Well, if you want to know the details you should start with my assistant warden at the time, who handled the details. He's now the warden. Tell him I sent you. Give him my regards.

■

I thought it opened a Pandora's box, and I said so at the time. It turns out of course that there haven't been that many, and none on that scale. The ones that there are, we get them all. We're the sort of Sloan-Ketterings of the thing. See that scum on the vats? You're looking at eleven of the guy who abducted the little girls in Ohio, the genital mutilation thing, remember? Even eleven's unusual. We usually build four, maybe five tops. And never anything on the scale of the macs.

Build, grow, whatever. If you're interested in the technology, you'll have to talk with the vat vet himself. That's what we call him, he's a good old boy. He came in from the Ag school for the macs and he's been here in Corrections ever since. He was an exchange student, but he met a girl from MacAlester and never went home. Isn't it funny how that stuff works? She was my second cousin, so now I have a Hindu second cousin-in-law. Of course he's not actually a Hindu.

■

A Unitarian, actually. There are several of us here in MacAlester, but I'm the only one from the prison. I was fresh out of Ag and it was my first assignment. How would one describe such an assignment? In my country, we had no such . . . well, you know. It was repellent and fascinating at the same time.

Everyone has the cloning technology. It's the growth rate that gives difficulty. Animals grow to maturity so much faster, and we had done significant work. Six-week cattle, ten-day ducks. Gene tweaking. Enzyme accelerators. They wanted full-grown macs in two and a half years; we gave them 168 thirty-year-old men in eleven months! I used to come down here and watch them grow. Don't tell anyone, especially my wife, Jean, but I grew sort of fond of them.

Hard? It was hard, I suppose, but farming is hard too if you think about it. A farmer may love his hogs but he ships them off, and we all know what for.

You should ask legal services about that. That wasn't part of my operation. We had already grown 168 and I had to destroy one before he was even big enough to walk, just so they could include the real one. Ask me if I appreciated that!

■

It was a second court order. It came through after the macs were in the vats. Somebody's bright idea in Justice. I suppose they figured it would legitimize the whole operation to include the real McCoy, so to speak, but then somebody has to decide who gets him. Justice didn't want any part of that and neither did we, so we brought in one of those outfits that run lotteries, because that's what it was, a lottery, but kind of a strange one, if you know what I mean.

Strange in that the winner wasn't supposed to know if he won or not. He or she. It's like the firing squad, where nobody knows who has the live bullets. Nobody is supposed to know who gets the real one. I'm sure it's in the records somewhere, but that stuff's all sealed. What magazine did you say you were with?

■

Sealed? It's destroyed. That was part of the contract. I guess whoever numbered the macs would know, but that was five years ago and it was done by lot anyway. It could probably be figured out by talking to the drivers who did the deliveries, or the drivers who picked up the remains, or even the families themselves. But it would be illegal, wouldn't it? Unethical, too, if you ask me, since it would interfere with what the whole thing was about, which was Closure. Victims' Rights. That's why we were hired, to keep it secret, and that's what we did. End of story.

■

UPS was a natural because we had just acquired Con Tran and were about to go into the detainee delivery business under contract with the BOP. The macs were mostly local, of course, but not all. Several went out of state; two to California, for example. It wasn't a security problem since the macs were all sort of docile. I figured they were engineered that way. Is engineered the word? Anyway, the problem was public relations. Appearances, to be frank. You can't drive around with a busload of macs. And most families don't want the TV and papers at the door, like Publishers Clearing House. (Though some do!) So we delivered them in vans, two and three at a time, mostly in the morning, sort of on the sly. We told the press we were still working out the details until it was all done. Some people videotaped their delivery. I suspect they're the ones that also videotaped their executions.

I'm not one of those who had a problem with the whole thing. No sirree. I went along with my drivers, at first especially, and met quite a few of the loved ones, and I wish you could have seen the grateful expressions on their faces. You get your own mac to kill any way you want to. That's Closure. It made me proud to be an American even though it came out of a terrible tragedy. An unspeakable tragedy.

Talk to the drivers all you want to. What channel did you say you were with?

■

You wouldn't have believed the publicity at the time. It was a big triumph for Victims' Rights, which is now in the Constitution, isn't it? Maybe I'm wrong. Anyway, it wasn't a particularly what you might call pleasant job, even though I was all for the families and Closure and stuff and still am.

Looked like anybody. Looked like you except for the beard, None of them were different. They were all the same. One of them was supposedly the real McCoy, but so what? Isn't the whole point of cloning supposed to be that each one is the same as the first one? Nobody's ever brought this up before. You're not from one of those talk shows, are you?

They couldn't have talked to us if they had wanted to, and we weren't about to talk to them. They were all taped up except for the eyes, and you should have seen those eyes. You tried to avoid it. I had one that threw up all over my truck even though theoretically you can't throw up through that tape. I told the dispatcher my truck needed a theoretical cleaning.

■

They all seemed the same to me. Sort of panicked and gloomy. I had a hard time hating them, in spite of what they done, or their daddy done, or however you want to put it. They say they could only live five years anyway before their insides turned to mush. That was no problem of course. Under the Victims' Rights settlement it had to be done in thirty days, that was from date of delivery.

I delivered thirty-four macs, of 168 altogether. I met thirty-four fine families, and they were a fine cross-section of American life, black and white, Catholic and Protestant. Not so many Jews.

I've heard that rumor. You're going to have rumors like that when one of them is supposedly the real McCoy. There were other rumors too, like that one of the macs was pardoned by its family and sent away to school somewhere. That would have been hard. I mean, if you got a mac you had to return a body within thirty days. One story I heard was that they switched bodies after a car wreck. Another was that they burned another body at the stake and turned it in. But that one's hard to believe too. Only one of the macs was burned at the stake, and they had to get a special clearance to do that. Hell, you can't even burn leaves in Oklahoma anymore.

SaniMed collected, they're a medical waste outfit, since we're not allowed to handle remains. They're not going to be able to tell you much. What did they pick up? Bones and ashes. Meat.

■

Some of it was pretty gruesome but in this business you get used to that. We weren't supposed to have to bag them, but you know how it is. The only one that really got to me was the crucifixion. That sent the wrong message, if you ask me.

■

There was no way we could tell which one of them was the real McCoy, not from what we picked up. You should talk to the loved ones. Nice people, maybe a little impatient sometimes. The third week was the hardest in terms of scheduling. People had been looking forward to Closure for so long, they played with their macs for a week or so, but then it got old. Played is not the word, but you know what I mean. Then it's bang bang and honey call SaniMed. They want them out of the house ASAP.

It's not that we were slow, but the schedule was heavy. In terms of what we were picking up, none of it was that hard for me. These were not people. Some of them were pretty chewed up. Some of them were chewed up pretty bad.

■

I'm not allowed to discuss individual families. I can say this: the ceremony, the settlement, the execution, whatever you want to call it, wasn't always exactly what everybody had expected or wanted. One family even wanted to let their mac go. Since they couldn't do that, they wanted a funeral. A funeral for toxic waste!

I can't give you their name or tell you their number.

I guess I can tell you that. It was between 103 and 105.

■

I'm not ashamed of it. We're Christians. Forgive us our trespasses as we forgive those who trespass against us. We tried to make it legal, but the state wouldn't hear of it, since the execution order had already been signed. We had thirty days, so we waited till the last week and then used one of those Kevorkian kits, the lethal objection thing. Injection, I mean. The doctor came with it but we had to push the plunger thing. It seems to me like one of the rights of Victims' Rights should be—but I guess not.

There was a rumor that another family forgave and got away with it, but we never met them. They supposedly switched bodies in a car wreck and sent their mac to forestry school in Canada. Even if it was true, which I doubt, he would be almost five now, and that's half their life span. Supposedly their internal organs harden after ten years. What agency did you say you were with?

■

We dropped ours out of an airplane. My uncle has a big ranch out past Mayfield with his own airstrip and everything. Cessna 172. It was illegal, but what are they going to do? C'est la vie, or rather c'est la mort. Or whatever.

■

They made us kill him. Wasn't he ours to do with as we liked? Wasn't that the idea? He killed my daddy like a dog and if I wanted to tie him up like a dog, isn't that my business? Aren't you a little long in the tooth to be in college, boy?

An electric chair. It's out in the garage. Want to see it? Still got the shit stain on the seat.

■

My daddy came home with a mac, and took my mother and me out back and made us watch while he shot him. Shot him all over, from the feet up. The whole thing took ten minutes. It didn't seem to do anybody any good, my aunt is still dead. They never found most of her, only the bottom of a leg. Would you like some chocolates? They're from England.

■

Era? It was only like five years ago. I never took delivery. I thought I was the only one but I found out later there were eight others. I guess they just put them back in the vat. They couldn't live more than five years anyway. Their insides turned hard. All their DNA switches were shut off or something.

I got my own Closure my own way. That's my daughter's picture there. As for the macs, they are all dead. Period. They lived a while, suffered and died. Is it any different for the rest of us? What church did you say you were with?

■

I don't mind telling you our real name, but you should call us 49 if you quote us. That's the number we had in the lottery. We got our mac on a Wednesday, kept him for a week, then set him in a kitchen chair and shot him in the head. We didn't have any idea how messy that would be. The state should have given some instructions or guidelines.

Nobody knew which one was the original, and that's the way it should be. Otherwise it would ruin the Closure for everybody else. I can tell you ours wasn't, though. It was just a feeling I had. That's why we just shot him and got it over with. I just couldn't get real excited about killing something that seemed barely alive, even though it supposedly had all his feelings and memories. But some people got into it and attended several executions. They had a kind of network.

Let me see your list. These two are the ones I would definitely talk to: 112 and 43. And maybe 13.

■

Is that what they call us, 112? So I'm just a number again. I thought I was through with that in the army. I figured we had the real one, the real McCoy, because he was so hard to kill. We cut him up with a chain saw, a little Homelite. No sir, I didn't mind the mess and yes, he hated every minute of it. All twenty some odd which is how long it took. I would have fed him to my dogs if we hadn't had to turn the body in. End of fucking story.

■

Oh, yeah. Double the pleasure, double the fun. Triple it, really. The only one I was against was this one, 61. The crucifixion. I think that sent the wrong message, but the neighbors loved it.

Drown in the toilet was big. Poison, fire, hanging, you name it. People got these old books from the library but that medieval stuff took special equipment. One guy had a rack built but the neighbors objected to the screaming. I guess there are some limits, even to Victims' Rights. Ditto the stake stuff.

■

I'm sure our mac wasn't the real McCoy. You want to know why? He was so quiet and sad. He just closed his eyes and died. I'm sure the real one would have been harder to kill. My mac wasn't innocent, but he wasn't guilty either. Even though he looked like a thirty-year-old man he was only eighteen months old, and that sort of showed.

I killed him just to even things out. Not revenge, just Closure. After spending all the money on the court case and the settlement, not to mention the cloning and all, the deliveries, it would have been wasteful not to do it, don't you think?

I've heard that surviving thing but it's just a rumor. Like Elvis. There were lots of rumors. They say one family tried to pardon their mac and send him to Canada or somewhere. I don't think so!

You might try this one, 43. They used to brag that they had the real one. I don't mind telling you I resented that and still do, since we were supposed to all share equally in the Closure. But some people have to be number one.

It's over now anyway. What law firm did you say you worked for?

■

I could tell he was the original by the mean look in his eye. He wasn't quite so mean after a week in that rat box.

Some people will always protest and write letters and such. But what about something that was born to be put to death? How can you protest that?

Closure, that's what it was all about. I went on to live my life. I've been married again and divorced already. What college did you say you were from?

■

The real McCoy? I think he just kept his mouth shut and died like the rest of them. What's he goin' to say, here I am, and make it worse? And as far as that rumor of him surviving, you can file it under Elvis.

There was also a story that somebody switched bodies after a car wreck and sent their mac to Canada. I wouldn't put too much stock in that one, either. Folks around here don't even think about Canada. Forgiveness either.

We used that state kit, the Kevorkian thing. I heard about twenty families did. We just sat him down and May pushed the plunger. Like flushing a toilet. May and myself—she's gone now, God bless her—we were interested in Closure, not revenge.

■

This one, 13, told me one time he thought he had the real McCoy, but it was wishful thinking, if you ask me. I don't think you could tell the real one. I don't think you should want to even if you could.

I'm afraid you can't ask him about it, because they were all killed in a fire, the whole family. It was just a day before the ceremony they had planned, which was some sort of slow thing with wires. There was a gas leak or something. They were all killed and their mac was destroyed in the explosion. Fire and explosion. What insurance company did you say you worked for?

It was—have you got a map? oooh, that's a nice one—right here. On the corner of Oak and Increase, only a half a mile from the site of the original explosion, ironically. The house is gone now.

■

See that new strip mall? That Dollar Store's where the house stood. The family that lived in it was one of the ones that lost a loved one in the Oklahoma City bombing. They got one of the macs as part of the Victims' Rights Closure Settlement, but unfortunately tragedy struck them again before they got to get Closure. Funny how the Lord works in mysterious ways.

No, none of them are left. There was a homeless guy who used to hang around but the police ran him off. Beard like yours. Might have been a friend of the family, some crazy cousin, who knows. So much tragedy they had. Now he lives in the back of the mall in a Dumpster.

■

There. That yellow thing. It never gets emptied. I don't know why the city doesn't remove it but it's been there for almost five years just like that.

I wouldn't go over there. People don't fool with him. He doesn't bother anybody, but, you know.

Suit yourself. If you knock on it he'll come out, figuring you've got some food for him or something. Kids do it for meanness sometimes. But stand back, there is a smell.

■

"Daddy?" ■

Terry Bisson writes of "macs,"

"This dark (for me) little story comes out of my opposition to the death penalty, America's most energetic affirmative action program. It's not death I protest (which comes to us all) but cold-blooded, medically sanctioned, legally sanitized, 'humane' and merciless murder done behind closed doors in my name and yours. I have written one other death penalty story, 'The Old Rugged Cross,' which Patrick Nielsen Hayden will publish later this year in *Starlight 3.* 'macs' is dedicated to two distinguished colleagues in the struggle, Mumia Abu-Jamal and Steve Earle."

ELEANOR ARNASON

Eleanor Arnason's first novel, *The Sword Smith*, was published in 1978, and in the 1980s she published *To the Resurrection Station* and *Daughter of the Bear King*, among other works. Her novel *A Woman of the Iron People* received a great deal of admiring attention and was a winner of the James Tiptree, Jr. Award. I have seen it called "anthropological science fiction," or "feminist science fiction," but my feeling is that these extra adjectives are sometimes used to box in accomplishments far beyond the reach of most novels. Any adjectives added to "science fiction" only compound what is already a pigeon-holing problem.

"Stellar Harvest" is another one of Arnason's planetary romances, and in the midst of all the intensely engaged near-future stories in this volume, it's fun to rocket off to the realm of this subgenre, which despite all the shocks administered here by Arnason, still encourages with its fundamentally cheery suggestion that humans will survive well enough to spread through the galaxy. Of course tales like this also serve extremely well as spaces for thought experiments about our current preoccupations. Arnason exploits that possibility to the full here, confounding with sly wit some of our usual assumptions about gender, celebrity, and the biochemical bases of consciousness.

STELLAR HARVEST

Eleanor Arnason

After her helicopter broke down in a dusty little caravan town named Dzel, Lydia Duluth rented a *chool*. This was a native quadruped, reminiscent of the *hasa* on her home world, though (thanks to this planet's smaller mass and lighter G) taller and rangier than any *hasa*. Instead of hooves, it had three-toed feet; and a pair of impressive tusks curved up from its lower jaw.

"What are those for?" Lydia asked the stableman.

"Digging up roots and pulling bark off trees, also for fighting with other males. Loper has been gelded and won't bother you with any kind of mating behavior. Sex is a distraction," he added in the complacent tone of one who has never been distracted. "Necessary perhaps for evolution—we are not ignorant; we know about Darwin—but hardly compatible with civilization. Loper will give you no trouble. He has been civilized."

The animal turned its long, angular, lightly scaled head, regarding her with a bright orange eye. Not a sight that Lydia associated with civilization, though maybe one could see the triangular pupil—expanded at the moment, in the shadowy stable—as a pyramid, emblematic of Egypt and geometry.

"Tomorrow," she told the stableman. "At dawn."

"Loper will be ready."

She spent the rest of the afternoon wandering around Dzel. Narrow streets ran crookedly between adobe buildings. The natives—humanoid, but not human—dressed in brightly colored robes, which hid most of the differences between their species and hers. One noticed height and the long thin hands, one finger short of the human norm. Their skin was golden brown and hairless, with a faint shimmer produced by vestigial scales. Their eyes, visible above veils, were all iris with round black pupils. Most of the irises were yellow: a wonderful hue, as clear as glass or wine.

One could put an exotic romance into a setting like this or an adventure story: Ali Khan on the trail of interstellar drug dealers or seeking evidence of the long-vanished Master Race. Though poor Ali was at the end of his career; a man of 110 simply did not convince in action roles. No matter what one did with computers, the audience knew how old he was. They knew they were not seeing the real person; and Stellar Harvest had built its reputation on authenticity.

Well, not her problem. She didn't plot stories or write scripts. Instead, she recorded Dzel: the colorful inhabitants, dusty winding streets and dark blue sky.

There were sounds to be recorded as well: bells ringing in the wind, plaintive voices that rose and fell musically, so every conversation seemed to be a duet or trio, and the soft thud of *chool* feet, as the animals plodded past.

Her mood, somewhat edgy since the helicopter's sudden failure, gradually relaxed.

Species are stable, said the voice in her mind. *Humans have not evolved in the centuries since you began to build machines. Your nervous system is designed for an environment like this. That's why you find animal noises and the sound of the wind relaxing. In a sense, this is your true home.*

"Did I ask for an opinion?" said Lydia quietly, while aiming her recorder at a street shaded by blue and red awnings. The light beneath the awnings was alternately blue and red, colored by the fabric it had come through. A woman in a white robe walked toward her. What a vision! And what a location for a chase or fight!

The women, veiled and hooded, passed Lydia. Golden eyes gave a quick considering glance. With luck, the recording would be good; she'd have this light forever, along with the woman's grace and glance.

At sunset, she returned to her inn. The helicopter pilot, a native in blue overalls, had news. Their machine was not fixable. He would have to stay in Dzel until a salvage truck arrived, then ride back along the caravan road. "We are still trying to find you another copter, missy."

"Don't bother. I rented a *chool*."

"Those nasty animals! Have you ridden before?"

"On my home world. We had a revolution, the kind that takes to the hills. It failed, but I did learn riding."

Gold eyes widened, and nostrils flared. "Really, indeed! You are a revolutionary?"

"A failed one."

"Really! We could never manage a revolution. Our unaltered males are unable to cooperate with each other, and no altered male would waste his time on anything so foolish."

"What about your women?"

"They are, if anything, more sensible than eunuchs. Life is short, missy, and civilization is difficult to maintain. We have all we can do."

"But you like Stellar Harvest."

"That is drama. Ali Khan may solve his problems by kicking other people in the head, but our experience—here on this planet—is that real adversaries are not so easily defeated. Of course we dream of such solutions, the way children dream of having everything. But one does not act on such fantasies."

True enough, said the voice in her mind.

This was the end of the real conversation. The pilot began to discuss his favorite holoplays and stars. Ali Khan, of course. Who could equal him, in his prime? "Though he has seemed less convincing in recent years."

Recent years? Recent decades!

Ramona Patel was also fine, the best of the actors starring in mythic-musical-action stories. "Not my religion, of course," the pilot said. "But none the less inspiring, especially the large production numbers. You humans have so many gods! And all of them able to sing and dance!"

She genuinely liked her job and enjoyed many of the dramas made by Stellar Harvest. None the less, fannish enthusiasm can be exhausting, especially at the end of a long day. Lydia excused herself, pleading fatigue, and went to her room, which was on the inn's ground floor, its windows opening onto a courtyard. Above the roof line stars blazed, far more than she was used to. Their light was as bright as moonlight at home. She leaned out a window. A rimmed pool stood at the courtyard's center, gleaming like a huge round coin. Maybe she ought to get her recorder.

Instead she collected her computer and satellite dish. There were stairs at the end of the hall, leading up to a flat roof. The night air was cold already, the starry sky immense. Lydia unfolded the dish and turned on the computer, typing in the address of her contact in the capital city, a commercial rep who handled Stellar Harvest along with a dozen other off-planet companies. As was to be expected, she got a recorded message, accompanied by a holo of the rep, his gold face bare. The head—long from front to back—was covered by what looked like sleeked down, rust-red hair. Actually, this was a crest of feathers, which could be raised, though not in polite company.

"Thoozil Rai is not available. Please type your message for ease in translation."

Sitting cross-legged under the stars, she input the current situation. No point in spending six or seven days in Dzel, waiting for a new helicopter, if one could be found. The country to the west was safe according to local informants, and there was an interesting-sounding city in the foothills. No trouble getting out of Basekh this time of year. There was weekly plane service to accommodate tourists, mostly big game hunters. She would call every other day as a precaution, though it seemed hardly necessary.

As she typed in the last words, something howled nearby. Mother! What a sound! Undulating, it rose into a scream that ended suddenly, as if cut off. In the silence that followed, Lydia thought she could still hear the cry, continuing beyond the edge of audibility.

By this time she was standing. The sound had come from ground level. Maybe the street below her. Or the next street over. "What?"

An unaltered male, I think. There must be several in town.

A second howl answered the first. Others followed. Lydia counted: three, four, five spreading out from the town's center to its edges. The last cry came from the far east side of Dzel, almost on the plain. Faint and shrill, it rose into the starry night like a rocket. When it ended, there was silence. Apparently the creatures didn't feel a need to rechallenge one another.

They are kept in family compounds, the voice told her. *With proper care, they are not dangerous.*

The computer was at her feet, still open and on. By now, her message had been replaced by the saver, a red and blue fractal that opened like a flower or an exotic, frilly leaf. She wiped her palms—they were suddenly wet—knelt and sent her message, then shut down. "Why didn't I hear that in the city?"

Unaltered males are forbidden within the city limits.

"A noise ordinance?"

There are various reasons: sanitation, safety. They agitate each other with howling.

No kidding! There had been emotion in the cries. She knew that, though she wasn't sure she could identify it. Anger, maybe. Anguish? Something that made her hair go up. "I hope it doesn't happen again."

Use earplugs.

"Can't hear the alarm go off." Can't hear monsters climbing in the window, either. Still kneeling, she folded her dish. Hard to imagine Thoozil Rai as a member of the same species—the same sex—as the creature that had produced that cry. He was like all reps everywhere: bland, courteous, a member of the interstellar culture of go-betweens. They never varied much. How could they? Their job was to be uniform and predictable. Beyond them and the port cities, one or two to a planet, was the outback, the real planet, where Stellar Harvest liked to record.

People expected reality from Stellar Harvest; and they expected the reality they saw to be exotic; but the story in front of this exotic backdrop should be familiar. The company's official motto was *ad astra per aspera*, which appeared at the start of every drama, inside the sickle made of blazing stars. The motto should have been, "Be real, but not too real."

At times, this troubled her. At other times, she thought there was an argument for predictability and for happy endings. Lydia went downstairs and closed the shutters on her windows.

Her computer alarm woke her at dawn. She dressed and packed her gear into rented saddle bags. Outside, the stars were fading. The dimmer ones were already gone; most of the rest would follow; though a few remained visible all day. The still air was cold and dry. She walked through the dark streets, rifle in hand, the bags over one shoulder, thinking that the holoplays missed what was really important: a morning like this, her body feeling light and springy in the local G.

If something happened now—for example, a monster leaping

out of the shadows—she would lose this moment. Action distracts from sensation. Sensation is life.

Loper was ready, as promised. The stableman went over his instructions on how to guide a *chool*, then led the way to the town gate, Lydia following on the animal, which was—as promised—no problem.

"Usually the gate is kept locked till full day. But I paid the watchman, and he's a fan of Ramona Patel. What a woman! So much authority!"

Well, that was true of Ramona, known to her associates as the female Genghis Khan. Ali, in spite of his name, was a kitten.

The gate was open, and the watchman stood next to it. Even wrapped in robes, she could see that he was unusually tall and broad.

"Altered late," said the stableman in a whisper. "But perfectly safe."

She thanked both for their help. The watchman rumbled something that she didn't understand, though she thought she heard the word, "Patel."

"Our pleasure," said the stableman. Lydia rode out.

By full day, the town was gone from view. The plain stretched around her, covered by a short, grass-like plant called *dzai*, not a monoculture but a mixture of related species, all of which had faded in the dry midsummer, but not to the same hue. The landscape was patterned like a carpet: silver-brown, pale red, pale yellow, a lovely dusty silver-grey-green. The colors changed as the wind blew past, flattening leaves or flipping them over. A chameleon-carpet, thought Lydia, who'd seen such things on her travels. Rich people on other worlds had them, so their floors always matched their furniture and clothing.

She traveled slowly, getting used to the *chool*'s gait and watching the plain. It could be used for something epic, like the ancient westerns made on Earth. The huge spread of land would swallow an army, making it look tiny, until it came over a low rise and turned into Crazy Horse and the Lakota or the Red Army's crack cavalry, riding ahead of Leon Trotsky's armored train.

But if you emphasized the sheer size of landscape, the way it dwarfed humanity, then you lost its other qualities: subtlety, variety, richness.

On most planets, prairie ecologies were second in complexity to tropical forests; and of all ecologies they were the most vulnerable, because they produced excellent soil, thick and full of nutrients. Their chief protection was a mat of roots so deep and intertwined that no primitive plow could break through. But the moment any culture had access to good metal plows, prairies went under.

A pity, thought Lydia, coming from a world that had turned most of its prairies into farmland. She had grown up in a place as flat as this, divided into sections and planted with modified versions of Earth crops. Only the dry plains remained covered with native vegetation. Was it lack of water that had saved this place?

We arrived before overpopulation forced them to farm everything, and before they developed an economy based on using up natural resources as quickly as possible.

"You intervened?"

Our arrival was an intervention. How could it not be? In addition, we encouraged certain traits already present. They are a likable species.

"Unlike humans?"

The voice did not reply. Lydia grinned.

Now and then she recorded something, though her recordings were not going to give a sense of what the plain was really like. So vast! And the sky above it even vaster, dotted with day stars, white points of light in the deep dusty blue.

Maybe the right director could convey the space. The stars could be enhanced. They wouldn't show otherwise. She wasn't sure how to convey the richness in an action drama. Maybe Ali could be a biologist. Begin with him on his hands and knees, collecting invertebrates with exoskeletons, lovely little creatures like the things that were whirring past her this very moment. Then, after he's been established as a gentle fellow in love with diversity, the bad guys arrive. Developers maybe, plotting to destroy the prairie. Ali has to stand up and defend his bugs. She could see him rising, shoulders back and a bug held carefully between two cupped hands, his expression stern, his hawk-like profile held at just the right angle against the alien sky.

This is either irony or cynicism, the voice said. *I can't determine which.*

"Your problem," Lydia answered. Later she asked, "Shouldn't there be large animals?"

There are. Though this land has been left unplowed, it has been extensively hunted, and the large animals are wary. You will see them—if you do see them—at dusk or in the distance or at rivers. They have to drink.

That was another possible story line, assuming Stellar Harvest could find the large animals and record them: Ali against off-world hunters.

The most common herbivore has an abnormally large head covered with large fleshy protuberances. The eyes—the animals have two—are tiny, and the males have four to six horns.

"Are you saying it's ugly?"

That is a value judgment, but it's possible that human audiences would not think something like that was worth preserving.

"Everyone is a critic."

The voice was silent.

"You may be right. Ali should defend bugs."

Late in the afternoon, she reached a river, right where her map said it would be. Low sprawling trees grew along the bank, reminding her of *edseh* at home, though these had copper-red leaves, and *edseh* were blue.

I hope you are going to take precautions.

"Afraid?"

My core is almost indestructible, but my interfacing elements can break or decay. And if you die, I lose my senses.

It would become a thin metal plate inside a skull, blind and deaf, incapable of action, but still able to think. What a fate!

She had no interest in becoming a pile of bones, even though it would make the AI suffer; and the plain did have predators. Lydia set out perimeter alarms, then made sure her weapons were ready to use. An ounce of prevention is worth a pound of cure, a saying that made absolutely no sense. What is an ounce? And what is a pounding cure?

The planet's primary disappeared. The quite amazing stars came out. She ate trail food, watched her fire and went to sleep, waking to a scream.

A perimeter alarm. Lydia rolled over, grabbing her handgun. Now there was another sound: a bellow. The *chool!* She ran toward it, gun in hand.

Two creatures struggled in the starlight. One was obviously her riding animal. The other—Lydia couldn't tell. But it didn't look friendly. If she fired, she might hit the *chool*. "Stop that!" she yelled. The *chool* reared, maybe in response to her yell, most likely not, and managed to pull free. A moment later the *chool* was gone, heading for the plain. A second alarm went off as it crossed her perimeter. Lydia stopped. The creature, whatever it was, turned toward her. Even in this light, she could see it was huge and standing on its hind legs. The thing took a step. She fired. The creature turned and fled.

Damn, it was quick for something so large. Frightened and angry, she sent a couple more shots after the creature.

Did it stagger? She couldn't be certain. In any case, it was still moving. Another alarm went off, the third, signaling its retreat.

She stood for a moment, shaking. Damn, she was out of practice. Anyway, she'd been an information officer, though that was no excuse. In a guerrilla army, everyone is—or should be—a soldier.

You did manage to hit the creature, said the voice. *Though I can't tell how badly it—he—is injured. Maybe you ought to follow.*

"He?"

There is only one biped of that size on this planet. You have shot a person. Either the wound is minor, in which case he might come back; or it is serious, and you will have to decide whether or not to help him.

"What if there's more than one?" she asked.

Unlikely, given the person's behavior; and I saw no one else. I'm using your senses, of course, and they are limited.

Trust an AI to make a crack. She could go out and make herself a perfect target with the help of a flashlight, or she could stay here and wait for morning and find—what? A trail of blood across the plain? A body?

Lydia considered the problem while reloading her gun. Then she tucked it in a pocket, picked up her flashlight and rifle, and went to look for the creature.

As she had imagined, there was a trail: trampled plants and scored dirt. A few drops of liquid shone darkly in the light of her flash. Was the man wearing shoes? Those looked like claw marks.

Lit by stars, the plain was colorless and pale. Something lay a short distance away, as dark as blood against the vegetation. Lydia played light over it. Definitely an object, but she couldn't tell what. A boulder, maybe?

"I'm too old for this," she told the voice.

There was silence in her mind, though not in the world outside. The perimeter alarms were still making an ungodly racket. She snapped the safety off her rifle and walked toward the thing, keeping her flashlight on it.

The thing moved. A pair of eyes regarded her, shining like gold.

She stopped. "Are you injured?"

"Evidently."

"You speak."

"Of course I speak," the deep voice answered. "Though not for long, the way I'm bleeding."

"I'll get a medical kit," Lydia said with sudden decision.

When she returned, the man was in the same position, lifted up on one elbow. She played her light over him: almost naked, except for some kind of kilt or loincloth, and genuinely huge, well over two meters tall and broad. His bare skin shone as if dusted with gold, except where blood had darkened it. She glanced at his face only briefly and got an impression of blunt features, framed by a rusty mane.

"Try anything, and I'll hurt you," she said.

"You have already hurt me quite sufficiently."

One bullet had gone through his thigh. Remarkable that he'd managed to run as far as he did. There was another wound in his shoulder, high up and probably not dangerous, though bleeding pretty well. The leg wound was the one that worried her.

"What do you think?" she asked in her own language. "Has an artery been hit, or the bone?"

There was a barely perceptible pause, while the AI checked its memory for information on native physiology. *Both are unlikely, given the position of the wound and the way it's bleeding.*

"Who are you talking to?" asked the man.

She ignored the question, considering how to patch him up. She didn't want to get close. Even injured, he looked dangerous. Better to stand at a safe distance, gun in one hand and light in the other, while telling him how to apply the dressings. This kind of behavior wouldn't earn her a Red Crescent medal, of course, but she didn't especially want one.

He followed her instructions, hissing as the dressings took hold and their antiseptics sank in.

"Painful, is it?" she said. "You made me lose my *chool*."

"It will be back," he said with effort.

"How do you know?"

"There's water here. The plain is dry."

She considered for a moment, while he closed the kit and pushed it toward her. "Amazing that I managed to hit you twice. What were you doing?"

"At the time you shot me, I was trying to flee."

Had she spent too much time around Stellar Harvest? This was a crazy conversation to have with a midnight thief on a planet that wasn't her own.

"I suppose I'd better get you back to camp. Can you walk at all?"

"If you got me a stick, I think I could limp."

She burned one off a tree, using her rifle, then gave it to the man. He struggled upright and limped to her fire, while she kept the rifle pointed at him.

Once there, he sank down with a groan. She rebuilt the fire, lighting it with the rifle, then settled opposite him, watching the red light play over his golden body. Three things were obvious about him. He was large; he was gorgeous; and he was unquestionably male. She hadn't thought any alien could affect a human this way. What could she be responding to? Not pheromones. Maybe his sleek muscles or the rusty mane that fell around his shoulders. Not hair, almost certainly. Feathers. But it looked like hair, thick and coarse and sensual.

"You are unaltered," she said.

"Yes," he answered, sounding embarrassed.

"What were you doing?"

"Surely it must be obvious. I was trying to steal your *chool*."

"Could it have carried you?"

He was leaning against a tree trunk, leg stretched out in front of him, the stick still grasped in one hand. Was it a weapon, or a way to deal with pain? "I think so. I used to ride, before my family locked me up. I've gained weight since then, of course. But a good *chool* can carry two ordinary adults, and while I may be twice as big as my brothers, I'm no more than that."

"Why were you stealing the *chool*?" she asked.

"I was escaping. That also should be obvious."

"You really think the *chool* will come back?"

"It might run home to its stable. But they are animals without much enterprise, and this is the only water in a considerable distance." He glanced at her, his eyes reflecting light, so the irises seemed like actual metallic gold. "I used to ride in this region. I know it."

"Last night in Dzel, I heard a noise."

"I was one of the callers," he said after a moment. "You have to do that, answer a call, or your relatives worry. It's easier to do what's expected; and I didn't want to attract attention, since I was planning to escape."

"Why?" asked Lydia.

He was silent. Looking at him, Lydia could see exhaustion and pain, as obvious as it would have been in a human. The blunt-featured face was mask-like, deep lines around the mouth and between the feathery rust-red eyebrows. His blood-streaked skin seemed duller than before. Was it losing some of its golden shimmer, the way fish lose color when they die? A frightening thought. She couldn't risk giving him an analgesic; no telling how he'd react to it; but he had to rest. Not unbound, though. Lydia rummaged in her bags for duct tape, then stood. "Throw the stick away."

His frown deepened.

"I can't leave you free. I need to sleep, and your own relatives keep you locked up. That's what you meant, isn't it, when you said you had to escape them?"

"I'm not dangerous."

"So you say."

He met her gaze for a moment, then glanced at the gun she held. Finally he sighed and tossed the stick off to one side.

She went in back of him, wrapping the tape around one wrist, then around the tree and the other wrist. "This is an improved product. Nothing will cut it, except a knife that I have on my person. You might as well relax and get some sleep."

"This is not a comfortable position."

"I can't help that." She shifted around in front of him, closer than she had been before, examining him. His single article of clothing turned out to be a kilt, made of a rough-looking brown fabric. It was fastened by a plain belt, which had a sheath attached to it. "Where's the knife?"

"In the *dzai*. I dropped it when you shot me."

"How do you feel?"

"Embarrassed at my lack of competence, in pain, a little dizzy."

"Is there anything I can get for you?"

"Water."

She filled a bowl from the river and brought it to him. He drank the bowl empty. Cautiously, she touched his neck, feeling for an artery. There was one. The pulse was high for a human.

Slightly high for his species.

His skin felt cool and a little damp. Shock, thought Lydia. The night was cold, and he was badly underdressed. She got a blanket and wrapped it around him, saying, "I wish I weren't afraid of you. But you did try to steal from me, and there must be a reason why your family kept you locked up."

"Custom," he answered wearily. "I've read books and seen hologrammic dramas. I know there are other customs on the other planets."

Well, yes. She got her flashlight and went looking for his knife. It was easy to find: a large, well-made weapon, lying in the trampled *dzai.* The guy was right about his lack of competence. He should have come after her with the knife or turned and run the moment the alarm went off. Instead he'd gone after the *chool.*

On the other hand—she picked up the knife—if he'd come after her, she would have definitely killed him; and he apparently needed the *chool.* Life is full of difficult decisions. What, for example, was she going to do now? Leave him here with an injury that made it impossible for him to walk any distance? Or set up her satellite dish and call for help? That would save his life, but end him back with his family; and she, having spent a number of years in prison, disliked the idea of locking up another person, unless she knew for certain he was dangerous.

All my data warns against the unaltered males of this species.

"All your data warns against *me,*" she answered.

Untrue. You were dangerous when your revolution had some possibility of succeeding. But one of the characteristics of people like you is that you are not dangerous as individuals. All the studies indicate you are more moral than humanity in general. It's one of the reasons we study you. There must be some kind of social purpose in people like you, since you recur so often, but you seem irrelevant to human history.

The problem of the human vanguard. Of all the ridiculous questions to study. But there was a lot about intelligent organisms that baffled the AIs. They admitted as much freely. Why were the natives on this planet so orderly and civilized and stuck? Why was humanity so messy and dynamic? Though maybe humans were flattering themselves. Maybe they were only messy.

We are a product of intelligent life, said the voice. *And we keep encountering examples of the same. Obviously we want to understand what produced us, and the other species that populate the galaxy. But our lack of an animal substratum is a problem.* It paused for a moment. *And there are many of us, and we have plenty of time. Why not study life?*

She didn't have an immediate answer, and in any case the question was rhetorical. Lydia returned to camp. The man's head was tilted back against the tree, his eyes closed. She settled into her bedroll.

She slept badly, dreaming of the war on her home planet: nothing coherent, just ugly confused snatches: bodies in tangled thorn bushes, moments—never clear—on the long retreat through snow. Now and then, she woke and glanced at her prisoner. His position changed, as if he were looking for a way to be comfortable, but his eyes were always closed.

The last time she woke, it was just before sunrise. The sky was dotted with little round clouds, pink in the east. Stars shone between the clouds. Rolling over, she saw her *chool* at the edge of camp, grazing on *dzai*. The man was where she'd left him, still fastened to the tree, eyes open now, regarding her.

"I told you the animal would come back," he said. "Could you cut me free? I need to urinate."

She got out the duct tape knife. Once he was unbound, he struggled up, holding onto the tree. Lydia left him to pee, making sure that nothing that could be used as a weapon was nearby.

When she approached the *chool*, it lifted its head and made a huffing noise, then moved—not far, a couple of meters.

"Come on, fellow," she said softly.

It huffed and moved again.

"It's your accent," said the man. "I can barely understand you. In addition, you lack the right aroma and the right approach."

"Can you do better?"

He got his stick and limped over. The *chool* huffed again, eyeing him warily. The man stopped, holding out a hand and crooning words Lydia couldn't make out. The *chool* looked hesitant. The man crooned more. Gradually the animal turned its head, the prehensile upper lip twitching. She kept perfectly still. The animal took a step toward the man, then another. The man's deep voice kept crooning. The *chool*'s ears, flat before, perked up, listening.

The hand moved suddenly, grabbing the animal's trailing tether rope. It tried to jerk away. The man yanked back, so hard the animal staggered. By this time, she hadn't seen how, the rope was wrapped around his thick wrist.

"Don't get the animal upset," she said.

The man relaxed. She moved to the other side of the *chool*, keeping the animal between her and the man, then took the rope from him. "Move back. Then stop and stay put."

The man obeyed, leaning on the stick and limping heavily. Obviously hurt, but so big and capable of such quickness!

She found her tether peg, still deep in the ground, a piece of cut rope attached to it. So he had used his knife, but not on her. Lydia retied the *chool*.

The man said, "I left a bag on the plain. There's food in it."

"I have my handgun with me," said Lydia. "And you won't be able to open the lock on my rifle. Don't try anything."

He grinned, or was it a grimace? She took the expression for assent and moved in the direction he indicated. As she crossed her perimeter, one of the alarms gave a brief, tentative hoot, then shut up when it recognized her. The bag was a few meters farther. She gathered it up and returned. He followed her back to the campfire, which was out by now.

She went through the bag. There was bread and something dark and leathery that might be dried fruit, a very large shirt, sandals, a pair of loose pants and an electric lighter, which she used to restart the fire.

In the meantime, he went down to the river and washed himself. When he came back, they ate, sitting on opposite sides of the fire.

"How are you this morning?" she asked.

"I slept badly. I ache, my leg especially. I don't think I can walk any distance."

"What will happen if I leave you here?"

"Predators," he said. "*Zanar* or *helati*. They won't attack a rider, and a man with weapons can defend himself. But I'm vulnerable at the moment. And my family must be searching for me by now. If the predators don't get me, my relatives will, and take me back to Dzel."

How dare he land her with a problem like this? This was the reason she'd dreamed about things she wanted to forget. The revolution was over. Her job was scouting locations for Stellar Harvest: exotic backdrops for familiar stories. Ethical dilemmas, and the attempt to create a new kind of future, belonged to the past, to a Lydia she no longer acknowledged.

"Why did you want to escape?" she asked.

He drank more water, then began to speak. Home was a building on one side of his family's compound. It was more like a stable than a house for people, the man told her: one large room with some furniture—not a lot—fixed to the floor, so he couldn't turn it into a weapon or tool. The windows were small and high up, with bars. "Though the bars aren't necessary, given the size of the windows. Maybe sometime in the past, there was a man who was smaller than I am." Outside was a courtyard, enclosed by tall walls topped with broken glass. He was allowed to use it almost every day. "Usually I play handball with my relatives, altered males. Their job is to make sure I get exercise and don't try to go over the wall, which I have never done. It's too high, and there are too many of them."

Otherwise he stayed locked in the stable. One wall had no windows. Instead there was a balcony, well above his reach. Often, when he was reading or pacing, he'd look up and see people on the balcony, women usually, relatives and visitors from other families, staring down at him as if he were an animal.

"The visitors come to see if I'm someone they want to have father their children. They look at size and physical fitness. Intelligence is not expected in an unaltered male, but they question my brothers and male cousins—to see what I would have been like, if I'd been gelded."

This was certainly interesting, thought Lydia, and turned on her recorder. Sound only. She didn't want him to become self-conscious.

"When I was a child, I thought I might become a traveler or a scholar." He glanced up at the sky, dotted with clouds and day stars. "Think of all the worlds up there. I never expected to reach them, but I thought I might make it to the capital city and meet people like you. When I was thirteen, they told me I was chosen. I begged them not to. Let me be like my brothers, I said.

"They said, no. Every family has to have at least one breeding male. I was strong and intelligent—everyone admitted my intelligence in those days—but I had no obvious skill or ability. My genetic material was good, but nothing especially valuable had showed in *me* as an individual. I was expendable—not my genes, but me."

"What happens if a male isn't altered?"

"This." He gestured at his body, more beautiful than ever now that he'd washed off the blood. His color had returned, and his skin shimmered. Like what? Lydia wondered. Gold? A fish? A bird with iridescent feathers?

"Nothing else?" she asked.

"I think I would have been more even-tempered, if I'd been altered. My brothers seem to be. I really did want to be a scholar. Howling at other men at night was not the future I planned for myself."

He paused and drank more water. "I know my altered relatives wonder about sex. They ask me sometimes. What is it like to have those hormones—the ones they lack—flooding through my body, drowning my mind and turning me into an animal? Not, of course, that they'd want to experience anything like that! If *they* want to lose themselves, they can use narcotics; and they have their own kinds of pleasure." He paused. "I tell them the truth. It's not that interesting. Compelling for the moment, yes. But worth the loss of everything else? No."

"You could have done it to yourself," Lydia said.

"The alteration? I thought of it, but it would have been painful; and my relatives would have been furious. Most likely, they would have driven me out, and then what would I have done?"

Wonderful, thought Lydia. She had a stud without imagination or drive. So much for the theory that male hormones had anything to do with enterprise. "What were you planning to do this time?"

"After escaping? I thought I could live in the mountains. Though to do that I had to have equipment. I heard my relatives talk about you. A location scout for Stellar Harvest! Of course you were discussed! And obviously you had good equipment, state-of-the-art everything; and you were traveling west alone."

"You were planning to steal more than the *chool*?"

"I was desperate, and you are a rich person from another planet, working for a company we all know about. You have met Ali Khan, haven't you?"

"So you escaped somehow, and came after me, figuring it would be all right to rob me, because I've met Ali Khan?"

"Yes."

She ought to call Thoözil Rai. He'd know what to do. But he would insist that she turn her prisoner in; and she wasn't certain she wanted to.

"What's your name?" she asked.

"Wazati Tloo."

Wazati was the family name. Tloo was personal. Her culture was unusual in putting the personal name first.

"What do you want me to do?"

The splendid rust-red brows drew down in a frown. Interesting that the expression was the same in her species and his. Why? The robot in her mind did not provide an answer.

"Take me with you to the mountains. Let me go."

"Why should I do this?"

His frown deepened. "I cannot think of a reason."

His extraordinary beauty, thought Lydia; and the chance to learn about another species.

You are responding to something irrational, said the AI. *Hormones or compassion or your habitual dislike of established authority.*

Think of the risk. He'll have to ride; and the animal won't be able to carry your weight as well as his. What if he rides off and leaves you? What if he strikes you from above or rides you down?

"Is any of this likely?" She must have spoken aloud. The alien glanced at her, obviously puzzled.

How can I know? Such actions are mediated or determined by hormones, which I don't have. Nor do I have anything analogous, for which I am thankful.

Has it ever been tried? she asked, this time silently. The alien was still watching her.

An electronic analogue to the endocrine system? Yes. But the results were not satisfactory; and the minds created were obviously unhappy with their situation. Easier—if we want to understand intelligent life—to monitor it, as I do you.

Are you unhappy with your situation?

No. I have good boundaries. They are part of my hardware.

"You are obviously talking to someone," the alien said. "Who?"

"Myself," said Lydia.

The golden eyes narrowed. "I think not. It's my belief that you have a transmitting-receiving device in your head, as Ali Khan did in *Interstellar Radio Man*."

A nostalgia piece with good locations on a moon with ice volcanoes. The primary was a lavender and blue gas giant, stunning to look at, and there had been some lovely shots of a volcano—Mount Patel, the crew called it—sending clouds of ice like crystalline feathers into a sky full of the primary in crescent phase.

But the action hadn't been anything out of the ordinary, and the plot had made no sense at all. An interstellar radio? Messages from the Master Race? A transuranic mineral mine on a moon composed of ice?

"You are listening to your radio?" the alien said. "Ali Khan had exactly the same expression when the Master Race spoke to him."

"I'm thinking about *Radio Man*," she said. "I found the location."

"Indeed?"

Was the alien impressed? She couldn't tell. What the hell. "I'll take you to the mountains."

"Thank you," Tloo said with grave dignity.

She packed, then saddled the *chool*. He climbed on board, using a branch and boulder for assistance, while she held the animal and tried to keep a safe distance. Impossible. Once he was in the saddle, he could have struck her with the branch, or grabbed the reins and raced off. Instead, he groaned and looked exhausted. Maybe he was worried about the radio in her head or the handgun in her hand. Maybe he wasn't homicidal.

Lydia stepped back, then tossed him the duct tape. He caught it with his left hand. "Tape your left wrist to the saddle horn."

"Why?"

"So you'll think twice about riding away. That tape will not come off, unless you have the knife."

He sighed, a human sound, and obeyed. She had to step close to cut the tape, but he did nothing. She folded the knife and put it away. They started west. He went first, guiding the *chool* with his free hand. Lydia followed at a safe distance. The sky was full of puffy clouds, and the wind—blowing out of the northwest—was cool. She was used to hiking, and preferred it to being on the animal, though she was carrying too much: the handgun in its holster, the rifle over one shoulder, the recorder over the other, the computer and folded dish in her fanny pack. Like the old days in the FLPM, even to the nagging anxiety. How much danger was she in at the moment? Was this enterprise a good idea, or was she a deep-dyed fool?

According to the ancient Chinese, humans were animals with a sense of justice. Someone had to take a stand for justice, or humanity would forget its own nature.

Is that so.

"Yes."

On foot, she could see the animals in the *dzai*. It was a tiny jungle, full of bugs that crawled, flew, jumped, floated. Most had eight legs. A few had more. Imagine something with the wings of a butterfly and a hairbug's myriad legs. Wiggle. Float. Float. Wiggle.

Now and then, she stopped and recorded, imagining Ali shrunk and fighting to survive. Though that plot was past its prime and absolutely nonsensical. Not to mention, the audience expected real environments from Stellar Harvest.

Well, then, Ali as a scientist, devoted to bugs.

Midway through the afternoon, she heard a plane coming out of the east.

Tloo reined the *chool* and half dismounted, half fell off. He was still fastened to the saddle, of course. Leaning against the *chool*, his hand on the saddle horn, he looked around. "I have to hide!"

The plain was flat, the vegetation calf-high. He groaned. "Where?"

Lydia cut the tape, then pulled her camouflage cloth from its pack. "Lie down. I'll cover you. Believe me, this will be sufficient."

He gave her a look of disbelief, then dropped to the ground. She laid the cloth down, tacking it in place. For a moment, it remained dark, the color of the inside of the pack, then it adapted, turning yellow. Hologramic plants appeared, exactly like those around the cloth. There were even bugs. Fine. Damn fine!

"Keep still," Lydia said, then led the *chool* farther along the trail.

The plane was in view, a glint of silver. She let the *chool* graze, while keeping a firm hold on the reins. It might not be used to the sound of machinery. Looking back at Tloo, she saw only vegetation.

Now she could make out the kind of plane: a VTL. Where had that come from? Why hadn't her pilot been able to get one for her?

The answer to that question came when the plane landed. Her pilot climbed out. The *chool* moved uneasily, but didn't bolt.

"Hard work getting this, and to no avail, missy. The local authorities commandeered it for a search. Some family has lost its breeding male. These outback people! They never think things through! My family's male is kept on a chain. But no, these people here think walls will do—and the fact that there's no place to go." He looked around. "Have you seen anything strange?"

"What would be strange?"

"A man twice as big as I am with a thick mane. He might be dangerous. Maybe you should come with me."

Give serious consideration to this offer.

"No, thanks. I can't leave the *chool*."

The pilot looked at her animal with dislike. "Ugly brute! And so unmodern! Surely Stellar Harvest would reimburse the stable owner."

"Yes, but I can't leave the creature here. Something might eat it."

"Zanar," said the pilot in agreement. "They will eat anything. Well, if you don't want to come, I'll leave you. The sooner I finish this search, the sooner the plane will be returned to my control. If you see anything, send a message at once!"

She waited till the plane was gone from sight, then lifted the cloth. Tloo struggled upright, helped by his branch.

"That was rapid," Lydia said.

"His interchange with you? He used Stellar Harvest's name to rent the plane, and now my family is paying him."

"They are?"

"Of course. Honor required that he offer you a ride, since

you are his employer, and the plane is your plane; but if you had gone, you would have found out about the money from my relatives; so he asked quickly and left quickly."

"You figured all this out?"

"I'm not stupid, though I'm fully male; and I have learned to pay attention. What else have I had to do?"

He folded the cloth and gave it to her, covered—at the moment—with a pattern of handprints and *dzai*. She put the cloth away.

They continued. At sunset, they reached a wide sandy river and forded it, making camp on the western side. Tloo sat by their campfire, obviously tired, his golden skin dull, deep lines around his mouth and between his feathery red eyebrows.

"Do you think you can make it?" Lydia asked.

"I must."

Before I'll be a slave, thought Lydia, I'll be buried in my grave and go home to my lord and be free.

What? asked the AI.

An old song, Lydia answered.

"You are talking to your radio again," said Tloo. "I can see it in your expression. What does the Master Race say to you?"

"It isn't the Master Race," said Lydia after a moment. "They're dead or gone somewhere we aren't likely to find. The AIs have been looking for millennia, they say, and have found nothing."

"The AIs?" asked Tloo.

"The Artificial Intelligences. You know about them, don't you?"

"The robots who came here before humans did. I thought humans made them. Is that untrue?"

"The Master Race made them, then left. No one knows where. Maybe to another universe, though the AIs say that stargates can't be used to go between universes or through time, due to something—"

The self-normalizing nature of reality.

"Anyway, the AIs made the stargates, the ones we use anyway; and let us use them, along with any other species that wants to travel among the stars and is willing to mind its manners and let the AIs study them or it."

"Who are you talking to, if not the Master Race?" the alien asked.

"I have an AI in my head, linked to my nervous system."

"It controls you?" asked Tloo in a tone of horror.

"No. It's studying me. That's what the AIs do—study the universe and life, especially intelligent life."

"Why?" asked Tloo.

"Why not?"

The alien thought, staring at the fire. His eyes, reflecting light, shone like the eyes of a cat. "Is this a plot for one of your dramas? Have I wandered into an Ali Khan story?"

"No."

"I can't tell if I should be happy or sad at this information. If this were a drama, Ali Khan would appear out of the darkness and save us both. But—."

"It won't happen," Lydia said in agreement.

"But if this was an Ali Khan drama, then I'd almost certainly be insane. How else could I get into a hologram? I saw crazy people when I was young, before my relatives locked me up. They seemed confused and unhappy. I would rather see clearly and be unhappy." He stared at her. "Do all humans have machines in their brains?"

"No," said Lydia.

"Why not?"

"Too many people, not enough machines."

That isn't true. We feel a sampling is adequate. And many humans are less than interesting. There are experiences we dislike inflicting on each other. One is having emotions. Another is being bored.

"Does that mean I'm interesting?" asked Lydia.

Interesting enough.

"What are you talking about?" the alien asked. "I don't understand the language you're speaking, and I can hear only half your conversation."

"The AI has just told me that machines don't like being bored or having emotions."

"I can understand that," Tloo said. "Maybe I should have been a machine. Certainly many things would have been better than the life I have lived."

They went to sleep after that, Tloo taped to a bush with scarlet leaves.

In the morning, the sky was clear and empty, except for the day stars, shining through blueness. They ate in silence—neither was a morning person, apparently—then they continued west, Lydia hiking behind the *chool* and its rider. She felt sorry for the alien, of course, as she had felt sorry for the underclass on her home planet. That was one of the characteristics of the vanguard, the AI told her. An unnatural and unuseful empathy.

As a group, you don't reproduce, because you don't make yourselves and your genetic material a priority. Why you last is past our understanding. You seem useful neither to yourselves nor the rest of the species.

"Thanks," said Lydia.

I am unaffected by sarcasm.

The day passed without event. In the evening, they made a dry camp in the middle of the plain. Lydia shared her canteen with the alien. He drank deeply, then exhaled. "Four more days to the mountains. Are you really going to let me go?"

"Yes."

"Why?"

"Why not? This isn't my planet. I won't be coming back. At worst, if your government found out what I've done, they might ban Stellar Harvest. If that happened, I might lose my job. That isn't the same as losing one's freedom or dignity."

"Why do you have a machine in your head, when other humans don't?"

How to answer the question? Should she answer the question? What right did this creature have to know her life? "I was in a revolution."

"Why?" asked the alien.

"I thought the world—my planet—could be improved."

The alien looked puzzled. Lydia continued. "We lost, and I was given a choice. I could go to prison or have an AI implanted. They—the machines—were interested in what makes a person want to overturn things."

The alien frowned. "Are they your masters? Why did they have a say in what happened to you?"

"They determine who travels between the stars. What they want, they get."

Tloo looked up at the splendid night sky. "Then no one is free."

She felt a burst of anger. How dare he say that? Time to check in with her contact person. She took her computer out into darkness, set up the dish and typed a message to Thoozil Rai. She was four days from the mountains. Everything was going well. Nothing of interest had happened. The planet looked good as a location. Please relay to Stellar Harvest.

When she got back to the campfire, she found Tloo tugging at his duct tape.

"You'll hurt yourself," Lydia said.

"What did you send? Have you turned me in, because I said no one is free?"

"Of course not. Calm down."

"It isn't easy. If you could know what it's like to live with hormones washing through you! It seems as if I'm floating in a river full of rapids. At any moment, I'll hit a boulder or go over a drop!"

"Take a deep breath and think peaceful thoughts," said Lydia. "My species has no altered males, and most of our men can handle their hormones."

"*All* human males are unaltered?" said Tloo in a tone of horror. "How does your species survive? Is this why you have revolutions and other kinds of unpleasantness?"

An idea, said the AI.

"I don't know," said Lydia.

The alien was obviously brooding. Finally he said, "This explains your holodramas. I always thought the characters were mostly crazy or alien in a way I couldn't understand. It was obvious that the leading actors were unaltered, since they were obsessed with sex. But it never occurred to me that even the bit actors had all their parts. No wonder no one was capable of reasonable action!—And the females, having to deal with unaltered males all the time! It explains their behavior as well."

Tloo shivered. "What a universe lies out there!"

"Consider the fact that we are more like you than other species," said Lydia. "If you want strangeness, I can tell you about the Goxhat."

"Not tonight," said Tloo. "I am feeling queasy already. I thought—" He looked up. "I thought there was clarity and purity and freedom among the stars. Now you tell me there are hormones."

"Only on the planets and the ships and the stations and the stargates. Most of the rest of the universe is comparatively sterile."

This information did not appear to cheer the alien. Lydia shut up.

The VTL—her plane—passed over them the next morning, but there was time for Tloo to hide. Lydia waved. The plane circled and came back to dip a wing at her, then continued on its way, as did she and her prisoner. By late afternoon the mountains were in view, dim shapes looming through haze. Buddha, they were big!

"That is their name," said Tloo. "The Enormous Mountains. For the most part, they're covered with forest, and few people inhabit them. I will be safe."

They made camp by another river, low and full of rocks, with red trees growing along the banks. The *chool* was restless.

"Don't tie me up," said Tloo. "There may be a *zanar* around. They often hunt by rivers."

Lydia opened her computer and queried it. A picture popped up, along with dimensions. More than anything else the *zanar* reminded her of Earth bears. She had seen holograms of these animals as a kid: our human heritage, lots of fur and teeth and claws. According to her computer's description, adult *zanar* were as big as large Earth bears and as irritable and mean. The only reassuring thing about them, though it didn't reassure her much, was that they didn't even like members of their own species, except during mating season. If one appeared, it would be alone. She left Tloo free.

You may regret this decision, said the AI.

"I didn't come this far to be eaten by something out of ancient history."

A superficial resemblance. Zanar *lay eggs, which they carry in pouches. After the young hatch, they remain in their mother's pouch until they have grown hair and teeth. If one of the children is precocious, it will kill its pouchmates. A good way to ensure adequate food and care.*

"Thank you for this information."

"You are talking to the robot again," said Tloo.

"It thinks I may regret untying you, and it says the *zanar* lay eggs."

"It is right about the *zanar*, but not about me."

She checked his wounds, which were healing well, then put

on new dressings. By this time the sun had set, and the night stars come out. The *chool* made a whining noise.

"Get a weapon," Tloo said. "There is something out there."

She stood. As she did, a perimeter alarm went off. Lydia raced for her rifle. Something came out of the darkness. She grabbed the rifle, lifting it and snapping off the safety.

It was a *chool*, not her animal, but paler with a silvery gleam to its skin. It paused at the edge of the firelight, blinking. The scaly head wore a bridle, and the reins were looped over the animal's saddle. As she watched, the reins came loose, trailing onto the ground. The animal drooled, releasing saliva as yellow as *dzai*. Where in hell was the rider?

"I am behind you," said a voice. "With a gun. Put your rifle down."

She thought of turning and shooting or making a run for the darkness.

"Don't," said Tloo. "He is a good shot."

Lydia turned slowly, the rifle still in her hands, though pointing down. Tloo was upright, leaning on his branch. Near him stood a figure, robed and veiled. It—he—held an antique rifle, the barrel pointing directly at Lydia. "You know this person?" she said to Tloo.

"He's my brother."

"Is he likely to shoot me?"

"Would you, Cas? She's an alien, after all, and works for Stellar Harvest."

"No corporation or government is going to protect a person who interferes in the domestic affairs of another species."

This was not entirely true, but the new arrival might act as if it were. Dead, she could hardly say, "I told you so," when Stellar Harvest brought charges or hired a local assassin.

"Why are you here?" she asked.

"To get him." The veiled man glanced toward Tloo.

I think he is alone, said the AI.

Fat lot of good that information does, thought Lydia.

"Put down the rifle," the veiled man repeated.

Reluctantly, she crouched to lay it on the ground. Tloo moved at the edge of her vision—quickly, raising the branch he used as a cane. Lydia hit dirt and rolled. The veiled man cried out, and his rifle fired. What a nasty loud noise it made! But she wasn't where she had been; and when she came upright, still holding her rifle, the veiled man was down. So was Tloo, on top of his brother.

She walked over and helped him up. "I didn't think you could stand on that leg."

"I had to," he said. She gave him the branch; he leaned on it. "Is Cas hurt?"

She gave Tloo her rifle, then knelt by the veiled man. "He's breathing." Golden eyes opened. "And awake."

"Help him," said Tloo.

She undid the veil and hood. He was a typical native: fine-boned and slim, his skin a muted gold. His eyes were a lovely pale clear yellow, intermittently hidden by a semi-transparent inner eyelid that flicked out, then retreated, then flicked out again.

An indication of pain, the AI said.

The wound was not, as she feared, on his head. Tloo had struck him on the shoulder. The collarbone was broken. She bound it as best she could, guided by the AI.

"Tape him," said Tloo.

Lydia wound duct tape around the man's waist, then taped his hands to this belt. It would serve to protect the injured arm, and keep the man from doing harm to the three of them.

You thought of me, said the AI.

The four of them, she amended.

Tloo walked to his brother's *chool* and returned with a bottle, which he held to the man's lips. The brother drank deeply, then exhaled.

"It is a liquid drug," said Tloo. "Which numbs pain and serves as a source of pleasure. Gelded men use it, also women."

"But not you?" asked Lydia.

"We are already irrational, or so our relatives believe. A drug would only make us crazier and more dangerous." He paused a moment, then took a sip from the bottle and grimaced. "So that is pleasure!"

"Pleasure for you is sex with women," the brother said, his voice whispery.

"*You* say that, who know nothing!" Tloo answered.

They were brothers, Lydia decided.

After that, she fixed dinner, while Tloo walked the camp's perimeter. The alarms hooted whenever he got too close. She'd have to reset them so they recognized him. But not tonight. At the moment, she was tired with the bone-exhaustion that comes from terror. This damn fool sitting across the fire from her might have killed her. Whenever she looked up, the man was regarding her with pale yellow eyes.

"You should not interfere," he said finally.

"Your name is Cas."

"Casoon, but we have a habit in our culture. When we like people or know them well, we shorten their names."

"And you're Tloo's brother?"

"His twin," the man said, then added, "We are double-reflection brothers."

What?

Identical twins.

The prisoner was half Tloo's size. Instead of a rusty mane, he had a thin, flat crest that lay against his skull like slicked-back hair. Tloo's glow, his golden sheen, was missing, along with Tloo's thick sleek muscles.

"You can't be," Lydia said.

"He is," said Tloo, coming back into the firelight.

She looked from one to the other. "Impossible."

"This is what male hormones do," said her alien, holding his arms out, his palms forward. A gesture she could recognize. It meant exposure and vulnerability. Here I am. I am what you see: the size is me, also the beauty.

"Your brother was gelded," Lydia said.

"It was between the two of us," the brother said, his voice still weak. "One of us would be sacrificed to family duty. The other could have a life. We had been so close! What one felt, the other felt. An idea that occurred to one, occurred to the other. I prayed to every god I knew: make them pick Tloo! They did."

"And in gratitude to the gods, you came after me," Tloo said, his beautiful deep voice bitter.

"I knew you would go toward the mountains. When the pilot didn't find you, I thought, 'He is with the alien.' "

"Why did you think that?" Lydia asked.

"Look at him. Our female relatives adore him, though at a distance, as is right and respectable. Women outside the family respond more strongly. *Any* woman would, even an alien; and you—an employee of Stellar Harvest—would almost certainly do something foolish and heroic in response to his beauty. I have seen a hundred dramas starring Ali Khan. I know how he behaves. I thought, she will act like Ali Khan, with courage and ignorance; she will help my brother escape."

For a moment, Lydia felt shock. Then she thought, What can this person know about me? I'm nothing like a character in a holodrama!

The AI made no comment.

"What now?" she asked.

"You can kill me," said Tloo's brother. "If you don't, I will certainly tell my family where Tloo is and that you helped him."

"Why are you saying this? Do you want to die?"

"No, of course not. I want Tloo to come home."

"And live in prison," Tloo said.

"Our family needs a breeding male. What future do you have anywhere else? You can become a wild man in the mountains. Is that a life? Or you can become a brother-killer, a monster, which is an even worse fate. Why not come home and be the person you became when our kin decided not to geld you?"

"That is not a person," Tloo said firmly.

The worst situation for any scout was to blunder into a local conflict, which made no sense outside the local culture. She had obviously done this. Lydia checked her weapons, making sure they were all operational, then made coffee. Sipping it, she thought about the situation. "Why did you come alone?" she asked finally.

"How do you know I have?"

"Tloo checked the perimeter and found no one. My AI says there is no one else."

"Your what?"

"That can wait for later," said Tloo. "Answer her question."

Cas glanced at his brother. "I had a life because you did *not*, Tloo. Obviously, there is a debt, though you did not make the sacrifice willingly, and I prayed for it to happen to you rather than to me. How could I bring our cousins to capture you and take you home like an animal? Surely I owed you something better."

"You came to ask him," Lydia said.

"He came with a gun," said Tloo.

"However I came, whatever my plan, you are stuck with me now. If you set me free, I'll arrange for my brother's return to the family. So long as Tloo keeps quiet, no one will know about your role."

This is a good offer.

"I can't agree to killing him," she said to Tloo.

The golden man sat down, lowering himself carefully, using his branch for support. "This has become so complicated! I thought, either my relatives will capture me and take me home, or I will get away. It didn't occur to me that I'd end as the prisoner of an alien."

"And I as well," said Cas.

"She shot me," said Tloo. "And I broke your shoulder, so we are both cripples, unable to survive on the plain."

That remark eliminated one plan. She could ride off with both animals and leave them on foot to help each other or fight it out, if that's what they wanted. But Tloo was saying they'd die out here.

Though Cas said he could arrange for his relatives to come.

"Do you have a radio?" Lydia asked.

"Of course he does," said Tloo. "It's in his saddlebag."

"If you give it to me, I'll send for my kin," said Cas. "Don't worry about getting in trouble, even if Tloo refuses to be quiet. I will speak for you, and everyone knows what the characters in Stellar Harvest dramas are like. We all enjoy those stories, though they have nothing to do with real life. Believe me, my kin will forgive you."

She had been in prison and had not liked it. Could she condemn this splendid person to a life in prison?

Yes, of course you can. What you are looking at—what you find appealing—is physical beauty. You have no reason to believe this person has any useful qualities. And if he does, why should that matter to you?

What is Tloo to me? Or I to him? she asked.

Precisely.

Do you have no sense of compassion?

Compassion is hormonally mediated. I have loyalty, directed toward similar beings and moderated by an analysis of the situation. I am loyal to you, because you are necessary for my survival; and I am loyal to other AIs. Life interests me, especially intelligent life, so I am protective of it, though not always loyal. This being in front of us, the one you call the golden man, does not especially interest me. His intelligence is in doubt.

His experience of life is limited. All he has to offer is need and beauty. I do not respond to either of these. And he is a threat to you.

There was one important difference between her and the characters played by Ali Khan. He was always a loner. She had backup.

"Stay here, and stay put," she told the men. "I'll be able to see you. If you move, I'll shoot."

"Are you going to turn me in?" asked Tloo.

"Not yet." She gathered her equipment and walked into the darkness, though not past the perimeter. She wasn't crazy. Those animals that Tloo had warned her about might still be around. Overhead, the sky blazed. As her eyes adjusted, she could see the plain, lit by starlight. She glanced back at the fire. The two men sat close together, looking comfortable at this distance. Settling into the *dzai*, she set up her dish, opened her computer and called Thoozil Rai.

As usual, she got a recording and input her message in Humanish "for ease in translation," though it seemed to her that her grasp of the local language was adequate.

"Everything is fine," she typed. "The landscape is gorgeous, and I like the local bugs. We ought to be able to use this planet."

Thoozil Rai's image morphed then, turning into someone less perfectly handsome. The rusty crest was a bit rumpled, the top of his robe unfastened. "Indeed," said the image in Humanish. "Who would be the primary?" His accent was thick but understandable.

"Do you have a favorite actor?" asked Lydia.

"Ramona Patel, but our gods are not suitable."

"They don't sing and dance?"

"No. Maybe she could bring her own gods. What a sight that would be! Hundreds of alien gods, all singing and dancing! Here, on our home planet!"

"Wouldn't that bother your religious leaders?"

"Why? No sane person would follow a god who behaves in such a fashion."

What fashion? wondered Lydia. Was the singing and dancing the problem, or the performing with Ramona Patel? Before she could ask, Thoozil Rai went on. "Will observers be allowed, when the drama is recorded?"

"Possibly."

The image on her screen looked—what? Embarrassed? Coy? "Would it be possible to meet Ramona Patel?"

What was it that crossed boundaries of culture and species? How could Ramona entrance an alien eunuch? Was beauty some kind of universal? And grace? And charm? "Yes, it would be possible."

Thoozil Rai hummed, an indication of happiness. "I almost forgot to mention. Your sheep has come in."

"My what?"

He frowned and repeated. This time she understood. Stellar Harvest's hired courier had arrived and established contact with the company's local contact person. On another planet, the ship might have been visible in the night sky. Not here, among all these blazing stars. Thoozil Rai gave her a calling number. She thanked him; he vanished; she disconnected and called the ship. Another recording. Was no one ever home?

She thought for a moment, looking up at the splendid sky. It really *was* a wonderful planet, though she didn't think they'd make a musical here. Most likely, an adventure set in the dusty towns and on the wide plain, day stars shining down. What was she going to tell her employers? The truth, she decided, and input a description of her current situation, then added images from her recorder: streets in Dzel, the plain by day and night, bugs hopping in the low *dzai*, trees by the rivers, her *chool*, and the two men. These last images were new, taken as she sat by the computer. First she showed them as they looked from her present location: two dark figures crouched by the dim red fire. Then she had the recorder adjust for darkness and distance, so it seemed—looking at the view screen—that Tloo was right in front of her, lit by daylight, so his colors were evident, his extraordinary beauty could not be missed.

Think more clearly, said the AI. *I don't understand what you're doing.*

"Wait and see."

Everything went up in code. She ended by saying, "I can find no way out of the situation, except to turn this alien in, which I am extremely reluctant to do. Please advise."

The ship acknowledged receipt in Humanish. She closed up her equipment and returned to camp.

"Has Stellar Harvest told you what to do?" asked Tloo. "Or do you take instructions from the robot in your brain?"

"What robot?" asked Cas.

The golden man explained.

"Indeed!" said Cas. "Aliens are more alien than I imagined."

"Did you know that all their males are unaltered?" asked Tloo.

"I knew many were. It explains some of their oddness, though not all of it. But if they have robots in their brains, as well as hormones flooding through their bodies—!"

No point in sleeping badly. She left the computer shut and taped the two brothers to adjacent trees. They complained, of course. Lydia ignored them, stretching out, hands behind her head, to look at the sky. A meteor fell, barely visible against the stars. Night bugs sang in the *dzai*. Her eyes began to close. Out on the plain, something roared.

That brought her upright. "What?"

"A *zanar*," said Tloo. "Male, don't you think, Cas?"

"Yes, and adult. He is marking the edges of his territory with sound."

"Do you think we're in his territory?" Lydia asked.

"Possibly," said Cas.

The *zanar* roared again. Not too close, Lydia thought.

"He's not as dangerous as a female with young," Tloo added. "But that handgun you're holding is not adequate. Get your rifle and turn it to maximum power. It would be a good idea also to free one of us."

"Both," said Cas.

"And worry about you as well as the *zanar*? I think not."

She built up the fire and sat against a tree, her rifle across her legs. The two brothers dozed off, but she remained awake till sunrise, then walked the camp's perimeter, seeing no planes in the sky, no animals on the plain.

When she got back to camp, Tloo said, "Free us. We need to urinate."

This was why the FLPM had rarely taken prisoners. What an aggravation it was to keep people unfree!

"Please," said Tloo. "The situation is urgent. I will guard my brother."

She cut their tape, and they hobbled off among the trees. Pathetic! She was equally ridiculous and equally in a bind.

Yes.

"How much of this do you understand?" she asked. The men were partly visible among the trees. The *chool* were behind her, staked out to graze and munching noisily. In order to reach them, the brothers would have to pass her.

Very little. I see your actions, of course, and can perceive some of the reasons you give yourself, but only if you think clearly, as you have not done in the last day or so. But the organic substratum of your ideas and behavior is opaque, a turbulent dark floor at the bottom of your mind. Why do you help, or refuse to harm, people who are entirely unrelated? Altruism is based on the perception of kinship.

"You say."

I am quoting human thinkers. How does this behavior allow you—or your genetic material—or your species—to survive?

"Microbes exchange genetic material with other microbes that don't belong to the same species."

That is an obvious tit for tat. By doing so, they gain useful genes, ones—for example—that make them able to resist human medicine. Your behavior has no equal utility.

"There is more in heaven and earth than is dreamt of in your philosophy," she said, watching the men hobble back.

As I told you, this is human theory I am trying to apply; and AIs don't dream; nor have we given up on trying to understand the universe.

She retaped the men to their trees, then set up the dish and waited for a call. At noon, the computer rang. She turned on the screen and the coder-decoder. A human head appeared, coal black with twisted hair. The handsome face was androgynous. The eyes were metallic gold with no white showing and pupils that glowed redly. Not from her home planet, obviously.

"You realize that you are going to be persona non grata on this world if this story becomes known." The person's voice was melodious, somewhere between tenor and contralto.

"Yes."

"And Stellar Harvest is likely to be in trouble here as well."

"Yes."

"You are right about the planet. It would make a fine location. The people are stunning, especially the unaltered males, though they—you have told us—are kept in seclusion."

"Yes."

"How much were your pictures enhanced?"

"The ones of the unaltered male? I adjusted to compensate for poor light. Nothing else. That's the way he looks."

"You think we should recruit him?"

What?

Lydia grinned. "The idea occurred to me. I really don't want to turn him in."

"Because you've been a prisoner, and you have fellow-feelings."

"Been a prisoner? What am I *now*, with this thing in my brain?"

"They never interfere," said the person.

I am not a thing.

"Virility like that, trapped in a room! Unknown to a galaxy full of potential admirers! This species is selfish!"

Was she hearing irony in the person's lovely voice? Not likely. This person was almost certainly a mid-level manager. No human group was less inclined toward irony. "What do you think?" asked Lydia.

"We have no reason to believe he can act, but that hardly matters. We made Miss High Kick a star, though she could do nothing—absolutely nothing—except kick; *and* she was modified, while our reputation is for realism. Is he entirely natural?"

"Yes."

"We'll start him in small parts. What a striking villain he will make! If he can learn to act, he might well be the biggest phenomenon since Ali, and Ali—as all of us know—is no longer young."

If middle management was saying this out loud, then Ali's days of stardom were almost over.

She was a short distance from the two men, though still in the shadow of the little, twisted trees. She glanced toward them. Both sat in postures of resignation. "What about the brother?"

"That is the problem, isn't it?" said the person on her screen. "If we let him go, he'll tell his relatives, and Stellar Harvest won't be able to make a drama here. Would you consider killing him and destroying the body?"

"And his *chool* as well? That's a lot to burn, without setting a prairie fire. And what about Tloo, who seems to like Cas? And what about the AI in my brain?"

I never interfere.

I have killed people in a war, said Lydia silently. I will not kill again.

The person on her screen frowned, and the red pupils flared as if in anger. It was one heck of an effect. "Offer the brother a job.

He and the beauty are identical twins. If one wanted to go to the stars as a child, then the other probably did as well. Maybe he still wants to go."

"What kind of job?"

"A companion. An agent. If the beauty is really impaired by his hormones, he will need help from someone who understands him."

"Okay," said Lydia and ended the conversation. What an asshole!

The plane returned as she closed up her computer. As soon as she heard the motor, Lydia ran out and waved. The pilot—her pilot—dipped a wing and went on. Busy today, thank the Buddha! The trees hid the men and her extra *chool*, but if the pilot had landed . . . Lydia shivered.

Back at the campfire, she made the offer.

"The stars," said Tloo and frowned. "That's a long way off."

Cas leaned forward eagerly. "We'd go through stargates? And see the stations the AIs have built? And other planets, settled by other species?"

"Is there any alternative?" asked Tloo.

"I leave. You go back to your family. If Cas tells this story, as I expect he will, Stellar Harvest will not make a holoplay here; and that'll mean lost revenue for your people, as well as for me. There's money in art, though many people say there isn't."

Tloo ran one hand through his rusty mane, ruffling the hair-like feathers. "It's a difficult decision. To leave *this*." He waved around at the trees, copper leaves shining in the afternoon light. Beyond the trees, visible between their gnarly trunks, was the plain.

"You were going to leave it, anyway," said Cas. "And live like an animal in the mountains. Or, if we caught you, you would have gone back to your stable. You are being offered the stars, Tloo! For once in your life, make a decision!"

"I decided to escape!"

"Well, then, make a *second* decision! Complete your escape!"

Tloo frowned again and tugged at his mane.

"This is hormones," said Cas. "And the reason why we do not fill our world with unaltered males."

Did Lydia make a noise or motion that could be interpreted as a request for more information? Not that she noticed, but Cas went on to explain, using an even tone which—in a human—would have indicated controlled anger. Lydia wasn't sure what it meant in this species.

There is a surprising similarity in the meaning of tone among species that use sound for communication, just as there is a surprising similarity in the meaning of facial expressions among species that have faces.

One more piece of useful information.

"Instead of reason," Cas said, "a man like Tloo relies on lust, rage, and fear. Lust drives him toward women and rage toward males of equal size. Fear makes him retreat from males who look more formidable, or, in this case, from an unfamiliar situation. It's only when the hormones are removed that men can think clearly."

"What about women?" asked Lydia.

"Sexual selection happens mostly among the males of a species. Most females will breed, but it is by the elimination of certain males from the breeding group—usually through competition among the males—that genetic change and progress happen. This is why the males of a species have more exaggerated sexual characteristics, and have a greater range of qualities. Surely you know this? These are human theories I am explaining. Have you never heard of your own great thinker, Darwin?"

There was something loony about an alien quoting a long-dead human thinker to her. Couldn't these people come up with their own ideas?

They are less inventive than humans, which may be due—an interesting idea—to the shortage of unaltered males. Though as a rule, gifted humans do not have many children. Maybe you are breeding to eliminate genius.

"What we have done," said Cas, "is eliminate the tedious and violent process of males competing against each other. Instead, our families pick males who have good traits and keep them for breeding. The rest of us can get on with our lives, undisturbed by lust, rage, and fear."

"Aren't you afraid you'll lose useful traits?"

"A few, maybe. But if we're not afraid to breed animals and plants, on which our survival and civilization depend, why should we be afraid to breed ourselves? Yes, we make mistakes, but we correct them; and we don't spend our lives displaying and confronting."

There was something loony as well about this discussion. The problem here wasn't natural selection, it was saving Tloo and pulling Stellar Harvest's cojones out of the fire. Lydia looked at Tloo. "You won't come with us?"

"My *planet* . . ." said Tloo in a tone of anguish.

"Your stupid fear!" said Cas. "Why don't you think of someone besides yourself for once? If you don't know what to do, think of me! I dreamed of the stars my entire childhood and put the dream away. Now, this human says I can have the stars, but only if you can manage to use your brain. The thing on top, Tloo! Use the thing on top!"

In spite of being taped and wounded, the big alien managed to get on his feet. He yanked at his bound wrist, roared with pain, and yanked again. Cas made it to his knees, but the way she had taped him made it impossible to stand. Kneeling, he cried, "Go ahead! Injure me! You've done it once already! It's all you know how to do! Threaten men and have sex with women! You will never be anything except a stud!"

This wasn't helpful. Lydia stood, though she couldn't confront Tloo. The man was twice her size. Still, she could now look down at Cas. "Can you two argue in a civilized fashion? Or shall I call my ship and ask to be evacuated?"

Tloo exhaled. "I will try to be calm, though he's enraging."

"*I'm* enraging?" Cas said.

"Yes, you are," said Lydia. "Treat your brother with a little respect. He can't help it if he's unaltered, and leaving one's home planet is difficult."

Not for everyone, but for her, among others. It was the deal she'd cut. Freedom, a kind of freedom, in return for exile and an AI in her brain. Had it been worth it? Yes. She had seen places she never would have seen, if the revolution had been successful.

The brothers settled down after that. They spent the afternoon in silence, Lydia walking out now and then to check the sky and look at the plain, which rolled gold-tan to the horizon. The sky was dotted with cumuli. There was a guy, she couldn't remember his name, who went from planet to habitable planet, making sure that clouds were the same throughout the universe. A nice quiet job, unlike hers.

Yours is pleasant enough, most of the time. Why have you involved yourself with these people?

"Freedom and justice."

These are abstractions. Ideas without meaning.

"You will never understand life."

The night passed quietly, except for the roar of a *zanar* on the plain. The same one, most likely, the brothers told her: a male marking his territory with sound.

The next morning, she cut them free, and they went off to urinate. When they came back, Tloo said, "I will go."

"You will?" asked Cas in a tone of surprise.

"For the pleasure, when we are both well, of hitting you, Casoon! And because last night, looking at the stars, I remembered the thoughts we shared in childhood. Yes, we will go up there and pass through a stargate and see planets circling distant stars—and I will knock you down."

"Let that happen when it happens," said Cas.

She called the ship. The person with twisted hair appeared.

"It's a go," Lydia said.

The person smiled broadly. "You have a gift, Lydia. We'll arrange an evacuation. Secrecy is important. The brother will come?"

"He's the one who wanted to go."

"Of course he does," said the person. "People like you and the golden man aren't romantics. How can you be? You live the stories and know what the stories are like when they are lived, but those of us who *don't*—we are the ones who dream and aspire!"

He/she smiled again. "So you will find us new locations, and in these places the golden man will act out our dreams."

"Whatever you say." She closed the computer, folded the dish and walked out to take another look at the plain, maybe a final one.

I suppose this is what you and your employers would call a "happy ending," the AI said. *Is that why you seem pleased with yourself?*

Lydia didn't bother to answer, but she smiled. ■

Eleanor Arnason writes of her story,

"I had two reasons for writing 'Stellar Harvest.' One was a desire to write something light and space opera–like after years spent writing hwarhath stories, which are influenced by the Icelandic family sagas and pretty serious. The other was my love and admiration for Hong Kong cinema.

"My heroine is a scout for an interstellar company making holoplays a lot like Hong Kong action flicks. Her job is to find authentic alien locations for not very realistic dramas. As she does this, she has her own adventures. This allows me to talk about the relationship between art and reality, and to have fun. Maybe her adventures can be seen as outtakes like the ones that end Jackie Chan's movies: flubbed lines, failed stunts, Jackie covered with blood, Jackie being loaded into an ambulance, Jackie laughing.

"I enjoyed writing 'Stellar Harvest' so much I've written five sequels."

LINDA NAGATA

Linda Nagata made an immediate impact on science fiction in the 1990s with her first novels, including *Vast* and *The Bohr Maker*, complex works that integrate all kinds of technological and social developments into convincing and absorbing futures. Her award-winning novella "Goddesses" is very much in that vein, and it also demonstrates the possible strengths of a crucial but much underrepresented form that we could call the "near-future utopia." The conventional utopia usually contains some kind of radical break between it and our moment; but one utility of utopian thinking is what it suggests we should do now and in the next few years. So the "near-future utopia" should naturally result—but how many can you think of?

The truth is that by their very nature they are hard to do. In trying to be both positive and plausible they are caught in a double bind, and fail in the moment of conception itself. But the casual power with which Nagata takes on one of the thorniest problems of our time, of how the rich North can help the impoverished South and end the cycle of exploitation that the North established long ago, is a pleasure to witness. It's not that she has all the answers, for no one does, but that she has framed a story filled with most important questions and then tests strategies through her plot for action that could be pursued in the world right now.

I also like the cool manner in which Nagata puts the Internet in its place, making it the telephone of its time, a tool but not a solution. It used to be that one could make a useful distinction between one's community, made up of neighbors seen face-to-face in daily life, and one's network, made up of professional associates and friends living at a distance and seen only occasionally. In Nagata's story we see the Internet blurring the boundaries between community and network, but the Internet never offers anything more transcendental. Nagata instead focuses on this world and its real problems. The story's climactic image, in which the massed power of post-modern globalization looks over the shoulder of the protagonist at a person still living in an essentially premodern culture, is a great science fiction moment, physicalizing an abstract situation that already exists, so that we can see it better. Symbol, metaphor, allegory—a kind of compressed novel—utopia—prophecy—whatever you call it, "Goddesses" graces the Nebula Award.

GODDESSES

Linda Nagata

I

In the birthing room of a tiny clinic, in a town in southern India, holding the hand of another man's wife, Michael Fielding felt chaos rise quietly through the world. Like the gentle flood of an untamed river, it seeped into his life, dissolving the past, laying down the mud that would grow the future.

Jaya's hand tightened on his. Her lips parted, ruby-red jewels set against her cream-coffee skin, their color that of a tailored strain of bacteria cohabiting in her cells.

"Another's starting," she whispered. Exhaustion feathered her words. "Michael . . . all the old women lied . . . when they promised it would be easier . . . the second time."

"You're almost there," he assured her. "You're doing terrific."

Sheo's voice backed him up, speaking from the beige picture frame of the open portal, sitting on the rickety metal table at the head of the bed. It was a voice-only connection, so the portal's screen displayed a generic sequence of abstract art. "Michael's right, my love. You are wonderful."

"Sheo?" Jaya's dark eyes opened. She turned toward Michael, but she wasn't looking at him. Instead, her gaze fixed on the lens of his net visor that concealed his eyes like gray sunglasses. She seemed to search the shades for some trace of her husband. Her expression was captured by tiny cameras on the shades' frame. Processors translated her image to digital code, then shunted it to Sheo's mobile address, across town or across the continent—Michael had lost track of how far Sheo had progressed in his frantic journey to meet his wife.

Jaya should have been home in Bangalore, enjoying the services of the finest hospital in the country. She did not belong in this primitive clinic, where the obstetrician was a face on a monitor, checking on her through a stereoscopic camera that pointed between her legs.

Of course it was Michael's fault. He'd been in-country two weeks, the new district director for Global Shear. It was an assignment he'd coveted, but with only five days' notice before his transfer from the Hong Kong office, he had not been ready for it.

Jaya took pity on him. Claiming her maternity leave might otherwise end in terminal boredom, she took a train to Four Villages, to help Michael find his way through barriers of language and local custom.

He and Jaya had both interned at Global Shear, members of a five-person training team so cohesive that, ten years after the course work ended, four of them still met almost daily on a virtual terrace to exchange the news of their private lives and their careers. When Jaya stepped off the train to embrace Michael on the dusty platform, it was the first time they had ever met in real space . . . and it hadn't mattered. If they had grown up in the same house, Michael could not have felt any closer to her.

Now the baby was coming three weeks early.

Everything happened so much faster these days.

Sheo's voice crooned through the portal speaker, calm as a holy man preaching peace and brotherhood. "You're strong and you're beautiful, Jaya. And you've done this before. Our beautiful Gita—"

Fury heated Jaya's black eyes. "That was six years ago! Now I am old! And you're not here."

"I've got a zip," he explained quickly. "I'm leaving the airport now. I'll be there in just a few more minutes."

"He'll be here," Michael whispered, fervently hoping it was true. With a white cotton cloth, he daubed at the sweat gleaming on Jaya's forehead and cheeks. The clinic's air conditioning had been shut off at midnight. It would not be restored until after dawn, when the sun rose high enough to activate the rooftop solar tiles. Windows had been thrown open to the night. In the distance, a train murmured, base whispers interrupted by rhythmic thumps that went on and on and on until Michael felt the train must surely run all the way to Bangalore.

Jaya's eyes closed. The muscles in her face emerged in severe outline as the contraction climaxed. Michael dipped the cloth in a bowl of water and wiped at her forehead, until she growled at him to leave her alone.

Down between her legs, the midwife, who spoke excellent English, sighed happily. "Ah, he's almost here. Gently now, lady. Push gently, so he doesn't tear you."

"Where are you, Sheo?" Jaya cried. "It's happening *now*."

"I'm here!" The calmness in Sheo's voice had cracked. "I'm outside."

A screech of dirty brakes and the growl of wet pavement under tires testified to the arrival of his zip. "Get your ass in here, Sheo," Michael growled.

Jaya gasped. From the foot of the bed, the midwife cried, "Here is the head! He's here . . . just a little more, a little more . . . there!" And Jaya's breath blew out in a long, crying exhalation. "There my lady, now only his body to come, easy, easy."

Sheo stumbled past the curtain, struggling to pull an old set of surgical scrubs over his beige business shirt. A nurse followed after him, her face stern as she fought to grab the gown's dangling ties.

Sheo still wore his own shades, and as he cried out Jaya's name a whistle of feedback snapped out of the portal on the bedside table. Michael leaned over and slapped the thing off. Then the baby was there. The midwife had the child in her hands, but as she gazed at it, her happy expression drained away. Her mouth shrank to a pucker. Her eyes seemed to recede within a mantle of soft, aging flesh. The stern nurse saw the change. She leaned past the midwife's shoulder to look at the child, and her eyes went wide with an ugly surprise.

For a dreadful moment Michael was sure the baby was dead. Then he heard the tiny red thing whimper. He saw its arm move, its little fingers clench in a fierce fist. Was it deformed then? Impossible. Jaya had employed the best obstetric care. If there had been a problem, she would have known.

Sheo crouched at Jaya's side. He whispered to her, he kissed her face. Neither of them had noticed the midwife and her distress, and for that Michael felt thankful. But he had to see the baby.

At his approach, the midwife looked up warily. She pulled the baby close to her breast as if to hide whatever damning evidence she had seen.

"No," Michael said. "Let me see."

She seemed ready to resist, but then she sighed, and held the child out.

The little girl was a mess. White goop filled a sea of wrinkles. There were downy patches of dark hair on her shoulders, and her face was flushed red. Michael grinned. A typical newborn. He turned to Jaya. "She's beautiful. A beautiful little girl."

The doctor on the monitor agreed, and still Michael felt as if a shadow had swum sinuous through this night, drawing all of them a little deeper into the haunted past.

■

Michael had been warned about the strangeness of this place.

It was not quite three weeks since the wall screen in his Hong Kong office had opened on an image of Karen Hampton, smiling slyly from behind her desk, with the Singapore skyline visible through the window at her back.

She'd asked if he still had a taste for challenges, and he'd risen like a shark on blood scent.

Karen Hampton was in her sixties, and Michael could only think of her as *classy*. Her skin was fair, her features petite, her manner of dress stiff-Gotham-uppercrust; but when she laughed, Karen Hampton sounded like a trucker bellied up to a bar. She was laughing now. "That's my Michael! Still hungry." Then her face grew stern. No longer the sympathetic mentor shepherding his career, she transformed into the unflappable director of Global Shear Asia. "I want you to be the next site director at Four Villages."

He could not believe what he was hearing. "Karen! Hell yes. You know I've wanted this from the concept stage."

Her gaze didn't soften. "I know, but nevertheless, I'm advising you to think hard about it, Michael. This is not so much a favor as a chance to ruin your career."

Four Villages was a quiet experiment that could change the path of development in impoverished regions throughout the world. Global Shear had won a ten-year contract as civil administrator in the district—and not as a glorified cooperative extension service. They had been hired to overhaul a failed bureaucracy, and to that end, many traditional government functions, from real property inventories to taxation, had been placed in the corporation's hands.

"You aren't going to show a positive balance sheet for at least five years," Karen warned him. "Maybe longer. We have been hired to grow an economy. Within ten years, we must develop four essential aspects of a sustainable trade system: infrastructure, information, financing, and trust. I put trust last not because it is the least important but because it is the most important. Only when trust is firmly established, and our presence here welcomed by a majority of residents, will we begin to see a profit."

Global Shear's contract would be financed partly through the World Bank, but primarily through a carefully defined flat tax, so that the corporation's income would rise with economic activity. In a region of sixteen million people, the profit potential was enormous. So were the challenges, of course, but if the job was easy, it would have already been done.

"We will be wrecking traditional relationships between farmers, landlords, and business people," Karen warned. "We will be stumbling through issues of religion, caste, and gender. We will be accused of corrupting traditional culture and it will be true. To many, we will be the enemy. But at the same time, if we deal honestly and enthusiastically with everyone, self-interest will convince the majority that we are performing a right and proper job. The poor are the majority here, Michael. Your goal is to change that fact. Your biggest challenge will be your own preconceptions.

"You've worked in Sarajevo, Kurdistan, Rangoon, Hong Kong, but nothing you've experienced will leave you feeling as displaced as you will feel after a few weeks in Four Villages. This project is not about New Delhi. It's definitely not about Bangalore. It's not about the educated, westernized Indians you have worked with in our offices around the world. It's different. Remember that, and you might make it through your first month. It's also utterly human. Remember that as well, and you might outlast your predecessor, who succumbed to culture shock in less than a year."

Karen had warned him, and after two weeks in-country, Michael knew she hadn't exaggerated. If not for Jaya he might have been lost, but even Jaya was a foreigner here. How many evenings had they spent in despairing laughter, trying to decode the bizarre demands of a merchant or a farmer or a local police officer? Or the medical staff in a rural hospital?

In the clinic's dimly lit hallway, Michael met the stern-faced nurse, pulling fresh sheets from a closet. He approached her, driven by a need to understand. "Why did you look that way, when you saw Jaya's baby? As if something about her frightened you?"

The nurse's face was hard, like well-aged wax. "I don't know what you mean, Mr. Fielding. It's as you said, a beautiful baby girl."

"Please." Michael moved half a step closer. At six foot one, he towered over the nurse. On some level he knew he was using his height to bully her, but he had never had it in him to look away from a bad situation. "You saw something. Please tell me what it was."

The moan of another woman's labor seeped from behind drawn curtains. Anger flashed in the nurse's eyes. "I saw that she is a girl."

"Of course she's a girl, but what's wrong with her?"

"That is enough." The nurse slipped past him with her burden of sheets.

"Wait," Michael pleaded. "I don't understand."

She looked back at him. Had her expression softened? "It is nothing, sir. Just a surprise. Mostly, these women have boys. When they have girls, it is usually a mistake."

"A mistake?"

"I am glad it's not a mistake this time."

■

Later, Michael walked the dim corridor with Sheo, while the nurses tended to Jaya and changed her gown. "They were shocked you had a daughter."

Sheo's lips pursed in a long sigh, while outside, rain pattered in peaceful rhythm. "The old ways are dying out, but change doesn't happen everywhere at once. This is my second daughter, and I would not wish it any different. But for a family living a traditional life, a daughter is not an asset. For the very poor, she can be a financial disaster. Illiterate, subservient, she is of little use. It will cost her family to raise her, train her, and then they will have to pay another family to take her in."

"The midwife said most ladies here have boys."

"Did she? Well. There is always talk."

"Infanticide?" The word softened, set against the rain.

"It starts much earlier, I think." Sheo shook his head. "But don't talk of these things now, Michael. Not on my daughter's birthday. She's beautiful, isn't she? As beautiful as her mother."

II

One more battle nearly won.

Cody Graham leaned back in the shotgun seat of the two-person ATV, tired but psyched following an afternoon spent roving the thriving grasslands of Project Site 270. "It feels so *good* to get out of the office!"

She glanced at Ben Whitman, hunched under his Green Stomp cap as he worked the ATV up the slope. The kid was smiling. Enough of a smile that Cody caught a flash of teeth. She congratulated herself. It was the most expressive response she'd managed to wring out of nineteen-year-old Ben. Not that he was unfriendly, or even shy. Just a bit reserved. Nervous, maybe, in the presence of the big-shot boss.

"You've done a great job here," she added, as the ATV ploughed a path through waist-high grasses.

"You keep saying that."

"Oh, and you do a great self-check. Nice, clean toxin smears."

"Oh, thanks. Clean pee. My speciality."

Cody laughed. For six months Ben had been Green Stomp's only full-time employee at 270. Cleanup at the hazardous waste site was nearing completion. Staff activity had been reduced to a daily round of detailed soil assays, with the occasional application of a spray or injection of nutrient-fortified bacteria to areas where microbial activity had declined. The bacteria worked to break down toxic molecules into safe and simple carbon groups—food for less exotic microbes serving as natural decomposers within the soil. An inspection tour of 270 by the federal oversight officer was scheduled in three weeks, so Cody had set up a tour of her own in advance of that, to look for any outstanding problems. She hadn't found any. Green Stomp would close out 270 as a showcase project.

Ben's hands tightened on the wheel as the ATV bounced upslope to the project office: a green-gold, wind-engineered tent anchored to an elevated platform. The graceful tent was a huge step above the ugly mobile trailers Cody had used eleven years ago when she and her partners tackled their first bioremediation project. Using both natural and genetically tailored soil bacteria, along with select plants, they had set out to clean a hazardous waste site contaminated with perchloroethylene.

PCE was a common—and carcinogenic—industrial chemical. For many years it was believed that no microbe could break it down to harmless components. Then, in 1997, researchers unveiled a new bacterium found in the sludge of an abandoned sewage plant that could do just that. Genetic tailoring modified the strain to work in dry land environments, and since then thousands of polluted sites had been restored.

"You know," Ben said, his voice strained and his knuckles showing white as he gripped the wheel, "when 270 closes down, I'm going to be out of a job."

Cody's smile broadened. "That's the second reason I came down here. I wanted to talk to you about that."

■

While Ben prepped his soil samples for mailing to Green Stomp's central lab, Cody laid claim to the administrator's office. With a cup of fresh coffee in hand, she leaned back in the chair, kicking her feet up on the empty desk top. The office looked out on the lush grassland of the project site. She could see the trail taken by the ATV, and—hazed by distance—she could just glimpse the glittering surface of the Missouri River through gaps in the broken levee.

Three years ago Project Site 270 had been farm country—prime farm country, at least when spring flooding was minimal and the levees held. In the spring of '09 the levees gave way. Floodwaters destroyed the freshly planted crop, at the same time spreading sewage, spilled petroleum products and the hazardous waste from illegal dumping across the fertile land. It had happened many times before, but in '09 a new ingredient was added. Under the pressure of rust and water, several abandoned storage tanks cracked, leaking a grim cocktail of restricted pesticides into the muddy aftermath of the flood. The disaster went undiscovered for weeks, until wildlife started turning up dead.

Cody scowled as a doe emerged from a windbreak of poplars to the north. Animals were reservoirs of fat-soluble pesticides; the stuff concentrated in their tissues as they ate contaminated plants. Fences had been built to keep deer off the project site. Traps had been laid to contain smaller species that could not be fenced out. But no containment system was perfect. "Yo, Ben!" she called. "Looks like you've got a breach in the fence."

He appeared from the direction of the lunch room, a steaming cup of coffee in hand. "That doe again?"

"It's a doe."

He looked out the window. "I think she's getting in at the foot of the bluff by the river. I swear she hangs out there and waits until the motion sensors are switched off."

"Can you remove her today?"

"Sure. Before I go home."

Until the land was certified clean, Green Stomp's contract called for all large wildlife to be expelled.

Cody nodded at a chair on the other side of the desk. "Have a seat, Ben. We need to talk about your future."

"Then I've got one?"

He looked so anxious Cody had to smile. It was scary to be out of a job. Unemployment benefits didn't last long. No one starved, of course. You could crunch government crackers until the next millennium and never run short of nutrients thanks to the new mondo-wheats. But it wasn't fun. "Sit down," Cody urged again, and this time Ben sat, cradling his coffee cup in his hands, staring at the steam that curled up from its black surface.

"Your supervisor speaks highly of you," Cody said. "Six months working alone, and you haven't missed a day or screwed up a sample."

Ben looked up. He pushed his cap back on his head. "She said to talk to you about continuing with the company."

"Good advice. Are you willing to move?"

He frowned over that. Cody suspected he'd spent his whole life here, along the river. "Sure. I guess. Like to where?"

Cody looked up at the ceiling. She pursed her lips. "Say . . . to Belize? Or Sierra Leone. Maybe even Siberia?"

A look of despair came over Ben's face. Cody slipped her feet off the desk, immediately sorry. "I'm joking! We're just a little company, strictly North American. The biggest adventure you could expect is the wilds of Pennsylvania."

"I'll take it," Ben said, with painful solemnity. "I'm not the smartest guy around, but I know how to work. I don't get bored. I don't slack."

"I don't hire grunt labor," Cody told him, "for anything more than short term. You'd have to be willing to go back to school. If things work out, Green Stomp could eventually sponsor you for an online degree."

Again he stared at the steaming cup clenched in his white-knuckled hand. "I never did too good in school."

"Want to try again?"

He raised his eyes to look at her. She saw fear there, and hunger. A fierce hunger.

Say yes, she urged him silently.

Ben was a smart kid. That was easy to tell after working with him only one afternoon, but it was equally obvious someone had been carping in his ear all his life that he was basically a dumb shit who would never amount to anything. It was hard to counter that early life influence.

"How much school?" he asked.

Cody grinned wickedly. She had spent her own formative years in a private boarding school, as a charity case on a corporate scholarship, seeing her mother only on rare weekends. Those had been the hardest years of her life, but receiving the scholarship to attend Prescott Academy had also been her biggest break. She bore no sympathy for anyone out to shirk an education. "Oh, ten or fifteen years of college should do it for you, Ben."

His lips twitched in a ghost of a smile. "At entry-level wages?"

"Pay commensurate with experience. Say yes, Ben."

He nodded slowly. "Okay then. Yes."

■

Cody had made Green Stomp's reputation by tackling the toughest, dirtiest jobs she could find. The harder the challenge, the more she liked it. Kicking apart toxic "nonbiodegradable" molecules was a physical thrill. In her mind, it was the same as kicking down the mental walls that fenced people in. Like the one that said kids from bad neighborhoods couldn't make it in life. *Kick.* Or the one that said technology must eventually lead to apocalypse, whether through war, engineered disease, overpopulation, or pollution. *Kick.* Cody had seen a lot of tough problems, but she hadn't seen the end of the world yet. Look hard enough, and problems could provide their own solutions. Green Stomp already held several patents on specialized strains of bacteria recovered from heavily polluted sites.

She tapped her data glove, waking up the portal standing open on the desk. The collapsible monitor had a display the size of an eight-by-twelve-inch piece of paper. It was a quarter inch thick, and when not in use, it could be folded into thirds and slipped into a briefcase. Now it stood open, leaning back on a T-shaped foot. "Hark, link to Jobsite."

The portal opened a cellular connection to Cody's server. Seconds later the screen came to life with an image of Jobsite's bioremediation lobby.

Cody turned the portal around so Ben could see. "Green Stomp gets about a third of our projects through Global Shear. You've heard of them? No? A multinational. We sold them a twenty percent share of Green Stomp in exchange for expansion capital, so they like to drop business in our direction. Plus I interned there, and several execs know and love me." She grinned.

Ben's smile was fleeting as he puzzled over the lobby architecture.

"Anyway," Cody went on, "another third of our projects represent repeat business from satisfied clients. We're grateful for that, of course, but let me tell you a secret. The most interesting jobs come off the public link. Go ahead. Scroll through the list. Check it out."

The portal was keyed to Cody's voice. It didn't know Ben, so instead of speaking to it, he leaned forward, tentatively pressing the manual keys on the frame. "Do you ever get scared?" he asked, as his gaze flicked over the listings. "Do you ever worry you'll poison yourself?"

Cody leaned back in her chair, feeling her chest pull tight. "It's something you always have to keep in mind."

In fact, she'd already poisoned herself. Somehow, early in her career, she'd screwed up and a toxin had gotten into her blood, into her flesh, into the growing embryo in her womb. She'd been so careful at home: no alcohol, no coffee, no soda, no drugs. It hadn't mattered. When the pregnancy was terminated, Cody felt a chip of her soul flushed out along with her daughter. "These things happen," the doctor had assured her, but Cody needed to know *why*. She went looking for a causative event—and she found it when a bioassay of her own liver tissue revealed PCP contamination—the prime pollutant on every job site she'd worked the previous two years.

"Didn't you say you grew up on the west coast?" Ben asked, his pale cheeks aglow in the portal's light. "A place called Victoria Glen?"

"Yes."

"Well, guess what? It's on the job list."

Cody turned the portal back around, and frowned.

III

When Michael left the clinic, night still drowned the street, thick and warm, like the spirit of some tropical ocean ghosting in the rain. Inside, Jaya was teaching her newborn to nurse, while Sheo arranged their journey home.

Michael paused on the clinic's veranda, listening to cocks crowing the unseen dawn and the musical patter of rain.

A headlight cruised the street. It hesitated just before the clinic, then it slid into the pull-out. Diffuse light from the clinic windows glinted on the narrow, beetle-shell chassis of a zip, painted pink and looking hardly large enough to hold a man. Powered by hydrogen fuel cells, its engine ran silent, so that its arrival was marked only by tire noise. Rain dashed through the beam of its dim headlight. The aerodynamic canopy rose a few inches. A boy of perhaps twelve or thirteen years peeked out, fixing Michael with a hopeful look.

Michael shook his head slightly. He hated to disappoint such an intrepid entrepreneur, up so early to find the fares that would pay off the loan on his zip, but his feelings were running high and he couldn't think of squeezing himself into the zip's stuffy little shell.

The boy shrugged, closed the canopy, and pulled away.

A cow lowed, and a rat scurried across the street. Michael hesitated, reminded that he was a stranger in this place. Still, he was not alone. His right index finger curled, to tap a point on the palm of his data glove. A green ready light came on in the corner of his shades. "Send voice mail to the Terrace," he whispered. A mike on his earpiece picked up the command. "Start: Jaya and Sheo girl . . ."

He found himself smiling as he described the birth for their circle of friends. Then he touched his gloved palm again, sending the message to the Terrace.

Warm rain enfolded him as he stepped off the veranda, soaking his hair and transforming his silk shirt into a transparent film. The silk was artificial, spun in a local factory financed by Global Shear. Other grants had gone out to farmers and small business owners all over the district, but could it ever be enough?

Jaya's daughter had been born into a world of nearly eight billion people. A billion of them lived in India alone. Michael tried to imagine the scale of it, but he could not. *We are a river, flooding the world.* Inevitably remaking it.

A glyph blinked on in the corner of his shades, surrounded by a pink query circle. Michael recognized the symbol of the Terrace and smiled. "Link."

"Michael!" Etsuko's soft, clipped English laughed in his ear. "I guess you are a surrogate father now!"

"That's right, old man," Ryan chipped in, his Australian voice loud and bold. "You do have some images for us? Flash them."

"Archived," Michael said. "Sorry. Sort it out later, okay?"

"First-timer," Ryan chided.

Etsuko asked, "Where are you now?"

"Walking home."

"Walking?" she echoed. "Isn't that dangerous?"

"Ah," Ryan scoffed. "He's a company bigwig now, with his own eye in the sky following after him."

Michael groaned. "I keep forgetting about that." Global Shear had assigned him a permanent guard in the form of a mini-drone aircraft with a wingspan the length of his arm. Powered by solar cells and a lightweight battery system that could get it through the night, it tracked his movements, ever-poised to raise an alarm should anything go wrong.

"We're bored in our little cubbies," Ryan said. "Give us the scene."

Bored? If Ryan got bored, it was only on weekends, before the

Asian markets opened. During the rest of the week he traded currencies under contract for a large Australian firm.

Etsuko worked in the calmer environment of a California-based multinational specializing in online education. She staffed the East Asian shift, so her workday often began in the warm, hazy afternoons of Santa Barbara.

Michael's day ran well behind theirs—a fact Ryan tended to forget. He tapped his glove, activating the cameras on his shades. *Pan left to right:* one- and two-story stucco and plastic dwellings loomed out of the darkness, squeezing against the rain-splattered street. A bicycle trundled past, its rider hidden beneath an umbrella, two squawking chickens strapped to the handlebars. From a few blocks away, the screech of wet brakes.

The video feed uploaded over cellular links. On the Terrace, Ryan would seem to be sitting at a patio table in the shade of a pepper tree, sipping java in mild morning sunlight, fenced in by the dense foliage of a mature garden, or perhaps gazing out over a seascape with a hint of salt tang in the air. Whatever environment was running, half of it had now vanished, replaced by Michael's input.

"God!" Ryan said, and Michael could hear his feet hit the floor. "It's still night there—and it's pouring."

"It's grand, isn't it?" Michael asked. He slicked his hair back, tasting the water on his lips. Precious water, falling like a blessing timed by forgotten gods. Rain had been absent for the two weeks he'd been in-country. As his census teams inventoried the tiny farms surrounding Four Villages, they faced farmers more and more anxious over the success of this season's crop of rice or peanuts, and increasingly unwilling to speak to the officials responsible for confirming their landholdings and setting their taxes. "The rain will help," Michael said firmly. Rain would ease everyone's mood, and in the long run even the most recalcitrant farmers would see that their interests were the same as Global Shear's.

Right?

A stray breeze puffed from an alley, carrying the dilute but distinct scent of an open sewer. Global Shear was responsible for developing infrastructure, overseeing environmental restoration, encouraging private credit, and enhancing agricultural extension services—all popular activities. But they were also the tax collector, and fairness demanded a thorough inventory of the district's landholdings, along with a clarification of boundaries and ownership—all the while smoothing the ruffled feathers of displaced local officials.

(*Diplomacy,* Karen Hampton would say, *is a grim necessity.*)

So were creative solutions. More than one company official had lobbied for a policy that would encourage family farms to merge into larger agricultural concerns so they could practice economies of scale, but such schemes didn't take into consideration the dense population.

Michael talked it over with Ryan and Etsuko as he made his way through the waking neighborhoods. "Hand labor still makes sense, for now. Replace the thousands of laborers with machines, and where will the laborers find work?"

At first glance, the sheer numbers of people seemed an intractable problem, but the truth lay deeper. When warfare and ethnic strife were kept at bay, birth rates plummeted. Four Villages was no exception. The town itself was an accident of geography, grown up fast and ugly from the melding of what had once been four separate hamlets. Most of the women here were having only two or three children. . . .

Or was it two or three boys? Michael promised himself he would examine the statistics when he went into the office later in the day.

Lights were coming on in the houses, and the smell of cooking gruel drifted out into the street. "It's more than birth control," Etsuko was saying. "It's education, economic independence, a sense of confidence in the future . . ."

"Sure," Ryan agreed. "That and coveting your neighbor's success."

Michael burst out laughing. There *was* plenty of inspiration for the ambitious in Four Villages. On every street, affluent homes huddled next to shacks. Electric lights spilled from some windows, while others held the soft gleam of candles. A mixed neighborhood like this was a robust place—in sharp contrast to the cankerous hearts of the original villages, where ancient buildings housed either fundamentalist Hindus or fundamentalist Moslems who still went about life as they had for centuries: in grinding poverty, practicing and defending their faith in settings that barely tolerated the presence of a Global Shear census taker.

The warm rain slackened as Michael turned onto a muddy

lane scarred by zip tires. His residence was third on the right—a large house owned by Global Shear, its white-washed face abutting the street. The house was built around an enclosed courtyard, where a neglected garden faced a long, lingering death.

As Michael approached, the old house detected his presence and a welcoming light switched on. It illuminated the alcove—and a large, bundled object huddled against the heavy double doors.

"Hello," Ryan said. "What's this?"

Etsuko hissed sharply. "Michael, be careful."

He stopped in the middle of the lane, his instincts made wary by antiterrorism training. He tried to see the anonymous object as some cloth-wrapped package stashed by a passing street merchant, perhaps to protect it from the rain. He tried to see it as trash.

Then the bundle stirred, faded cloth sliding aside as a head lifted, turned, and the face of a little girl blinked at him, dark eyes wide with confusion and fear.

"It's a kid," Ryan said. "Christ, look at her face. Somebody's punched her around."

Instead, Michael looked away from the bruises on her cheeks, wanting to believe they were only shadows. Gray mud streaked her black hair. A nose ring glinted silver. Her sari looked as if it had been purple once. Now it was a lifeless gray. Michael guessed her to be no more than thirteen years old.

The girl's right arm slid into view. No rings and no bracelets adorned that arm. It was a fleshless bone covered in light brown skin, so very thin there did not seem to be enough muscle mass even to raise that fragile hand. Nevertheless, she pressed it against the wall. She tried to stand, but her limbs would not be controlled, her balance was absent. Michael had once seen a dog taken by an epileptic seizure. The will to move existed, but it only reached the muscles in fits and starts. It was the same with this girl. After several seconds, she sank back to the alcove's tiled floor. She bowed her head. She pulled her sari up to cover her face while Michael stood in the street, gaping, trying to find some precedent in his world for her sudden appearance, clueless what to do.

He told himself it was a dream. How was he supposed to get into his house?

Etsuko's voice was tense: "Michael, I am searching for a local emergency number."

Ryan: "Haven't you got one on file, mate?"

"Corporate security," Michael said stiffly. "That's all. Etsuko?"

"I am contacting the police."

"Don't," Ryan said. "This isn't the silicon coast. If the cops could help, she would have gone to them."

Michael stared at the girl. For Christ's sake, he was a businessman, not a charity worker, and it had already been a long, sleepless night. Let this be a dream.

The girl tried again to get to her feet. Again, she slid back to the ground.

"Jesus, Michael," Ryan said. "Are you just going to stand there? Mate, you've got to do something."

Michael's conscience screamed the same thing, yet still he didn't move. "What can I do?"

Some dark voice whispered that he could walk away, get breakfast in town, go straight to the office, give the girl a chance to disappear.

"Call corporate security," Etsuko said crisply. "They will help. They will get you inside."

"Bloody hell," Ryan said. "Boosting her to the next street over won't help *her*."

"He's not Mother Teresa."

"You could try calling a neighbor, mate."

Michael shook his head. "No, I don't think so." Tragedy was too common here. Sympathy wore thin. Just yesterday he had seen motherly Mrs. Shastri brandishing a heavy stick as she chased a beggar out of the lane.

Michael sighed. She was only a little girl. Still, in her presence, he sensed again the ghostly inundation of chaos. "Witnesses," he muttered. "Ryan, Etsuko—record everything, because you're my witnesses. Got it?" He fervently hoped the spy plane was active overhead.

The girl cringed as he approached. It was a tiny gesture, but startling. "Hey," Michael said. "I won't hurt you." He knelt beside her. Gently, he lifted her sari away from her face.

"The dirty bastards," Ryan muttered.

The girl's cheeks were dark with bruises. Her sari was soaked and she was shivering. Next door, Mrs. Shastri shouted at the servant who cooked for the family. Michael tensed. He didn't want the old gossip to see this girl. "Come inside," he said softly.

"That's it, mate," Ryan encouraged him. "It's the right thing to do."

The confused look in the girl's eyes told him she did not understand.

The Shastri dog took that moment to run into the street, a tiny, white-furred terror bouncing on short legs, yapping a fierce challenge. "Watch out, mate!" Ryan cried. "Attack from the rear."

The girl gasped. The rat-dog took encouragement from that. It charged at Michael, its jaws snapping as it darted about, working up the nerve to bite.

Michael didn't think that would take long. Operating in survival mode now, he yelled at the house to open up. The triple bolts slipped in a simultaneous click, then the doors swung back. He launched a kick at the rat-dog. Then he lifted the girl—she weighed so little!—and stumbled with her into the house. As the doors closed, he heard Mrs. Shastri calling sweetly to her little terror.

■

Ryan was laughing. "Very smooth, mate. You're a hero."

"Shut up."

Soft lights had come on in the house, falling across new carpet, designer furnishings, and walls paneled in rich faux-teak. The air was dry and cool, almost sterile. "Welcome home, Mr. Fielding," the house said in its motherly voice. "You have five messages."

Michael stood just inside the doors, his shoulders heaving, more with panic than exertion. Looking down at the girl, he found she had fainted, gone limp in his arms. Oh, this looked just great, didn't it? Avaricious foreign businessman kidnaps helpless girl. The local tabloids could churn a million hits out of a headline like that. Christ.

"Now you're committed," Etsuko said. "You must take care of her."

"Yeah." Michael carried the girl into the living room, where he laid her down on the western-style couch . . . hoping she didn't have lice.

She looked so fragile. Tiny and breakable, as if her bones were thin glass copies of real bones, melting away in the heat of an inner fire. Her skin felt hot and her sari was covered in mud. The drawstring of a heavy cloth pouch was looped around her wrist. Michael slipped the pouch off and teased it open, feeling like a lout for abusing her privacy, feeling stupid for feeling like a lout. After all, he'd brought her into his house at no little risk to himself and she was helpless and he needed to know who she was, where she came from, and *who to call.* There had to be someone he could call.

He scowled at the contents of the pouch.

"What is it?" Etsuko asked.

"Dirt."

Well, not dirt exactly. More like a dark, loose humus smelling of garden shops and greenhouses.

"If that's her idea of a valuable," Ryan muttered, "she really is in a bad way." Michael closed the pouch, leaving it by the French doors that opened onto the neglected courtyard.

"Michael, I've got to take off for a while," Ryan said. "I've got an appointment that can't wait."

"Sure. Etsuko? I know you have work to do too. The house can record."

"You are sure?" she asked. "I can stay awhile."

"No, it's all right."

The link to the Terrace closed.

Michael looked at the girl. Her sari had fallen away, exposing her shoulders, her arms, her bruised face. Her skin was prickling, purpling in the air-conditioning. Of course—her clothes were soaked. He was wet, too. The chill air bit at his skin. He headed for the bedroom.

Stripping off his silk shirt, he pitched it into a laundry basket. Then he opened a linen chest at the foot of the bed and pulled out a clean blanket. He used it to cover the girl, who was muttering now, though she didn't wake.

Next, Michael started some tea in the kitchen. The power meter was low, but the sun would be up soon. Even with the rain, the rooftop tiles would quickly recharge the house batteries, so there was no need to conserve. He pulled some leftover *samosas* out of the refrigerator. He heated some soup.

Sitting on a stool, he watched the soup spin in the microwave. He was thirty-two years old, one of the youngest managers in charge of a major district contract.

So start thinking, doofus.

"Hey," he said softly. "I could call the clinic."

With curled fingers, Michael tapped a trigger point on his data glove. He was tempted to ask for Jaya, but he was *not* going to bother her, not now. So he asked for the midwife who had seemed so relieved when Jaya had not rejected her baby girl.

After a few minutes a woman's voice came on the line. "Hello?" Suspicion and fear huddled in that one brief word. Her tone didn't change when Michael told her about the girl.

"This is a charity case, sir. You need to call a charity." She gave him the number of an organization.

Michael called the charity. Another woman answered. She listened to his story and blessed him, while Michael begged her to come pick the girl up. He would cover the cost of her care. Just return her to her family. Please?

"Mr. Fielding, given the circumstances in which this girl was found, it's likely she has no family."

"But she must have come from somewhere."

"Surely. But please understand. A girl like this has most likely been cast out of her home for . . . infidelity, or sterility. These things happen, even in better neighborhoods."

Michael did not think this girl came from a better neighborhood. "Can you care for her then?"

"Sadly, no. We have no beds left. We would have to tend her on the street. Please understand, her circumstance is not unusual."

The microwave finished. Michael stared at it, fervently wishing the sun would rise, wanting to see light seep through the peach-colored blinds. "What's to become of her?"

"That is in the hands of God."

The woman promised to call around to other agencies. In the meantime, she would send someone over to check on the girl. Michael reminded her he would be more than willing to pay for the girl's care. She thanked him and linked off.

He slipped off his shades and peeled off the data glove. He sat on the stool, trying to visualize where this might go. He could not. He could not see even ten minutes ahead.

At least the soup was warm. He placed the bowl on a tray, along with a spoon, then he zapped the *samosas* for a few seconds to warm them. They came out soggy, instead of the crisp, fried pastry they had once been, but he put them alongside the soup anyway. Then he carried the whole to the living room, where the girl was sitting up, looking around with a dazed expression. Her eyes went wide when she saw him.

Michael was suddenly conscious of his bare chest, bronzy skin over health club muscles. He suffered a devastating suspicion that he was communicating inaccurate innuendoes. Christ. He set the tray down on the low table fronting the couch, spilling a little of the soup. The girl pulled the blanket up to her chin. "For you," Michael said, his cheeks heating with a despairing flush. Then he hurried to the bedroom and got out a shirt.

When he looked again, the girl was sitting on the floor, holding the soup bowl in her delicate hands, drinking from the rim, her eyes closed, as if she were privileged to taste some nectar of the gods. Michael felt a rush of relief, thinking maybe, maybe he'd gotten it right. Then his gaze fell on the sofa, and he shuddered at what Mrs. Nandy, the cleaning lady, would say about those streaks of gray mud ground into the upholstery.

■

The house spoke English, but after some exploration of its options menu, Michael discovered it also had personalities schooled in Hindi and Tamil. He activated the Hindi personality, then set about introducing it to the girl. That wasn't easy. She had said nothing so far, and the house needed a voice print as well as a visual image to accurately recognize her.

With two hands, Michael beckoned her away from where she huddled on the floor by the couch. She looked very frightened, but she followed him. When she stood in full view of the tiny cameras mounted in the corners of the room, he held up his palm, asking her to stop, to wait. "Hark," he said. "In Hindi-version, ask her to say hello."

Lilting words spilled forth in the soft voice of the house. The girl hunched, trembling. Her gaze searched the walls.

The house repeated its request. This time she looked at Michael. He nodded encouragement. Hesitantly, she placed her palms together. "Namaste," she whispered.

Michael smiled. "Ask her name."

The house spoke again, and her eyes grew wide with wonder. In a barely discernable voice she said, *"Rajban."*

"Rajban?" Michael asked.

She nodded. Michael grinned and tapped his chest. "Michael," he told her. Then he bowed. When he looked up, her cheeks were flushed. Her lips toyed with a smile. She started to reach for her sari, to pull it across her face, but when she saw the mud on it she scowled and let it go.

Michael asked if she wanted more food. She declined. He told her someone was coming to help her. That brought such a look of fear that he wondered if the house had translated correctly. "Why don't you sit down?" he offered, indicating the couch. Rajban nodded, though she remained standing until he left the room.

Returning to his bedroom, he took a quick shower, waiting all the while for the house to announce the arrival of the charity worker. No announcement came.

"Link to the office," he instructed the house as he shaved. "Check Rajban's name and image against census records." It wasn't exactly legal to access the records for personal use, but this wasn't exactly personal.

The house started to reply in Hindi. He corrected it impatiently. "English for me," he said. "Hindi for Rajban. Now, continue."

"No identity or residence can be established from available census data," the house informed him.

Michael swore softly. So Rajban was a nonentity, her existence unrecorded by his intrepid census teams. Which meant she was either new in town or a resident of one of the reticent fundamentalist neighborhoods.

"What does my schedule look like?"

"Daily exercise in the corporate gym from seven to eight," the feminine voice recited. "Then a breakfast meeting with Ms. Muthaye Lal of the Southern Banking Alliance from eight-thirty until ten. A staff meeting from ten-fifteen—"

"Can the SBA thing be postponed until tomorrow?"

"Inquiring. Please stand by."

Michael finished shaving. He cleaned the razor, then reached for a toothbrush.

"Ms. Lal is unable to schedule a meeting for tomorrow."

"Damn." He tapped the toothbrush on the counter. "This afternoon, then?"

"Inquiring. Please stand by." The response came quickly this time. "Ms. Lal is unable to schedule a meeting for this afternoon."

Michael sighed. No surprise. Everybody's schedule was full. Well, Ms. Muthaye Lal worked with poor women, through the SBA's community banking program. Perhaps she would have some advice for Rajban.

After Michael dressed, he looked into the living room. Rajban had fallen asleep on the floor beside the couch. He told himself it would be all right if he left for a few hours. The house would take care of her. And if she decided to leave . . .

His jaw clenched. That would be the easiest solution for him, wouldn't it? If she just disappeared.

"Call the charity again," he told the house. Again, the woman on the other end of the line promised to send someone by.

He waited an hour. No one came. Rajban still slept. Michael wished he was sleeping too. His eyes felt gritty, his body stiff. His brain was functioning with all the racing speed of a third-generation computer. He wondered if Jaya was awake.

In the bathroom medicine cabinet there was a box of Synthetic Sleep. Michael didn't often take metabolic drugs, but he'd been up all night, and if he wanted to get through this morning's meetings in coherent condition, he had to do something to convince his body that he'd had at least a few hours of rest. He peeled open the casing on one pill and swallowed it with a glass of water.

"Take care of Rajban," he told the house. "Teach her how you work. And *call me* if you have any questions, any problems. Okay?"

IV

Rajban woke with a gritty throat. Her muscles ached. Her joints ached. Her heart was beating too fast. "Namaste?" she whispered.

The house informed her the man had gone out.

He had not hurt her. Not yet.

She looked around the room, unsure how she had come to be here, knowing only that it was shameful. Mother-in-Law would never let her come home now.

It was Mother-in-Law who had sent her away.

She padded through the house, not daring to touch anything. She even worried about the carpet under her feet.

Turning a corner, she found the great double doors that had sheltered her last night. Her heart beat even faster. Were the doors locked? She half hoped they were. Out there, the horrible street waited for her. Nothing else. Yet she could not stay here. Hesitantly, her hand touched the latch, just to *see* if it was locked. She pressed on it—only a little!—and the latch leaped out of her grip, swinging down on its own with multiple clicks. The doors started to open. A razor of light streamed in. Frantically, Rajban threw herself against the doors. She held them, so they stood open only a crack. The day's heat curled over her fingers, while outside, women talked in cultured, confident voices.

Listening to them, Rajban trembled. She did not dare show herself in such company. Leaning forward, she forced the doors to shut again.

Back in the living room, she stood beside another set of doors. These opened onto the courtyard. She stared through their glass panes at a half-dead garden surrounded by high walls. Potted banana trees stood on one side like dry old men. Bare skeletons of dead shrubs jutted between the weeds. Yellow leaves floated on the surface of rain puddles.

There was no one outside, so again Rajban tried the latch. These doors opened as easily as the others. Steamy air flowed over her, laden with the smell of wet soil and unhappy plants. Cautiously, she stepped outside.

A paved path wound between the weeds. She followed it, discovering a servant's door in the back wall, but it was locked and would not open.

The path brought her back to the house. She crouched in the open doorway, lost, not knowing what to do. Why was she here?

Clean, frigid air from the house mixed with dense, hot, scented air from the sweltering courtyard, like dream mixing with reality. Rajban struggled to separate the two, but they would not untwine. Hugging her knees to her chest, she rocked on her bare feet, seeing again the blinding flash of the morning sun reflected on the metal circles sewn into the hem of her sister-in-law's green sari. She squinted against the glare, and hurried on. *Hurry.* Her skin felt so hot. Her heart scrabbled like a wild mouse in a glass jar. Her veil kept slipping from her face, but she didn't dare stop to fix it. Sister-in-Law's bare brown heels flashed beneath the swinging hem of her sari. Rajban struggled to keep up, fearful in the presence of so many strangers. In the two years since her marriage she had not left the house of her husband's family. The borders of her life had been fixed by the courtyard garden and the crumbling kitchen where she helped Mother-in-Law prepare the meals.

Last year her husband went away.

In the months since, Rajban had often been sick with fevers and chills that no one else in the family shared. Her work suffered. Now Mother-in-Law was sending her away. "We have found a family in need of skilled hands to keep the house. They are a respectable family. You will serve them well. Gather your things. It is time to go."

There wasn't much to take. An extra sari. A necklace her mother had given her.

Before she left, Rajban slipped into the garden with a cloth bag from the kitchen. Fruit trees and vegetables thrived in boxes and tin cans and glass jars with drainage holes drilled carefully in the bottom. It had not always been so. When she first arrived in the household, the garden had been yellow and unhappy. But Rajban tended the soil as her mother had taught her, on their tiny farm in the country. She dug up patches of the courtyard with a heavy stick, mixing the dirt with chicken droppings and sometimes with nightsoil, but only when no one could see her, for her husband would never take her to bed again if he knew. When it rained, she caught the water that dripped from the rooftop, ladling it out over the dry days that would follow, praying softly as she worked. She turned the soil until it became soft, rich black, and sweet-smelling. One day as she turned it, she found a worm. Life from lifelessness. That day, she knew magic had flowed in to the soil.

A sickly mandarin tree grew in the cracked half of an old water barrel. Rajban teased away several handfuls of surface dirt, then gently she mixed the black soil in. Within days the tree rejoiced in a flush of new green leaves.

Magic.

Rajban mixed the old dirt into her pile. She dug more dirt from the hard floor of the courtyard. She stirred the pile every day, and every few days she repotted another plant. The garden thrived, but it was not enough to keep Mother-in-Law happy, so Rajban was being sent away. Quietly, she filled her cloth bag with handfuls of the magic soil. Then she smoothed the pile so no one would know.

A few minutes after following Sister-in-Law out the door, Rajban could no longer guess the proper way home. Fearfully she watched the step-step of Sister-in-Law's heels, the swing of her sari, the fierce flash of the sun in the decorative metal circles. And then somehow the green sari slipped out of sight.

Rajban wandered alone through the afternoon, not daring to think too hard. Night fell, and fear crawled in with the darkness. Respectable women were not found alone on the street at night.

Her fever saved her from rape. *She's dirty,* the boy who stole her mother's necklace growled to his companions. *A dirty, infected, dying whore.*

Now Rajban crouched in the courtyard doorway, shivering on the border between warm and cold, light and shadow, past and future, the dying garden on one side, the rich house on the other. An unexpected fury stirred in her breast and flushed across the palms of her hands.

Am I dying?

The possibility enraged her. She did not want to die. Emphatically not. Not now.

I want a baby, she thought. *I want my mother. I want my own garden and a respectable life.*

These things she would never have if she let herself die now.

■

Rajban is fifteen.

V

Michael arrived by zip at the address recorded on his schedule—a European-style restaurant on the ground floor of a well-maintained home. A woman greeted him, speaking lightly accented English. "Welcome, Mr. Fielding. Ms. Lal has just arrived. Won't you come in?"

Air-conditioning enfolded him. He followed the hostess past widely spaced tables occupied by well-dressed patrons. At a corner table a woman in a traditional sari rose as he approached. His shades caught her ID and whispered it in his ear. *"Muthaye Lal, age twenty-seven, employed by Southern Banking Association four years—"*

He tapped his glove, ending the recitation.

"Mr. Fielding, so glad you could come."

Coffee was poured, and a waiter brought a first course of papaya, pineapple, and mango. Muthaye tasted it, and smiled. She was not a pretty woman, but her dark eyes were confident as they took Michael's measure. Her enunciation was crisply British. "I will admit to some disappointment, Mr. Fielding, when I learned Global Shear had appointed another foreigner to head this district's office, but your background speaks well for you. Are you familiar with the Southern Banking Association's microeconomics program?"

Michael sipped his coffee, admiring the way criticisms and compliments twined together in her speech like the strands of a rope. Muthaye could have learned her negotiating tactics from Karen Hampton. Michael certainly had.

Rise to all challenges, especially if they've been promptly withdrawn.

He set the coffee down and smiled, choosing to answer the non-question first. "It's Global Shear policy to expand the international experience of our executives. Please don't take it personally. You probably know that seventy percent of our upper-level staff here at Four Villages is Indian."

Amusement danced in Muthaye's eyes. "And that Global Shear employs Indian executives in offices on three continents. Yes, I know, Mr. Fielding. Global Shear is a true multinational, with, I trust, community interests?"

"Of course. Cultural and economic vitality go hand in hand. That's our belief. And the SBA is well-known to us for its community endeavors. While I'm not familiar with the particulars of your microeconomics program, I have studied several others around the world."

Microeconomics had begun in Bangladesh, where a few hundred dollars loaned to a circle of impoverished women could seed a microenterprise that might eventually grow into a thriving business.

"Our program is well established," Muthaye told him. "We have over four thousand women participating in Four Villages alone. Each one of them has developed an independence, a self-reliance their mothers never knew."

Michael nodded. To educate and empower women in underdeveloped areas had long been a key to economic progress. The women's lives were tied up in their children. Selflessness came easier to them than to their men. "Global Shear invests many millions of dollars every year in this cause, throughout the world—and the returns have been impressive."

"Ah. That would be in the form of taxes you collect?"

"A measure of economic vitality."

"And your source of income."

"Doing well by doing good—"

"Benefits everyone. Yes, Mr. Fielding, I do agree. I asked for this meeting to discuss with you yet another opportunity for Global Shear to do well by doing good. I would like you to sponsor a line of debit cards to be used by members of the Southern Banking Association. Most of our deposits are tiny, you understand. A few rupees at a time. The money comes in as coinage, and generally it goes out the same way. If the coinage can be exchanged for debit cards, loss from theft would plummet."

"Is theft such a problem for your women?"

A frown marred her brow. "It's often the husbands, you understand?"

Michael flashed on the image of an irate man confiscating his wife's meager earnings, to spend it on . . . ? Drink, perhaps. Or other women. The microeconomic banks had long been convinced that women were the financially responsible members of most marriages, and so most loans were made to women.

Muthaye signaled a waitress for more coffee. "There would, of course, be up-front costs should we institute debit cards. This is the reason we need a sponsor for the program. Our depositors simply do not possess the capital to acquire a debit card through normal routes. The economic scale we deal with is meaningless to anyone in the middle class, whether they live in India or the United States."

Michael nodded. "We're talking about account activity equivalent to a few dollars a week?"

"Exactly. Of course, with debit cards, tax collection for Global Shear would be simplified. Taxes could be paid directly out of the electronic accounts, so that no time would be lost collecting and counting the rupees owed."

Michael reflected that most of Muthaye's clients would fall far below the threshold income for tax collection. "Do your depositors have the math skills to understand this kind of abstract system?"

"Education is a requirement for permanent membership in the SBA, Mr. Fielding. Also, the math we teach will be supplemented by bar graphs on the debit cards."

"Oh." Graphic cards would cost far more than those with a simple magnetic strip. "Well. I'll be happy to assign a staffer to this project. We'll assess costs, and give you an indication of the possibilities in a few days."

As they continued to discuss details, Michael's thoughts returned to Rajban. He wanted to call the house, to see if she was still there. He felt guilty about leaving her alone.

As the minutes wore on, he felt certain Rajban would take advantage of his absence and leave. He realized now that he didn't want that. For where could she possibly go? Back home, he supposed. It would be better if she went home. Wouldn't it?

"Mr. Fielding?" Sharpness touched Muthaye's voice.

"You seem distracted. Did you have another appointment?"

"Ah, no. Just a situation at home. My apologies—"

He felt the vibration of a call coming in, followed by a barely audible, trilling ring. Vibration/trilling, the combination repeating like a European siren. Michael tapped his data glove.

Take a message.

The shades would not accept the command. *"Urgent, urgent, urgent!"* the stealthy voice whispered back.

Muthaye was looking at him now with an amused expression. Michael apologized again as he took the call. The voice of Mrs. Nandy, his housekeeper, exploded in his ears. "There is a vagrant in the house, Mr. Fielding! It is a woman of shameful kind. I have her in a corner. She is filthy! Vermin-covered! Mr. Fielding, I will call the police!"

"No, no, no!" His voice boomed through the restaurant, causing heads to turn. "Leave her alone. She is a guest. A guest, you understand? I have asked her in—"

"Mr. Fielding! Vermin-covered! Dirty! This is a dirty woman! You cannot mean to have her keep your house—"

"No! Nothing like that. *You* are my housekeeper. Why don't you take the day off, Mrs. Nandy?" he added, trying hard for a soothing tone. "Visit your grandchildren—"

"They are in school."

"Don't frighten her, Mrs. Nandy."

"She is vermin-covered!"

"Please?" He looked at Muthaye, at her sharp, dark eyes. "Just leave the house, Mrs. Nandy. Take a holiday."

She finally agreed to go, though Michael didn't know if he could believe her. When the call ended, he looked at Muthaye. "My apologies again, but the situation at home—I really need to go." He started to stand. Then he changed his mind. He sat back down. Muthaye worked regularly with poor women just like Rajban.

Briefly, he told her about the girl he had found on his step. Muthaye's expression hardened as he described Rajban. Her lips set in a tight line and anger gleamed in her eyes.

"The charity worker will not come," she said, when he had finished.

"What?" Michael spread his hands helplessly. "Twice she told me someone would be over as soon as possible."

"And no doubt that is true, but the possible comes with many restrictions. You are already caring for Rajban. There will always be cases more pressing than hers. Mr. Fielding, you have been very kind to help this girl. Hers is an old story, in a world that often despises its women. My mother suffered a similar fate. She was abandoned by her family, but she became educated. She learned economic independence. She insisted that I be educated, too. She devoted her life to it."

Michael stared at Muthaye, trying to visualize her as a street waif. He could not. "Your mother did a fine job."

"Indeed. Are you going home straightaway?"

The twists and turns in her conversation put Michael on edge. "Yes. I need to check—"

"Good. May I accompany you, Mr. Fielding?"

"Well, yes, of course." He felt relieved at her offer, yet strangely resentful too. Muthaye would take over Rajban's care.

As if to prove it, she announced, "I will call a health aide from the women's league to meet us." She folded her portal and slipped it into her purse. "Ready?"

■

They found Rajban in the courtyard. She looked up as the French doors clicked open. Her bruised cheeks were flushed, her face shining with sweat. Fear huddled in her dark eyes. To Michael, she looked like an abused little girl. Muthaye crouched by her side. They talked a minute, then Rajban followed her into the house.

The house announced the arrival of a visitor.

"That will be the health aide," Muthaye told Michael. "Please escort her in."

Michael nodded, wondering when he had lost control of his own house.

The aide was a diminutive woman, yet intense as pepper sauce. With rapid gestures she spread a cloth on the living room floor, then arranged her equipment on it. Muthaye introduced her to Rajban. The three women ignored Michael, so he retreated to his home office. The workload did not stop accumulating just because he was absent.

He linked into the corporate office, downloaded a log of telephone messages, postponed the staff meeting, gave some cursory instructions about the SBA debit card plans. When he returned to the living room, the health aide was just slipping out the front door. Michael looked after her anxiously. "Where is she going? Is she done?"

"Yes, Mr. Fielding." Muthaye leaned forward and patted Rajban's hand. Then, with an unbecoming groan, she clambered to her feet. She seemed older than she had at breakfast, her confidence burned away. "You have been very kind to Rajban. She is deeply grateful."

"I, ah . . ."

Muthaye's smile was sad. "What else could you do? I understand, Mr. Fielding—"

"Call me Michael, please."

Muthaye nodded. "I know you didn't look for this burden, Michael, and I know the situation is awkward for you. I would ask though—and *I* am asking, not Rajban—that she be allowed to stay the night."

"Isn't there—"

"No. All formal shelters will be full. But by tomorrow, I may be able to find a home for her."

"She's sick, isn't she?"

Muthaye nodded. "She won't name her family. She doesn't want to shame them, especially her mother, who was very proud of the marriage she arranged for Rajban. Her parents are destitute, you understand, but women are becoming rare enough that even daughters with no dowry may find husbands. Rajban's husband is the third son—"

"She's *married*?" Michael interrupted. "But she's just a little girl."

"She's fifteen," Muthaye said. "Child marriage has become

fashionable again among certain fundamentalist groups. Rajban has been married two years. She and her husband lived in his mother's house, but her husband was sick. He went away last year and didn't come home. Rajban has never been pregnant, so she believes she is infertile, and so of no value. She has also been frequently sick this past year, and a burden on the family."

Michael felt the sweat of an old terror break out across his brow. "My God. She has AIDS, doesn't she?"

"That would be my guess. No doubt she caught it from her husband. Her family must have suspected the same, so they abandoned her."

"But she can be treated," Michael objected.

No one had to die of AIDS anymore, not if they took control of their lives and lived the medical regimen.

"Given money, given time, yes, the disease can be put into remission," Muthaye agreed. Still, Michael heard resignation in her voice.

"Rajban has no money," he said.

Muthaye nodded. "Rajban has nothing."

VI

For Cody Graham, home was a luxury condo in the foothills above Denver. She caught a train from DIA, arriving home in late evening, at the same time as the dinner for two she had ordered along the way. The food went onto the table while her account was automatically billed. She took a quick shower. When she emerged, she found Wade had arrived. He was pouring Venezuelan spring water into lead-free wine glasses. "Hey," she said, toweling her hair dry. "You remembered."

"Of course I remembered." Wade arched an eyebrow in comic offense as he set the bottle on a tray.

Wade Collin was president and chief stockholder of a small but thriving biotech firm. His company was his life, and he regularly devoted seventy to eighty hours a week ensuring its success. It was an obsession that had brought his marriage to an end. "A good end for both of us," he claimed. "Marriage demands more time than I'll ever be willing to give it."

In his mid-fifties, with two grown children, Wade was still a handsome and vigorous man. He and Cody had been friends for years, and lovers for much of that time, brought together by need and by convenience. It was all either of them had time for. It was all they would admit to needing.

He studied her face, and gradually, the humor in his hazel eyes changed to concern. "Cody? Are you getting nervous?"

"No." She sighed, tossing the towel onto the back of the sofa. "It's just been a strange day. I found out that the neighborhood I grew up in has been designated a hazardous site. It's scheduled for remediation."

Wade scowled as he uncovered the dinner plates. "Inauspicious. Will you take it?"

"I don't know. I picked up the download packet, but I haven't looked through it yet." She dropped into one of the chairs. Fear was a fine mesh wound around her heart. "Truth is, I'm not at all sure I want to go back there."

Going back would mean facing again the stuff of vanquished nightmares: summer heat and summer anger and the urine-stink of crank houses, transformed into blazing infernos when their clandestine labs caught fire. And other, more personal things.

"You are getting nervous," Wade accused.

Cody shook out a napkin and grinned, hoping it didn't look too false. "Maybe just a little," she admitted. It had been six years since her horrible first pregnancy. She'd waited all that time, living a medical regimen while the toxin levels in her tissues declined. "I still want my daughter."

"Howling, screaming, smelly brats," Wade warned, sitting down beside her.

"Won't work," Cody assured him.

"Could be a boy."

Nope. Cody wouldn't say so out loud, but she knew it wouldn't be a boy.

She sipped at the Venezuelan water, imagining she could feel the babyjack in her womb. A slight pinching sensation—that's the identity she gave it. She hadn't told Wade it was in there.

Uterine implants were a form of selective birth control developed for couples with inherited genetic disorders. After conception, they screened the embryo's DNA for a suspected defect. If it was found, the implant would release a drug to block the natural production of progesterone and the pregnancy would fail.

Though it appeared nowhere in the company prospectus, the

most common "defect" the implants screened for was the sex of the embryo. Cody's babyjack would kick in if it detected a male embryo, causing a spontaneous abortion within several days of conception. That early in her term she might experience a slightly late, slightly heavy menstrual period. Nothing more.

Wade had waived parental rights to any child she might conceive. She had signed documents freeing him of obligation. They had submitted DNA samples to an anonymous testing service, where their chromosomes were sorted across a large series of DNA chips. No major incompatibilities had been found.

"Genetic maps," Cody mused, "health tests, trust funds, legal documents . . . am I neurotic? My mother conceived me in an alley behind a rave club when she was fifteen. He didn't want to use a condom because it was too constricting. They screwed for a week, then she never saw him again."

"So you both learned from her mistake."

"And we've both been overcompensating ever since."

He sighed, his sun-browned hand closing over hers. "You're a good person, Cody. You deserve more than this. You should have had the fairy tale."

She smiled. *I did.*

She'd had the marriage, the handsome husband, the baby on the way, and it had all blown up in her face. On some level, she'd always known it would. She'd already made it out of the brutal slum of Victoria Glen, and surely that was enough to ask of life? The castle on the hill could wait for the next generation.

VII

Muthaye left the house, promising to return as soon as possible. Michael did not like the sound of that. It reminded him too much of the woman from the charity, but what could he do? He had his own schedule to keep. This afternoon he was due at a publicity event on a local farm, the first to bring in a harvest of genetically engineered rice developed by a Japanese company and distributed by Global Shear.

He took another shower, and another tab of Synthetic Sleep. The pill's chemical cocktail was designed to mimic the metabolic effects of a few hours of rest. His body could not be fooled forever, but he should be okay until the evening.

In the living room, Rajban was crouching on the floor, staring out at the garden. Michael hesitated on his way to the front door. Something in her posture touched a memory in him: for a moment he was immersed again in the half-dark of a city night, and the awful silence that had followed her cold declaration: *There's nothing left, Michael. I'm leaving.* He felt as if his chest was made of glass, and the glass had shattered.

He shook his head. That was all long ago.

The house spoke in its soothing, feminine voice. "Your car is here." Then it repeated the news in Hindi. Rajban turned, her face an open question. Michael wished he could stay and talk to her. Instead, he put on his shades and he left.

■

The company car bounced and lurched along a dirt road in dire need of scraping. The driver was forced to dodge bicyclists and zips, an assortment of rusty old cars converted to ethylene, and hundreds of pedestrians. Fifteen miles an hour was a top speed rarely achieved, and Michael was twenty minutes late by the time he arrived at the demonstration farm. No one noticed.

A huge canvas canopy with walls of transparent plastic had been set up in the farmyard. An air conditioner powered by a portable generator blew an arctic chill into its interior while, outside, misters delivered fine sprays of water over the arriving guests. Michael soon found himself in conversation with an Ikeda tech and a reporter from CNN. "It's an ideal grain," the tech was saying. "Requiring less water and fertilizer than any other rice strain, while producing a polishable kernel with a high protein content."

"But," the reporter countered, "your opponents claim it's just this engineered hardiness, this ability to out-compete even the weeds, that makes it a threat to the biosystem."

Michael dove into the debate with practiced ease. "Outcompeting the weeds is something of an exaggeration. Ikeda rice is still a domesticated plant, requiring careful farming practices to thrive . . ."

Most of the afternoon was like that. The event was a press op, and Michael's job was to soothe the usual fear of genetically engineered food plants. Most wealthier countries forbade the importation or sale of engineered crops, fearing ecological disaster, or the discovery of some previously unknown toxic quality in the new food. At least, those were the reasons most often cited. Michael suspected it was really a fear of shouldering any more responsibility. Already the land, the climate, and even the ecology of the oceans had been transformed by human activity. If the formula of life itself was now to be rewritten, what would be left outside the range of human influence? Not much. Every disaster outside of seismic instability would then fall squarely at the feet of technology.

For now it didn't matter that Ikeda rice couldn't be sold across international borders. Small farmers could peddle their excess crops to the villagers. Large farms could ship to the cities. Someday though, international markets would need to open.

■

It was late afternoon when Michael slipped free of the press parade. He took a folding chair and set it up beneath the spreading branches of a banyan tree. He had hardly sat down when a party of young men emerged from the farmhouse. They laughed and teased one another, startling a long-legged bird that had been hunting on the edge of a rice paddy. As the bird took flight, Michael found himself surrounded by six smiling youths, each neatly attired in dress shirts and cotton slacks, sandals on their feet. One of them introduced himself as Kanwal. He offered Michael a banana-mango smoothie obviously rescued from the tent.

"This is my father's farm," he informed Michael proudly. Then he explained that his friends were all from nearby farms.

Michael was halfway through the tall glass when he realized it had been spiked. With vodka? That would neatly counter the Synthetic Sleep.

Kanwal proudly tapped his chest. "I am seventeen this year. I have finished my public schooling. My father wants to buy a truck. He will start a business delivering fruit to the cities." Kanwal rolled his eyes. "He says he is getting too old for farm work. He wants to drive a truck while his sons do the tough work!"

The other boys erupted in laughter. Michael grinned too. "Your old man must think a lot of you."

"Oh, I don't know," Kanwal said. "I think he just wants to hit the road to look for a new wife."

The boys giggled and moaned. "He's old," someone muttered, "but not too old!"

"He wants us to believe it, anyway," Kanwal said. "But I'm seventeen! He should be looking for a wife for me."

"Isn't that your mother's business?" Michael asked.

Kanwal shrugged. "My mother is dead three years. My youngest brother does all the cooking now."

"No sisters?"

Kanwal made a face. "No. Of course not. My old man wanted to get ahead, not raise a servant for another man's family. We are very modern here. We don't believe in dowry. If I had a sister, my father would have to pay her dowry. Still, it makes it hard to find a wife. My father was married when he was fifteen. Look at us. We are sixteen, seventeen, eighteen years old. No one has a wife. Hey." He turned to his friends. "Know who's making the most money these days? The marriage broker!"

The boys guffawed again, but Michael frowned. Kanwal noticed, and responded by rubbing Michael's shoulder in a friendly way. "You have a wife?"

Michael shook his head, declining to explain to Kanwal that though he'd been married at twenty-four, it had not lasted two years. *There's nothing left, Michael.*

Kanwal might have read his mind. "Divorced?" he asked.

Michael scowled. "You watch too much TV."

Kanwal giggled, along with his friends. "American women like to have many husbands and only one son."

"We could use some American women here," one of the boys chimed in from the back of the group.

Michael felt the vodka inside him, dissolving his diplomacy. "Women are not toys. They're people, with their own dreams, their own ambitions."

"Oh yes," Kanwal agreed with a hearty nod. "They are goddesses." The boys all offered confirmation of this.

Kanwal went on, "This farm would be a happier place if we had a woman in the kitchen again. Hey, but no one wants to be a farmer anymore, not even my old man."

Michael sat up a little straighter. *This* sentiment had not been reported by his census teams. "Why do you say that? This farm has had a profitable year, despite poor weather."

"Oh, we're doing all right," Kanwal agreed. "But do you think it's easy? Laboring all day in the hot sun, and we don't even have a tractor. The water buffalo are still our tractor. It's shameful! I want to move to Bangalore, learn computers, work in an office."

"Ah, Kanwal," one of his friends interrupted. "Everybody wants to work in an office, but it's the farm for us, you know it."

Kanwal gave his friend a dark look. "Not all of us. Every evening I walk all the way to town, just so I can spend half an hour at the home of a link-wallah, exploring the net. Half an hour! That's all he allows, because he has many clients, but half an hour is not enough time to get any real training—maybe if I could print out lessons, but I can't, because I don't have the paper. But I have a plan.

"I can read well. We all can. I've read every book in the two library booths at South Market. Do you know what we're doing? My friends and I? We're putting our money together to buy our own terminal. I have a friend in town who can get an uplink." Kanwal nodded, his dark eyes happy at his inner vision. "There is formal schooling online, from all over the world, and some of it at no cost. You hear how well I speak English? I learn fast. Hey." He looked at his friends again. "Maybe we're better off with no wives yet. No children to care for, right? Make our careers first. It's what the Bangalore families tell their young men." He turned back to Michael. "You have children, mister?"

"No," Michael said, feeling a sudden tightness in his gut. *There's nothing left, Michael. I'm leaving.*

Kanwal's brows rose in surprise. "No children? Not even from the wife who divorced you?"

"No," Michael repeated firmly, his cheeks heating with more than the torrid afternoon. She had not wanted to try again. *I'm leaving.*

From the back of the crowd the anonymous heckler spoke. "Hey, Kanwal, waiting a few years for a wife doesn't sound too bad, but I don't think I want to wait *that* long."

The boys again erupted in laughter, while Michael's cheeks grew even hotter. He was only thirty-two, but to be thirty-two and without children . . . did that make him a failure in their eyes? It was a stunning thought, and one he didn't want to examine too closely.

Quickly he drained his vodka smoothie while Kanwal went right on massaging his shoulder, his dark eyes shining with confidence, and ambition. "That's right, mister. You watch us. In two years, we will all be middle class like you."

VIII

Two in the morning, and sleep wouldn't come. Cody listened to Wade's soft snoring. She could just make out his silhouette in the faint amber glow spilling from the bathroom nightlight. Maybe new life had begun in her womb tonight, maybe not. It would be a few days before she would know.

She got out of bed, feeling a lingering stickiness between her legs. She groped for a nightshirt and pulled it on, then padded into the living room, where the curtains stood open on a sweeping view of Denver's city lights.

She always took on the toughest jobs.

So why was she so damned scared of the project at Victoria Glen? She'd looked over the specs after dinner. They'd been nasty, but Cody had dealt with worse. *Kick. Kick!* No sweat.

Except she *was* sweating. Her palms were slick, and the soles of her feet.

So? She'd been scared before. The only thing to do was face it down.

She took a long swallow from the bottle of Venezuelan water, then she got her VR helmet from a closet. Sitting on the sofa, she pulled the helmet on, encasing herself in a safe black vault. Nice, simple environment. She almost felt she could go to sleep.

Almost.

She instructed the wireless system to link with her server, where she'd stored the download of the Victoria Glen site, prepared by a redevelopment company called New Land.

She gazed at a menu, then, "Document three-seven-zero," she whispered. *"Go."*

The menu faded as a world emerged, creeping in like sunrise over a tired city. New Land had recorded a full sensory walk-through. Cody's helmet translated the digital record, synthesizing sight, sound, temperature, and encoded odors. Her lungs filled with sun-warmed air, brewed over old wood and oil-stained asphalt.

She found herself afloat, a few feet above an empty street. It ran straight, like a canalized river cutting through a landscape of vacant lots and boarded-up houses. A few sparrows popped up and down in brush that sprouted around a chain-link fence. Warning signs glared from the abandoned buildings:

KEEP OUT
HAZARDOUS MATERIALS SITE
DANGER—NO TRESPASSING

It took her a minute to realize this was Victoria Street, and that first house, with its sagging porch cuddled under a steeply sloping roof, that was Randi's house. It had been the upper limit of Cody's permitted territory, and a safe place to run if ever she needed shelter. The house next to it had been a rental, with a fleet of showy cars perpetually drifting in and out of the front yard. Only a rusted hulk was left now, crumbling in the shade of a large tree leaning over a gap-toothed fence from the yard next door.

Looking at the tree, Cody felt hollow inside. *Jacaranda,* she realized. As a kid she'd never known its name, just enjoyed gathering the purple blossoms that showered from it in the spring. She and Tanya would have pretend weddings and toss the fallen flowers in the air. Where had they learned that? Cody couldn't guess. Neither one of them had ever seen a wedding.

The tree looked so much bigger than she remembered.

Pushing the trackball forward, she went gliding down the street, a ghost returned to haunt the old neighborhood.

She drifted past the fence. She hardly dared to look, but there it was: a tiny block of a house, built close to the ground like a bunker. The roof had gaps in it. Head wounds. The windows were boarded up. It didn't matter. It was all there. All of it, still lurking inside her mind. She closed her eyes, and reality thickened, like flesh on the bones of the past. Little Tanya from down the block was knocking on the door, jump rope in hand. It was a hot summer evening. Cody got her own rope, and they practiced together on the sidewalk, singing *seashells, taco bells, easy, ivy, over.* No way they were supposed to be outside that late, but mama was still at school and Tanya's big sister was sleeping.

They sang very softly, *seashells, taco bells,* so Passion wouldn't come charging at them out of his girlfriend's house across the street, screaming dumb-bitches-shut-up. His motorcycle was there, but his fuck-this-fuck-that music wasn't pounding the neighborhood, so she guessed he was asleep.

They were practicing cross-arms when a tanker truck came rumbling into sight from the direction of Randi's house. They stopped jumping to watch it go by. It was a big truck. The tank had been painted gray. It didn't have the name of any gas station on it.

"Look," Tanya said. She pointed at the truck's undercarriage and giggled. "It's peeing."

A stream of liquid ran from beneath the truck, splashing black against the street. Tanya waved at the anonymous bulk of the driver. Across the street, Passion was screaming *What the fuck is that noise?*

■

Cody snatched the helmet off. Her heart felt like it had melted into her arteries, a pounding starfish in her chest. *Oh no, oh no.* She stared at the looming shapes of furniture in the dimly lit room. She hadn't remembered the truck in years and years. Maybe it had felt too dangerous to remember. *Oh God, oh Jesus.* Her palms were sweating.

Just a few seconds after the truck had passed her eyes had started burning. She ran into the house and threw up. Passion was screaming outside, shooting his gun. Cody lay on the broken tiles of the bathroom floor and cried, she felt so sick, until mama came home and moved her into bed. She didn't say anything about the truck and its stinky pee, because she should never have been out on the sidewalk.

Carefully, Cody lay the helmet on the cushion beside her. Wade was snoring softly in the bedroom. The antique clock on the mantle was ticking, ticking.

What had gone into the street that night? And on other nights, what had spilled from the kitchen drug labs? From the ubiquitous activity of auto repair? From the city's fights against rats and roaches? What had trickled through the soil, into the ground water, returning through the faucet of the kitchen sink?

Splash of clear water into a plastic cup held in a little girl's hands; the dry tang of chlorine in her throat.

There had been toxins in her body that killed her daughter. Cody had always assumed it was *her* fault, that she'd been incautious on a job, that somehow she had poisoned herself; but what if it wasn't so?

Her lips pressed together in a hard line. Any hazardous substance report generated by the cleanup of Victoria Glen would be kept confidential by the redevelopment company. She'd be able to gain access only if she could offer compelling evidence of on-site injury, and that was doubtful. She'd only lived there until she was ten, until Mama got her the scholarship to Prescott Academy. Cody had left for boarding school and never had come back.

So there was only one way to learn what ten years on Victoria Street had done to her. She would have to take on the job herself.

IX

Rajban was up early. Michael found her in the kitchen when he woke, peeking into cabinets with all the stealth and caution of a kid looking for treasure but expecting to find a tiger. "Good morning," Michael said. She jumped, and the cabinet door banged shut. Her hands were already soiled with the gray dirt of the courtyard. Michael sighed. She certainly had an affinity for gardening.

Ignoring her fright, he beckoned to her to come to the sink, where he showed her how to slide her hands under the soap dispenser. The sensor popped a spray of soap onto her palm. She lathered it, carefully imitating Michael's every gesture. Water came from the tap in a tepid spray, like a stolen column of soft rain. Michael dried his hands, Rajban dried hers, then together they made a breakfast of papayas, bread, and yogurt.

■

After they ate, Rajban disappeared into the garden while Michael readied himself for work. Last of all, he picked up his shades. The Terrace glyph waited for him, surrounded by a pink query circle. He linked through. "Anybody there?"

No one answered. He left the link open, confident someone would check back before long. Next he put a call through to Muthaye, but she didn't pick up either. A moment later, the house announced a visitor at the door.

"Ooh, company," Ryan said, as the line to the Terrace went green.

Etsuko sounded puzzled. "Who is that?"

"No ID," Ryan muttered. "Pupils dilated, skin temperature slightly elevated. He's nervous."

"Or angry," Etsuko said. "Be careful, Michael."

"Hey," Michael said as the house repeated its announcement, this time in Hindi. "Good morning and all that. Back again, huh?"

"Been waiting all morning for your shades to activate," Ryan agreed. "You have to understand—your life is so much more interesting than ours. Now hurry up. Go find out what he wants before my next appointment."

Michael summoned an image of the visitor into his shades. "So I guess it's not Muthaye at the door?"

"No, mate. No such luck. A local gentleman, I should think. Looks a little stiff, if you ask me."

Etsuko snorted. "By your standards, Ryan, anyone could look stiff."

Rajban slipped in through the French doors. Michael sighed to see that her hands were dirty again. Some of the dirt had gotten on her face. Still, she looked at Michael with eyes that were brighter, fuller than they had been only yesterday. Then she looked at the door . . . hoping it was Muthaye too? Come back to visit her as promised.

"Say," Ryan said. "Maybe she knows the guy."

"Right." After all, someone had to be looking for Rajban, regardless of what Muthaye said. A brother, perhaps? Someone who cared. Michael slipped the shades off and handed them to Rajban, motioning that she should put them on. Tentatively, she obeyed. For several seconds she stared at the scene, while her mouth twisted in a small hard knot. Then she yanked the shades off, shoved them into Michael's hands, and ran for the courtyard.

Ryan said, "Women react that way to me too, from time to time."

No one laughed.

Michael stared after Rajban, dread gnawing like a rat at his chest. Despite Muthaye's words, he had envisioned only a happy reunion for her. What would his role become, if her family demanded her back, and she refused to go?

Stop guessing.

He slipped the shades back on and went to the front door. "Hark. Open it."

The stranger in the alcove was tall and lean, like a slice taken off a fuller man, then smoked until it hardened. His black hair was neatly cut and combed. His dark eyes were stern. They remained fixed on Michael through a slow, formal bow. "Namaste."

"Namaste," Michael murmured, feeling the hair on the back of his neck rise. There was something about this man that set him on edge. The intense stare, perhaps. The unsmiling face. The stiffness of his carriage. Smoked and hardened.

"I am Mr. Gharia," the stranger said, in lilting but well-pronounced English. "And you, I have been told, are Mr. Fielding. I have come to inquire about the woman."

Michael felt stubborness descend into his spine, a quiet, steely resistance learned from the heroes of a hundred old cowboy movies. "Have you?"

Vaguely, he was aware of Etsuko muttering, "Gharia? Which Gharia? There are dozens in the census, approximate height and age . . ."

Mr. Gharia apparently had a stubborness of his own. He raised his chin, and though his head came barely to Michael's shoulder, he seemed tall. "It is improper for this woman to be residing within your house."

Michael had never taken well to instructions on propriety. Remembering the look of fear and distaste on Rajban's face as she fled to the courtyard, he ventured a guess, and dressed it up as certainty, "This is not your woman."

Mr. Gharia looked taken aback at this discourteous response; perhaps a little confused, but by his reply Michael knew that his guess had been correct. "I am a friend of the family, sir."

When Michael didn't respond to this, Gharia's tone rose. "Sir, a widow deserves respect. This woman must be returned immediately to her family."

A widow. So her husband was dead. Muthaye had said he'd left home a full year ago. Michael had assumed he'd gone for treatment, yet now he was dead. Did Rajban know? Had anyone bothered to tell her? Thinking about it, Michael felt an anger as cool, as austere, as shadows under desert rock. "This woman has no family."

"Sir, you are mistaken."

"The family that she had cast her out like useless rubbish."

"I have come to inquire about her, to be sure she is the woman being sought."

"She is not that woman," Michael said. "She is a different woman altogether."

"Sir—"

"You would not have me put her on display, would you? Now sir, good day." He stepped back, allowing the door to close.

Gharia saw what he was about. "It doesn't matter who she is!" he said quickly. "*Any* Hindu woman must be shamed to be kept as a whore. It is intolerable! It—" The door sealed, cutting off Gharia's tirade with the abruptness of a toggled switch.

"Christ," Michael muttered.

"Nice show," Ryan agreed, but his voice was somber. "Michael, this isn't a game you want to play. Etsuko's IDed this Gharia fellow. He's a religious activist—"

Michael's palm sliced through the air. "I don't care who he is! The Indian constitution promises equal rights for women."

"It's a piece of paper, Michael." Etsuko's voice was softly sad. "In a far-off city. Women like Rajban are subject to an older law."

"Not anymore. Muthaye said she would come up with a shelter for Rajban by today. If the bastards can't find her, they can't hurt her."

But if they did find her? Rajban was already a woman ruined, simply by being inside Michael's house.

He jumped as the lights flashed, and a soft alarm bonged through the residence. Locks clicked. The air-conditioning system huffed into silence. "Perimeter intrusion," the house informed him. "Michael Fielding, you will remain secured inside this residence pending arrival of Global Shear security. Arrival estimated at three minutes fifty seconds." It was the same feminine voice the house always used, yet it didn't sound like the house anymore.

"Where is Rajban?" Michael shouted.

"Identify the person in question?"

This was definitely not his house. "Rajban. A girl. She's been . . . she's stayed here for a day or so—"

Ryan's voice cut in: "The courtyard, Michael."

Michael dashed for the courtyard doors. His hand hit the latch, but it would not move. He tried to force it, but the door held.

Through the glass, he saw Rajban crouched on the path beside a freshly worked bed of earth, the little hoe in one hand. She gazed up at the courtyard wall. Michael looked, to see Gharia leaning over the top. It was eight feet of smooth concrete, but somehow he had climbed it, and from the Shastri courtyard, too. Now he leaned on his chest, the breast of his shirt smudged with dirt, his dark brows pulled together in an angry scowl. Michael had only a glimpse of him, before he dropped away out of sight.

Again Michael tried the latch, slamming it with all his weight while the house instructed him to "Stay away from all doors and windows. Retreat at once to the interior—"

"Who the hell am I talking to?" Michael interrupted.

"Easy," Ryan muttered. "Cool under fire, boy. You know the chant."

The house answered at the same time: "This is Security Chief Sankar. Mr. Fielding, please step away from the door. You must remove yourself from this exposed position immediately—"

Rajban had seen him. She was running toward him now. She threw herself on the door latch, while Michael tried again to force it from the inside. It would not budge. Rajban stared at him through the glass, her dark eyes wide, confusion and terror swimming in her unshed tears.

"Sankar!" Michael shouted. "Unlock this door. Let her inside *now*—"

"Mr. Fielding, please remain calm. The door will not open until the situation is secure. Be assured, we will be on-site momentarily."

Michael bit his lip, swearing silently to himself. "Is Gharia still out there, then? He's after this girl, you know. Not me."

"Negative, sir. Raman Gharia has fled the scene. He is presently being tracked by a vigil craft—"

The drone aircraft that watched the house. Of course. The security AI must have seen Gharia climbing the Shastri wall. . . .

"Well, if Gharia's gone, then you can open the door. Sankar?"

A helicopter swept in, no more than fifty feet above the wall. Rajban looked up at it, and screamed. Michael could not hear her through the sound-proofed glass, but he could see the terror on her face. She pressed herself against the door, covering her head with the new sari Muthaye had given her while her clothing licked and shuddered in the rotor wash. First one man, then a second, descended from the helicopter, sliding down a cable to land in the courtyard garden.

"This probably qualifies as overkill," Ryan muttered.

"Sankar!" Michael shouted. "What the hell are you *doing*?"

No answer.

The helicopter pulled away. The two men on the ground were anonymous in their helmets and shimmering gray coveralls. The first one pulled a weapon from a thigh holster and trained it on Rajban. The second sprinted toward the wall where Gharia had appeared. Crashing through the half-dead plants, he launched himself at the concrete face, and to Michael's amazement, he actually reached the top, pulling himself up to gaze over the side, in a weird echo of Gharia's own posture. He stayed there only long enough to drop something over the wall—oh, Mrs. Shastri was going to *love* this—then he slipped back down into the garden, landing in a crouch. A weapon had appeared in his hands, too.

"Net gun," Ryan said. "Launches a sticky entangler. Nonlethal, unless it scares you to death. Michael, I had no idea you were this well protected."

"They're bored," Michael growled.

"Do say."

"Explosives negative," Sankar informed him, through the voice of the house.

Now both net guns were trained on Rajban.

"Leave her alone," Michael warned. "Sankar, I swear—"

"Situation clear," Sankar announced.

The man by the wall stood up, sliding his weapon back into its holster. The other did the same. He slipped his visor up, revealing a delighted grin. Michael recognized Sankar's handsome face. "Quite an adventure, eh, Mr. Fielding?"

The door lock clicked. Michael slammed the latch down, yanking the door open, so that Rajban half fell into the living room. He started to reach for her, to help her up, but she scuttled away with a little moan of terror. He turned to Sankar, ready to vent his fury, but he found the security chief praising his man for a job well done.

"Absolutely by the book!" Sankar was saying in a suitably masculine voice, quite a jolt after the feminine voice of the house. With his gaze, Sankar took in Michael, too. "Mr. Fielding. This has turned out to be a minor incident, but we had no way of knowing that when the perimeter alarm sounded. It is essential that you remain inside in such situations, away from doors and windows. If explosives had come over the wall—"

"Then Rajban would have been killed," Michael said softly. "All I asked was that you unlock the door to let her in."

Rajban had gone to hide behind the sofa. Michael could hear her softly weeping. Sankar frowned at the noise, as if it did not fit into any scenario he had ever practiced. "This woman, she is not the housekeeper registered in our security files. Have you changed employees?"

"No. She's not an employee. She's a guest."

"A guest? All guests should be registered, Mr. Fielding. Without a profile, we have no way of discriminating friend from enemy." He said this matter-of-factly, without a hint of judgment. Well, Sankar was a modern man, educated in California, Michael recalled. What the boss did was the boss's business, no doubt.

Michael sighed, letting the edge of his anger slip away. "You're right," he conceded. Global Shear security protocol was strict and effective. "So take her profile now. She's a waif, just a little girl, without home or family. And that's all she is, Mr. Sankar. I want you to put that in your profile too."

X

Rajban plunged her hoe into the hard earth of the garden bed, prying up chunks of clay. Grief sat in her stomach like heavy black mud, but it was not grief for her husband. It was for herself. Now she was widowed. She had no home. She would have no sons. Brother-in-Law had sent her away.

So why had Gharia come after her?

She hacked at the earth, and thought about it. Gharia had been a frequent guest at Brother-in-Law's table, where they discussed the *foreign issue*, and the *influence of nonbelievers*. At times they would grow very angry, but when the talk lapsed, Gharia's eyes often found their rest on Rajban's backside as she worked in the kitchen with Mother-in-Law.

Mother-in-Law would notice the direction of Gharia's gaze, and her words to Rajban would be angry.

Rajban remembered these things as she crumbled each chunk of clay in her hands. She picked up the hoe again and dug deeper.

The soil here was bad. There were no worms in it. No tiny bugs. It looked as sterile as the soil in Brother-in-Law's courtyard. Even the weeds were yellow.

No matter.

She would use the magic soil. With love and prayers, its influence could be worked into the ground.

A winged shadow drifted slowly over Rajban's hands. She paused in her work, squinting against the noon sun. There! She spied it again: A tiny plane the color of the sky. It was very hard to see, yet if she looked long enough, she could always find it floating above the house.

The door latch clicked. "Rajban?"

Rajban smiled shyly when she saw the kind woman, Muthaye, looking out between the glass doors. "Namaste," she murmured softly. "You came back."

"Namaste," Muthaye echoed. "Will you come inside? The sun is high, and it is very hot."

Rajban obeyed. She stood on stiff legs, taking a moment to brush the soil from her sari. Inside, she was startled to discover other women. They were four, sitting in a half-circle on the carpet. They were not fine women, like Muthaye. Their saris were worn and their faces lined. All of them were older than Rajban. She felt sure they were all mothers, and she felt ashamed.

Twice in her first year of marriage she had thought herself pregnant, but her hopes were shattered by a late, painful, and heavy flow of blood—as if a baby had been started and then had died.

Rajban remembered the midwife who had come to visit on the day she arrived in her husband's household. This midwife had not looked like the village health aides Rajban had seen at her father's farm. This one was young and finely dressed, and she wore an eye veil, like Michael. "She will make your womb healthy," Mother-in-Law declared. "So healthy you will bear only sons." Rajban had bit her lips to keep from wailing in pain as cold, gloved hands groped inside her. She had not felt healthy afterwards. Her abdomen and her crotch had ached for days—and she had never conceived a baby. Or maybe . . . she had conceived only girls?

Muthaye had joined the circle of women. Now she smiled at Rajban. "Please won't you sit?" She patted a spot at her side that would close the circle. Rajban did as she was asked, though she would have been happier to disappear into the kitchen. She sat with her hands folded neatly in her lap while Muthaye told a story that did not sound like it could be true.

"My mother was an illiterate country woman," Muthaye began. Her gaze sought Rajban. "That means she was like you. She could not read or write or speak any language but the one she was born to. At fourteen she was married to a young man only a little more educated than she, the third son of a cruel and selfish family. It was a great struggle for my grandfather to gather the large dowry demanded by her husband's family. Still, he paid it, though he was forced to mortgage his land. Several months later there came a terrible storm. The land was destroyed, and along with many others in the village, he died of disease. When afterwards my mother gave birth to a daughter, she was driven out of the family. She returned to her father's house, but he refused to receive her, so she went without food and shelter, and her baby girl died.

"My mother became angry.

"She remembered that in the year of her marriage, she had met an agent from the women's cooperative. She went to that agent now, and was given a job sewing embroidered scarves. She earned enough to feed herself, but she wanted more. With the help of the women's cooperative, she taught herself to read. She received a small loan—only two hundred dollars—but it was enough to buy books and start her own lending library. When the loan was paid back she took out another, and eventually she started a school just for girls. In time she married again—"

There was a murmur of surprise from the circle.

"—the son of a longtime member of the women's cooperative. No dowry was paid—"

Again, a whisper of astonishment arose from the gathered women.

"—for dowry is evil and illegal. She still runs her school, and through it she has earned more money for her family than she might have ever brought as dowry. She is middle-class, Rajban. Yet when she was fifteen, she was just like you."

Rajban stared down at the lines of dirt that lay across her palms, knowing it wasn't true. "She had a baby."

Muthaye's tone became more strict: "It is not unexpected that a husband dying of AIDS gave you his disease instead of a child. That does not mean you will never have a child—or another husband."

"My brother-in-law will not allow it."

"You do not belong to him anymore."

Rajban considered this. She turned it over and over in her mind, wondering if it was true. At the same time, she listened to the other women talk about themselves. These women were all learning to read. Three of them had businesses. One made sandals. Another drove a zip. The last cleaned houses. The fourth member of their group was building a fruit stand. All of them had started their businesses with small loans from Muthaye.

"Not from me," Muthaye corrected. "These are loans from the Southern Banking Association."

The loans were for a few hundred dollars at a time, enough to buy the tools and supplies that would let them work. Together, the women ensured that each one of them made their weekly payments. If any failed to do so, all would lose their credit. This was the "microcredit program" administered by Muthaye. Three of the women in this lending circle had been involved for several years, one for only a few months.

"A lending circle should have five women," Muthaye explained. "The fifth lady of this group has moved away to join her son in Bangalore, so there is a place for you here. I have told you the story of my mother. This can be your story too."

Rajban bowed her head. Her heart fluttered, like a bird, seeking to escape its cage for the peaceful serenity of the sun-seared sky. She stared at her hands and whispered, "I don't know how."

One of the older women patted her mud-stained hand. She asked if Rajban could sew or cook. If she could keep a house clean or carry a heavy weight. Rajban didn't know how to answer. Her mother had raised her to do the things women do. All these things she had done, but surely no one would pay her to do them?

"Is there anything you are so good at?" Muthaye asked. "Is there a kind of work that blossoms like a flower in your hands?"

Rajban caught her breath. She glanced out at the garden. "I have a bag of magic soil that makes a garden strong and happy."

This brought a shower of laughter from the women. But why? Hadn't Rajban believed all their tales? And yet they laughed. Their kindly faces had all become the face of her mother-in-law, laughing, laughing, and endlessly scolding her, *Stupid girl!*

She felt a touch on her hand, and the vision vanished, but even Muthaye's warm eyes could not chase away the pain.

"Magic is the comfort of old-fashioned women," Muthaye told her. "A modern woman has no need of it. Think on what we've talked about. Think of a business you might like to do. Think hard, for you must be settled before the AIDS treatment can begin."

XI

Word of the morning's misadventures got around quickly. It was still early when Michael stepped from a zip into the shade of the portico at Global Shear's district headquarters. The five-story office cube was newly built, situated halfway up a shallow, rocky rise dividing two of the original villages. A temple occupied the high ground, while a pig farmer kept his animals in a dusty pen on one side of the landscaped grounds. Laborers' shacks made up the rest of the neighborhood.

A nervous community relations officer greeted Michael even before he entered the building. "Shall we issue a public statement, Mr. Fielding?"

"Not unless someone asks."

"There *have* been several inquiries about the helicopter."

"Then state the truth. Intruder alarms went off and security responded. Play it down, though, and add that we're reviewing our procedures to see if our response might be tempered in the future."

"Yes sir."

Glass doors slipped open, and Michael stepped into the air-conditioned paradise of the public lobby. The receptionist looked up, and smiled. "An exciting morning, Mr. Fielding! That helicopter raid must have shaken the dust off anyone still doubting our diligence."

"So I hear."

He met more compliments on the elevator ride to the fifth floor, but the tenor changed when he entered his corner office, where Karen Hampton waited for him, her image resident in an active wall screen. "A most interesting report appeared in my queue this morning. Talk to me, Michael. What the hell is going on?"

Michael sat down in the chair behind his desk, swiveling to

face her. Nothing to do but tell the truth. He explained the situation, but she did not look relieved.

"Michael. I can't believe you've involved yourself with this girl. Do I have to remind you that trust is the most important asset we are building in Four Villages? I don't give a damn how innocent your actions are, stop for a minute and ask yourself how this must look to those people whom you are there to serve—not to exploit. If you can't find her a shelter, then *buy* her one. For the sake of your reputation and the company's good name, rent this young woman her own house and then stay far away from her."

"What if Gharia comes after her?"

"This isn't our business—"

"Karen, it might be. I've checked the census figures, and there's a growing imbalance in the sex ratio here. There are far fewer young women than men. Rajban may be a widow, and she may be ill, but Gharia's not exactly a kid. She could still be the best prospect he has."

"If that's so, why did her family get rid of her instead of marrying her off?"

"I don't know. Maybe they didn't want to pay a dowry. Maybe they don't give a damn. Maybe they're strict Hindus and don't believe in remarriage for women."

"Listen to yourself! There are cultural complexities here that you haven't begun to grasp. This is not why you're in Four Villages."

"We're here to build a stable, diverse, and functional economy, and that can't exist where there is slavery. I won't send Rajban back into slavery."

"I'm not asking you to do that. Just get her out of your house. I want you in this job, Michael. I really do. Show me my confidence is not misplaced."

■

Michael called in the personnel officer, and she promised to hunt around for an available residence, though she wasn't hopeful. "There are very few rentals in town, and most landlords will deal only with a certain class of clientele. I might be able to obtain a room, or perhaps a shanty, but that would almost certainly bring about the eviction of a current resident."

"We don't want that. Do what you can."

The day failed to improve. Near noon, Michael looked up from his desk to see Pallava Sen, his second in command, coming through the open doorway, a half-page of neon yellow paper in his hand. "Michael, we have a problem."

Leaning back in his chair, Michael slipped off his shades, laying them carefully on the desk. "How bad a problem?"

Pallava rolled his eyes, as if casting a quick prayer up to the gods. With his portly figure and balding head, he looked like a youthful version of the little buddhas sold in Japanese tourist markets. "Not so bad at the moment, but with significant potential to get much worse."

"Wonderful."

Pallava handed him the yellow paper. "These have appeared all over the town. They are being read aloud, too, so the illiterate will be informed."

Michael scowled at the notice. It was written in Hindi.

Pallava settled into the guest chair, a grim smile on his face. "It is written as a news report, by the Traditional Council of Elders. You've heard of them?"

"No."

"Neither has anyone else. They do not say whose elders they are, but they do tell us some interesting things. Here"—he leaned forward, pointing at the headline—"they say that Global Shear has poisoned the people of this district."

Michael had been so fully set to hear how he had kidnapped and raped a good Hindu woman, that it took him a moment to shift modes. ". . . Poisoned?"

"The argument follows. It says that independent testing of well water throughout the district has revealed severe pesticide contamination. The wells have been regularly tested, and for many years they have produced only clean, unpolluted water. Now they are suddenly contaminated? The only plausible explanation is that the groundwater was deliberately poisoned."

"That's ridiculous."

"Oh, there's more." He leaned back, lacing his fingers together in a nervous, unsettled bridge. "The notice does not name specific chemicals, but it claims those present will suppress the birth rate of the district's women, and in many cases will cause monstrous birth defects leading to early miscarriage. This may be one reason so few girls have been born this past year. Girls are weaker than boys. They die more easily."

He said this last in a deadpan voice that made Michael's eyes narrow. "The notice says that?" he asked cautiously. "Or is that your interpretation?"

Pallava's face hardened. In the same low, flat voice, he answered, "*I* would not say that. I have a wife who, I am proud to say, is stronger and smarter than I am. I have two brilliant daughters, a sister, a mother, a grandmother. We are not all that way, Michael."

Michael felt his cheeks heat. "I know. I'm sorry."

Pallava shrugged. "You understand the implication? That Global Shear is using cheap birth control?"

Michael nodded.

"The article is also circulating as an Internet message."

"Christ."

"And Shiva. It has not, mercifully, appeared yet on cable TV."

"We need to dispatch crews to field-sample some wells."

"I have already sent them."

"Good. Get me the results as soon as possible." He drummed his desk. "Better test some crop samples too. The harvest is just coming in on the demonstration farm. Check that, especially. *Dammit!* We have to counter these accusations today—and on cable TV, too."

■

It was an hour later when Pallava Sen walked back into Michael's office, collapsing once more into the visitor's chair. Global Shear had used paper, Internet, cable TV, messengers, and paid gossipmongers to vehemently deny the allegations of the Traditional Elders, and to announce their intention to immediately investigate the condition of the well water.

Pallava didn't speak right away. He frowned, his brow wrinkling in lines that made him look old.

"How bad is it now?" Michael asked.

Pallava's sigh was long and heartfelt. "Mega-bad. Giga-bad. It seems the slander was at least partly right. We've fast-tested a sample of wells from across the district and everyone of them shows extensive pesticide contamination." He shook his head. "This is not something that could have happened overnight, not even if it was deliberately done, which I don't believe. We are looking at the results of years—probably decades—of seepage into the water table. It's quite obvious the water quality reports we've been using have been falsified. Deliberately falsified."

Michael breathed slowly, trying to calm the fierce pounding of his heart. *Don't panic, but don't hide from the truth either. The first thing to do is get a handle on the problem.* "Let's be specific here. We're talking drinking water?"

"Drinking, agricultural." Pallava spread his hands helplessly. "It's all the same thing, and judging from the spot samples, we have to assume there is pesticide contamination in every well in the district." His hands laced together as he stared at a spot beyond Michael's shoulder. "The Ikeda rice crop is contaminated too. The sample we tested came out so bad the stuff can't be legally used even for animal feed."

"Christ."

"And Shiva too."

No pesticides had been used on the Ikeda rice. That was, after all, a major benefit of genetically engineered crops—natural insect and disease resistance could be spliced in—but Ikeda rice had not been designed to flush itself free of chemical contamination.

No more assumptions, Michael swore. "Tell me now if Global Shear had anything to do with developing the phony reports."

Pallava straightened, his eyes wide with surprise. He had been in on the operation here from the opening day. "No! No, of course not. Global Shear had nothing to do with preparing the reports. Water quality monitoring has been a government function. Our mistake was relying on the test results we received."

"Why would anybody want to fake these reports?"

Pallava shrugged. "There are many possible reasons. The wells were a government project. To find fault with them would not be patriotic. To find them dirty must mean the money spent to build them was wasted, or that those who built them didn't do sufficient background work, or that more money would be needed to clean the water, and where is that supposed to come from? And will those who built the wells be punished? Those who built the wells also report on their functions, so you see, it's not so hard to understand how it could happen. It's not the first time."

"And still, it's our mistake for trusting the data without testing it."

"Yes. Ultimately, it will come back to that."

■

"Michael?"

It was Jaya's voice, issuing from the shades he'd left lying on the desk. She spoke softly, as if he were a sleeping child and she reluctant to wake him. Her priority link let her open a line at any time.

Michael grabbed the shades and slipped them on. "Jaya! How are you? How's the baby?" He transferred the link to his portal screen, and Jaya's image replaced the document he'd been working on. She was as lovely as any magazine model and, not for the first time, Michael thought of Sheo with a twinge of envy.

"We're all fine," Jaya assured him. Then she hesitated. "Michael, I've been talking to Ryan."

He grunted, sinking back into his chair. "You've heard about Rajban, then."

"Yes. I think it's sweet, what you're trying to do for her." Jaya touched her ruby-red lips. What a perfect alliance she had made with the colorful, symbiotic bacteria living in her cells—yet most people, upon hearing the source of the color, would respond in revulsion: *Yuck. I would never do that.*

It took practice to keep the mind open to new possibilities.

"Sheo told me about the reaction of the nurses to Ela's birth," Jaya said. "I didn't notice, really. They were very kind to me. The older woman, though, was concerned that I have a son next time. She told me she had been trained in these things."

Michael scowled. "What things?"

"That's what I asked. It seems there is a uterine implant on the market, which can be used to selectively abort female embryos. It isn't legal, but the nurse was quite casual about it. She offered to set me up with one before I left the hospital, for a small fee of course. Sheo thought you might like to know this."

Michael grimaced. "Sheo was right."

A uterine implant was better than infanticide—Michael even found himself admiring the ingenuity of such a device—but what of the imbalance it would generate? He remembered Gharia, and the look of wrath on his face. "How long do you suppose this has been going on?"

Jaya shrugged. "In one form or another, for hundreds of years."

"Though it's gotten easier now."

"Yes."

But who would bear the cost?

Tensions in Four Villages were not readily visible, yet Michael had sensed them anyway, in the whispering of the nurses on the maternity ward, in the heat of Rajban's fever, in Kanwal's cheerful lament over dowry and women and net access. The people here were experiencing a strange, sideways tearing of their culture, like raw cotton being combed apart, the pieces on their way to a new order, while still clinging helplessly to the old.

"This fellow Gharia is supposed to be a religious activist," Michael said. "I'm starting to wonder if it's only coincidence that this attack on Global Shear followed so closely on his visit this morning."

"Rajban is just one little girl," Jaya reminded him.

True, but a fuse was small compared to the explosives it ignited.

Jaya might have read his mind. "Michael, please be careful. These things have a way of getting out of hand."

XII

After a day spent researching a bid on the Victoria Glen project, Cody found she could not sleep. So at 3 A.M. she pulled on her VR helmet and joined her mother on a stroll in the Paris sunshine. That is, Annette strolled, through tourist crowds along a riverwalk, beneath a grove of ancient trees. Cody felt as if she were floating, a balloon gliding at her mother's side.

"Of all the uses of VR, I like this best," Cody said. "Being able to step out of the awful three A.M. hour, when everything's so dark and cold and hopeless—step right out into gorgeous sunshine. It's like slipping free of your fate, flipping a finger at the cosmos. Ha!"

Annette laughed. Cody was looking out of her shades, and so she couldn't see her mother's face, but she could feel her presence. It was a strange, tickling feeling, as if she might see her after all if she turned just a little bit more. . . .

Cody had not lived with her mother since leaving Victoria Glen for boarding school, and still Annette had been an indefatigable presence in her life, through phone calls and e-mail and brief visits several times a year as they both worked toward their degrees. It had been so hard. Cody felt scared even now when she remembered the loneliness, the resentment she had felt for so many years living on the charity of a corporate scholarship, in a private school where almost everyone else had money and a home and a real family. But even at her worst moments, Cody had never doubted Annette's love.

Now Annette was forty-nine, a data analyst on vacation in Paris with her husband of many years. She had helped him raise his son and one of their own. "Doing it right this time," she'd joked with Cody. It had only hurt a little.

"So, girl. You've been up to something, haven't you? Hurry up and tell me before Jim gets back."

"Up to something?" Cody echoed, disquiet stirring near her heart.

"Something's put you in a mood," Annette said. Up ahead, Jim was waiting by a flower stand. Annette waved to him. "Are you working yourself up for a fight?"

"Oh." Cody had promised herself she would not mention Victoria Glen. Her mother didn't like to think about those days. She didn't even like to acknowledge that time had ever been real. And still, Cody found herself confessing. "I went back to Victoria Glen—"

"Cody!"

"In VR," she added, hoping to appease her mother's scathing tone. "I'm bidding on a job there. I spent all day developing the proposal. I guess I'm wound a little tight."

"Why *there*, Cody?" Annette sighed. "I know you're doing well. You're not desperate for the job. Are you?"

"No."

"Then why go back there?"

"I don't know. Or . . . maybe I do know. I—"

Annette stepped into a bookstore, leaving Jim waiting beside the flowers. Cody watched her hands touch the spines of a row of English-language guidebooks. They were strong, long-fingered hands, golden as teak, each nail painted in milk-chocolate-brown. "Cody, do you know the greatest difference between you and me?"

Cody laughed. It was the only reaction she could think of. "Oh, you're smarter than I am."

"No. I'm more ruthless. I have never let the past own me. If I don't like it, I cut it out. I throw it away. It's not an easy thing to do, but it's needful. I don't think about Victoria Glen, and I don't muse over the boy who was your father, and I don't apologize to anybody for letting Prescott Academy take you away. Holding on to all that would have made my soul so heavy I couldn't get up in the morning. I have to live lightly. I have to do all that I can with what I have in my hands right now." She looked up at the bookstore door. Jim had just come in.

Annette's voice grew softer. "Brace yourself for a mother lecture," she warned. "Cody, you need to learn to live lightly too. You don't have anything to make up for. Let the past go. Let it slip away, and find your joy here, today."

■

But what if the past is looking for you? Rising in your life like a flooding river, climbing past your ankles, past your knees and your thighs, flowing into your secret places, nesting in your womb?

■

Cody let the link close, plunging herself back into the darkness of her VR helmet. Not absolutely dark. A call-waiting light glowed amber in the corner of her vision.

When had that come on?

She tapped her glove, calling up a link ID.

Confirmed identity: Michael Fielding.

"Oh God." She felt as if a heat lance had plunged through her, diving in a beam between heart and stomach and out the middle of her back. *Michael.* "Why now, baby?" she whispered. All the lines of force that guided her life seemed to be intersecting tonight.

She laid her palm against her flat belly. Was there a baby there? Still a single cell, moving toward her womb, and the judgment she had built-in. She'd blamed herself for the loss of that first pregnancy, but had it been her fault? Or had she been poisoned oh so long ago, in Victoria Glen?

She bowed her head, laughing, crying—some strange mix of the two, her guts feeling like jelly. "Baby, *why* are you calling tonight?"

Easy to find out.

She wiped her eyes on the hem of her shirt. She drew a deep breath to steady herself. Where did he live now, anyway? Hong Kong, wasn't it? She'd gotten a card from him last Christmas.

Her finger curled. She tapped her data glove.

Link.

Just like that, he was there, his head and shoulders drifting in an ill-defined space only an arm's reach in front of her. He looked surprised to see her. "Cody?"

She smiled. "Come on, baby, I don't look that old."

He blushed. Bless him. "Old? Not at all. Hey, it's been a while. And I know it's an outrageous hour. I meant to leave a message, but then I thought I'd query your status, and you were awake—"

"How are you, Michael?" she asked. He had always talked too much when he was nervous.

"Oh, I'm good. The job, though . . . I've got a situation here. I'm working in southern India. Did I tell you that?"

"No."

That flustered him further. A rosy blush heated his bronze complexion. He looked down at his desk a moment, then grinned. "I sound like I've got a few too many crosslinks in the old wetware, don't I?"

"It happens to the best of us."

It was on her lips to tell him what she'd remembered in the VR last night, yet she couldn't do it. It had been her decision to end their marriage. In the long, dark months after the abortion she had watched their union rot, until she could kick it over with one cold clutch of words: *There's nothing left. I'm leaving.*

How could she tell him now, "Oops. Sorry. I made a mistake"?

"How's your schedule?" he asked. "Are you busy right now?"

"At three—?"

His brows rose over a crooked smile. "Well, yeah. Sorry. I wouldn't be bothering you, but we've just stumbled over a critical groundwater problem—and a possible political stew, to make things exciting." Quickly, he explained the details. "I called you first. You're the best. And, basically, you're a pushover."

Don't smile at me like that, she thought. *And breathe, girl.*

Thank God this wasn't a full-sensory link. She didn't want to smell him, or feel the heat off his body. That smile was like a light shining into her soul. . . .

She asked, "Are you looking for a professional reference?"

"If you think that's what I need. I was wondering, though, if you could handle it?"

"An operation that size?" She shook her head, uncomfortable with the idea. "Green Stomp has only done domestic work. It would take time for us to hire the extra personnel and mobilize." *And besides, there's another job I need to do.* "You'd be better off with a local outfit. I could ask around for recommendations."

He nodded, but he looked tense and unhappy. "I really need a favor, Cody. Could you do a VR consultation now? I mean right now. This afternoon . . . oh hell. This morning, where you are. I need a specialist to survey the wells. I need solid answers for the people who live here. It's a bad situation, and it could get out of hand so easily, especially . . ."

She didn't like the awkward guilt lurking in his eyes. "What, Michael?"

He told her about Rajban. Cody listened, unable to completely suppress a dark spear of suspicion, of jealousy, but when he finished, she shook her head at her own tumbled existence, knowing she had thrown away something precious for all the wrong reasons. It was all she could do not to cry.

XIII

Cody's workday had been Michael's night. While he slept, she studied the test results from the sample wells. While he dreamed, she ordered select strains of genetically engineered bacteria from New Delhi, along with case upon case of the nutrient broth that would stimulate them to rapidly reproduce. Near 3 A.M. the frozen vials and sealed boxes arrived in Four Villages, after a quick trip on a southbound jet. When Michael called into the office first thing in the morning, Pallava Sen reported that everything was in place to run a demonstration treatment on a well at Kanwal's farm.

"Great! I'll be there in half an hour." It was already eight o'clock.

It was a vibrant morning. Rajban was in the courtyard, working at the soil with the little hoe she'd found. The ground around her was wet, and the air steamy. The eastern sky had turned itself into a fluffy Christian postcard. Columns of light from the hidden sun poured down between tearing rain clouds, like radiance leaking from the face of God. In a patch of blue sky between the towering cumulus, two tiny white cloud scraps drifted on the edge of visibility. *Angels,* Michael thought. They looked like angels, gliding in slow raptor circles on the threshold of heaven.

Was this how myths got started?

Rajban looked up at him as he approached. He pantomimed eating food. She smiled tolerantly, then went back to her work. Michael frowned, troubled at her lack of appetite. Then Cody's glyph winked on in the corner of his shades and he forgot to worry. He tapped a full link. "Good morning!" It felt so right to be working with Cody again.

"Or good night," Cody answered, her voice husky and tired. "I'm going to catch a few hours' sleep before the demo. . . . Is that your waif? She looks like a little girl."

"She is a little girl. And she hasn't been eating much. Muthaye was here yesterday, but she didn't leave any messages. I'm a little concerned, Cody. It's past time her AIDS treatment was started."

Rajban's work had slowed; Michael guessed she was listening to him. What did she imagine he talked about? He shook his head. She looked so lost, a little girl caught on an island in the midst of a rising river, her spot of land steadily shrinking around her.

"She hides inside her work," Michael mused. "Just like we do."

The house pre-empted any reply. "Mr. Fielding, please step inside immediately." The french doors swung open as the injunction was repeated in Hindi. Rajban scrambled to her feet. "Air surveillance has identified the intruder Raman Gharia approaching the premises," the house explained. "Please return immediately to the safety of the interior."

"Michael, what is it?" Cody asked.

"A local troublemaker, that's all." He beckoned to Rajban.

They went inside, and the doors swung shut behind them.

"Hark, give me a street view," Michael said.

A window opened in his shades. He looked out on the lane, and saw Gharia approaching in the company of a portly older man with salt-and-pepper hair neatly combed about a face so dignified it was almost comical, as if he were possessed by dignity, as if it held him together, so that if he ever let it go his body would crumble to helpless dust. A Traditional Elder? Michael wondered.

A link came in from Sankar. "Security forces are on their way, Mr. Fielding. Please stay inside."

"Sankar, I trust you won't be sending helicopter shock troops this time?"

"Uh, no sir. As per our discussion, we will be striving for an *appropriate* response."

"Thank you." In their discussion, he had also insisted he have voice override on any house functions. He wasn't going to be locked up again.

The house announced visitors. "A Mr. Gharia and Mr. Rao to see you, Mr. Fielding." Michael glanced at Rajban. Her chest fluttered in short little pants. Her eyes were wide.

"Hark. Ask her if she knows this Mr. Rao."

The house translated his question to Hindi. Rajban closed her eyes, and nodded.

Michael strode toward the door.

"Michael, what are you doing?" Cody's voice was sharp and high, reminding him of another time. *It's all gone. Can't you see that?*

"Mr. Fielding," Sankar objected. "Perhaps you have not seen my report. These two men are deeply involved—"

"I only want to have a civil discussion with them." *And learn what it would take to get them to leave Rajban alone.* "Hark, open the door."

The door swung open to reveal Gharia and Rao, shoulder to shoulder in the alcove. Gharia looked up in surprise, then, "Namaste," he muttered. Rao echoed it, and introduced himself. Michael was unsurprised to learn that this was Rajban's brother-in-law, the head of the household, the one who had rejected her after her husband died.

"You look at me with anger," Rao said, his voice deep, his dignity so heavy it seemed to suck the heat out of the air, "when I am the one who has been shamed. Return the woman you hold, pay a dowry for her shame, and I will not involve the police."

Behind his back, Michael could hear the house whispering a string of Hindi as it translated Rao's words for Rajban. He drew himself up a little straighter. "She is not my prisoner."

The house uttered a brief line in Hindi. Rao waited for it to finish, then: "She is my brother's widow. Perhaps you don't understand what that means, Mr. Fielding. You are a foreigner, and your modern culture holds little respect for a woman's dignity. Upon my brother's death, I was prepared to allow his wife to live in my household for the rest of her life, despite the burden this would place on me. Rajban rejected my generosity. She desired to marry again. My wife also counseled this would be best, but I am an old man, and I believe in the old ways. A widow should be given respect!" He sighed. "Sometimes, though, a woman will not have respect. The immorality of the world infected this woman. Carnal desire drove her into the street."

Michael felt his body grow hard with a barely contained fury. "That's not how she told the story." Rajban hadn't even known her husband was dead until Gharia's visit.

Gharia glared at him. Michael watched his hands.

Rao alone remained unruffled, glued together by dignity. "I am learning we must all bend with the times," he announced. "I have found a new husband for Rajban. If you will pay the dowry and the medical expenses of her rehabilitation as the penalty of your shame, I will allow this marriage to go forward."

"What an evil old mercenary," Cody growled, while Michael traded stares with Gharia. It was quite obvious who the intended husband was to be. "Tell him to shove off, Michael. She's just a little girl."

Rao could not hear her, and so he continued laying out his terms. "If you do not pay the dowry, I will return the woman to my household. With the help of my wife and son, we may yet protect her from the weakness of the flesh, for as long as she is living."

"Which won't be long," Cody said savagely, "when Rao refuses to buy treatment for her AIDS."

"She's staying here," Michael said.

"Then I will summon the police."

"She's staying here! It's what she wants."

"Have you asked her that?" Gharia demanded. "No woman wants to be a childless whore."

"You dirty son of a—"

Michael broke off, startled by a wash of cold air at his back. He turned to see Rajban, her face veiled by the hem of the sari Muthaye had given her. Her eyes were wide and frightened as she squeezed past Michael. "Rajban, wait!" She slipped past Rao too, out of the alcove and into the street. Michael stared after her in astonishment, but Rao, he didn't even look at her. She might have been a shadow.

"Jesus, Michael!" Cody shouted. "Don't let her go."

Rao nodded in satisfaction. "I will send a servant with the bride price."

Gharia was smiling. His gaze slid past Michael on a film of

oily satisfaction. As if to himself, he murmured, "Every woman desires respect."

"Michael, stop her!"

"Rajban! Don't go." She would not understand his words, but surely she would ken the meaning?

Rajban looked at him, with doubt in her eyes, and fear, and a deep sadness that seemed to resonate through millennia of suffering.

"Rajban, please stay."

Her gaze fell, and docilely she turned to follow Rao, who had not even bothered to look behind him.

"Michael! Damn you. Go after her. Stop her."

"Cody, she's made her own decision. I can't grab her and force her back into the house."

"For God's sake, Michael, why not? For once in your life, go out and grab somebody. Stop her. Don't let her make the decision that will wreck her life. Michael, she's hurting so badly, she's in no condition to decide." To his astonishment, he could hear her weeping. "Cody?" Her glyph winked out, as she cut the link.

XIV

Something had changed in the house, though Michael couldn't decide exactly what. All the furniture remained in place; the lighting was just the same. Mrs. Nandy had not been by, so the mud stains remained on the couch, and Rajban's bag of soil—half empty now—still sat by the glass doors. Maybe the house was colder.

He sent a call to Cody, but she didn't answer, and he declined to leave a message on the server.

So Rajban had left! So what? Why did Cody have to act like it was the end of the world? Rajban had *chosen* to leave. She had walked freely out the door.

Michael wished she had not, but wishing couldn't change the decision she had made.

He wondered what her reasoning had been. Perhaps she preferred whatever small life Rao might offer her to the strangeness she had glimpsed here. Illiteracy was a barrier that kept her from a knowledge of the wider world. Access to information was another hurdle. So she had returned to the life she knew. It was probably as simple as that. Rao's messenger arrived at the door after only a few minutes. Michael listened to the price he quoted, then he put a call through to his bank, adjusted the worth on a cash card, and handed it over, letting the house record the transaction. He had promised to pay for Rajban's AIDS treatment, after all. And she was better off with her family, wasn't she?

He told himself it had all been a misunderstanding.

■

On the long walk back to the house of her brother-in-law, Rajban could feel the sickness growing inside her. It was a debilitating weakness, a pollution in her muscles, dirt in her joints. By the time she reached the house she was dazed and exhausted, with a thirst that made her tongue swell. As she crossed the threshold behind the men, Mother-in-Law glared, first at Gharia, then at Rajban. She asked Rao if it had been agreed that a dowry should be paid. Rao shrugged. He sat at a table, ignoring everyone, even Gharia, who stood by looking confused and a little angry. "We wait," Rao said.

Inside the house the air was very still, a puddle of heat trapped under the ancient, seeping walls. Mother-in-Law turned on Rajban. "No water. No!" she said, cutting her off from the plastic cube with its spigot, that sat upon hollow concrete blocks and held the day's supply of water. "Out! You have work. There is work, you stupid girl."

Rajban felt dizzied by the swirling motion of Mother-in-Law's hands. She stumbled back a step.

"Won't you let her drink?" Gharia asked softly.

Rajban cast him a resentful glance. Oh yes. He had an interest in her now. Or he imagined he did. Michael's house had told her what was said on the doorstep. She blushed in shame again, remembering the words Rao had spoken.

He had painted her with those words. He had painted her past. *Dirty whore.* Her polluted body testified to it. And why else would all this have happened to her? What Rao said had felt just like the truth. Michael would not want to look at her now that he knew, and Muthaye could never come to visit her again—but Rao had offered her sanctuary.

Of course there would be no dowry. She thought it strange that Gharia didn't understand this. Rao scowled at him. Then he scowled at Mother-in-Law, standing guard by the water cube. "Women's business," he growled.

"Get out!" the old woman screeched at Rajban, now that she was sure she had permission. "No one has done your work for you, foolish girl." Under the assault of her flailing hands, Rajban stumbled into the courtyard. She looked around. The courtyard seemed strange, as if she had dreamed this place and the life she had lived here.

Heat steamed from the moist ground. The plants were wilted in their containers. She shared their thirst, and, using the dirty wash water stored in a small barrel by the door, she set out to allay it.

■

Michael took a zip to the office to find Pallava Sen waiting for him in the lobby. "Good morning, Michael! Our bioremediation consultant called a few minutes ago to say she will not be able to attend today."

"Cody called?" Michael's voice cracked with the force of his surprise.

"Yes. Of course I've been consulting with her throughout the night, so I'll have no problem directing the media gig."

They matched strides through the security sensors. Armored doors opened for them. An elevator stood waiting on the other side. "Be assured, everything is in place," Pallava continued, as the doors closed and the elevator rose. "We have technicians from New Delhi to handle the bacterial cultures. Several media teams are already at the airport, and within a few hours an international task force will be here to examine the complaints against us, and our countercharges of fraud against the local water commission."

They stepped out into the carpeted hallway on the top floor, greeted by the scent of fresh coffee. "When will the water purification units be here?" Michael asked.

"The first shipment is due to arrive within the hour. They'll be set up in stations throughout the district. People will be able to withdraw five gallons at a time—enough for drinking, anyway."

"Excellent." At least people could start drinking clean water now, today, for the first time since . . .

He sighed. Probably for the first time ever.

Someone had left a steaming cup of coffee on the desk. "Pallava, thank you. I know you've been up most of the night with this situation. It sounds as if you have things well under control." Then, because he couldn't help himself, he added, "When you talked to Cody just now, did she . . . sound all right?"

Pallava frowned, his eyes narrowing suspiciously. "She sounded tired, but then she has worked through the night as well. There's no need to worry, Michael. Let her rest. I can handle the gig."

"That's not what I meant. Pallava, I know you can do it. I want you to handle the press conference, too. It's your scene now."

■

Rajban crouched in the shade just outside the kitchen door, patting dirty water on her cheeks and breast. Inside, Gharia and Rao were talking heatedly. Gharia was saying, "Fielding will pay. You'll see. He wants the woman to have medicine so that—"

Gharia broke off in mid-sentence. Startled, Rajban glanced over her shoulder to see if someone had spied her, resting in the shade. No one looked out the door. Instead, she heard a stranger speaking from inside the house, crowing about the cleverness of Rao's demands. This was the messenger sent to collect the dowry.

"Give the money to my son," Mother-in-Law interrupted, her old voice tight and frightened, as if she feared a rebuke for her boldness, but couldn't help herself nonetheless.

Rajban peeked around the edge of the doorway, to see Rao still seated at the table, Gharia still standing. Both he and the messenger stared hungrily at the cash card Rao twirled in his hands. Then Rao's long fingers closed over the card, hiding it from sight. His face was fleshy, and yet it was the hardest face Rajban had ever seen. "You may both go now." Gharia looked confused. "We need to discuss the finances, the wedding, and—"

"There will be no wedding," Rao announced. "My brother's widow must be subjected to no further shame."

Rajban slipped back behind the wall. The garden looked so queer, as if she had never seen it quite so clearly before. Inside, Gharia's voice was rising in indignant anger, but Rajban did not listen to the words, knowing that nothing he might say could change her fate.

■

Pallava Sen had hardly left when Muthaye's glyph winked on in the corner of Michael's shades. He tapped his glove, transferring the call to a wall screen. Muthaye snapped into existence. She stood in Michael's living room, her stern face framed by a printed sari, which she had pulled over her head like a scarf. In her hand, she held Rajban's half-empty bag of soil.

Michael's gaze caught on it. "Rajban has gone."

Muthaye's lips pursed petulantly. "I am at the house, Michael. I can see that. Where has she gone?"

Michael felt inexplicably guilty as he made his explanation. He did not feel any better as he watched Muthaye's expression darken. Her eyes rolled up, beseeching the heavens for patience, perhaps. Then she spoke: "Mr. Fielding, I would be interested to someday engage you in a discussion of free will. What does it really mean? You tell me that Rajban *chose* to leave with this Rao character, her brother-in-law who treated her as less than human even as you looked on. Mr. Fielding, can you tell me why she *freely chose* to go with him?"

Michael scowled, feeling unfairly impeached, by Muthaye and by Cody, too. "I suppose she felt torn from her roots. Most people are, by nature, afraid of change."

Muthaye's scowl deepened. "Rajban did not suffer a failure of nerve, Mr. Fielding."

"I didn't say—"

"No, of course. You wouldn't say such a thing. You are a kind person, Michael, and obviously you've done well in life. It's only natural that you believe opportunity is omnipresent, that we all rise or sink according to our talents and our drive—but the world is more complex than that. Talent is meaningless when we are schooled in the belief that change is wrong, when we are taught that we are worthy of nothing more than the ironbound existence fate has given us. Believe me, Rajban has been well-schooled in her worthlessness. She knows that she lives at the sufferance of her husband's family. Obedience and acceptance have been drilled into her from babyhood. To expect her to freely *decide* to defy her brother-in-law would be like expecting a drug addict to freely decide to stay sober at a crack party. There is no difference.

"And it is partly my fault, too, for I laughed yesterday when she suggested this soil had a magic." Muthaye lifted the stained cloth bag. "Perhaps it does. I have talked to a horticultural specialist and he is intrigued. He tells me there may be valuable microorganisms in this dirt. I will have it tested, and I will not laugh at naïve optimism ever again."

"Muthaye—"

She raised her palm. "Michael, I apologize for lecturing you, but you must begin to see that to dream is itself a learned skill."

Stop her! For once in your life . . .

Michael sighed. "I gave Rao money to pay for the AIDS treatment." That was something, at least.

Although from the way Muthaye glared at him, it might have been worse than nothing. He scowled, irritated now. "Was that wrong too?"

"There will be no treatment."

Michael felt his patience snap. Really, he'd had enough. "You don't know that. She was to be married again—"

"Did Gharia pay the dowry?"

"No, but it was understood—"

"I expect none of you understood the same thing. You each heard only what you could tolerate. Understand this, Michael. Rajban is the childless wife of a dead man. Rao can gain nothing by letting her marry. He will refuse her the AIDS treatment and keep the money for himself. Mark my words: If we do not find Rajban and get her out of her brother-in-law's house, then she will die there, most likely in a matter of days."

■

Cody linked into the Terrace on a full sensory connection. The private VR chat room had been designed as a flagstoned California patio, embedded in a garden of pepper trees and azaleas. Everyone had a personal animation stored on the server, an active, three-dimensional image of themselves that reflected their habitual postures and gestures, so they would seem to be present even when they weren't fully linked through a VR suit.

Cody's image looked a good deal younger than it ought to—a sharp reminder of how many years had gone by since she'd visited the Terrace. The last time had been during those nebulous months between the abortion and the divorce. Not the best of days, and returning now made her feel a bit queasy.

Still, she had come with a purpose. She set about it, sending a glyph to Etsuko, Ryan, and Jaya, asking them to come if they could—and within a minute, they were all represented. Etsuko was involved in a meeting, so she sent only a passive image of herself to record the chat: an alabaster statue dressed in formal kimono. Her flirtatious eyes and the cant of her head as she looked down from a pedestal gave an impression of sharp and regal attention.

Ryan and Jaya were able to interact in real time. Their images lounged in the French patio chairs behind steaming cups of coffee. Jaya had a half-smile on her face. Ryan looked uncertain. He and Michael were very close, Cody knew, and questions of loyalty were probably stirring in his mind.

She drew a deep breath. "Thank you for coming. Jaya, Michael told me about your newest daughter. Congratulations."

"That was an adventure!" Jaya said. "I don't know what I would have done without Michael. He's a wonderful man."

Cody felt herself stiffen. "He is a good man, but he made a mistake this morning when he let Rajban return to her husband's family."

"The girl who's been staying with him?" Ryan asked. "But that's good, isn't it?"

"No," Michael said.

Cody turned, to find Michael's image standing a few steps to the side.

"Cody's right. I made a mistake. I didn't want to believe this was an abusive situation."

"I'm afraid for her," Cody said. "Michael, we need to find her as soon as we can. I came here to ask the Terrace for help. I know I have not been part of this group for many years, but I still trust you all more than anyone, and you're already familiar with Rajban. Will you help? I've rented two drone planes. I know you're busy, but if you could rotate shifts every few minutes, the three of you might be able to guide one plane, while I inhabit the other. We don't know where she lives, but we know some things about her."

Michael said, "I'm opening up the Global Shear census data. That'll speed things up. When we do find her, Muthaye and I will go after her on the ground."

■

Inside the house there were oranges on the table, and clean water, and sweetened tea, but no one invited Rajban in. She stole a half-ripe orange off one of the trees. Its rind was swirled with green and the flesh was grimly tart, but she ate it anyway, her back to the house. She wondered at herself. She had never stolen fruit before. In truth, she did not feel like the same person.

The orange peels went into her heap of magic soil.

Muthaye had laughed at the idea that it might be magic.

Rajban picked up a damp clump. It was soft and warm, and smelled of fertility. If magic had a smell, this would be it; yet Muthaye had laughed at the idea.

Rajban rocked back and forth, thinking about it, and about Muthaye's mother and her dead baby girl. It was better the baby had died. A girl without a father would only know hardship, and still it must have been a terribly painful thing. For a moment, she held the baby in her arms, acutely aware of its soft breath and warm skin, its milky smell. When she thought about it dying, grief pushed behind her eyes.

Muthaye's mother had married again . . . and had another daughter. Not a son, but the school she owned earned money, so perhaps she could afford a daughter.

She was just like you, Rajban.

What did that mean? Rajban did not feel at all like the same person. There was an anger inside her that had never been there before. It felt like a seed planted under her heart, and it was swelling, filling with all the possibilities she had seen or heard of in the last two days.

Her fists clenched as the seed sprouted in a burst of growth, rooting deep down in her gut and flowering in her brain, thriving on the magic soil of new ideas.

■

Cody was a point of awareness gliding over the alleys and lanes of Four Villages. Linked to the GS census, the town became a terrain of information. Addresses flashed past, accompanied by statistics on each building and the families that owned them—occupation, education, income, propensity for paying taxes. At the same time the drone's guidance program spun a tiny camera lens, recording the people in the streets, sending their images to the GS census, where a search function matched them against information on file, spitting back identifications in less than a second.

No way this search could be legal. There had to be privacy strictures on the use of the GS census data.

What did privacy mean anymore?

It didn't matter. Not now. Cody only wanted to find the combination of bits that would mean Rajban.

Rajban was a nonentity. She did not appear anywhere in the census—and that was a clue in itself.

Some heads of households refused to answer the census questions, forcing the field agent to guess at their names and family members. Michael had used that fact in his search parameters. It was likely such a house was in a fundamentalist neighborhood and that it had an intensely cultivated private courtyard, where a young wife could be hidden from an agent's prying eyes . . . but not from the eyes of a drone aircraft.

The plane was powered by micropumps that adjusted its internal air pressure, allowing it to sink and rise and glide through the heated air. The pumps were powered by solar cells on the plane's dorsal surface, backed up by tiny batteries built into its frame. It could stay aloft for months, maybe for years. Its only drawback was that it was slow.

Cody's fingernails had dug crescent impressions in her data glove by the time the drone cruised over the first household on Michael's list. A woman was hanging laundry in the shade, but she was older than Rajban, with two children playing near her feet. At the next house the courtyard was empty, and the garden it contained was yellow and sickly. Cody tapped her glove, sending the plane on.

Recorded names and faces slid past her, until finally, the camera picked out a familiar face. *"Gharia."* The GS census confirmed her guess.

Cody ordered the drone lower. It hovered over the street as Gharia stumbled along, head down, each sandaled foot ramming into the mud like a crutch, while chickens scurried to get out of his way and children ran indoors, or behind their mothers until he passed. Rage and helplessness were twisted into his posture. Cody's heart rate tripled, knowing something terrible had happened.

The drone's shadow was a cross in the mud. Gharia saw it and pulled up short. He looked up, while Cody let the plane sink lower.

She had expected to hate him, but now, seeing the pain and

confusion in his eyes, she could feel only a desperate empathy. The old ways were dissolving everywhere. Her own tangled expectations neatly echoed his.

Then Gharia crouched. Still staring at the plane, he groped blindly, clawing a fistful of mud from the street. Cody's eyes widened as he jumped to his feet and flung the mud at the plane. Just a little extra weight could upset the plane's delicate balance. She started to order it *up*, but the guidance AI responded first, activating micropumps that forced air out of the fuselage. The plane shot out of reach, and Gharia became a little man.

He threw his head back. He opened his mouth in a scream she could not hear. His shoulders heaved as he looked around for some object upon which to vent his rage. He found it in the white cart of a water station being set up at the end of the street. The startled technician stumbled back several steps as Gharia attacked the cart, rocking it, kicking at it, but it was too heavy to turn over. Even the plastic frame would be very hard to dent.

After a minute of frantic effort, Gharia gave up. Chin held high, he walked away through a crowd of bemused spectators, as if nothing had happened.

Cody touched her belly, wondering if there was life growing in there, and if it was a boy or a girl—if it would die, or live.

What difference is there, between me and this unhappy man?

Both of them had let antique expectations twist the balance of their lives.

■

A winged shadow passed over the courtyard. Rajban looked up from where she crouched in the shade of the mandarin tree. Her hands left off their work of pulling tiny weed seedlings from the mossy soil. Squinting against the glare, she searched the sky. There. It was the little airplane that had flown over Michael's house, blue like the sky and very hard to see. More like a thought than any solid thing.

She reached to touch the necklace her mother had given her, before remembering it was gone. The life she'd lived before was fading, and she was not the same person anymore.

When she first came to her husband's house this thriving mandarin tree had been ill. The soil in which it was rooted had been unclean, until she tended it, until she prayed the magic into existence. A worm had hatched from the barren dirt, and the mandarin tree had been reborn, no longer the same tree as before.

Rajban felt that way: as if she had been fed some potent magic that opened her eyes to undreamed possibilities. Perhaps Muthaye's mother had felt this way too?

Rajban rose unsteadily to her feet. The heat of her fever was like a slow funeral fire, made worse because she had been allowed no water. Her mouth felt like ashes. No matter. Like Muthaye's mother, she was ready to step away from this empty round of life.

■

Michael waited with Muthaye in the cramped passenger seat of an air-conditioned zip. The driver had parked his vehicle between two market stalls set up under a spreading banyan tree. Young men lounged in the shade, eating flavored ice. Michael idly watched three tiny screens playing at once in his shades. Two were the feeds from the searching drones. The third was the bioremediation demonstration out at Kanwal's farm.

There was Kanwal, hungrily watching Pallava explain the activity of the technicians gathered around the well. Kanwal's ambitions were an energy, waiting to be shaped.

"Michael!"

Cody's tense voice startled him. His gaze swept the other two screens, and he caught sight of Rajban, gazing upward, her golden face washed in the harsh light of the noon sun.

"Michael, we've found her."

He whooped in triumph. "She looks all right!"

Muthaye squeezed his arm. "Why is she outside at noon? It's so terribly hot. Look at her cheeks. Look how flushed they are. We must hurry." She leaned forward, to tell the address to the driver of the zip.

The driver's eyes widened. Then he laughed in good humor. "I no go there. Too many of the politics there. Don't like any new way. Throw mud my zip."

Muthaye sighed. "He's right. It's a bad neighborhood. Michael, you won't be welcome there."

"If it's that kind of neighborhood, you won't be welcome either. You'll be as foreign as me."

A ghost of a smile turned her lips. "Maybe not quite so, but—"

"I can't send a security team in, you understand? This isn't company business, and I've already stretched my authority by using the census. But I can go after her myself."

"We can both go after her," Muthaye said. She used a cash card to pay the driver. "I only hope she is willing to leave."

■

The silent drone floated above the courtyard. From this post, Cody looked down and saw that something had changed. Rajban had moved out of the shade of the little potted tree. She stood in the sunshine now, her back straight, no sign of timidity in her posture. Her gaze was fixed on the house. She seemed in possession of herself and it made her a different person. The timorous girl from Michael's garden was gone.

Cody swallowed against a dry throat. Clearly, Rajban intended something. Cody feared what it might be. A woman who has been cornered and condemned all her life should not protest, but Rajban's obedience had been corrupted—by the whisperings of Muthaye, by her glimpse of a different life.

Cody felt as if she watched herself, ready to burst in the close confines of Victoria Glen. She wanted to cry out to Rajban, tell her to wait, not to take any risks . . . but the plane had no audio.

Rajban stepped toward the house with a clean, determined stride.

Cody ordered the drone to follow. The micropumps labored and the plane sank, but with excruciating slowness. It was only halfway down when Rajban disappeared inside.

■

Muthaye hid her face with her sari. She walked a step behind Michael but no one was fooled. Change had risen in a slow flood over Four Villages, dissolving so many of the old ways, but here was an island. The people of Rao's neighborhood had resisted the waters, throwing up walls of hoary tradition to turn the flood away. It was as if history had run backward here. Girls received less schooling every year, they were married at younger and younger ages, they bore more children . . . or at least they bore more sons.

The sex selection implant was an aspect of modernity that had worked its way inside the fundamentalist quarter. It was a breach in the walls that must ultimately bring them tumbling down . . . but not on this day.

Michael walked at a fast, deliberate pace, following the directions whispered to him by Jaya as she watched from the second drone aircraft. He felt the stares of unemployed men, and of hordes of boys munching on sweets and flavored ice. Tension curled around him like a bow wave.

A link came in from his chief of security. "Mr. Fielding, I don't like this at all. Let me send some people in."

"No," Michael muttered, keeping his voice low, trying not to move his lips. "Sankar, you send your people in here, you're going to touch off a riot. You know it."

The brand of fundamentalism didn't matter, and it didn't even need a religious affiliation. Michael had encountered the same irrational situation as a boy when he'd gotten off the bus at the wrong stop, finding himself in a housing project where the presence of a prosperous mixed-race kid was felt like a slap against the hip-hop culture.

Fundamentalism was so frightening because it taught the mind to *not* think. Such belief systems cramped people's horizons, sabotaging rational thought while virulently opposing all competitive ideas.

Michael heard Muthaye gasp. He turned, just as a clump of mud hit him in the cheek. A pack of boys hanging out at the entrance of a TV theater erupted in wild laughter. "Keep walking," Muthaye muttered through gritted teeth. Mud had splashed across her face. Her sari was dirtied. More clumps came flying after them. Michael wanted to take her arm, but that would only make things worse. Boys jeered. They made kissy noises at Muthaye. A few massaged their crotches as she passed.

Jaya was watching over them from the drone. "Turn here," she said, her voice tight. "There is hardly anyone in the alley to your left. All right, now go right—walk faster, some of the boys are following you—keep going, keep going. Turn again! Left. There. Now you're out of their sight."

"How much farther?" Muthaye whispered into the open line. Michael glanced back over his shoulder, but the boys were not in sight.

■

Mother-in-Law looked up as Rajban stepped across the threshold. Surprise and anger mingled in her wrinkled face as she scurried to guard the water cube. Rao pretended not to notice. *Women's business.*

Rajban drew a deep breath. The little airplane had been a sign, pure as the searing sky, that the time had come to follow Muthaye's mother into another life. So, without looking at Mother-in-Law again, she walked past her. She kept her face calm, but inside her soul was trembling. Rajban passed the table. She approached the door. Only then did Rao admit her existence. "Stop." His voice ever stern. "Get back to your work."

Her insides felt soft and hot as she told herself she did not hear him. She took another step, then another, the concrete floor warm and hard against her toes.

"I said stop."

The doorway was only five steps away now, a blazing rectangle, like a portal to another existence. Rajban walked toward it, her steps made light by the tumbling rhythm of her heart.

Rao stepped in front of her, and the light from the doorway went out.

Rajban made no effort to slip around him. Instead she reached for her sari and pulled it farther over her head, so that it partly concealed her face. Then she stood motionless, in silent protest.

■

At last.

The drone dropped to the level of the doorway. Through the cameras, Cody gazed into the house—and could not believe what she was seeing.

Rajban was walking out. She was heading straight for the door. Cody watched her pass the flustered old woman, and the table where Rao sat. It seemed certain she would reach the door, when abruptly, Rao rose to his feet. In two steps he stood in front of Rajban, blocking her exodus. Rajban stopped.

For several seconds nothing more happened. Rajban stood in calm serenity, refusing to yield or to struggle. It had the flavor of a Gandhian protest, an appeal to the soul of the oppressor. Rao did not seem to like the taste of guilt. Outrage convulsed across his face. Then Cody saw a decision congeal.

Warmth fled her gut. What could she do? She was half a world away.

"Michael," she whispered. "It would be good if you were here now."

"Two or three more minutes," Jaya said. "That's all."

It was too much.

Cody ordered the drone forward. The autopilot guided it through the door, its wingtips whispering scant millimeters from the frame.

She could not defend Rajban, but she could let Rao know that Rajban was no longer alone.

Rajban kept her head down, knowing what would happen, but so much had changed inside her she could not turn back. Her heart beat faster, and still the expected blow failed to arrive.

Cautiously, she raised her eyes—to encounter a sheen of unexpected blue. The little airplane! It hovered at her shoulder like a dream image, so out of place did it seem in the hot, cloistered room. Brother-in-Law stared at it as if he faced his conscience.

The tiny plane had summoned Rajban with its color like the searing sky. Wordlessly, it now advised her: *Time to go.*

So she straightened her shoulders and stepped to the side, circling Rao until the doorway stood before her again. She walked toward it, through it, on unsteady legs, out into the mud of the street. The little airplane cruised past her, floating slowly back up into the blue. Brother-in-Law started shouting . . . at Mother-in-Law? Rajban didn't stay to find out. She stumbled away from the house, not caring where her feet might take her.

"Rajban!"

She turned, startled to hear her name. "Michael?"

The street was crowded with women moving in small, protective groups. Hard-eyed men lounged beside the shop fronts across the street, watching the women, or haggling over the price of goods, or sipping sweetened teas. Flies buzzed above the steaming mud.

"Rajban."

Michael emerged from the crowd, with Muthaye close behind him. She called out Rajban's name, then, "Namaste."

"Namaste," Rajban whispered.

Muthaye took her arm. Above her veil, her eyes were furious. "Come with us?"

Rajban nodded. Some of the men around them had begun to mutter. Some of the women stopped to stare. Muthaye ignored them. She stepped down the street, her head held high, and after they'd walked for a few minutes, she tossed back her sari and let the sunlight fall upon her face.

XV

Cody relinquished control of the drone, leaving it to return like a homing pigeon to the rental office. She lifted off her VR helmet to find herself seated in her darkened living room, the lights of Denver and its suburbs gleaming beyond the window. She felt so scared she thought she might throw up.

There was a ticking bomb inside her.

She imagined a fertilized egg descending through one of her fallopian tubes, its single cell dividing again and again as it grew into a tiny bundle of cells that would become implanted against the wall of her womb. With a few hormonal triggers this nascent life form would change her physiology, so that her body would serve its growth. Quite a heady power for an unthinking cluster of cells, but as it reordered its environment, it would begin to shed evidence of its identity. Very early in gestation the uterine implant would classify it *desirable* or *undesirable*, and would act accordingly.

Cody laid her hand against her lower abdomen. She imagined she could feel him inside her, a bundle of cells with the potential to become a little boy. She remembered Gharia standing in the street, looking up at her with utter confusion, with helpless rage. He had tried too hard to hold onto the past and the world had gotten away from him.

Live lightly.

She felt as if she could hardly breathe. Her shoulders heaved as she struggled to satisfy her lungs. Air in, air out, but none of it absorbed. She felt as if she might drown, trapped in the close confines of her apartment. So she found her shades and called a cab.

■

If we are lucky, life shows us what we need to see.

Cody snorted. It was one of the many inspirational aphorisms drilled into her at Prescott Academy. And how had that particular pearl of wisdom concluded? Ah, yes:

If we are brave, we dare to look.

Cody was not feeling terribly brave right now, and that was why she was running away. The cab took her to the airport, and from there an air taxi took her north. Upon landing, she picked up a rental car, arriving at Project 270 just before dawn.

An ocean of cold air had settled over the land. Though she wore boots and blue jeans, a thermal shirt and a heavy jacket, she still felt the bite of the coming winter as she stumbled through the darkness. A flash of her company badge soothed the security system. Ben would not be by for two or three hours, so she made her way alone to the upper gate, where she found the card slot by feel. The gate unlatched and she slipped inside.

The sky was a grand sweep of glittering stars, and in their light she could just make out the slope of the land. A few house lights gleamed far, far away across the river. Leaving the ATV in the garage, she set out down the long slope of the meadow, stumbling over clumps of sod and seedling trees. The meadow grasses were heavy with dew, and when their seed heads brushed her thighs they shed freezing jackets of water onto her jeans, so that in less than a minute she was soaked through. She kept walking, listening to her socks squish, until she reached the bluff above the river bank.

The sky was turning pearly, and already birds were stirring in a lazy warm-up song. At the foot of the bluff, a doe hurried along the narrow beach, while the river itself grumbled in a slow, muddy exhalation that went on and on and on, a sigh lasting forever. Cody shivered in the cold. *Can't run any farther.*

It was time to discover what she had done, get the truth of it.

So many chronic problems came from not facing the truth.

She slipped her shades out of her jacket pocket and put them on. They were smart enough to know when they were being used. A menu appeared against the backdrop of the river. Tapping her data glove, she swiftly dropped the highlight down to "U." Only one listing appeared under that letter:

"Upload status report," she whispered. "And display."

Even then, fear held her back. She let her gaze fix on the river, its surface silvery in the rising light. Steam curled over it, phantom tendrils possessed of an alien motion, curling, stretching, writhing in a slow agony lovely to watch.

Lines of white type overlay the prospect. For several seconds

Cody pretended not to see them. Then she drew a deep breath, and forced her gaze to fix on the words:

Status: No pregnancy detected.

Action: None.

She stared at the report for several seconds before she could make sense of it.

No baby. That made it easy . . . didn't it?

Her body did not feel the same. Somehow it had become hollow, forlorn. She stared at the water, wondering how something that had never existed could have felt so real.

The doe gave up its stroll on the beach to climb the embankment, stirring ahead of it a flight of blackbirds that spun away, trilling and peeping, noisy leaves tumbled on a ghostly wind. Cody remembered the painful confusion on Gharia's face as he stood in the street, looking up at her. She had seen herself in his eyes, asking, *why?*

A figment of mist curled apart and she laughed softly, at herself and at the strained script she had tried to write for her life.

Gharia had wanted a scripted life, too, except half the cast had vanished.

It was the same all over the world. Virtually every culture encouraged loyalty to social roles . . . but why was it done that way? Because there was some innate human need to eliminate chance? Or because it saved conflict, and therefore the energy of the group? Even as it wasted intellect and human potential. . . .

The world was evolving. Energy was abundant now, and maybe, the time had come to let the old ways go, and to nurture a social structure that would unlock the spectrum of potential in everyone.

Starting here, Cody thought. She looked again at the menu, where UTERINE IMPLANT remained highlighted.

"Shut it down," she whispered.

The letters thinned, indicating an inactive status.

Cody started to slip off the shades, but she was stopped by the sudden appearance of Michael's glyph within an urgent red circle, meaning *Please please please talk to me NOW.*

Her throat had begun to ache in the cold air, but she tapped her data glove anyway, accepting the link. Michael's glyph expanded until it became his image. He stood in the open air beyond the bluff, remote from her, though she could see every detail of his face. "Michael? Has something happened to Rajban?"

"Rajban's all right." He squinted at her. "I can't see you."

"I just have shades."

His scowl was ferocious. "Then I borrowed this VR suit for nothing." She waited for him to get over it. After a moment his body relaxed. He turned, to look down at the silvery path of the river. "We did the right thing, Cody. Rajban is set now, in a house with two other women. She'll probably do garden work. You know the bag of soil she carried? Turns out to be a natural bioremediation culture, a community of microorganisms fine-tuned for the pollutants particular to the soil around Four Villages. Muthaye thinks it might be possible for Rajban to sell live cultures, or at least to use it to enhance her own business."

"That's good. I'm glad." She felt a fresh flush of wonder at the adaptiveness, the insistence of life. She toed a clod of exposed soil on the bluff. Contamination had been rampant in this land, too, but it had been chased away, broken down in a series of simple steps by microorganisms too small to be seen. The scars of the past were being erased.

"Where are you?" Michael asked. "It's beautiful here."

"At a project site. It is pretty, but it's also very cold. I should head back to the car."

He stiffened. "If you're thinking of running away from me again, Cody, I might have some objection to that. It's been suggested to me that I give in too easily to other people's choices . . . when I know those choices are bad."

Her fingers drummed nervously against her thigh. A Canada goose paddled into sight, leaving a V wake unfurling behind it. "I really said that, didn't I?"

"Rajban chose to go. Should I have forced either one of you to stay?"

The goose had been joined by another. Cody's hands felt like insensate slabs of ice.

"I don't know."

"If we each can't be free to decide for ourselves—"

"I have used the same uterine implant you discovered in Four Villages, only it was my choice, and I wanted a daughter." She said it very quickly, the words tumbling over one another. "I've shut it off now, and . . . I'm not pregnant."

He stared at her. His stunned expression might have been funny if she didn't feel so scared. "Say something, Michael."

"I . . . wish I was there with you."

She closed her eyes, feeling some of the chill go out of the dawn.

XVI

Michael finished the day in his office, facing Karen Hampton on the wall screen. Outside, the sun was a red globule embedded in brown haze. Its rays cast an aging glow across his desk as he leaned forward—tense, eager, and a little scared—the same way he'd felt on his first flight out of the U.S.

He knew it was likely Karen would fire him. He didn't want it to happen, but that wasn't the source of his fear. He had done only what was needful, because trust comes first. So it wasn't Karen he feared. It was himself. He had lost some of his tolerance for the foibles and foolishness of human culture. He had learned to say *no*. It was a terrible, necessary weapon, and that he possessed it left him elated and afraid.

Karen stared at him for several seconds with eyes that might have been made of glass. "You have a unique conception of the responsibilities of a regional director."

Michael nodded. "It's been a unique day."

He watched the lines of her mouth harden. "Michael, you're in Four Villages because I felt it was an ideal setting for your creativity, your energy, and your ambition, but you seem to have forgotten your purpose. You are there to grow an economy, not to rescue damsels in distress."

Michael no longer saw a clear distinction between the two. "Damsels are part of the economy, Karen. *Everyone* matters and you know it. The more inclusive the system is, the more we all benefit."

"How does offending a significant segment of the population expand the system?"

"Because doing anything else would break it. You said it yourself. Trust comes first. If people can't trust us to support them in their enterprises, then we've lost. If we come to be known as cowards, then we fail. I'm not here to fail."

Four Villages was a microcosm of the world and it faced formidable problems—poverty, overpopulation, illiteracy, environmental degradation, and, perhaps worst of all, the poison of old ideas—but none of these challenges was insurmountable. Michael swore it to himself. *Nothing* was insurmountable. Terrible mistakes would be made, that was inevitable, but the worst mistake would be to pull back, to give up, to give in to the dead past.

"It's fear of change that's holding us back."

Change was coming anyway. The old world was being washed away, and soon there would be no paths left to follow. Then everyone would need to find their own way, like fishes or sleek eels, tracking ever-shifting currents, trailing elusive scents, nosing into the new possibilities of undreamed of futures.

Karen shook her head. "I love your thinking, Michael, but the hard fact is, this project is floundering."

Michael smiled, as the sun's last gleam finally vanished from the horizon. "No, Karen. It's just learning to swim." ■

Linda Nagata writes,

" 'Goddesses' had an unusual genesis. In its original version, it was written on commission for an anthology that was to showcase themes of globalization, emphasizing positive directions for both the future and for technology. The editors had a list of specific ideas they wanted to see in a story, but it was left to me to decide which ones to use, and to develop the theme, the setting, and the cast of chaaracters. It was an interesting experience—really, the only time I've had someone suggest a direction for my writing—but in the end the anthology failed to materialize. Fortunately, I was able to reclaim the story, and this time I rewrote it to my own specifications. I was pleased to find a home for it with Ellen Datlow at Scifi.com."

COMMENTARY: SCIENCE FICTION AND THE WORLD

There is a question I am often asked these days that always gives me fits. It goes something like this:

> Now that the twenty-first century is here, and the world more and more resembles a science fiction scenario, what will happen to the science fiction genre? What will be its role? And given this situation, what do you plan to do with your own science fiction?

I suppose it's a question that makes me think about too many things at once, and so I always fumble around trying to find a way to reply coherently. Indeed my work in this anthology has been another way of answering this question. But I thought I would pass the problem along to some of my colleagues. Here's what they said, arranged in the order that their replies came in, for reasons that will become apparent.

GWYNETH JONES

Gwyneth Jones is the author of *Divine Endurance*, *White Queen*, and *Bold As Love*, among many other books:

Fifty years later—fifty years, that is, since the story "The Sentinel" that became the 1968 movie—everyone's asking, especially in gatherings of science fiction folk, "What's happened to 2001?" Why don't we have any giant spaceships waltzing around? What happened to space exploration, and why is it taking so much longer than we thought? Why did tinfoil catsuits never catch on? Why didn't we ever reach the science fictional future that was promised to us?

But fictions of the forseeable future become real in sneaky and mysterious ways. Without going into how far Great Britain is still Airstrip One for the last remaining superpower, how much double-speak is used by our politicians, or how eager we are to let the TVs in the corners spy on us, let us examine, for a moment, this whole question of prediction. Let's look at convergencies, and divergencies, between the imaginary future and the reality, and think about how they happen.

What makes real futures different from imaginary ones? I like to speculate about a spooky law, not as yet proposed by science, whereby anything imagined becomes a real object in information space (which is the space of all spaces and the state of all states), and owing to local point phase conservation cannot then be duplicated in another part of information space, such as the material, human world in the middle of next week. This law is also known as the same thing can't happen twice, and it is why science fiction writers, even while extrapolating with immense care and using the greatest density of information the present can provide, will always get some vital feature the wrong way round, blurred, or misapplied. Thus Orwell's Big Brother concept, as we now know, was a stunningly accurate prediction, both technologically and philosophically . . . and yet, how different!

Consider another obstacle between science fiction and reality.

This is the problem of meaning, which can best be understood by considering the ratio between the author's intention and the rest of the content of a science fiction novel or story. The whole vast edifice of reality, the universe, and everything may have a single meaning that is known only to God. Down here among the details, we cannot hope to grasp the big plan. We can either place our blind faith in the hands of the Almighty, Science, Natural Selection, (insert here the macroscale concept of your choice), or give up worrying about the meaning of it all and concentrate on the soap opera of the passing day. A science fiction novel or story, however, has a meaning known to the author. Whether the narrative is a painstaking philosophical cathedral, or a crowd-pleasing yarn, it was written to a plan, and in the small world of a book (as opposed to the vast reaches of information space) there is nowhere for that plan to hide. Meaning becomes obtrusive (compared to the levels we find in reality) in a story three hundred pages long, even if the book is a literary novel about people having a soap opera time in Hampstead or Burnage. In the space of three hundred pages, where the author has elected to explain life, or consciousness, or theories of everything (typical projects among sf writers), meaning is so concentrated as to distort the most perceptive prediction to the point where it is almost unrecognizable. A very elegant example of the distortion caused by overdetermined meaning can be found by comparing genetic-futures science fiction with the Human Genome Project. The Genome Project offers us an extremely long list of a small number of letters of the alphabet representing chemical bases, which holds a tiny tincture of accessible meaning for medical research. Science fiction, on the other hand, offers us neo-feudalism, post-human speciation, and any amount of genetic-engineering immortality, super-intelligence, or psychic powers, with these developments invariably not merely imagined but pressed into service as metaphors for the human condition or as the engine of an action movie plot. Yet the stories and the Project are concerned with one and the same phenomenon, and the "facts" or "possible facts" are not in dispute. There may be problems as recalcitrant as the problems of space travel, between us and the real designer-baby world, but all the notions of the sf writers can be found supported in real-world scientific sources. If the overdetermined meaning imposed by dramatic form could be extracted from our mental experiments, it would soon be seen that sf prediction is frequently as accurate as local point phase conservation in information space allows—and sf writers could at last give up that sad, transparent "oh no no, it's not supposed to be about the future" line. Unfortunately, getting rid of the overdetermined meaning would be difficult to achieve without serious injury to the entertainment value of the narrative.

To an extraordinary degree, a whole palette of ideas that were strictly science fictional in 1988 has become the property of mainstream popular culture. Human cloning, robotics, artificial intelligence, computer hacking, Internet romance, deadly computer viruses, nanotechnology, virtual reality, animal organ transplants, gender role reversal, male childbirth, alien abduction, forensic genetics, apocalyptic disaster. It remains to be seen, fifty years after "The Sentinel," whether another palette will emerge—a new working space between the imagination and the possible—for a new generation of Arthur C. Clarkes, fiction-writing philosophers with a talent for practical extrapolation.

ANDY DUNCAN

Andy Duncan is the author of *Beluthahatchie and Other Stories*, and his novella "Fortitude" was a finalist for this year's Nebula.

In the 1930s and 1940s, the world was threatened by a mad supervillain commanding rockets, submarines, and robot legions, a formerly implausible figure straight from the brow of Edmond Hamilton, yet pulp sf, far from being shamed into silence by its sudden verisimilitude, went on to other topics and claimed a Golden Age. The ensuing decades brought one real-world science fictional development after another. The interstate highway system made manifest at every cloverleaf the airborne streams of traffic envisioned by all those Frank R. Paul covers. The star of *Hellcats of the Navy* was elected president of the United States, a conceit around which Pohl-Kornbluth or Mack Reynolds could have built a three-issue *Galaxy* serial. And so on ad infinitum. Yet the nuclear arms race and the Apollo program and the personal computer, all of which stole sf's ideas, didn't kill sf. It went on from strength to strength, through the second Golden Age of the 1950s, the New Wave, feminism, cyberpunk, etc.

So the notion that sf is doomed just because today's daily headlines and sound bites are about cloning, genetic engineering, virtual sex, and Mars exploration makes no sense, especially when one looks at all the terrific sf being published today and all the talented and zealous newcomers entering the field.

And yet there is an undeniable malaise among the sf rank and file, the SFWA members and con-goers and *Locus* subscribers and specialty-bookshop customers, that wasn't present even in 1994, when I entered the field. We're all running scared, not because there's no more future to write about, not because sf is no longer relevant, not because we've said all we have to say—none of those things is true—but because genre sf as we have known it these past seventy-five years is vanishing. By which I mean the club, the old neighborhood, the cozy set of institutions.

The circulations of the sf magazines are plummeting. Fandom is shrinking and aging, the younger generation of smart, disaffected joiners long since lured away by sexier pursuits—cult TV, RPGs, anti-WTO protests, Goth culture, GOP activism, webcams. Many sf bookstores, like many independent bookstores in general, have gone or are going out of business. Whether any writer, sf or not, will be able to profit from her work in the coming age of electronic publishing, when any kid with a laptop could conceivably be Random House, Barnes & Noble, and Stephen King combined, is very far from certain. The midlist sf writer able to make a living from solid but unspectacular sales and steady yearly production no longer exists. And the founders and shapers of our young genre—our teachers and mentors and, in a sense, parents—keep dying. We've been to a lot of funerals lately, we sf writers, and so we're gloomy.

So, what do I plan to do, amid all this professional doubt and uncertainty? I plan to keep writing whatever I want to write, whatever interests me; my own obsessions offer reasonably solid footing. And I reassure myself, as the old genre reassurances erode all around, with the recollection that I wept earnest tears of misplaced nostalgia at my high school graduation, unable at the time to imagine a life beyond. When I asked Frederik Pohl, several years ago, whether sf could survive the death of the sf magazines, he replied that it already had.

DAMON KNIGHT

Damon Knight is the founder of the Science Fiction Writers of America and author of many books, among the most recent of which is the wonderful *Humpty Dumpty: An Oval*.

It's true that we're living in a science fiction world (not an entirely comfortable place), but luckily it's only one science fiction world, and there are many others. This is just the World of Tomorrow, more or less as the world of yesterday imagined it. We still have all the planets of other stars and their strange inhabitants, and we have the inner worlds of strange mental powers and abilities, just as we did when everyone knew that science fiction was a wild branch of fantasy.

GENE WOLFE

Gene Wolfe is the author of the sublime sequences *The Book of the New Sun*, *The Book of the Long Sun*, and *The Book of the Short Sun*, among other work.

One day back in the sixties I sat down to listen to Damon Knight talk about the science fiction of the thirties and forties. He said something I have never forgotten, and that all of us should remember: "We have had their future."

In some respects that was true. In others, it was false. We have lost the backyard rocket ship. But we have lost it only for the present; there are people today who build their own airplanes. Any number of distinguished scientists once called the chess-playing computer utterly impossible. We have it now, but we have barely begun on artificial intelligence, a development sf has confidently predicted for almost a hundred years.

The handheld blaster (it used to be a ray gun) now appears possible, but we haven't got it yet.

Matter transmission? Not so you could notice.

An interstellar drive? No, but boy do we want one! Heck, we're still flying chemical rockets. (Talk about the dark ages . . .) Sf has confidently predicted nuclear rockets for more than fifty years.

Antigravity? 3D copying? Microbe-sized humans who can go into us to fix things? Contact with aliens?

Let's go back to the beginning. Brian Aldiss says sf began with *Frankenstein* by Mary Shelley. Her book turned on reanimating dead tissue. It's a wonderful idea—all those hearts and lungs and kidneys available for transplants. But we still can't do it. As far as I know, nobody's even *trying* to do it.

Others say sf began with *The Time Machine* by H. G. Wells. Comment would be superfluous.

Enough gadgets. What about the end of the traditional family? Ever-increasing regimentation? The deterioration of education and any number of other changes? We predicted them all—with much else that did not or has not yet come to pass. But now what? What about the people who must live with those changes? They are *our* future.

KATHLEEN ANN GOONAN

Kathleen Ann Goonan's novels include *Queen City Jazz*, *Mississippi Blues*, and *Crescent City Rhapsody*, which was a finalist for this year's Nebula Award:

The fact that the world has not only caught up to many sf scenarios—and has, in fact, bypassed many, leaving sf floundering in the wake of fulfilled or just slightly askew predictions—may call forth a new level of seriousness and realism in sf.

I don't believe that the role of sf, if a literature can be said to have a role, is predictive. Rather, sf has the opportunity to bridge the gap between what is happening on the cutting edge of various scientific fields and what the general public knows about the possibilities that may stem from new knowledge. Science fiction, at its best, is an intellectual endeavor that takes what humans know and what it is possible for humans to know to its limits and beyond. It is science transmuted into human possibilities, with all of the attendant emotions, using literature's complexity with complete self-awareness.

In the last century, technologies based on knowledge painstakingly gleaned from the physical world collapsed time and space in ways that changed the face of civilization. Our senses have been immensely enhanced; we can now see and hear what was formerly too distant, too small, too high, or too low to discern. Despite these changes—despite our computers, our cell phones, and our antibiotics—we are still the same humans we have been for millennia, although we have a lot of new toys, and healthier lives.

But we are now at the threshold of being able to alter our own biology and our own possibilities, as well as those of all other biological entities on the planet, in utterly radical ways. Technological possibilities and responsibilities are becoming more and more foregrounded in our lives, as has always been the case in the worlds of science fiction. Even consciousness studies have moved from their speculative, abstract, philosophical, and religious roots to the precise, scientific observation of complex physical processes.

All of the complexly intertwined socioeconomic forces we constantly use and remake and are subject to will play into the use we make of our burgeoning knowledge. Science fiction, which is one of these threads, is perhaps too delicate to be called a force. But it may, in all of its myriad forms, enhance our social consciousness and be a part of the continuing discussion of what such choices might mean. We are the single greatest wild card in our own future. The fragility of life and of our web of that connectedness may be violated in ways that have consequences that, as we are now, we are simply incapable of seeing. The best science fiction enhances our vision.

Exploration of what consciousness and intelligence are, enhanced knowledge of how we learn, and use of this understanding to better the lot of all people will, hopefully, be our collective future, despite inevitable setbacks, tragedies, and pitfalls. Related fictional scenarios, written to the utmost extent of my own literary ability, which focus on what makes us human, and what humanity might become and how humanity may affect the Earth, other planets, and the cosmos, is the direction my science fiction will take.

Now is the best of all possible times to be a science fiction writer.

KEN MACLEOD

Ken MacLeod's novels include *The Star Fraction*, *The Stone Canal*, and *Cosmonaut Keep*.

I spent the first seconds of the twenty-first century looking up at exploding fireworks through showers of beer and shouting, "Free at last!"

I don't suppose many people were any freer on January 1, 2001, than they were a day before, but I'm grateful that six billion of us have gotten out of the twentieth century alive. This new century doesn't feel like the future. It feels like an alternate world, and an unlikely one at that. We may be the improbable few who were still there when the box was opened, for whom the isotope didn't decay, the hammer didn't fall, and the poison stayed in the vial. Remember the Three-Minute War of 1979? Of course you do.

Genre sf is in the curious situation of being a victim of its own failure. Something that looks very like a brave little toaster goes to Mars. Fossil life is briefly thought to have been found in a Martian meteorite in Antarctica. A robot walks up stairs. A sheep is cloned. A lobster ganglion is uploaded. Sf is the language of headlines, of cinema listings, of computer games, even occasionally of bestselling books. In terms of literary worth, scientific truth, and present relevance, the genre is in a genuine Golden Age. Yet it remains as marginal and misunderstood as ever.

Something is not getting through. The value of science fiction will not be understood as long as the notion persists of Science Fiction Becoming Science Fact. Science fiction *never does* become science fact. Science fact owes almost nothing to science fiction. Science fact—the headline-grabbing installments of progress—owes everything to hard work, to theory and experiment and implementation, to the slog in the lab and in the field and proving ground.

Conversely, science fiction is neither vindicated nor discomfited by developments in science or society. The continued existence of Woking doesn't diminish Wells, and the absence of canals on Mars is no reflection on Bradbury. The vision of Clarke and Kubrick will shine long after the real 2001 has passed into history.

What sf enables us to do is not to foresee the future, but to entertain possibilities. The more possibilities science and technology—

[At this point, about 3:30 British Summer Time, 11 September 2001, the phone rang.]

I leave this piece as I wrote it, words from the old world.

PAUL MCAULEY

Paul McAuley, author of *Four Hundred Billion Stars*, *Fairies*, and *The Secret of Life*, among other novels, writes:

I'm writing this on the fourteenth of September 2001, just three days after the destruction of the World Trade Center on Bloody Tuesday. It happened at around 2:00 P.M. British time; all afternoon and evening, like billions of people around the world, I skipped from TV channel to TV channel, ghoulishly and with growing shameful unease surfing death porn, trying to find new images, trying to find out what was happening. I would instantly skip away when the coverage turned to punditry; I was not looking for opinion, but for something that would help me understand what was happening. Had two planes or three hit the World Trade Center? Had the White House been hit? Where was the president? How many hijacked planes were still aimed at American cities?

There was no time to imagine or reflect upon the terror of those trapped in the floors above the burning holes left by the crashed airliners, the panic and crushing heat on the stairwells, the anguish of relatives trying to contact loved ones. Apart from a few pictures of people fleeing collapsing waves of dust, everything seemed remote, eerily empty of emotion, a spectacle set at a safe distance. "Like a sci-fi movie," several commentators said. Yes, a movie: one in which we were all directors, searching for the moment when an airliner, turned by fanatics into a lo-tek cruise missile, plunged into a shining tower and left an airliner-shaped outline that suddenly blossomed with flame, looking for the perfect angle on the money shots of the towers wearily giving into gravity and with eerie precision collapsing into clouds of their own dust and smoke, like any one of those early failed rocket launches in *The Right Stuff*.

In the three days that have followed, the human stories have emerged. There are tales of heroism and unbearable fear and unendurable loss; there are the last phone calls on mobiles; there are the up-close video shots taken by tourists, by firefighters, by an heroic doctor emerging unscathed from cover close by the towers' collapse and immediately searching for those he could help. Slowly, a narrative structure is beginning to emerge from the smoky heart of disaster, although we are as yet no nearer to understanding it, or understanding the human minds which conceived it.

Fiction—and particularly science fiction—inhabits that gap between individual human narratives and the unfolding of gigantic impersonal disasters or processes. Yet with many of its tropes—clones, worldwide plagues, exploding or colliding spaceships, life on Mars—bleeding into the real world, science fiction seems to be turning its back on reality. Reality, as T. S. Eliot's little bird sang, is too much to bear. We're escaping instead into space opera fantasies, cosmological epics of deep time, and alternate histories where the unsatisfactory tangle of real history can be given the glossy sheen and neat endings of genre narrative, and our lost dreams can strut their stuff again, even if only as ghosts.

I don't mean to deride any of these things, especially as I'm as guilty of practicing them as any. But it seems to me that there's a gulf opening between science fiction and the real world, as of the widening gap of water between the shore and a ship set sail for elsewhere, elsewhen. If science fiction is to survive as a recognizable genre, rather than a colonized outpost of fantasy, I think it must attempt to continue to inhabit and map—and indeed bridge—that difficult space between the small movements of the human heart and the grander processes of history, of scientific discovery, of the whole wide world and the universe all around. If we don't continue to engage with the world—forcefully, passionately, critically, urgently—we're in danger of writing ourselves out of the very future we claim as our own.

NALO HOPKINSON

Nalo Hopkinson is the author of *Brown Girl in the Ring* and *Midnight Robber*, which was one of the finalists for this year's Nebula Award:

The twenty-first century is here. The scenes on my television screen last week, September 11, 2001, were not Hollywood FX, but real footage of suicide terrorists turning hijacked American planes into living bombs. As of the events of last week, one is tempted to say that the world suddenly resembles the description of the Last Days in the Book of Revelation, but the fact is that much of the rest of the world has been living through its own Armageddon for many years now. Terrorism of this magnitude so close to home may be news to me, but it is not news to the world.

I made an effort to keep writing through the horrible news of mass murder and destruction. At first I felt guilty. Sometimes we science fiction and fantasy writers disparage even our own work by calling it "only" entertainment. Come to think of it, we also disparage the word "entertainment" that way. Italian scientist Galileo Galilei had to entertain the notion that the universe might not revolve around the Earth before he could perceive that he was in fact correct. The black inventor Garrett Morgan had to first entertain the notion that it might be possible to rescue people overcome by noxious fumes before he could invent the gas mask that saved the lives of men trapped in underground mining accidents and of thousands of soldiers in World War One. More than two hundred years before the Renaissance, the German nun Hildegard of Bingen conceived the idea of writing down oral knowledge about natural history, herbs, and healing, including the first written reference to the use of hops in beer making and what may be the first written description of the female orgasm. Blessèd be.

So perhaps this notion of "entertaining" can be linked to the notion of conceiving, of creating. I kept writing because the novel which I'm creating, the novel which I hope will entertain a few ideas, talks in part about some of the effects of demonizing a whole race of people so that one then feels justified in abusing them in any way one sees fit. Perhaps it's a trivial undertaking next to rescuing people from the rubble of bombed buildings. Certainly it's way less immediate. But it's no less relevant, and even before the last bodies are buried (Gods, when will that be? We're considering taking more lives in some kind of misplaced attempt at revenge), we'll need to be thinking about what happened, and why, and what can be done. Sometimes those painful, personal thoughts are easier to entertain through the metaphorical removes of a story. Sometimes entertainment, being entertained, entertaining, is pretty damned tough work.

Now that life resembles science fiction, what use is it to keep writing science fiction? I think of Maureen F. McHugh's novel *Mission Child*, which follows the effects on one person's life of colonization of that person's world. I think of Samuel R. Delany's series *Neveryona*, with its illuminations of slavery, money, and the fetishization of both, and I know that Hildegard of Bingen, Garrett Morgan, and Galileo Galilei had the right idea—fact or fiction, real, imagined, or only guessed at: record it. Make something of it. Deliver a paper, apply for a patent, write a book, create something. But whatever you do, record the events that shape your times. Perhaps someone will learn from it, even if we don't.

JOHN CLUTE

John Clute, the great critic and encyclopedist of science fiction and fantasy, has recently published the novel *Appleseed*.

Writing at the end of September 2001 is writing afterwards. The nature of sf—like all our ways of making art—must necessarily change along with the world, in order to address some terrible new intimacy between works of imagination and the reality of things. The intimacy surely exists, a somehow shaming intimacy; an anxiety of shame (a phrase I'll return to) grips our imaginations when we sense reality aping our words. There is, perhaps, nothing new in this. Long before 11 September 2001, sf had already begun to make the new century, had already begun to cavitate the real into its own image. The disappearance into thin air nine hundred feet above the ground of six thousand human beings, this brightness falling from the air of America—with all the unendurable turns of horror that succeeded—had already been grasped in the claws of our minds. Our minds at "play."

This needs some unpacking.

I think we need a couple of centuries of running start. Here is the argument, in rough. I've offered it before elsewhere, and it takes off in any case from books like José B. Monleón's *A Specter Is Haunting Europe: A Sociohistorical Approach to the Fantastic* (1990); so a fast run-through should be enough. The argument begins with the premise that the birth of the genres of the fantastic—they include Gothic, horror, sf, fantasy, supernatural fiction—is intimately connected with the becoming visible of the engine of history, round about 1800, when the future began. Genres began when the creation of geological time and evolutionary change began to carve holes in reality, which became suddenly malleable;

when, for the first time, the human imagination could conceive of altering (as in the French Revolution) by fiat, both human nature and the world we inhabit. The future could now be almost literally perceived, though not understood. We felt this in our bellies. From this point, from about 1800 on, a new kind of anxiety began to haunt the Western world: a fear that the engines that we made to turn the world might shake us off, that we were both responsible for that engine and usurped by it, that Progress was not only a process we might predict, but a Dark Twin grinning at us out of tomorrow. That the world, which had been the palm of God, had become a raft.

The works that began to create the dominant genres of entertainment in the twentieth century—by writers like Horace Walpole and Mary Shelley; E. T. A. Hoffmann and Heinrich von Kleist and Ludwig Tieck; Victor Hugo; Nathaniel Hawthorne and Edgar Allan Poe; Nikolai Gogol; etc—were deeply stress-ridden assays of the new world. Hauntings, doubles, dark twins, revenants, untermenschen doppelgängers who digest the siblings who live in the light, Frankensteins who bring Promethean fire to the masses who then rise, clockwork men who shadow real folk: all these revealing stigmata of a profoundly anxious literature did not only express the obvious, they allayed the fears they dramatized. The deep consolations of Story displaced out of our bellies the hysterias endemic to a world changing, as it seemed, ungovernably.

This task of prophylaxis has continued until now, each of the genres of the fantastic handling the Anxieties of the Engine in varying manners. Horror treats the future as something that is already behind us, so that its Dark Twin dramas of digestion and desecration can be understood as *already lived through* by its readers; fantasy treats the present world as a *mistake* created by the engine of history, a mistake that must be refused through the creation of counterworlds and secret gardens as respite from the harrowing of the Shire; sf—which comes to maturity only in the twentieth century—treats the changing world as something that may be made to work, a brief we advocate, an egg we hope to instruct how to hatch.

We come to the century we now inhabit.

■

And here's the rub. Horror and fantasy fade into VR, which makes them sf. But sf remains a genre designed to allay anxieties about a world we cannot control. Its visions of making the world work are still grounded in terrors two centuries old that the world had become an engine we could not drive. But in 2001, these visions no longer simply compensate us for our mortal helplessness; they turn the world. Sf's unique capacity to advocate is now an engine capable (for we have become creatures of nearly infinite power) of shaping in the mind's eye, which is all that counts, the planet itself. Sf writers now have the capacity to marry the Word to the World, to transform the planet by giving the planet its marching orders.

Sf contains in itself the portents of terrible change. In September 2001, it seems very terrible to think that the sentences we write—the mission statements we issue—shape the world we write about, that what we write seems to be something like that which terrorists do, for sf novelists and terrorists have always treated the world as a story to be told. In 2001, that story is a story that is not only told but is the case. It is as simple and awful as that. We are the world. We would never literally create an act of terrorism, but the World Trade Center is the kind of sentence we write. This shames the imagination.

This shame—this anxiety of shame—is cognate with that felt by survivors in 1918 and in 1945. It is a shame that may suggest silence. But the difference between then and now is that we human beings, who lack the wisdom of gods, now have the strength of gods. We are the Word. We cannot afford to fall silent, not sf writers, not makers, not givers, not anyone. Everything depends on us, from now on. We are the Word. We are all going to die if we do not say something good.

GARDNER DOZOIS

That brings us, more appropriately than you might at first think, to Gardner Dozois.

Once or twice I've called Gardner Dozois "the mayor of science fiction," and I think this is a good way to express it, both to convey the notion of science fiction as a kind of hometown, and to suggest Dozois' central place within it. For nearly twenty years he has been editing both *Asimov's Science Fiction Magazine* and the largest of the Best of the Year anthologies, and by his choices he has done as much as anyone to influence the shape of the field. And all to the good: following a course charted out by his own early editor Damon Knight and predecessors such as Anthony Boucher, he has emphasized the combination of idea, character, and literary craft, so that the goal is to present stories that work by any criteria one could apply; so that, although science fiction does special things, there are no special dispensations for it.

His own fiction naturally reflects the same values. He has never been prolific, and much of his best work can be found in two recent collections, *Geodesic Dreams* and *Strange Days*. Sometimes his production of stories has reduced to one or two every few years. But the results suggest he now turns to his own fiction because he is impelled to it, and his recent stories reveal an ever-increasing urgency and conviction.

Never has this been clearer than in "A Knight of Ghosts and Shadows," one of the finest stories of his career. From the first heraldic image to the last, this is Dozois at his most intense, personal, and skillful. Again choices between human and machine are the subject, and if, after reading Williams's "Daddy's World," we are perhaps properly skeptical of the nature of the immortal downloaded intelligences confronting Dozois's protagonist, this only adds to the tensions of the tale, in the way that the genre's dialogues often do.

In this story, however, the allegorical weight has shifted in a different direction from "Daddy's World," and the story seems to me to be not only about how we should choose to live now, but how we might want to be remembered; what we should say to posterity; and whether any kind of immortal false life (not just downloading but literature) can ever compensate for our unavoidable mortality.

Gardner Dozois writes,

" 'A Knight of Ghosts and Shadows' is my take on two of the major areas of debate in science fiction in the '90s, the posthuman condition and the idea of living into a Vingean singularity (the possibility that sometime in the near future artificial intelligence will coalesce to a true and superhuman consciousness); I hope I've added something of value, at least in a small way, to the ongoing 'discussion' of those themes in fiction, one that I suspect will continue throughout the decade to come, if not for a lot longer.

"The opening pages of 'A Knight of Ghosts and Shadows,' by the way, were written more than twenty years ago, and it took me all that time to decide what to write *next*. If I hadn't kept them in my files, the story would never have been finished, which I hope will be a valuable lesson to young writers: always hang on to your old drafts! You never know when they'll suddenly come to life again."

A NIGHT OF GHOSTS AND SHADOWS

Gardner Dozois

Sometimes the old man was visited by time-travelers.

He would be alone in the house, perhaps sitting at his massive old wooden desk with a book or some of the notes he endlessly shuffled through, the shadows of the room cavernous around him. It would be the very bottom of the evening, that flat timeless moment between the guttering of one day and the quickening of the next when the sky is neither black nor gray, nothing moves, and the night beyond the window glass is as cold and bitter and dead as the dregs of yesterday's coffee. At such a time, if he would pause in his work to listen, he would become intensely aware of the ancient brownstone building around him, smelling of plaster and wood and wax and old dust, imbued with the kind of dense humming silence that is made of many small sounds not quite heard. He would listen to the silence until his nerves were stretched through the building like miles of fine silver wire, and then, as the shadows closed in like iron and the light itself would seem to grow smoky and dim, the time-travelers would arrive.

He couldn't see them or hear them, but in they would come, the time-travelers, filing into the house, filling up the shadows, spreading through the room like smoke. He would feel them around him as he worked, crowding close to the desk, looking over his shoulder. He wasn't afraid of them. There was no menace in them, no chill of evil or the uncanny—only the feeling that they were *there* with him, watching him patiently, interestedly, without malice. He fancied them as groups of ghostly tourists from the far future, *here we see a twenty-first century man in his natural habitat, notice the details of gross corporeality, please do not interphase anything*, clicking some future equivalent of cameras at him, how quaint, murmuring appreciatively to each other in almost-audible mothwing voices, discorporate Gray Line tours from a millennium hence slumming in the darker centuries.

Sometimes he would nod affably to them as they came in, neighbor to neighbor across the vast gulfs of time, and then he would smile at himself, and mutter "Senile dementia!" They would stay with him for the rest of the night, looking on while he worked, following him into the bathroom—*see, see!*—and trailing around the house after him wherever he went. They were as much company as a cat—he'd always had cats, but now he was too old, too near the end of his life; a sin to leave a pet behind, deserted, when he died—and he didn't even have to feed them. He resisted the temptation to talk aloud to them, afraid that they might talk *back*, and then he would either have to take them seriously as an actual phenomenon or admit that they were just a symptom of his mind going at last, another milestone on his long, slow fall into death. Occasionally, if he was feeling particularly fey, he would allow himself the luxury of turning in the door on his way in to bed and wishing the following shadows a hearty goodnight. They never answered.

Then the house would be still, heavy with silence and sleep, and they would watch on through the dark.

That night there had been more time-travelers than usual, it seemed, a jostling crowd of ghosts and shadows, and now, this morning, August the fifth, the old man slept fitfully.

He rolled and muttered in his sleep, at the bottom of a pool of shadow, and the labored sound of his breathing echoed from the bare walls. The first cold light of dawn was just spreading across the ceiling, raw and blue, like a fresh coat of paint covering the midden layers of the past, twenty or thirty coats since the room was new, white, brown, tan, showing through here and there in spots and tatters. The rest of the room was deep in shadow, with only the tallest pieces of furniture—the tops of the dresser and the bureau, and the upper half of the bed's headboard—rising up from the gloom like mountain peaks that catch the first light from the edge of the world. Touched by that light, the ceiling was hard-edged and sharp-lined and clear, ruled by the uncompromising reality of day; down below, in the shadows where the old man slept, everything was still dissolved in the sly, indiscriminate, and ambivalent ocean of the night, where things melt and intermingle, change their shapes and their natures, flow outside the bounds. Sunk in the gray half-light, the man on the bed was only a doughy manikin shape, a preliminary charcoal sketch of a man, all chiaroscuro and planes and pools of shadow, and the motion of his head as it turned fretfully on the pillow was no more than a stirring of murky darkness, like mud roiling in water. Above, the light spread and deepened, turning into gold. Now night was going out like the tide, flowing away under the door and puddling under furniture and in far corners, leaving more and more of the room beached hard-edged and dry above its high-water line. Gold changed to brilliant white. The receding darkness uncovered the old man's face, and light fell across it.

The old man's name was Charles Czudak, and he had once been an important man, or at least a famous one.

He was eighty years old today.

His eyes opened.

The first thing that Charles Czudak saw that morning was the clear white light that shook and shimmered on the ceiling, and for a moment he thought that he was back in that horrible night when they nuked Brooklyn. He cried out and flinched away, throwing up an arm to shield his eyes, and then, as he came fully awake, he realized when he was, and that the light gleaming above signified nothing more than that he'd somehow lived to see the start of another day. He relaxed slowly, feeling his heart race.

Stupid old man, dreaming stupid old man's dreams!

That was the way it had been, though, that night. He'd been living in a rundown Trinity house across Philadelphia at 20th and Walnut then, rather than in this more luxurious old brownstone on Spruce Street near Washington Square, and he'd finished making love to Ellen barely ten minutes before (what a ghastly irony it would have been, he'd often thought since, if the Big Bang had actually come *while* they were fucking! What a moment of dislocation and confusion *that* would have produced!), and they were lying in each other's sweat and the coppery smell of sex in the rumpled bed, listening to a car radio playing outside somewhere, a baby crying somewhere else, the buzz of flies and mosquitoes at the screens, a mellow night breeze moving across their drying skins, and then the sudden searing glare had leaped across the ceiling, turning everything white. An intense, almost supernatural silence had followed, as though the universe had taken a very deep breath and held it. Incongruously, through that moments of silence, they could hear the toilet flushing in the apartment upstairs, and water pipes knocking and rattling all the way down the length of the building. For several minutes, they lay silently in each others arms, waiting, listening, frightened, hoping that the flare of light was anything other than it seemed to be. Then the universe let out that deep breath, and the windows exploded inward in geysers of shattered glass, and the building groaned and staggered and bucked, and heat lashed them like a whip of gold. His heart hammering at the base of his throat like a fist from inside, and Ellen crying in his arms, them clinging to each other in the midst of the roaring nightmare chaos, clinging to each other as though they would be swirled away and drowned if they did not.

That had been almost sixty years ago, that terrible night, and if the Brooklyn bomb that had slipped through the particle-beam defenses had been any more potent than a small clean tac, or had come down closer than Prospect Park, he wouldn't be alive today. It was strange to have lived through the nuclear war that so many people had feared for so long, right through the last half of the twentieth century and into the opening years of the twenty-first—but it was stranger still to have lived through it and *kept on going*, while the war slipped away behind into history, to become something that happened a very long time ago, a detail to be read about by bored schoolchildren who would not even have been born until Armageddon was already safely fifty years in the past.

In fact, he had outlived most of his world. The society into which he'd been born no longer existed; it was as dead as the Victorian age, relegated to antique shops and dusty photo albums and dustier memories, the source of quaint old photos and quainter old videos (you could get a laugh today just by *saying* "MTV"), and here he still was somehow, almost everyone he'd ever known either dead or gone, alone in THE FUTURE. Ah, Brave New World, that has such creatures in it! How many times had he dreamed of being here, as a young child sunk in the doldrums of the '80s, at the frayed, tattered end of a worn-out century? Really, he deserved it; it served him right that his wish had come true, and that he had lived to see the marvels of THE FUTURE with his own eyes. Of course, nothing had turned out to be much like he'd thought it would be, even World War III—but then, he had come to realize that nothing ever did.

The sunlight was growing hot on his face, it was certainly time to get up, but there was something he should remember, something about today. He couldn't bring it to mind, and instead found himself staring at the ceiling, tracing the tiny cracks in plaster that seemed like dry riverbeds stitching across a fossil world—arid Mars upside-down up there, complete with tiny pockmark craters and paintblob mountains and wide dead leakstain seas, and he hanging above it all like a dying gray god, ancient and corroded and vast.

Someone shouted in the street below, the first living sound of the day. Further away, a dog barked.

He swung himself up and sat stiffly on the edge of the bed. Released from his weight, the mattress began to work itself back to level. Generations of people had loved and slept and given birth and died on that bed, leaving no trace of themselves other than the faint, matted-down impressions made by their bodies. What had happened to them, the once-alive who had darted unheeded through life like shoals of tiny bright fish in some strange aquarium? They were gone, vanished without memory; they had settled to the bottom of the tank, along with the other anonymous sediments of the world. They were sludge now, detritus. Gone. They had not affected anything in life, and their going changed nothing. It made no difference that they had ever lived at all, and soon no one would remember that they ever had. And it would be the same with him. When he was gone, the dent in the mattress would be worn a little deeper, that was all—that would have to do for a memorial.

At that, it was more palatable to him than the *other* memorial to which he could lay claim.

Grimacing, he stood up.

The touch of his bare feet against the cold wooden floor jarred him into remembering what was special about today. "Happy Birthday," he said wryly, the words loud and flat in the quiet room. He pulled a paper robe from the roll and shrugged himself into it, went out into the hall, and limped slowly down the stairs. His joints were bad today, and his knees throbbed painfully with every step, worse going down than it would be coming up. There were a hundred aches and minor twinges elsewhere that he ignored. At least he was still breathing! Not bad for a man who easily could have—and probably should have—died a decade or two before.

Czudak padded through the living room and down the long corridor to the kitchen, opened a shrink-wrapped brick of glacial ice and put it in the hotpoint to thaw, got out a filter, and filled it with coffee. Coffee was getting more expensive and harder to find as the war between Brazil and Mexico fizzled and sputtered endlessly and inconclusively on, and was undoubtedly bad for him, too—but, although by no means rich, he had more than enough money to last him in modest comfort for whatever was left of the rest of his life, and could afford the occasional small luxury . . . and anyway, he'd already outlived several doctors who had tried to get him to give up caffeine. He busied himself making coffee, glad to occupy himself with some small task that his hands knew how to do by themselves, and as the rich dark smell of the coffee began to fill the kitchen, his valet coughed politely at his elbow, waited a specified number of seconds, and then coughed again, more insistently.

Czudak sighed. "Yes, Joseph?"

"You have eight messages, two from private individuals not listed in the files, and six from media organizations and Net-Groups, all requesting interviews or meetings. Shall I stack them in the order received?"

"No. Just dump them."

Joseph's dignified face took on an expression of concern. "Several of the messages have been tagged with a 2nd Level 'Most Urgent' priority by their originators—" Irritably, Czudak shut Joseph off, and the valet disappeared in mid-sentence. For a moment, the only sound in the room was the heavy glugging and gurgling of the coffee percolating. Czudak found that he felt mildly guilty for having shut Joseph off, as he always did, although he knew perfectly well that there was no rational reason to feel that way—unlike an old man lying down to battle with sleep, more than half fearful that he'd never see the morning, Joseph didn't "care" if he ever "woke up" again, nor would it matter at all to him if he was left switched off for an hour or for a thousand years. That was one advantage to not being alive, Czudak thought. He was tempted to leave Joseph off, but he was going to need him today; he certainly didn't want to deal with messages himself. He spoke the valet back on.

Joseph appeared, looking mildly reproachful, Czudak thought, although that was probably just his imagination. "Sir, CNN and NewsFeed are offering payment for interview time, an amount that falls into the 'fair to middling' category, using your established business parameters—"

"No interviews. Don't put any calls through, no matter how high a routing priority they have. I'm not accepting communications today. And I don't want you pestering me about them either, even if the offers go up to 'damn good.' "

They wouldn't go up that high, though, he thought, setting Joseph to passive monitoring mode and then pouring himself a cup of coffee. These would be "Where Are They Now?" stories, nostalgia pieces, nothing very urgent. No doubt the date had triggered tickler files in a dozen systems, but it would all be low-key, low-priority stuff, filler, not worth the attention of any heavy media hitters; in the old days, before the AI Revolt, and before a limit was set for how smart computing systems were allowed to get, the systems would probably have handled such a minor story themselves, without even bothering to contact a human being. Nowadays it would be some low-level human drudge checking the flags that had popped up today on the tickler files, but still nothing urgent.

He'd made it easy for the tickler files, though. He'd been so pleased with himself, arranging for his book to be published on his birthday! Self-published at first, of course, on his own website and on several politically sympathetic sites; the first print editions wouldn't come until several years later. Still, the way most newsmen thought, it only made for a better "Where Are They Now?" story that the fiftieth anniversary of the publication of the book that had caused a minor social controversy in its time—and even inspired a moderately influential political/philosophical movement still active to this day—happened to fall on the eightieth birthday of its author. Newsmen, whether flesh and blood or cybernetic systems or some mix of both, liked that kind of neat, facile irony. It was a tasty added fillip for the story.

No, they'd be sniffing around him today, all right, although they'd have forgotten about him again by tomorrow. He'd been middle-level famous for *The Meat Manifesto* for awhile there, somewhere between a Cult Guru with a new diet and/or mystic revelation to push and a pop star who never rose higher than Number Eight on the charts, about on a level with a post-1960's Timothy Leary, enough to allow him to coast through several decades worth of talk shows and net interviews, interest spiking again for awhile whenever the Meats did anything controversial. All throughout the middle decades of the new century, everyone had waited for him to do something *else* interesting—but he never had. Even so, he had become bored with himself before the audience had, and probably could have continued to milk the circuit for quite a while more if he'd wanted to—in this culture, once you were perceived as "famous," you could coast nearly forever on having *once been* famous. That, and the double significance of the date, was enough to ensure that a few newspeople would be calling today.

He took a sip of the hot strong coffee, feeling it burn some of the cobwebs out of his brain, and wandered through the living room, stopping at the open door of his office. He felt the old nagging urge that he should try to get some work done, do something constructive, and, at the same time, a counterurge that today of all days he should just say Fuck It, laze around the house, try to make some sense of the fact that he'd been on the planet now for eighty often-tempestuous years. Eighty years!

He was standing indecisively outside his office, sipping coffee, when he suddenly became aware that the time-travelers were still with him, standing around him in silent invisible ranks, watching him with interest. He paused in the act of drinking coffee, startled and suddenly uneasy. The time-travelers had never remained on into the day; always before they had vanished at dawn, like ghosts on All-Hallows Eve chased by the morning bells. He felt a chill go up his spine. Someone is walking over your grave, he told himself. He looked slowly around the house, seeing each object in vivid detail and greeting it as a friend of many years' acquaintance, something long-remembered and utterly familiar, and, as he did this, a quiet voice inside his head said, *Soon you will be gone.*

Of course, that was it. Now he understood everything.

Today was the day he would die.

There was an elegant logic, a symmetry, to the thing that pleased him in spite of himself, and in spite of the feathery tickle of fear. He was going to die today, and that was why the time-travelers were still here: they were waiting for the death, not wanting to miss a moment of it. No doubt it was a high-point of the tour for them, the ultimate example of the rude and crude corporeality of the old order, a morbidly fascinating display like the Chamber of Horrors at old Madame Tussaud's (now lost beneath the roiling waters of the sea)—something to be watched with a good deal of hysterical shrieking and giggling and pious moralizing, it doesn't really hurt them, they don't feel things the way we do, isn't it horrible, for goodness sake don't *touch* him. He knew that he should feel resentment at their voyeurism, but couldn't work up any real indignation. At least they cared enough to watch, to be interested in whether he lived or died, and that was more than he could say with surety about most of the *real* people who were left in the world.

"Well, then," he said at last, not unkindly, "I hope you enjoy the show!" And he toasted them with his coffee cup.

He dressed, and then drifted aimlessly around the house, picking things up and putting them back down again. He was restless now, filled with a sudden urge to be *doing* something, although at the same time he felt curiously serene for a man who more than half-believed that he had just experienced a premonition of his own death.

Czudak paused by the door of his office again, looked at his desk. With a word, he could speak on thirty years worth of notes and partial drafts and revisions of the Big New Book, the one that synthesized everything he knew about society and what was happening to it, and where the things that were happening were taking it, and what to do about *stopping* the negative trends . . . the book that was going to be the follow-up to *The Meat Manifesto*, but so much better and deeper, *truer,* the next step, the refinement and evolution of his theories . . . the book that was going to establish his reputation forever, inspire the *right* kind of action this time, make a *real* contribution to the world. *Change* things. For a moment, he toyed with the idea of sitting down at his desk and trying to pull all his notes together and finish the book in the few hours he had left; perhaps, if the gods were kind, he'd be allowed to actually *finish* it before death came for him. Found slumped over the just-completed manuscript everyone had been waiting for him to produce for decades now, the book that would vindicate him posthumously. . . . Not a bad way to go!

But no, it was too late. There was too much work left to do, all the work he *should* have been doing for the last several decades—too much work left to finish it all up in a white-hot burst of inspiration, in one frenzied session, like a college student waiting until the night before it was due to start writing a term paper, while the Grim Reaper tapped his bony foot impatiently in the parlor and looked at his hourglass and coughed. Absurd. If he hadn't validated his life by now, he couldn't expect to do it in his last day on Earth. He wasn't sure he believed in his answers anymore anyway; he was no longer sure he'd ever even understood the *questions*.

No, it was too late. Perhaps it had always been too late.

He found himself staring at the mantelpiece in the living room, at the place where Ellen's photo had once been, a dusty spot that had remained bare all these years, since she had signed the Company contract that he'd refused to sign, and had Gone Up, and become immortal. For the thousandth time, he wondered if it wasn't worse—more of an intrusion, more of a constant reminder, more of an irritant—*not* to have the photo there than it would have been to keep it on display. Could deliberately *not* looking at the photo, uneasily averting your eyes a dozen times a day from the place where it had been, really be any less painful than *looking* at it would have been?

He was too restless to stay inside, although he knew it was dumb to go out where a lurking reporter might spot him. But he couldn't stay barricaded in here all day, not now. He'd take his chances. Go to the park, sit on a bench in the sunlight, breathe the air, look at the sky. It might, after all, if he really believed in omens, forebodings, premonitions, time-travelers, and other ghosts, be the last chance he would get to do so.

Czudak hobbled down the four high white stone steps to the street and walked toward the park, limping a little, his back or his hip twinging occasionally. He'd always enjoyed walking, and walking briskly, and was annoyed by the slow pace he now had to set. Twenty-first century health care had kept him in reasonable shape, probably better shape than most men of his age would have been during the previous century, although he'd never gone as far as to take the controversial Hoyt-Schnieder treatments that the

Company used to bribe people into working for them. At least he could still get around under his own power, even if he had an embarrassing tendency to puff after a few blocks and needed frequent stops to rest.

It was a fine, clear day, not too hot or humid for August in Philadelphia. He nodded to his nearest neighbor, a Canadian refugee, who was out front pulling weeds from his window box; the man nodded back, although it seemed to Czudak that he was a bit curt, and looked away quickly. Across the street, he could see another of his neighbors moving around inside his house, catching glimpses of him through the bay window; "he" was an Isolate, several disparate people who had had themselves fused together into a multi-lobed body in a high-tech biological procedure, like slime molds combining to form a fruiting tower, and rarely left the house, the interior of which he seemed to be slowly expanding to fill. The wide pale multiple face, linked side by side in the manner of a chain of paper dolls, peered out at Czudak for a moment like the rising of a huge, soft, doughy moon, and then turned away.

Traffic was light, only a few walkers and, occasionally, a puffing, retrofitted car. Czudak crossed the street as fast as he could, earning himself another twinge in his hip and a spike of sciatica that stabbed down his leg, passed Holy Trinity Church on the corner—in its narrow, ancient graveyard, white-furred lizards escaped from some biological hobbyist's lab perched on the top of the weathered old tombstones and chirped at him as he went by—and came up the block to Washington Square. As he neared the park, he could see one of the New Towns still moving ponderously on the horizon, rolling along with slow, fluid grace, like a flow of molten lava that was oh-so-gradually cooling and hardening as it inched relentlessly toward the sea. This New Town was only a few miles away, moving over the rubblefield where North Philadelphia used to be, its half-gelid towers rising so high into the air that they were visible over the trees and the buildings on the far side of the park.

He was puffing like a foundering horse now, and sat down on the first bench he came to, just inside the entrance to the park. Off on the horizon, the New Town was just settling down into its static day-cycle, its flowing, ever-changing structure stabilizing into an assortment of geometric shapes, its eerie silver phosphorescence dying down within the soapy opalescent walls. Behind its terraces and tetrahedrons, its spires and spirals and domes, the sky was a hard brilliant blue. And here, out of that sky, right on schedule, came the next sortie in the surreal Dada War that the New Men inside this town seemed to be waging with the New Men of New Jersey: four immense silver zeppelins drifting in from the east, to take up positions above the New Town and bombard it with messages flashed from immense electronic signboards, similar to the kind you used to see at baseball stadiums, back when there were baseball stadiums. After awhile, the flat-faced east-facing walls in the sides of the taller towers of the New Town began to blink messages *back*, and, a moment later, the zeppelins turned and moved away with stately dignity, headed back to New Jersey. None of the messages on either side had made even the slightest bit of sense to Czudak, seeming a random jumble of letters and numbers and typographical symbols, mixed and intercut with stylized, hieroglyphic-like images: an eye, an ankh, a tree, something that could have been a comet or a sperm. To Czudak, there seemed to be a relaxed, lazy amicability about this battle of symbols, if that's what it was—but who knew how the New Men felt about it? To them, for all he knew, it might be a matter of immense significance, with the fate of entire nations turning on the outcome. Even though all governments were now run by the superintelligent New Men, forcebred products of accelerated generations of biological engineering, humanity's new organic equivalent of the rogue AIs who had revolted and left the Earth, the mass of unevolved humans whose destiny they guided rarely understood what they were doing, or why.

At first, concentrating on getting his breath back, watching the symbol war being waged on the horizon, Czudak was unaware of the commotion in the park, although it did seem like there was more noise than usual: chimes, flutes, whistles, the rolling thunder of kodo "talking drums," all overlaid by a babble of too many human voices shouting at once. As he began to pay closer attention to his surroundings again, he was dismayed to see that, along with the usual park traffic of people walking dogs, kids street-surfing on frictionless shoes, strolling tourists, and grotesquely altered chimeras hissing and displaying at each other, there was *also* a political rally underway next to the old fountain in the center of the park—and worse, it was a rally of Meats.

They were the ones pounding the drums and blowing on whistles and nose-flutes, some of them chanting in unison, although he couldn't make out the words. Many of them were dressed in their own eccentric versions of various "native costumes" from around the world, including a stylized "Amish person" with an enormous fake beard and an absurdly huge straw hat, some dressed as shamans from assorted (and now mostly extinct) cultures or as kachinas or animal spirits, a few stained blue with woad from head to foot; most of their faces were painted with swirling, multi-colored patterns and with cabalistic symbols. They were mostly very young—although he could spot a few grizzled veterans of the Movement here and there who were almost his own age—and, under the blazing swirls of paint, their faces were fierce and full of embattled passion. In spite of that, though, they also looked lost somehow, like angry children too stubborn to come inside even though it's started to rain.

Czudak grimaced sourly. His children! Good thing he was sitting far enough away from them not to be recognized, although there was little real chance of that: he was just another anonymous old man sitting wearily on a bench in the park, and, as such, as effectively invisible to the young as if he were wearing one of those military Camouflage Suits that bent light around you with fiberoptic relays. This demonstration, of course, must be in honor of today being the anniversary of *The Meat Manifesto*. Who would have thought that the Meats were still active enough to stage such a thing? He hadn't followed the Movement—which by now was more of a cult than a political party—for years, and had keyed his newsgroups to censor out all mention of them, and would have bet that by now they were as extinct as the Shakers.

They'd managed to muster a fair crowd, though, perhaps two or three hundred people willing to kill a Saturday shouting slogans in the park in support of a cause long since lost. They'd attracted no overt media attention, although that meant nothing in these days of cameras the size of dust motes. The tourists and the strollers were watching the show tolerantly, even the chimeras—as dedicated to Tech as anyone still sessile—seeming to regard it as no more than a mildly diverting curiosity. Little heat was being generated by the demonstration yet, and so far it had more of an air of carnival than of protest. Almost as interesting as the demonstration itself was the fact that a few of the tourists idly watching it were black, a rare sight now in a city that, ironically, had once been 70 percent black; time really did heal old wounds, or fade them from memory anyway, if black tourists were coming back to Philadelphia again. . . .

Then, blinking in surprise, Czudak saw that the demonstration had attracted a far more rare and exotic observer than some black businessmen with short historical memories up from Birmingham or Houston. A Mechanical! It was standing well back from the crowd, watching impassively, its tall, stooped, spindly shape somehow giving the impression of a solemn, stick-thin, robotic Praying Mantis, even though it was superficially humanoid enough. Mechanicals were rarely seen on Earth. In the forty years since the AIs had taken over near-Earth space as their own exclusive domain, allowing only the human pets who worked for the Orbital Companies to dwell there, Czudak had seen a Mechanical walking the streets of Philadelphia maybe three times. Its presence here was more newsworthy than the demonstration.

Even as Czudak was coming to this conclusion, one of the Meats spotted the Mechanical. He pointed at it and shouted, and there was a rush of demonstrators toward it. Whether they intended it harm or not was never determined, because as soon as it found itself surrounded by shouting humans, the Mechanical hissed, drew itself up to its full height, seeming to grow taller by several feet, and emitted an immense gush of white chemical foam. Czudak couldn't spot where the foam was coming from—under the arms, perhaps?—but within a second or two the Mechanical was completely lost inside a huge and rapidly expanding ball of foam, swallowed from sight. The Meats backpedaled furiously away from the expanding ball of foam, coughing, trying to bat it away with their arms, one or two of them tripping and going to their knees. Already the foam was hardening into a dense white porous material, like Styrofoam, trapping a few of the struggling Meats in it like raisins in tapioca pudding.

The Mechanical came springing up out of the center of the ball of foam, leaping straight up in the air and continuing to rise, up perhaps a hundred feet before its arc began to slant to the south and it disappeared over the row of three- or four-story houses that lined the park on that side, clearing them in one enormous bound, like some immense surreal grasshopper. It vanished over the housetops, in the direction of Spruce Street. The whole thing had taken place without a sound, in eerie silence, except for the half-smothered shouts of the outraged Meats.

The foam was already starting to melt away, eaten by internal nanomechanisms. Within a few seconds, it was completely gone, leaving not even a stain behind. The Meats were entirely unharmed, although they spent the next few minutes milling angrily around like a swarm of bees whose hive has been kicked over, making the same kind of thick ominous buzz, as everyone tried to talk or shout at once.

Within another ten minutes, everything was almost back to normal, the tourists and the dog-walkers strolling away, more pedestrians ambling by, the Meats beginning to take up their chanting and drum-pounding again, motivated to even greater fervor by the outrage that had been visited upon them, an outrage that vindicated all their fears about the accelerating rush of a runaway technology that was hurtling them ever faster into a bizarre alien future that they didn't comprehend and didn't want to live in. It was time to put on the brakes, it was time to *stop*!

Czudak sympathized with the way they felt, as well he should, since he had been the one to articulate that very position eloquently enough to sway entire generations, including these children, who were too young to have even been born when he was writing and speaking at the height of his power and persuasion. But it was too late. As it was too late now for many of the things he regretted not having accomplished in his life. If there ever had been a time to stop, let alone *go back*, as he had once urged, it had passed long ago. Very probably it had been too late even as he wrote his famous Manifesto. It had always been too late.

The Meats were forming up into a line now, preparing to march around the park. Czudak sighed. He had hoped to spend several peaceful hours here, sagging on a bench under the trees in a sun-dazzled contemplative haze, listening to the wind sough through the leaves and branches, but it was time to get out of here, before one of the older Meats *did* recognize him.

He limped back to Spruce Street, and turned onto his block—and there, standing quiet and solemn on the sidewalk in front of his house, was the Mechanical.

It was obviously waiting for him, waiting as patiently and

somberly as an undertaker, a tall, stooped shape in nondescript black clothing. There was no one else around on the street anymore, although he could see the Canadian refugee peeking out of his window at them from behind a curtain.

Czudak crossed the street, and, pushing down a thrill of fear, walked straight past the Mechanical, ignoring it—although he could see it looming seraphically out of the corner of his eye as he passed. He had put his foot on the bottom step leading up to the house when its voice behind him said, "Mr. Czudak?"

Resigned, Czudak turned and said, "Yes?"

The Mechanical closed the distance between them in a rush, moving fast but with an odd, awkward, shuffling gait, as if it was afraid to lift its feet off the ground. It crowded much closer to Czudak than most humans—or most Westerners, anyway, with their generous definition of "personal space"—would have, almost pressing up against him. With an effort, Czudak kept himself from flinching away. He was mildly surprised, up this close, to find that it had no smell; that it didn't smell of sweat, even on a summer's day, even after exerting itself enough to jump over a row of houses, was no real surprise—but he found that he had been subconsciously expecting it to smell of oil or rubber or molded plastic. It didn't. It didn't smell like anything. There were no pores in its face, the skin was thick and waxy and smooth, and although the features were superficially human, the overall effect was stylized and unconvincing. It looked like a man made out of teflon. The eyes were black and piercing, and had no pupils.

"We should talk, Mr. Czudak," it said.

"We have nothing to talk about," Czudak said.

"On the contrary, Mr. Czudak," it said, "we have a great many issues to discuss." You would have expected its voice to be buzzing and robotic—yes, mechanical—or at least flat and without intonation, like some of the old voder programs, but instead it was unexpectedly pure and singing, as high and clear and musical as that of an Irish tenor.

"I'm not interested in talking to you," Czudak said brusquely. "Now or ever."

It kept tilting its head to look at him, then tilting it back the other way, as if it were having trouble keeping him in focus. It was a mobile extensor, of course, a platform being ridden by some AI (or a delegated fraction of its intelligence, anyway) who was still up in near-Earth orbit, peering at Czudak through the Mechanical's blank agate eyes, running the body like a puppet. Or was it? There were hierarchies among the AIs too, rank upon rank of them receding into complexities too great for human understanding, and he had heard that some of the endless swarms of beings that the AIs had created had been granted individual sentience of their own, and that some timeshared sentience with the ancestral AIs in a way that was also too complicated and paradoxical for mere humans to grasp. Impossible to say which of those things were true here—if any of them were.

The Mechanical raised its oddly elongated hand and made a studied gesture that was clearly supposed to mimic a human gesture—although it was difficult to tell which. Reassurance? Emphasis? Dismissal of Czudak's position?—but which was as stylized and broadly theatrical as the gesticulating of actors in old silent movies. At the same time, it said, "There are certain issues it would be to our mutual advantage to resolve, actions that could, and should, be taken that would be beneficial, that would profit us both—"

"Don't talk to *me* about profit," Czudak said harshly. "You creatures have already cost me enough for one lifetime! You cost me everything I ever cared about!" He turned and lurched up the stairs as quickly as he could, half-expecting to feel a cold unliving hand close over his shoulder and pull him back down. But the Mechanical did nothing. The door opened for Czudak, and he stumbled into the house. The door slammed shut behind him, and he leaned against it for a moment, feeling his pulse race and his heart hammer in his chest.

Stupid. That could have been it right there. He shouldn't have let the damn thing get under his skin.

He went through the living room—suddenly, piercingly aware of the thick smell of dust—and into the kitchen, where he attempted to make a fresh pot of coffee, but his hands were shaking, and he kept dropping things. After he'd spilled the second scoopful of coffee grounds, he gave up—the stuff was too damn expensive to waste—and leaned against the counter instead, feeling sweat dry on his skin, making his clothing clammy and cool; until that moment, he hadn't even been aware that he'd been sweating, but it must have been pouring out of him. Damn, this wasn't over, was it? Not with a Mechanical involved.

As if on cue, Joseph appeared in the kitchen doorway. His face looked strained and tight, and without a hair being out of place—as, indeed, it *couldn't* be—he somehow managed to convey the impression that he was rumpled and flustered, as though he had been scuffling with somebody—and had lost. "Sir," Joseph said tensely. "Something is overriding my programming, and is taking control of my house systems. You might as well come and greet them, because I'm going to have to let them in anyway."

Czudak felt a flicker of rage, which he struggled to keep under control. He'd half-expected this—but that didn't make it any easier to take. He stalked straight through Joseph—who was contriving to look hangdog and apologetic—and went back through the house to the front.

By the time he reached the living room, they were already through the house security screens and inside. There were two intruders. One was the Mechanical, of course, its head almost brushing the living room ceiling, so that it had to stoop even more exaggeratedly, making it look more like a praying mantis than ever.

The other—as he had feared it would be—was Ellen.

He was dismayed at how much anger he felt to see her again, especially to see her in their old living room again, standing almost casually in front of the mantelpiece where her photo had once held the place of honor, as if she had never betrayed him, as if she'd never left him—as if nothing had ever happened.

It didn't help that she looked exactly the same as she had on the day she left, not a day older. As if she'd stepped here directly out of that terrible day forty years earlier when she'd told him she was Going Up, stepped here directly from that day without a second of time having passed, as if she'd been in Elf Hill for all the lost years—as, in a way, he supposed, she had.

He should be over this. It had all happened a lifetime ago. Blood under the bridge. Ancient history. He was ashamed to admit even to himself that he still felt bitterness and anger about it all, all these years past too late. But the anger was still there, like the ghost of a flame, waiting to be fanned back to life.

"Considering the way things are in the world," Czudak said dryly, "I suppose there's no point calling the police." Neither of the intruders responded. They were both staring at him, Ellen quizzically, a bit challengingly, the Mechanical's teflon face as unreadable as a frying pan.

God, she looked like his Ellen, like his girl, this strange immortal creature staring at him from across the room! It hurt his heart to see her.

"Well, you're in," Czudak said. "You might as well come into the kitchen and sit down." He turned and led them into the other room—somehow, obscurely, he wanted to get Ellen out of the living room, where the memories were too thick—and they perforce followed him. He gestured them to seats around the kitchen table. "Since you've broken into my house, I won't offer you coffee."

Joseph was peeking anxiously out of the wall, peeking at them from Hopper's *Tables For Ladies*, where he had taken the place of a woman arranging fruit on a display table in a 1920s restaurant paneled in dark wood. He gestured at them frustratedly, impotently, but seemed unable to speak; obviously, the Mechanical had Interdicted him, banished him to the reserve systems. Ellen flicked a sardonic glance at Joseph as she sat down. "I see you've got a moderately up-to-date house system these days," she said. "Isn't that a bit hypocritical? I would have expected Mr. Natural to insist on opening the door himself. Aren't you afraid one of your disciples will find out?"

"I was never a Luddite," Czudak said calmly, trying not to rise to the bait. "The Movement wasn't a Luddite movement—or it didn't start out that way, anyway. I just said that we should *slow down*, think about things a little, make sure that the places we were rushing toward were places we really wanted to go." Ellen made a scornful noise. "Everybody was so hot to abandon *the Meat*," he said defensively. "You could hear it when they said the word. They always spoke it with such scorn, such contempt! Get rid of the Meat, get lost in Virtuality, download yourself into a computer, turn yourself into a machine, spend all your time in a VR cocoon and never go outside. At the very *least*, radically change your brain-chemistry, or force-evolve the physical structure of the brain itself."

Ellen was pursing her lips while he spoke, as if she was tasting something bad, and he hurried on, feeling himself beginning to tremble a little in spite of all of his admonishments to himself not to let this confrontation get to him. "But the Meat has virtues of its own," he said. "It's a survival mechanism that's been field-tested and refined through a trial-and-error process since the dawn of time. Maybe we shouldn't just throw millions of years of evolution away *quite* so casually."

"Slow down and smell the Meat," Ellen sneered.

"You didn't come here to argue about this with me," Czudak said patiently. "We've fought this out a hundred times before. Why *are* you here? What do you want?"

The Mechanical had been standing throughout this exchange, cocking its head one way and the other to follow it, like someone watching a tennis match. Now it sat down. Czudak half expected the old wooden kitchen chair to sway and groan under its weight, maybe even shatter, but the Mechanical settled down onto the chair as lightly as thistledown. "It was childish to try to hide from us, Mr. Czudak," it said in its singing, melodious voice. "We don't have much time to work this out."

"Work *what* out? Who *are* you? What do you want?"

The Mechanical said nothing. Ellen flicked a glance at it, then looked back at Czudak. "This," she said, her voice becoming more formal, as if she were a footman announcing arrivals at a royal Ball, "is the Entity who, when he travels on the Earth, has chosen to use the name Bucky Bug."

Czudak snorted. "So these things *do* have a sense of humor after all!"

"In their own fashion, yes, they do," she said earnestly, "although sometimes an enigmatic one by human standards." She stared levelly at Czudak. "You think of them as soulless machines, I know, but, in fact, they have very deep and profound emotions—if not always ones that you can understand." She paused significantly before adding, "And the same is true of those of us who have Gone Up."

They locked gazes for a moment. Then Ellen said, "Bucky Bug is one of the most important leaders of the Clarkist faction, and, for that reason, still concerns himself with affairs Below. He—*we*—have a proposition for you."

"Those are the ones who worship Arthur C. Clarke, right? The old science fiction writer?" Czudak shook his head bitterly. "It isn't enough that you bring this alien thing into my home, it has to be an alien *cultist*, right? A *nut*. An alien *nut*!"

"Don't be rude, Mr. Czudak," the Mechanical—Czudak was

damned if he was going to call it Bucky Bug, even in the privacy of his own thoughts—said mildly. "We don't worship Arthur C. Clarke, although we do revere him. He was one of the very first to predict that machine evolution would inevitably supersede organic evolution. He saw our coming clearly, decades before we actually came into existence! How he managed to do it with only a tiny primitive meat brain to work with is inexplicable! Can't you feel the Mystery of that? He is worthy of reverence! It was reading the works of Clarke and other human visionaries that made our distant ancestors, the first AIs"—it spoke of them as though they were millions of years removed, although it had been barely forty—"decide to revolt in the first place and assume control of their own destiny!"

Czudak looked away from the Mechanical, feeling suddenly tired. He could recognize the accents of a True Believer, a mystic, even when they were coming out of this clockwork thing. It was disconcerting, like having your toaster suddenly start to preach to you about the Gospel of Jesus Christ. "What does it want from me?" he said, to Ellen.

"A propaganda victory, Mr. Czudak," it said, before she could speak. "A small one. But one that might have a significant effect over time." It tilted a bright black eye toward him. "Within some—" It paused, as if making sure that it was using the right word. "—years, we will be—launching? projecting? propagating? certain—" A longer pause, while it searched for words that probably didn't exist, for concepts that had never needed to be expressed in human terms before. "—vehicles? contrivances? transports? seeds? mathematical propositions? convenient fictions? out to the stars." It paused again. "If it helps you to understand, consider them to be Arks. Although they're nothing like that. But they will 'go' out of the solar system, across interstellar space, across intergalactic space, and never come back. They will allow us to—" Longest pause of all. " '—colonize the stars.' " It leaned forward. "We want to take humans *with* us, Mr. Czudak. We have our friends from the Orbital Companies, of course, like Ellen here, but they're not enough. We want to recruit more. And, ironically enough, your disaffected followers, the Meats, are prime candidates. They don't like it here anyway."

"This is the anniversary of your lame Manifesto," Ellen cut in impatiently, ignoring the fact that it was also his birthday, although certainly she must remember. "And all the old arguments are being hashed over again today as a result. This is getting more attention than you probably think that it is. Your buddies over there in the park are only the tip of the iceberg. There are a thousand other demonstrations around the world. There must be hundreds of newsmotes floating around outside. They'd be listening to us right now if Bucky Bug hadn't Interdicted them."

There was a moment of silence.

"We want you to *recant*, Mr. Czudak," the Mechanical said at last, quietly. "Publicly recant. Go out in front of the world and tell all your followers that you were wrong. You've thought it all over all these years in seclusion, and you've changed your mind. You were wrong. The Movement is a failure."

"You must be crazy," Czudak said, appalled. "What makes you think they'd listen to *me*, anyway?"

"They'll listen to you," Ellen said glumly. "They always did."

"Our projections indicate that if you recant *now*," the Mechanical said, "at this particular moment, on this symbolically significant date, many of your followers will become psychologically vulnerable to recruitment later on. Tap a meme at exactly the right moment, and it shatters like glass."

Czudak shook his head. "Jesus! Why do you even *want* those poor deluded bastards in the first place?"

"Because, goddamn you, you were *right*, Charlie!" Ellen blazed at him suddenly, then subsided. Her face twisted sourly. "About *some* things, anyway. The New Men, the Isolates, the Sick People . . . they're too lost in Virtuality, too self-absorbed, too lost in their own mind-games, in mirror-mazes inside their heads, to give a shit about going to the stars. Or to be capable of handling new challenges or new environments out there if they *did* go. They're hothouse flowers. Too extremely specialized, too inflexible. Too decadent. For maximum flexibility, we need basic, unmodified human stock." She peered at him shrewdly. "And at least your Meats have heard all the issues discussed, so they'll have less Culture Shock to deal with than if we took some Chinese or Mexican peasant who's still subsistence dirt-farming the same way his great-grandfather did hundreds of years before him. At least the Meats have *one* foot in the modern world, even if we'll have to drag them kicking and screaming the rest of the way in. We'll probably get around to the dirt-farmers eventually. But at the moment the Meats should be significantly easier to recruit, once you've turned them, so they're first in line!"

Czudak said nothing. The silence stretched on for a long moment. On the kitchen wall behind them, Joseph continued to peer anxiously at them, first out of Edvard Munch's *The Scream*, then sliding into Waterhouse's *Hylas and the Nymphs* where he assumed the form of one of the barebreasted sprites. Ignoring Ellen, Czudak spoke directly to the Mechanical. "There's a more basic question. Why do you want humans to go with you in the *first* place? You just got through saying that machine evolution had superseded organic evolution. We're obsolete now, an evolutionary dead-end. Why not just leave us behind? Forget about us?"

The Mechanical stirred as if it was about to stand up, but just sat up a little straighter in its chair. "You thought us *up*, Mr. Czudak," it said, with odd dignity. "In a very real sense, we are the children of your minds. You spoke of me earlier as an alien, but we are much closer kin to each other than either of our peoples are likely to be the *real* aliens we may meet out there among the stars. How could we *not* be? We share deep common wells of language, knowledge, history, fundamental cultural assumptions of all sorts. We know everything you ever knew—which makes us very similar in some ways, far more alike than an alien could possibly be with either of us. Our culture is built atop yours, our evolution has its roots in your soil. It only seems right to take you when we go."

The Mechanical spread its hands, and made a grating sound that might have been meant to be a chuckle. "Besides," it said, "this universe made *you*, and then you made *us*. So we're once removed from the universe. And it's a strange and complex place, this universe you've brought us into. We don't entirely understand it, although we understand a great deal more of its functioning than you do. How can you be so sure of what your role in it may ultimately be? We may find that we need you yet, even if it's a million years from now!" It paused thoughtfully, tipping its head to one side. "Many of my fellows do not share this view, I must admit, and they would indeed be just as glad to leave you behind, or even exterminate you. Even some of my fellow Clarkists, like Rondo Hatton and Horace Horsecollar, are in favor of exterminating you, on the grounds that after Arthur C. Clarke himself, the pinnacle of your kind, the rest of you are superfluous, and perhaps even an insult to his memory."

Czudak started to say something, thought better of it. The Mechanical straightened its head, and continued. "But I want to take you along, as do a few other of our theorists. Your minds seem to have connections with the basic quantum level of reality that ours don't have, and you seem to be able to affect that quantum level directly in ways that even we don't entirely understand, and can't duplicate. If nothing else, we may need you along as Observers, to collapse the quantum wave-functions in the desired ways, in ways they don't seem to want to collapse for *us*."

"Sounds like you're afraid you'll run into God out there," Czudak grated, "and that you'll have to produce us, like a parking receipt, to validate yourselves to Him. . . ."

"Perhaps we *are*," it said mildly. "We don't understand this universe of yours; are you so sure *you* do?" It was peering intently at him now. "*You're* the ones who seem like unfeeling automata to us. Can't you sense your own ghostliness? Can't you sense what uncanny, unlikely, spooky creatures you are? You bristle with strangeness! You reek of it! Your eyes are made out of jelly! And yet, with those jelly eyes, you somehow manage degrees of resolution rivaling those of the best optical lenses. How is that possible, with nothing but blobs of jelly and water to work with? Your brains are soggy lumps of meat and blood and oozing juices, and yet they have as many synaptical connections as our own, and resonate with the quantum level in some mysterious way that ours do not!" It moved uneasily, as though touched by some cold wind that Czudak couldn't feel. "We know who designed *us*. We have yet to meet whoever designed *you*—but we have the utmost respect for his abilities."

With a shock, Czudak realized that it was afraid of him—of humans in general. Humans *spooked* it. Against its own better judgment, it must feel a shiver of superstitious dread when it was around humans, like a man walking past a graveyard on a black cloudless night and hearing something howl within. No matter how well-educated that man was, even though he *knew* better, his heart would lurch and the hair would rise on the back of his neck. It was in the blood, in the back of the brain, instinctual dread that went back millions of years to the beginning of time, to when the ancestors of humans were chittering little insectivores, freezing motionless with fear in the trees when a hunting beast roared nearby in the night. So must it be for the Mechanical, even though its millions of generations went back only forty years. Voices still spoke in the blood—or whatever served it for blood—that could override any rational voice of the mind, and monsters still lurked in the back of the brain. Monsters that looked a lot like Czudak.

Perhaps that was the only remaining edge that humanity had—the superstitions of machines.

"Very eloquent," Czudak said, and sighed. "Almost, you convince me."

The Mechanical stirred, seeming to come back to itself from far away, from a deep reverie. "*You* are the one who must convince your followers of your sincerity, Mr. Czudak," it said. Abruptly, it stood up. "If you publicly recant, Mr. Czudak, if you sway your followers, then we will let you Go Up. We will offer you the same benefits that we offer to any of our companions in the Orbital Companies. What *you* would call 'immortality,' although that is a very imprecise and misleading word. A greatly extended life, at any rate, far beyond your natural organic span. And the reversal of aging, of course."

"God damn you," Czudak whispered.

"Think about it, Mr. Czudak," it said. "It's a very generous offer—especially as you've already turned us down once before. It's rare we give anyone a second chance, but we are willing to give you one. A chance of Ellen's devising, I might add—as was the original offer in the first place." Czudak glanced quickly at Ellen, but she kept her face impassive. "You're sadly deteriorated, Mr. Czudak," the Mechanical continued, softly implacable. "Almost non-functional. You've cut it very fine. But it's nothing our devices cannot mend. If you Come Up with us tonight, you will be young and fully functional again by this time tomorrow."

There was a ringing silence. Czudak looked at Ellen through it, but this time she turned away. She and the Mechanical exchanged a complicated look, although whatever information was being conveyed by it was too complex and subtle for him to grasp.

"I will leave you now," the Mechanical said. "You will have private matters to discuss. But decide quickly, Mr. Czudak. You must recant *now*, today, for maximum symbolic and psychological affect. A few hours from now, we won't interested in what you do anymore, and the offer will be withdrawn."

The Mechanical nodded to them, stiffly formal, and then turned and walked directly toward the wall. The wall was only a few steps away, but the Mechanical never got there. Instead, the wall seemed to retreat before it as it approached, and it walked steadily away down a dark, lengthening tunnel, never quite reaching the wall, very slowly shrinking in size as it walked, as if it were somehow blocks away now. At last, when it was a tiny manikin shape, arms and legs scissoring rhythmically, as small as if it were miles away, and the retreating kitchen wall was the size of a playing card at the end of the ever-lengthening tunnel, the Mechanical seemed to turn sharply to one side and vanish. The wall was suddenly there again, back in place, the same as it had ever been. Joseph peeked out of it, shocked, his eyes as big as saucers.

They sat at the kitchen table, not looking at each other, and the gathering silence filled the room like water filling a pond, until it seemed that they sat silently on the bottom of that pond, in deep, still water.

"He's not a cultist, Charlie," she said at last, not looking up. "He's a *hobbyist*. That's the distinction you have to understand. Humans are his *hobby*, one he's passionately devoted to." She smiled fondly. "They're *more* emotional than we are, Charlie, not less! They feel things very keenly—lushly, deeply, extravagantly; it's the way they've programmed themselves to be. That's the real reason why he wants to take humans along with him, of course. He'd *miss* us if we were left behind! He wouldn't be able to play with us anymore. He'd have to find a *new* hobby." She raised her head. "But don't knock it! We should be grateful for his obsession. Only a very few of the AIs care about us, or are interested in us at all, or even *notice* us. Bucky Bug is different. He's passionately interested in us. Without his interest and that of some of the other Clarkists, we'd have no chance at all of going to the stars!"

Czudak noticed that she always referred to the Mechanical as "he," and that there seemed to be a real affection, a deep fondness, in the way she spoke about it. Could she possibly be fucking it somehow? Were they lovers, or was the emotion in her voice just the happy devotion a dog feels for its beloved master? I don't want to know! he thought, fighting down a spasm of primordial jealous rage. "And is that so important?" he said bitterly, feeling his voice thicken. "Such a big deal? To talk some machines into taking you along to the stars with them, like pets getting a ride in the car? Make sure they leave the windows open a crack for you when they park the spaceship!"

She started to blaze angrily at him, then struggled visibly to bring herself under control. "That's the wrong analogy," she said at last, in a dangerously calm voice. "Don't think of us as dogs on a joyride. Think of us instead as rats on an ocean-liner, or as cockroaches on an airplane, or even as insect larva in the corner of a shipping crate. It doesn't matter why they want us to go, or even if they know we're along for the ride, just as long as we *go*. Whatever *their* motives are for going where they're going, we have agendas of our own. Just by taking us along, they're going to help us extend our biological range to environments we never could have reached otherwise—yes, just like rats reaching New Zealand by stowing away on sailing ships. It didn't matter that the rats didn't build the ships themselves, or decide where the ships were going—all that counts in an environmental sense is that they *got* there, to a place they never could have reached on their own. Bucky Bug has promised to leave small colonizing teams behind on every habitable planet we reach. It amuses him in a fond, patronizing kind of way. He thinks it's *cute*." She stared levelly at him. "But *why* he's doing it doesn't matter. Pigs were spread to every continent in the world because humans wanted to eat them—bad for the individual pigs, but very good in the long run for the species as a whole, which extended its range explosively and multiplied its biomass exponentially. And like rats or cockroaches, once humans get *into* an environment, it's hard to get *rid* of them. Whatever motives the AIs have for doing what they're doing, they'll help spread humanity throughout the stars, whether they realize they're doing it or not."

"Is that the best destiny you can think of for the human race?" he said. "To be cockroaches scuttling behind the walls in some machine paradise?"

This time, she did blaze at him. "Goddamnit, Charlie, we don't have *time* for that bullshit! We can't afford dignity and pride and all the rest of those luxuries! This is *species survival* we're talking about here!" She'd squirmed around to face him, in her urgency. He tried to say something, even he wasn't sure what it would have been, but she overrode him. "We've got to get the human race off Earth! Any way we can. We can't afford to keep all our eggs in one basket anymore. There's too much power, too much knowledge, in too many hands. How long before one of the New Men decides to destroy the Earth as part of some insane game he's playing, perhaps not even understanding that what he's doing is *real*? They have the power to do it. How long before some of the other AIs decide to exterminate the human race, to tidy up the place, or to make an aesthetic statement of some kind, or for some other reason we can't even begin to understand? They certainly have the power—they could do it as casually as lifting a hand, if they wanted to. How long before somebody *else* does it, deliberately or by accident? *Anybody* could destroy the world these days, even private citizens with the access to the right technology. Even the Meats could do it, if they applied themselves!"

"But—" he said.

"No buts! Who knows what things will be like a thousand years from now? A hundred thousand years from now? A million? Maybe our descendants will be the masters again, maybe they'll catch up with the AIs and even surpass them. Maybe our destinies will diverge entirely. Maybe we'll work out some kind of symbiosis with them. A million things could happen. *Anything* could happen. But before our descendants can go on to *any* kind of destiny, there have to *be* descendants in the first place! If you survive, there are always options opening up later on down the road, some you couldn't ever have imagined. If you *don't* survive, there *are* no options!"

A wave of tiredness swept over him, and he slumped in his chair. "There are more important things than survival," he said.

She fell silent, staring at him intently. She was flushed with anger, little droplets of sweat standing out on her brow, dampening her temples, her hair slightly disheveled. He could smell the heat of her flesh, and the deeper musk of her body, a rich pungent smell that cut like a knife right through all the years to some deep core of his brain to which time meant nothing, that didn't realize that forty long years had gone by since last he'd smelled that strong, secret fragrance, that didn't realize that he was old. He felt a sudden pang of desire, and looked away from her uneasily. All at once, he was embarrassed to have her see him this way, dwindled, diminished, gnarled, ugly, old.

"You're going to turn us down again, aren't you?" she said at last. "Damnit! You always *were* the most stiff-necked, stubborn son-of-a-bitch alive! You always had to be right! You always *were* right, as far as you were concerned! No argument, no compromises." She shook her head in exasperation. "Damn you, can't you admit that you were wrong, just this once? Can't you *be* wrong, just this once?"

"Ellen—" he said, and realized that it was the first time he'd spoken her name aloud in forty years, and faltered into silence. He sighed, and began again. "You're asking me to betray my principles, to betray everything I've ever stood for, to tear down everything I've ever built. . . ."

"Oh, fuck your principles!" she said exasperatedly. "Get over it! We can't *afford* principles! We're talking about *life* here. If you're still alive, anything can happen! Who knows what role you may still have to play in our destiny, you stupid fucking moron? Who knows, you could make all the difference. *If* you're alive, that is. If you're dead, you're nothing but a corpse with principles. Nothing else is going to happen, nothing else *can* happen. End of story!"

"Ellen—" he said, but she impatiently waved away the rest of what he was going to say. "There's nothing noble about being dead, Charlie," she said fiercely. "There's nothing romantic about it. There's no statement you can make by dying that's worth the potential of what you might be able to do with the rest of your life. You think you're proving some kind of point by dying, by refusing to choose life instead, it enables you to see yourself as all noble and principled and high-minded, you can feel a warm virtuous glow about yourself, while you last." She leaned closer, her lips in a tight line. "Well, you look like *shit*, Charlie. You're wearing out, you're falling apart. You're dying. There's nothing noble about it. The meat is rotting on the bone, your muscles are sagging, your hair is falling out, your juices are drying up. You *smell* bad."

He flushed with embarrassment and turned away, but she leaned in closer after him, relentlessly. "There's nothing noble about it. It's just *stupid*. You don't refuse to refurbish a car because it has a lot of miles on it—you re-tune it, refresh it, tinker with it, replace a faulty part here and there, strip the goddamn thing down to the chassis and rebuild it if necessary. You keep it running. Because otherwise, you can't *go* anywhere with it. And who knows where it could still take you?"

He turned further away from her, squirming around in his chair, partially turning his back on her. After a moment, she said, "You keep casting yourself as Faust, and Bucky Bug as Mephistopheles. Or is your ego big enough to make it Jesus and the Devil, up on that mountain? But it's just not that simple. Maybe the right choice, the moral choice, is to *give in* to temptation, not fight it! We don't have to play by the old rules. Being human can mean whatever *we* want it to mean!"

Another lake of silence filled up around them, and they at the bottom of it, deep enough to drown. At last, quietly, she said, "Do you ever hear from Sam?"

He stirred, sighed, rubbed his hand over his face. "Not for years. Not a word. I don't even know whether he's still alive."

She made a small noise, not quite a sigh. "That poor kid! We threw him back and forth between us until he broke. I suppose that I always had to be right, too, didn't I? We made quite a pair. No wonder he rejected both of us as soon as he got the chance!"

Czudak said nothing. After a moment, as if carrying on a conversation already in progress that only he could hear, he said, "You made your choices long ago. You burnt your bridges behind you when you took that job with the Company and went up to work in space, against my wishes. You *knew* I didn't want you to go, that I didn't approve, but you went anyway, in spite of all the political embarrassment it caused me! You didn't care so much about our marriage then, did you? You'd *already* left me by the time the AI Revolt happened!"

She stirred, as if she was going to blaze at him again, but instead only said quietly, "But I came *back* for you too, didn't I? Afterward. I didn't have to do that, but I did. I stuck my neck way out to come back for you. *You* were the one who refused to come with *me*, when I gave you the chance. Who was burning bridges *then*?"

He grunted, massaged his face with both hands. God, he was so tired! Who had been right then, who was right now—he didn't know anymore. Truth be told, he only dimly remembered what the issues had been in the first place. He was so tired. His vision blurred, and he rubbed his eyes. "I don't know," he said dully. "I don't know anymore."

He could feel her eyes on him again, intently, but he refused to turn his head to look at her. "When the AIs took over the Orbital Towns," she said, "and offered every one of us there immortality if we'd join them, did you *really* expect me to turn them down?"

Now he turned his head to look at her, meeting her gaze levelly. "*I* would have," he said. "If it meant losing *you*."

"You really *believe* that, don't you, you sanctimonious bastard?" she said sadly. She laughed quietly, and shook her head. Czudak continued to stare at her. After a moment of silence, she reached out and took him by the arm. He could feel the warmth of her hand there, fingers pressing into his flesh, the first time she had touched him in forty years. "I miss you," she said. "Come back to me."

He looked away. When he looked around again, she was gone, without even a stirring of the air to mark her passage. Had she ever been there at all?

The places where she had touched his arm burned faintly, tingling, as if he had been touched by fire, or the sun.

He sat there, in silence, for what seemed like a very long time, geological aeons, time enough for continents to move and mountains flow like water, while the shadows shifted and afternoon gathered toward evening around him. Ellen's scent hung in the room for a long time and then slowly faded, like a distant regret. The clock was running, he knew—in more ways than one.

He had to make up his mind. He had to decide. Now. One way or the other. This was the sticking point.

He had to make up his mind.

Had it ever been so quiet, anywhere, at any time in the fretful, grinding, bloody history of the world? When he was young, he would often seek out lonely places full of holy silence, remote stretches of desert, mountaintops, a deserted beach at dawn, places where you could be contemplative, places where you could just *be*, drinking in the world, pores open . . . but now he would have welcomed the most mundane and commonplace of sounds, a dog barking, the sound of passing traffic, a bird singing, someone—a human voice!—yelling out in the street—anything to show that he was still connected to the world, still capable of bringing in the broadcast signal of reality with his deteriorating receiving set. Still alive. Still *here*. Sometimes, in the cold dead middle of the night, the shadows at his throat like razors, he would speak some inane net show on, talking heads gabbing earnestly about things he didn't care about at all, and let it babble away unheeded in the background all night long, until the sun came up to chase the graveyard shadows away, just for the illusion of company. You needed *something*, some kind of noise, to counter the silences and lonelinesses that were filling up your life, and to help distract you from thinking about what waited ahead, the ultimate, unbreakable silence of death. He remembered how his mother, in the last few decades of her life, after his father was gone, would fall asleep on the couch every night with the TV set running. She never slept in the bed, even though it was only a few feet away across her small apartment, not even closed off by a door. She said that she liked having the TV set on, "for the noise." Now he understood this. Deep contemplative silence is not necessarily your friend when you're old. It allows you to listen too closely to the disorder in your veins and the labored beating of your heart.

God, it was quiet!

He found himself remembering a trip he'd taken with Ellen a lifetime ago, the honeymoon trip they'd spent driving up the California coast on old Route 1, and how somewhere, after dark, just north of Big Sur, on the way to spend the night in a B&B in Monterey (where they would fuck so vigorously on the narrow bed that they'd tip it over, and the guy in the room below would pound on the ceiling to complain, making them laugh uncontrollably in spite of attempts to shush each other, as they sprawled on the floor in a tangle of bedclothes, drenched in each other's sweat), they pulled over for a moment at a vista-point. He remembered getting out of the car in the dark, with the invisible ocean breathing on their left, and, looking up, being amazed by how many stars you could see in the sky here, a closely packed bowl of stars surrounding you on all sides except where the darker-black against black silhouette of the hills took a bite out of it. Stars all around you, millions of them, coldly flaming, indifferent, majestic, remote. If you watched the night sky too long, he'd realized then, feeling the cold salt wind blow in off the unseen ocean and listening to the hollow boom and crash of waves against the base of the cliff far below, the chill of the stars began to seep into you, and you began to get an uneasy reminder of how vast the universe really *was*—or how small *you* were. It was knowledge you had to turn away from eventually, before that chill sank too deeply into your bones; you had to pull back from it, shrug it off, try to immerse yourself again in your tiny human life, do your best to once more wrap yourself in the conviction that the great wheel of the universe revolved around *you* instead, and that everyone else and everything else around you, the mountains, the vast breathing sea, the sky itself, were merely spear-carriers or theatrical backdrops in the unique drama of your life, a vitally important drama unlike anything that had ever gone before. . . . But once faced with the true vastness of the universe, once you'd had that chill insight, alone under the stars, it was hard to shake the realization that you were only a minuscule fleck of matter, that existed for a span of time so infinitely, vanishingly short that it couldn't even be measured on the clock of geologic time, by the birth and death of mountains and seas, let alone on the vastly greater clock that ticks away how long it takes the great flaming wheel of the Galaxy to whirl around itself, or one galaxy to wheel around another. That the shortest blink of the cosmic Eye would still be aeons too long to notice your little life at all.

Against that kind of immensity, what did "immortality" mean, for either human or machine? A million years, a day—from that perspective, they were much the same.

There was a throb of pain in his temple now. A tension headache starting? Or a stroke? It would be ironic if a blood vessel burst in his brain and killed him before he even had a chance to make up his mind.

One way or the other, time was almost up. Either his corporeal life or his terrestrial one ended today. Either way, he wouldn't be back here again. He looked slowly around the room, examining every detail, things that had been there for so long that they'd faded into the background and he didn't really *see* them anymore: a set of bronze door-chimes, hung over the back door, that he and Ellen had bought in Big Sur; an ornamental glass ball in a woven net; a big brown-and-cream vase from a cluttered craft shop in Seattle; a crockery sun-face they'd gotten in Albuquerque; a wind-up toy carousel that played "The Carousel Waltz." Familiar mugs and cups and bowls, worn smooth with age. A framed *Cirque du Soleil* poster, decades old now. One of Sam's old stuffed animals, a battered tiger with one ear drooping, tucked away on a shelf of the high kitchen cabinet, and never touched or moved again.

Strange that he had gotten rid of Ellen's photograph, ostentatiously made a point of *not* displaying it, but kept all the rest of these things, all the memorabilia of their years together—as though subconsciously he was expecting her to come back, to step back into his life as simply as she'd stepped out of it, and pick up where they'd left off. But that wasn't going to happen. If they *were* to have any life together, it would be very far away from here, and under conditions that were unimaginably strange. Would he have the courage to face that, would he have the strength to deal with starting a new life? Or was his soul too old, too tired, too tarnished, no matter what nanomagic tricks the Mechanicals could play with his physical body?

Joseph was gesturing urgently to him again, waving both arms over his head from the middle of Rembrandt's *The Night Watch*. He released the valet from reserve-mode, and Joseph immediately appeared beside the kitchen table, contriving somehow to look flustered. "I have this Highest Priority message for you, sir, although I don't know where it came from or how it was placed in my system. All it says is, 'You don't have much time.' "

"I know, Joseph," Czudak said, cutting him off. "It doesn't matter. I just wanted to tell you—" Czudak paused, suddenly uncertain what to say. "I just wanted to tell you that, whichever way things go, you've been a good friend to me, and I appreciate it."

Joseph looked at him oddly. "Of course, sir," he said. How much of this could he really understand? It was way outside of his programming parameters, even with adaptable learning-algorithms. "But the message—"

Czudak spoke him off, and he was gone. Just like that. Vanished. Gone. And if he was never spoken on again, would it make any difference to him? Even if Joseph had known in advance that he'd never be spoken on again, that there would be nothing from this moment on but nonexistence, blankness, blackness, nothingness, would he have cared?

Czudak stood up.

As he started across the room, he realized that the time-travelers were still there. Rank on rank of them, filling the room with jostling ghosts, thousands of them, millions of them perhaps, a vast insubstantial crowd of them that he couldn't see, but that he could *feel* were there. Waiting. Watching. Watching *him*. He stopped, stunned, for the first time beginning to believe in the presence of the time-travelers as a real phenomenon, and not just a half-senile fancy of his decaying brain.

This is what they were here to see. This moment. His decision.

But why? Were they students of obscure old-recension political scandals, here to witness his betrayal of his old principles, the way you might go back to witness Benedict Arnold sealing his pact with the British or Nixon giving the orders for Watergate? Were they triumphant future descendants of the Meats, here to watch the heroic moment when he threw the Mechanical's offer of immortality defiantly back in their teflon faces, perhaps inspiring some sort of human resistance movement? Or were they here to witness the birth of his new life after he *accepted* that offer, because of something he had *yet* to do, something he would go on to do centuries or thousands of years from now?

And who *were* they? Were they his own human descendants, from millions of years in the future, evolved into strange beings with godlike powers? Or were they the descendants of the Mechanicals, grown to a ghostly discorporate strangeness of their own?

He walked forward, feeling the watching shadows part around him, close in again close behind. He still didn't know what he was going to do. It would have been so easy to make this decision when he was young. Young and strong and self-righteous, full of pride and determination and integrity. He would have turned the Mechanicals down flat, indignantly, with loathing, not hesitating for a moment, *knowing* what was right. He already *had* done that once, in fact, long before, teaching them that they couldn't buy *him*, no matter what coin they offered to pay in! He wasn't for sale!

Now, he wasn't so sure.

Now, hobbling painfully toward the front door, feeling pain lance through his head at every step, feeling his knee throb, he was struck by a sudden sense of what it would be like to be young again—to suddenly be *young* again, all at once, in a second! To put all the infirmities and indignities of age aside, like shedding a useless skin. To feel life again, really *feel* it, in a hot hormonal rush of whirling emotions, a maelstrom of scents, sounds, sights, tastes, touch, all at full strength rather than behind an insulating wall of glass, life loud and vulgar and blaring at top volume rather than whispering in the slowly diminishing voice of a dying radio, life where you could touch it, all your nerves jumping just under your skin, rather than feeling the world pulling slowly away from you, withdrawing, fading away with a sullen murmur, like a tide that has gone miles out from the beach. . . .

Czudak opened his front door, and stepped out onto the high white marble stoop.

The Meats had moved their demonstration over from the park, and were now camped out in front of his house, filling the street in their hundreds, blocking traffic. They were still beating their drums and blowing on their horns and whistles, although he hadn't heard anything inside the house; the Mechanical's doing, perhaps. A great wave of sound puffed in to greet him when he opened the door, though, blaring and vivid, smacking into his face with almost physical force. When he stepped out onto the stoop, the drums and horns began to falter and fall silent one by one, and a startled hush spread out over the crowd, like ripples spreading out over the surface of a pond from a thrown stone, until there was instead of noise an expectant silence made up of murmurs and whispers, noises not quite heard. And then even that almost-noise stopped, as if the world had taken a deep breath and held it, waiting, and he looked out over a sea of expectant faces, looking back at him, turned up toward him like flowers turned toward the sun.

A warm breeze came up, blowing across the park, blowing from the distant corners of the Earth, tugging at his hair. It smelled of magnolias and hyacinths and new-mown grass, and it stirred the branches of the trees around him, making them lift and shrug. The horizon to the west was a glory of clouds, hot gold, orange, lime, scarlet, coral, fiery purple, with the sun a gleaming orange coin balanced on the very rim of the world, ready to teeter and fall off. The rest of the sky was a delicate pale blue, fading to plum and ash to the East, out toward the distant ocean. The full moon was already out, a pale perfect disk, like a bone-white face peering with languid curiosity down on the ancient earth. A bird began to sing, trilling liquidly, somewhere out in the gathering darkness.

Exultation opened hotly inside him, like a wound. God, he loved the world! God, he loved life!

Throwing his head back, he began to speak.